Also by Lynda La Plante

Bella Mafia

Entwined

Cold Shoulder

Cold Blood

Cold Heart

Prime Suspect

Royal
Heist

Royal Heist

A NOVEL

Lynda La Plante

Random House
New York

A significantly different edition of this book was published in the United Kingdom under the title *Royal Flush* by Macmillan London, copyright © 2002 by Lynda La Plante.

This work was originally published in the United Kingdom by Macmillan in 2002.

Library of Congress Cataloging-in-Publication Data

La Plante, Lynda.
Royal Heist : a novel / Lynda La Plante.
p. cm.
ISBN 1-4000-6025-7 (acid-free paper)
1. Koh-i-noor (Diamond)—Fiction. 2. Jewel thieves—Fiction. 3. England—Fiction.
I. Title.

PR6062.A65R69 2003
823'.914—dc22   2003058519

Printed in the United States of America on acid-free paper

Random House website address: www.atrandom.com

1 2 4 6 8 9 7 5 3

First U.S. Edition

Text design by Meryl Sussman Levavi/Digitext

I dedicate *Royal Heist* to Stephen Ross and Duncan Heath, my two racing partners, who, with me, make up Action Blood Stock, a company that handles our jointly owned racehorses. We've had some lucky and exhilarating times as well as a few bad days, but overall the sheer joy our racehorses have brought us has been worth every hard-earned cent. I wish my partners good fortune and good health, and may the three of us one day have a Derby winner.

Royal
Heist

1

June 2001: Royal Ascot was into its third day, with crowds enjoying the unusually warm, sunny weather. There was a circus atmosphere at times, with clowns on stilts and booths selling racing memorabilia. A brass band was warming up, and the aroma of fish and chips still hung in the air. Ladies in extravagant hats were escorted by men in morning suits, and everywhere they walked, the champagne flowed. Affluent visitors headed toward private boxes or to the Royal Enclosure. Today, it was murmured, Her Majesty the Queen was present, for one of her own horses was running.

Outside the official car park, Rolls-Royces, Bentleys, and Mercedeses queued with buses, coaches, and station wagons. The car park closest to the main gates was only for owners and trainers, and rows of attendants checked the passes displayed on windscreens. Police and racecourse stewards directed pedestrians over a crossing that led to the gates and turnstiles. The stewards wore old-fashioned bowler hats, smart black suits, white shirts, and as requested by the track officials, sober ties.

Christina de Jersey pulled her navy Corniche, packed with two teenage daughters and their friends, into the closest car park. The girls all wore their large hats bedecked with flowers, while Christina's was stowed safely in the trunk.

She had invited several guests to lunch in the de Jersey box and overseen the menu with her usual meticulousness. Though it was not twelve o'clock yet, she had wanted to avoid the even greater crush that would ensue nearer to the start of the first race, to give herself time to check the table and greet her guests.

* * *

A couple of hours earlier, in his helicopter, her husband had piloted his jockey, Mickey Rowland, and trainer, Donald Fleming, to the track. Now, from the busy helicopter pad, he made his way toward the racing stables on the far side of the track. Though fifty-seven, Edward de Jersey was still athletic and exceptionally fit from daily exercising his vast stable of race-horses. At almost six feet three, with broad, strong shoulders, he cut a striking figure. He wore not a gray top hat but rather a black silk one with a slightly curved Victorian-style brim.

De Jersey had a tight sensation in his stomach. Even though he had kept in constant touch with his stable lads, who had traveled by road from his stud farm, he would not feel easy until he had seen his entry, Royal Flush, for himself.

"What stall is he in?" he bellowed to his trainer.

"Number four," said Fleming, breathlessly, catching up.

Fleming, too, had spoken frequently to the lads to make sure the prize colt had not suffered any adverse effects from the journey. Royal Flush could be moody; a horse that volatile might injure himself in or out of the horse box. He was to race in the three o'clock seven-furlong Chesham Stakes for two-year-olds with a 37,000-pound purse. Royal Flush had cost a fortune, and de Jersey was convinced that he was special enough to win the Derby the following year. He had won his maiden race at Lingfield by over a furlong: a spectacular result. Still, Royal Flush had to prove he wasn't a one-race wonder.

As de Jersey approached the stables, he greeted his two lads. "How's my boy?" Numerous other owners and trainers were also checking their horses. Royal Flush was draped in his blanket and appeared unruffled by the hubbub around him.

"He's been a right bugger, sir. We cladded the sides of the box, but you know what he's like, tried to bite me hand off earlier—and he's been kick-ing and bucking. We gave him a good walkabout, though, in the backfield after breakfast, so he's calmer now."

De Jersey bent close to kiss the horse's soft velvet muzzle. "You be a good fella now," he told him. Then he checked virtually every inch of the horse. As he ran his hand over the muscular, glossy flanks, he felt breath-less with anticipation. There was big competition against Royal Flush for the Chesham: the Queen's horse was the favorite, and the Sheikh had a runner worth over a million.

At last, satisfied that all was in order, de Jersey went off by himself to stride the famous racetrack. He thought how perfect it was for his colt:

well watered—and with the forecast of a hot summer day, he couldn't have asked for better—the track would be firm. Royal Flush did not run well on soft ground.

He turned to look back at the finishing post, then at the stands and boxes, and half-wished they had not invited so many guests. If his "boy" wasn't placed, he would be hard-pushed to remain the genial host.

"Good day for it, sir."

De Jersey didn't recognize the wizened little man in his suit and bowler hat.

"Harry Smedley, sir. Your lad came up earlier. Says to be sure Royal Flush goes into the starting gate last. Apparently he's got a bit of a temper on him."

"It's imperative," de Jersey replied. "He doesn't like being stalled, and with so many young colts there'll be a delay getting them in."

Smedley nodded. "I'll make sure of it. The lads working the starter stalls aren't due up here yet, not until just before the first race, but I'll warn 'em."

De Jersey felt for his wallet.

"No need, sir, but let's hope he runs a good race. Certainly ran a blisterer on his maiden."

De Jersey was eager now to return down the track.

"Your dad would have been proud." Smedley gave a knowing wink. "Right old character he was."

Smedley reminded de Jersey of a garden gnome, with his bulbous nose and flushed cheeks. "You knew him?" he queried.

The small man looked baffled. "I'm Margie Smedley's son. My family used to run the dairy at the end of your street, and we was at school together. Before you got into the grammar school. Long while ago now, but my mother knew yours."

De Jersey still had no recollection of the man, but he nodded and smiled anyway.

Smedley moved closer. "You remember the corner shop just up from the dairy, two doors down from your old fella's bettin' shop? Gawd almighty, she was in and out like a ferret, my mother, never could resist a bet, and with it being on her doorstep . . ." Smedley chuckled. "You was always held up as an example to me. First, the only lad from round our way to get into the grammar school, then you went off to that officers' training place, didn't you?"

"Sandhurst." Still de Jersey couldn't place him.

"Your dad, he used to show us your picture in your uniform, proud as punch he was. And you had that handsome fella staying. He was wiv you at Sandhurst, right?"

De Jersey was surprised at the old man's memory—he and Jimmy Wilcox had been very close; they had been at officers' training together, and Wilcox was to this day someone he trusted.

"Mind you, it's only cos I knew you way back that I've followed your career. I'd never have recognized you now, but being a racing man meself, I wondered if you was him. Then I spotted you at Epsom a few years back. Your dad was a card, wasn't he?"

"He died a long time ago."

"I know, but those were the days, eh? We was at his funeral. Wanted his ashes sprinkled over the Epsom racetrack, great character he was. Did you do it?"

"I'm sorry?"

"Do like he wanted, with his ashes?"

"No, they wouldn't give me permission. Well, it's been nice talking to you, Mr. Smedley," said de Jersey, turning away, but the man tapped his arm.

"It's Harry, sir, eh? Funny old life, isn't it? I heard you had to leave that military college. Hurt yourself, didn't you?"

"Yes, I injured my knee."

"Fell off a horse, was it?"

"Playing polo."

"It must have been fate. I mean, look at you now, eh? I hadda do National Service. Life's full of surprises, isn't it?"

"It certainly is, Harry," replied de Jersey.

"No one would believe it, you and I was at school together in the East End."

"Well, not many people know," said de Jersey. This time he took out two fifty-pound notes from his wallet, saying, "Have a flutter on Royal Flush for old time's sake." He tucked the notes into Smedley's top pocket and, before the man could say any more, walked off.

"Good luck today, sir," Smedley said and tipped his bowler hat.

As he walked back down the track, de Jersey thought of his dapper little father, Ronnie Jersey. The "de" had been acquired many years after his father's death: de Jersey thought it gave his name more of an upper-class ring. Once he had acquired the deep, rather plummy tones of an aristocrat, it was hard to detect any East End in his speech.

The injury to which Smedley had referred destroyed any hope of an army career; perhaps it *had* been fate, although at the time it had broken his heart. The fall damaged his kneecap so severely that he still limped and was often in pain, though he never allowed it to interfere with his grueling daily rides.

Down the track, Smedley was regaling one of the other stewards about his "school pal" Edward de Jersey.

"His father ran a bookies'—in fact, two of 'em. Nice earners, but back in the fifties he had a lot of aggravation from the villains. Word was, he was forced out of business and his son took 'em over but sold them fast. Looks a real toff now, but we was at school together. I tell you one thing, I'd like a share of his life. He's worth bloody millions!"

De Jersey headed past the winner's enclosure and through the famous hole-in-the-wall archway toward the boxes. On the third floor he got out of the lift and walked to his double box, pausing only to look over the railing at the throng below. The crowds were in good humor, standing almost shoulder to shoulder around the bandstand, where the brass band played a medley of old-time music-hall songs. The crowd joined in with the chorus: "Ohhhhh, there ain't a lady living in the world that I'd swap for my dear old dutch." As he listened, de Jersey remembered his dad standing at the piano in the pub close to their terraced house. His dad only had the nerve to get up and sing after he'd downed several pints. He'd sing at the top of his voice, button eyes focusing on his beloved wife, Florence. De Jersey laughed softly as the past swept over him and he heard his mother say, "Eddy, get your dad's hat. We're goin' home!"

Someone brushed against his shoulder, and he turned to find Lord Wilby offering his hand. "Hello, Edward, wonderful day for it." Wilby introduced his wife.

"Charming as ever." De Jersey gave her a small bow and tipped his hat.

"How do you rate your colt's chances?" Wilby had two runners himself that day.

"Rather good, as long as he keeps his head."

Wilby checked his race card. "Ah, Mickey Rowland, yes, he's a good jockey. Handled well at Lingfield." Then more owners were acknowledging de Jersey, and the conversation ended.

Christina had decorated the box navy and white, his racing colors, and had the table laid for twelve. On the balcony, rows of seats overlooked the track. De Jersey's box faced the large screen that would televise the races, situated opposite the winning post. There were television screens inside the box, where some preferred to watch the action, especially if the weather was bad. Today, though, it was perfect.

Christina was arranging the flowers on the table when he entered. She wore little makeup and, like him, was lightly tanned. Even after twenty years of marriage, de Jersey continued to be amazed by how attractive he found her. She was tall, almost five ten, with long, naturally platinum blond hair, which she wore loose or caught up in a wide-toothed butterfly clip. De Jersey loved the delicate wisps that fell down to frame her perfect face, chiseled cheekbones and full mouth, though Christina's eyes, a strikingly deep blue, were her best feature. She was de Jersey's second wife; his first was merely a distant memory. Christina had two children, yet she still had the body of a young woman. She also retained the lilt of her Swedish accent.

She was wearing a white, wide-brimmed hat, with a black band and a large bow draped down one side, a tailored white jacket, tight black pencil skirt, and high-heeled black sling-back shoes. She still had a wonderfully voluptuous figure. She looked so cool and sophisticated; it was easy to tell that she had once been a model.

De Jersey encircled her waist and kissed her neck.

"Mind my hat," she said, laughing.

"You look stunning," he said.

She cocked her head to one side. "You're quite appetizing yourself, Mr. de Jersey. Go, welcome your guests, there's champagne open."

"I was watching you and thinking what a lucky man I am. I do love you."

She stood on tiptoe to kiss his cheek. "Did he travel well?"

"He did, and he's behaving himself, but he's got serious competition. I'll be happy if he just gets placed."

"He's going to win," Christina said with certainty. She did not share his passion for this colt, though she liked horses and enjoyed riding. De Jersey had been in property development when they met and was already a very rich man, the cultured voice honed to perfection. She still knew little of her husband's past and would have been astonished to learn that he had come from London's East End. Christina had been at his side throughout his career in racing, watching with pride as the stud farm grew to be one of the biggest in England. She took no part in the running of the racing yard but had an important role in de Jersey's life, giving him a stability he had never previously believed possible.

She poured him a glass of champagne and prompted him to join his guests, watching him go. Their nineteen-year age difference had never been an issue. Christina was above all a contented woman. She knew that behind his extrovert image her husband was a private man and, at times, inadequate at small talk. She enjoyed entertaining and smoothing the way for him. They made a good team.

"We have a beautiful day for it." He shook hands and opened another bottle of Krug. She knew he would prefer water until Royal Flush's race was over. Aware that he would be totally focused on his horse, she had chosen her guests carefully. Donald Fleming's wife was there, and their local vicar, who had leapt at the chance of going to the races, with his wife, a shy, retiring woman. After the racing they could spend time box hopping with the Sangsters and the Henry Cecils.

Leonie and Natasha stood close by their father as he discussed the racing form with the overeager vicar. "Here's my tip: first race I'd say an each-way bet on Cold Stream and maybe a tenner on the outsider, Charcoal." Before he could continue, David Lyons, his business and financial adviser arrived with his wife, Helen.

De Jersey gave him a bear hug, dwarfing David, who was no more than five feet seven. The financial adviser's hired morning suit was a trifle large, and his prominent ears held up his top hat.

"And Helen, what a wonderful creation," de Jersey said, referring to her hat, a bright pink ensemble of huge roses that made her pinched, nervous face seem even paler.

"Thank you. David said it was awful." Helen, who had spent weeks shopping for her outfit, had been upset by her husband's criticism.

"It's stunning." Christina kissed her and passed Helen a glass of champagne.

"I'd say your husband has some nerve," de Jersey said, laughing as he tapped David's topper, which sank low on his red, sweaty face. "What happened, David? No suits in your size left at Moss Bros?"

David smiled self-consciously. Like his wife, he had never attended Royal Ascot. Normally he was fastidious in his dress, but unfortunately he had left it until the last moment to hire his suit.

"I think you look splendid," Christina said. "Champagne? Now, if you need any help placing bets, Natasha will guide you through the procedure. Edward's suggested a possible winner for the first race, but I never pay any attention to him. I bet on the horse whose name I like best."

Quickly, David removed his hat and went to sit on the far side of the box, where he lit a cigar. De Jersey joined him. "Glad you could make it. It's been months since I've seen you, and I have a lot to thank you for. You made me a wealthy man."

"I've been caught up with work, but I have tried calling you." David drained his glass, which de Jersey refilled. They had known each other for twenty-five years but rarely socialized. David's latest business venture on de Jersey's behalf, financing an Internet company, had proved a gold mine.

"What do you say is going to be a surefire bet? Come on now, you've got to have insider information, Edward."

"There never is one." De Jersey hesitated. David's words were an eerie reminder of his father, who always used to say the same thing. He suddenly felt like talking about his father but resisted. David would have heart failure if he knew some of the things de Jersey had done. He was straight and honest, the very reason de Jersey placed so much trust in him.

"David, I am really pleased you and Helen could join us today."

David smiled. He had whiter than white teeth and always appeared suntanned. His balding head and big ears were often a source of amusement, but he was, in actual fact, a very confident man. Now that he was flushed with champagne, David's discomfort at wearing an oversize morning suit was beginning to lessen.

"Edward, lemme tell you. What with Helen's ruddy flower garden hat and me in this suit, I was of two minds about whether to come today. I said to this bloke at Moss Bros, can't you take the trousers up? No, he said, then puts the jacket on me and the sleeves covered my hand. I said, I can't go to Royal Ascot looking like a chump. Can't you recommend someone that's got one more my size? And you know what he said? No one will notice! I said, They will when I do a pratfall in front of the Queen.

"And then I get the manager, and he starts kneeling down with these pins in his mouth. He says to me, Can you stand on the stool? And I says, That's not gonna help. I can't carry that around the racetrack!" David chortled with laughter and showed the wide hem on his trousers as Helen blushed with embarrassment.

By the time Christina suggested they sit down for lunch, everyone appeared to be enjoying themselves. The vicar had accompanied David to the Tote and appeared to have backed every horse in the first race. It was one thirty. More champagne was offered, then chilled white Chablis as the oysters were served. They were to be followed by wild salmon in aspic with new potatoes and salad. There would be a break between courses to watch the races from the balcony.

Just as they finished the oysters, the crowds below cheered wildly and everyone left the table to watch the Royal procession pass beneath the balcony. Moments later the first runners were under starter's orders, and they were off. Their guests, led by David, cheered on the winner—Charcoal at twelve to one—then David and the vicar rushed out to collect their winnings.

De Jersey felt the knot in his stomach tighten. Two more races, then he would go down to the stables.

David was making his way to the Tote on the floor directly below. Natasha had already placed her bet, but when she saw him join the line she waited, and they returned together. David hurried to the balcony, but Natasha joined her father.

"Daddy, David put on an enormous amount of money!"

"Shush," Christina admonished.

"He can afford it, sweetheart," de Jersey said, grinning. "What's he backed?"

"Classy Lady." Natasha giggled. "Maybe because of his wife's awful rose-garden hat."

Christina said sternly, "That will do, Natty. Edward, don't encourage her. They're your guests."

De Jersey pulled a po-face. "Me?"

Natasha stood on tiptoe to kiss him. "I'm on Blue Babushka, the outsider, a fiver on the nose."

"Then join the others or you'll miss the race." Christina glanced at the table, now freshly laid for the next course. Natasha left, and de Jersey watched the television screen as the horses cantered past, heading for the starting gate. "Royal Flush will go in last," he said. "He gets so frisky. I might go and have another look at him."

"Not before we finish lunch. You've got almost two hours yet. . . . Darling?"

He was staring into space. "Next year, the Derby. That's my dream, to have a Derby winner." He lapsed into silence again. Sometimes he wanted to tell her about his childhood, but so much of the past was buried beneath the person he had become that the less she knew the safer he felt.

They had just finished the main course when Donald Fleming came into the box. "Mickey's in the weighing room," he said.

"I won the last race!" his wife called to him.

Fleming blew her a kiss, then turned to Christina. "Thank you for inviting my wife."

Christina patted his arm. "She looks wonderful."

"Thanks to you, all those dresses you sent over—she was like a little girl at Christmas. And don't tell me they were ones you didn't wear anymore because a couple had the price tags still on them."

"You didn't mind, did you? I knew she hadn't been well enough to go shopping."

"Mind? Course not. Having her here today makes it even more special. Cream'll be if Royal Flush wins."

Fleming crossed to his wife. She was talking about her recent mastectomy with Helen Lyons, who found operations fascinating.

De Jersey turned to Christina. "What was that about his wife?"

"I sent over some dresses for her to choose something to wear. She's been very poorly."

"I thought the operation was a success," he said, looking at his watch. He was impatient to go to the stables.

"Yes, but she lost self-confidence." Christina touched the emerald-and-diamond brooch on her lapel. "Can you see if the safety catch is on?" Her husband bent to look. "I don't know why you wanted me to wear it. I'm always afraid of losing it, and with these crowds . . ."

"Looks okay. It suits that jacket."

Christina nuzzled his neck. "It would suit any jacket. It's magnificent."

De Jersey grinned boyishly. He adored buying her expensive gifts. This brooch, for her last birthday, had been especially costly. The matching earrings were in his pocket. He had intended to give them to her before he left that morning but then decided that if Royal Flush won they would make it a memorable day for her too.

The next race was ready for the off. Fleming beckoned to de Jersey; it was time to get Royal Flush saddled up. De Jersey asked Christina to take the girls to the parade ring; he would join them there. He leaned close. "Just you and the girls, darling. You know I don't like too many people around when we saddle up." She nodded. As de Jersey and Fleming left, she joined the guests on the balcony to explain they would return after the race. David was put out that he couldn't come, so Christina explained Edward's nervousness and suggested that David could make his way to the stands around the parade ring and watch the saddling from there.

"Will the Queen be with her horse?" he asked like a kid.

"Yes, I believe so. She has a runner in the same race."

"Bloody hell, I wouldn't miss that. We'll go over to the stands then after the next race. Which way do we go?" After giving him directions, Christina signaled to the girls, and the five of them left the box.

They passed under the archway and headed along the grass path toward the arena, where the horses would be brought to their owners and trainers. There, the jockeys received their last-minute instructions before mounting to ride down the track to the starting gate. Dense crowds lined the fenced walkway to watch the Queen as she, too, made her way toward the parade ring.

De Jersey arrived at the stables as the horses were being walked outside. They were unsaddled but draped in their owners' colors, and their numbers were attached to their bridles. The sun blazed, and some were already sweating. Royal Flush was number seven. He was playing up, tossing his head. A couple of other horses walked sideways; some were kicking out. Her Majesty's trainer walked with her to the ring, surrounded by bodyguards and security officers, six feet in front and behind. Although they had walkie-talkies and were monitoring the crowds, they were discreet, and there was a wonderful atmosphere of well-being. Here at Royal Ascot the Queen could relax and enjoy her favorite pastime. She acknowledged the cheers but was deeply engrossed in talking to her trainer.

Quite a way behind, Christina was strolling with the girls, who were agog at such glamour. They excitedly spotted stars of movies and television and kept taking secret glances ahead to the Queen's party.

Royal Flush was still acting up as he was led into a stable. Fleming and de Jersey saddled him. De Jersey dipped a sponge into a bucket and squeezed water into the horse's mouth past the bit, talking to him all the time, but the horse was increasingly hard to control. Finally, the saddle was on and he was led out, rearing and bucking, ears flattened. De Jersey looked on, concerned.

"He's in a right mood," muttered Fleming.

"It's bloody hot for him."

As the stable lad took the reins, de Jersey tapped his shoulder. "See you in the ring."

"Yes, sir. He'll calm down. He's just desperate to get onto that track."

De Jersey straightened his gray silk cravat and replaced his topper. "Let's go." Then he and Fleming walked side by side toward the parade ring.

At the center the crowds pressed against the railings, and the green was full of owners and trainers. The Sheikh was waiting for his runner to appear, and de Jersey could see Christina and the girls chatting to friends. Making his way toward them, he passed the Queen and tipped his top hat. He was astonished when she acknowledged him. He had seen her on several occasions, but never before had she spoken to him.

"Do you play cards, Mr. de Jersey?" the Queen asked, smiling.

"Infrequently, ma'am." He bowed.

"I wondered how your horse came about his name."

De Jersey flushed to the roots of his hair; the royal flush was an unbeatable poker hand. "Whether it will prove to be his rightful name remains to be seen, ma'am."

The Queen inclined her head; the conversation was over.

His heart pounding, de Jersey replaced his top hat and continued to cross the green. He could hardly believe that Her Majesty had known his name and stopped a moment to get his breath.

"You all right?" Fleming asked.

"I'm fine, just . . . She knew who I was, Donald!"

Fleming laughed. "She doesn't miss a trick. She's got a stable of horses on a par with yours, and I bet she knows just what the competition is from our boy. That's her horse being led into the ring now." He gestured to a magnificent bay draped in the Royal colors, bigger than Royal Flush, and calmer. Royal Flush, a deep, almost burnt chestnut, still tossed his head, and there was a white film of sweat on his neck.

"Bloody hot for his second time out," de Jersey said. Then he greeted Christina by slipping an arm around her waist, and they watched as his lad walked Royal Flush round the ring.

Mickey Rowland adjusted his chin strap, whip under his arm, and looked around. Spotting de Jersey, he came over. "Hot out here," he murmured, nodding to Christina.

"You've met my daughters, and these two young ladies are—" De Jersey suddenly saw that Leonie was about to take a photograph. "Not now," he snapped.

"But, Daddy—"

"No! Christina, take the camera off her *now*!"

Leonie looked frightened and lowered it. Christina took the camera, explaining, "It's supposed to be unlucky, sweetheart. Take as many as you like after the race."

De Jersey, Fleming, and Mickey were deep in conversation, the incident forgotten. "I think it's best to give him his head. With this ground it's going to be fast. Let's see what he can do, maybe give him a tap halfway, keep him off the rails, center of the course. It's already been churned up, so if it's too rough move him across."

Mickey's face was expressionless. He and de Jersey walked toward Royal Flush. De Jersey bent low, speaking privately: "You know him best, Mickey. Do what you have to do. Let's see how good he is."

Mickey smiled. "See you in the winner's enclosure, then, shall I?"

De Jersey laughed and gave his jockey a leg up. Mickey tightened his gloves, tapped his helmet with his whip, and urged Royal Flush to walk out of the ring. The crowd headed back for the stands to watch the race. The horses would take a good, easy canter to the starting gate.

De Jersey walked ahead toward the owners' and trainers' stand, leaving Fleming to guide Christina and the girls. He didn't see David and

Helen Lyons waving from behind the barrier, but they had seen him pause by the Queen; David had the photograph to prove it.

Christina fanned herself with her race card as they headed up the steps to the front row of the stand. They were all very hot. She knew not to speak to her husband as he trained his binoculars on Royal Flush cantering up to the starting gate. De Jersey lifted them, lowered them, looked to the wide screen, then went back to the binoculars. Fleming was more relaxed.

"He'll start his shuffle in a minute," he whispered to Christina. Whenever de Jersey watched one of his horses race, he would shift from one foot to the other as if he were standing on hot coals. They exchanged smiles.

Now the commentator was saying that all the horses were in the gates except Royal Flush. Then he was in, and the next second they were off. Fleming stood close by de Jersey, who muttered, "Came out well, but he's boxed in. Move him up, Mickey, that's it—good, he's in a nice position."

As Christina squinted at the screen, Natalie asked where Royal Flush was.

"I think he's fourth, no fifth—he's right in the center. See the star on Mickey's cap?"

De Jersey yelped, and everyone turned to look. He was hopping up and down. "He's dropped back! What the hell is he doing?" His face was like thunder. "Come on, come on, Mickey! *Ride him. That's it! That's it.*" He nudged Fleming so hard that he was almost knocked off his feet. "He's moving up, sitting in a lovely position, see him?"

But the Queen's bay was breaking away from the pack. He was almost a length in front of the rest of the field.

De Jersey lowered the binoculars as the horses thundered down the backstretch. Royal Flush was still in fourth but looked as if he was tiring. Boxed in on both sides, he was struggling to hold his position. Then, suddenly, he began to draw ahead of the horses, neck and neck on either side of him.

Christina turned to see her husband standing, as if frozen, his hands at his sides. Then she was shouting at the top of her voice: "Come on . . . *Come on. Yes, Yes. Come on!*"

Suddenly Royal Flush seemed to get a second wind. The horse flew, his stride never faltering as he moved up from fourth to third, and then he was unstoppable. He passed the winning post two lengths ahead of the field. Mickey, high in the saddle, turned to look behind as he raised his whip in victory.

Fleming and de Jersey looked at each other, speechless for a moment, then Fleming gasped. "He's done it, just like you knew he would." De Jersey blinked back tears. Then Christina was in his arms, and his girls were hugging him. There were congratulations from everywhere, but he could hear nothing, his heart was pounding fit to burst.

They hurried to the winner's enclosure. Mickey rode in to cheers. De Jersey and Fleming took the reins as the jockey slid off Royal Flush and wrapped his arms around the sweating horse's neck. Then he removed the saddle. As he loosened his chin strap, Mickey said, "He's got a lot more under the bonnet. I've never felt anything like it. I hardly had to touch him."

De Jersey held the horse's head. "Next year it's the Derby, my boy."

Fleming laughed. "Give him a break! He's just won the Chesham. That's good enough for now."

The prize giving was a blur. De Jersey forced himself to keep calm, though he wanted to shout out that he had found it, a champion of champions! The dream of every trainer and owner, the fulfillment of twenty years' hard work. It was his!

Moments later, Fleming was being interviewed by the television sports team, but de Jersey sidestepped them. He avoided publicity and always left the interviews to his trainer.

After seeing that Royal Flush was hosed down and made ready to be driven home, de Jersey returned jubilantly to his box. The guests had all bet on Royal Flush. David was standing on a chair waving a fistful of fifty-pound notes, singing, "We're in the money!" They celebrated well into the afternoon, and David and Helen Lyons were the last to leave. After monitoring him drinking numerous cups of black coffee, Helen assured Christina that David was sober enough to drive.

"Don't worry, it'll take us a good hour to get out of the car park," David said and then clasped de Jersey's hand. "This has been one of the best days of my life. Delicious food, the best champagne and . . . and . . . I'm going to get that photograph of you with the Queen framed. I'll have it on my desk!"

"It was a special day, David, and I am glad you were here to share it. If it wasn't for you I probably wouldn't have been able to afford it!" de Jersey said, shaking David's hand. His financial adviser's mood suddenly deflated. He looked as if he wanted to say something but decided against it, saying instead, rather briskly to his wife, "Let's go, Helen, we don't want to overstay our welcome or we won't be invited next year."

Then dropping his voice, David said soberly to de Jersey, "Everything is going to be all right." They were gone before a puzzled de Jersey could reply.

* * *

De Jersey sat down, exhausted, watching while Christina marshaled the girls. "Will you be all right to fly the helicopter?" she asked.

He made no reply. As she repeated the question, he reached out and brought her hand to his lips. "I'm going for a walk. I'll see you at home. Thank you for today. It was a good idea to invite David and Helen. I think it meant a great deal to them."

She laughed softly. "I don't know if it was such a good idea to invite the vicar. Donald's had to drive him home. He could hardly stand up."

De Jersey blew his daughters a kiss, then stood up. "Drive carefully. I won't be too late." He picked up his top hat and walked to the door. "There's something for you on the table," he said to his wife over his shoulder. Then he left.

De Jersey walked toward the winner's enclosure. It was cooler now, and thousands of race goers were streaming out of the gates. He went to the number-one post and stood there—it had felt so good to lead Royal Flush into the winner's position. Then he headed toward the helipad. His was the only helicopter left. He walked slowly, breathing in the scent of the grass, and remembered how his father had opened his betting shop. After placing a winning bet on an outsider, he made enough to open his own betting shop. He never laid another bet. "It's a fool's game, but sometimes the fool wins. And luck runs out, so I'm not takin' any chances," he had said.

Ronnie Jersey's luck had run out months after he opened his second betting shop. Cancer was diagnosed. Shortly before his death he told his son, "Eddy, you run those shops for me. Take care of your mother. I know it's not what you wanted, but you can earn a good living, an' there's a good kid that works for me. You know Tony Driscoll." Tony was the illegitimate son of the woman who cleaned the shops. He had been just a toddler when Ronnie took them under his wing, and they owed everything to him. De Jersey had trouble remembering Mrs. Driscoll's first name. What he did remember was how they both wept at his father's funeral. Ronnie had been a surrogate dad to Tony and had even left him a few hundred pounds. The boys had not been that close as youngsters, but years later, when de Jersey needed him, Tony Driscoll, like James Wilcox, was one of the few men he trusted.

"I was hopin' I'd see you."

It was Smedley. By the tilt of him he'd had more than a few beers.

"What a win, eh? Clean as a whistle! I nearly had heart failure—I'd put those two fifties you give me on him!"

"Really?" De Jersey moved away, wanting to avoid another conversation.

"All the lads was on him, I tipped them off." Smedley bumped against the fence, then ducked beneath it. There was no getting away from him. "You got anythin' running tomorrow?"

"No."

"Ah, well, maybe not push your luck too far, eh? You goin' down the track? I'll walk wiv you. I need to sober up. Been in the stewards' lounge."

De Jersey made no reply but strode off, leaving Smedley, swaying slightly, a hurt expression on his red face. "I'm sorry if I bothered you," he said loudly.

De Jersey stopped. "Sorry, I don't mean to be rude. I have to get a move on—don't like flying at night."

"Oh, understandable," Smedley said, trotting after him. When he approached the helipad, de Jersey could hear Smedley wheezing behind him. As de Jersey opened the cockpit door, Smedley gasped. "You'd never get me up in one of them." De Jersey climbed aboard, and Smedley held up his square rough hand. "I'd like to shake your hand, sir."

De Jersey bent down to grasp it. He was beginning to find the man unbearably irritating. "I'll tell my grandson about it, me and you being at the same school. You got any?"

De Jersey looked down into the gnomelike face. "Just two daughters."

"Ah, well, we can't all be blessed. I got four lads, three grandsons and . . ."

The engine started up, and de Jersey slid the door shut. He waited for Smedley to scuttle away to a safe distance; the blades began to turn. As the helicopter lifted into the air, de Jersey saw the man grow smaller, and he felt an odd mixture of emotions. Most of his life had been spent escaping his past, but despite his massive wealth, the Smedleys of the world proved that he could never let his guard down. He had far too much to lose, having acquired, by various means, everything he ever wanted in life. However, Smedley did have something he coveted, a son . . . in fact, four of them. De Jersey's good humor returned. He had Royal Flush. Today had been just the beginning. He would fulfill his dream to win the Derby, and if he did, he would kiss the track, like his dad had done the day he'd made the twenty-five-to-one bet on the Derby outsider.

The light was fading as the helicopter flew over his vast estate. He couldn't help smiling at what lay below, which included a racing stable, just twenty-five miles from Newmarket and its famous racetrack, and close to the famous Tattersalls bloodstock auctions; a stud farm at a separate holding, ten miles from the stables; vast tracts of land for training; and separate yards and paddocks for the brood mares.

The electronically controlled gates gave access to a three-mile drive leading to his mansion overlooking a lake. The drive branched off from the house toward the stables. There were garages set back from the house with living quarters above for the chauffeur. De Jersey owned a Silver Cloud Rolls-Royce, a Mercedes convertible, a Range Rover, two Aston Martins, three motorbikes, and four golf carts, all in the same dark navy as the stable colors. His personal favorite was his Mercedes, whose registration plate read CHAMPION.

The stable lads in the yard shaded their eyes when they saw de Jersey's helicopter. They waved their caps as he flew over the neat row of outbuildings that had been converted into their living quarters. Beyond was a complex of cottages for the jockeys, a sauna, swimming pool, and gymnasium. The estate and its occupants were valued at over a hundred million pounds. De Jersey employed head lads, yardmen, work riders, two assistant trainers, a head trainer, stable lads, and traveling head lads, and he contracted two top jockeys in addition to Mickey Rowland. There were three large stable yards, and Donald Fleming's house was on the northern side of the old yard. The office, in the newest yard, was manned by a personal assistant, a racing secretary, and two managers.

The stable lads were yelling as De Jersey landed, and when he jumped down from the helicopter there were cheers from his staff. "Champagne all round!" he shouted.

De Jersey had naturally a rather off-putting, steely manner, but if you got to know him it was soon dissipated when he gave one of his shy smiles. The trust, admiration, and respect he demanded from his staff were returned threefold. He was, as his wife knew, a very reserved man. He had never raised his voice to anyone at the stables. He'd never needed to. With the adroit management, competent secretaries, and loyal employees, there was little to criticize. De Jersey actually detested losing his temper; to him doing so was a sign of weakness. He had tight control of his emotions, but his charm made his employees guard his privacy ferociously. There was not a single member of staff's wife, husband, child, or grandchild whose name he couldn't recall, and now, surrounded by them all as the champagne corks popped, he toasted his success and was blissfully happy.

He raised his glass. "To Royal Flush and to next year—the Derby!"

The cheers intensified with the arrival of the horse box. As Royal Flush was led down, they grouped around him, and de Jersey cupped some champagne into his hand and patted the horse's head with it. Then he led the horse back to his stable and watched over him like a doting father. The traveling stable lads brought his feed, and de Jersey was pleased when

Royal Flush couldn't wait to get at it. It was always a good sign when a young horse was not put off his feed after a race.

"You'll wear it out," Christina said, putting down a tray of sandwiches and tea as de Jersey rewound the tape of the race.

The oak-paneled drawing room was comfortable, with polished pine floors and exquisite Persian rugs. Soft throws and cushions covered the sofa, and a fire blazed in the grate.

De Jersey pressed play and prepared to glory once more in Royal Flush's victory.

"I'm going to keep him under wraps for the rest of the season," he said. He ate the sandwiches hungrily. "Just some light training before he rests for the winter."

"Thank you for my beautiful earrings," Christina drew back her hair to show him she was wearing them.

He kissed her neck. "I'd give you the world if I could," he said. His eyes strayed back to the TV screen and the moment Royal Flush passed the winning post.

Christina switched off the television. "Can we go to bed so I can thank you properly?" she asked. Now she had his attention. As they kissed, he scooped her up into his arms, but they didn't make it to the bedroom. Later, as she nestled beside him in front of the fire, wearing nothing but the earrings, de Jersey sighed. "I'm a lucky man," he murmured.

2

R oyal Flush enjoyed the rest he deserved in the months after the flat season, while de Jersey was still busy. He entered many horses in international races during the winter, and there were frequent trips to Dubai and Hong Kong. By November the horse's program had consisted of walking and trotting, but after Christmas it would build up for a couple of preparation races. It was planned that he would run the Thresher Trial at Sandown in April and then the Lingfield Derby trial.

De Jersey drove a golf cart into the yard. He wore a checked cap, jodhpurs, and a yellow cashmere polo-neck sweater beneath his Harris tweed jacket. His hand-stitched, brown leather riding boots were highly polished. He paid his first call of the day to Royal Flush. The horse had not outgrown his moody temperament, and he still had a bullyboy streak to him. He'd given a couple of the lads nasty bites. De Jersey had been worried that if he remained a stallion Royal Flush would be a danger to the other horses—he had already attacked a few in the yard. It would have been heartbreaking to geld him, but Royal Flush, perhaps sensing what was at stake, at three years old was finally settling down.

After a while de Jersey drove over to the east wing of the yard to inspect a new filly from Ireland. When he started the engine again, his cell phone rang. It was his wife.

"What's up?" he asked.

"Helen called." Her Swedish accent was always more pronounced on the telephone. "She was very distressed. I think David is sick. You'd better call."

Back at the house, de Jersey scraped his boots outside the kitchen door.

De Jersey walked into the kitchen. The table was set for him with grapefruit juice, black coffee, two slices of Christina's homemade rye bread, and a lightly boiled egg. He picked up the phone, but David's number was engaged so he decided to have breakfast before trying again. De Jersey had not seen David since Royal Ascot, preferring to leave the financial side of his business to his adviser. Recently he and David had discussed liquidating some of his investments. The cost of running the stables was astronomical, and the foot-and-mouth outbreak had meant a hefty loss for the adjoining farm. His cash resources were stretched to the limit.

Christina came in, her arms filled with holly and fir branches for the hall. The tree would not arrive until a few days before the girls returned from boarding school.

"The line was engaged. I'll try again after I've had a look at the papers."

Christina spread some old newspaper on the floor and began to spray the branches silver. "Helen was crying. For her to call so early, something must be wrong."

"Okay, I'll try again now. I hope to God I don't have to go over there. I've got a hectic day ahead."

Moments later, after having spoken to Helen's sister, de Jersey was arranging to land the helicopter at the small airport close to David's house in Radcliff, a particularly affluent London suburb.

"What's the matter?" Christina asked.

"Not sure. I spoke to Helen's sister. I'll be back as soon as possible." He kissed her cheek and was gone.

David Lyons's house was set back from the road. The gates were open, so the taxi drove straight through. The white stucco house had fake Georgian pillars and latticed lead windows with Swiss-style shutters and a green slate roof. The front door was ajar.

De Jersey stepped into the hall and made for the lounge, a dreary sea of beige. It was eerily empty. "Helen?" he called.

Frustrated, he headed toward the ornate indoor swimming pool, returning to the hall just as a small, pale-faced woman appeared. After introducing himself, he asked where Helen was.

"I'm her sister, Sylvia Hewitt. I spoke to you earlier. Helen's upstairs. Shall I get her for you?"

"I'd be grateful if you could tell me what's going on. You just said that Helen had to see me. Is David all right?"

"No—no, he isn't." She started to cry.

"Has there been an accident?" De Jersey was worried now.

"I'll get Helen. Please go and sit in the lounge."

De Jersey sat on one of the overplump sofas and waited at least a quarter of an hour.

"Helen." He rose to his feet. She closed the door.

"Edward." Her face was drawn and her eyes red-rimmed.

"Helen, what on earth is wrong? Has David had an accident?"

She took out a tissue. "He's dead," she said, bursting into tears.

De Jersey was stunned. "I'm . . . so very sorry."

She perched on the end of the sofa, blowing her nose. "I found him this morning. He was still wearing his pajamas. He must have done it in the middle of the night."

"Found him?"

She nodded. "In the garage."

De Jersey sat down slowly.

"The engine was running. The car was full of fumes. The doctor said he'd taken some sleeping tablets. He'd left me a note on the kitchen table, said for me to call you and not go into the garage. But I did."

"Oh God."

"I found another letter in the car, on the dashboard, addressed to you." Helen took a blue envelope from her pocket and passed it to him. "The police took my letter, but I didn't give them this one. I'd forgotten about it."

De Jersey slipped the envelope into his pocket. "Helen, is there anything I can do?"

She shook her head, then broke down into shuddering sobs.

De Jersey walked to the waiting taxi and headed back to the local airport. David and Helen had been a childless but loving couple for thirty years. What on earth had possessed him to kill himself? De Jersey regarded the single sheet inside the blue envelope:

My dear Edward,
I am so sorry. It ran out of control and I was unable to do anything about it. You will find all the documentation in the second drawer of my office desk. Yours, David.

De Jersey arranged for the helicopter to land in London, at the Battersea heliport. He was met at David's office in the City by two shocked, weepy secretaries and David's longtime assistant, Daniel Gatley, who was white-faced and trembling. "So dreadful, and just before Christmas too," he whispered.

David's oval desk bore a bank of telephones, a computer, and a large silver-framed photo of de Jersey talking to the Queen.

"David was so proud to have been at Royal Ascot. He talked of nothing else for weeks after," Gatley said.

"He said something about the second drawer and some documents?"

Gatley took out a bunch of keys and opened the drawer. It contained a thin file and a small, square box. De Jersey's name was printed on both. "That's all. The box contains computer disks, and these are contracts that I believe you have copies of anyway." Gatley passed them to him.

De Jersey flipped open the file. "What's all this about?"

"He didn't tell me much, but I knew he was in big trouble. He has been here most nights for the past few months."

"Financial?" asked de Jersey crisply.

"Two days ago he gave everyone here a month's notice."

"Embezzlement, or what?"

"Good heavens, no. David was one of the most honest men I've ever met."

De Jersey opened the box to find four unlabeled disks. "What are these?"

"I don't know. His drawer was always locked."

"But you have a key."

"Only since this morning, and I hadn't opened the drawer until now. I've been calling his clients and his friends."

"So, you have no idea what is on these?" de Jersey asked, holding up the disks.

"No, but I can open them for you and print them out."

"I can just about manage that." De Jersey attempted to make light of the situation, but he knew that something was very wrong. He wanted to leave so that he could find out what it was.

Christina was as stunned as her husband. David was so dependable. For him to have committed suicide was unthinkable.

"No, I don't know why he did it, but I've got to go over some disks he left me. They may give me the answer," de Jersey told her.

"What time would you like dinner?" she asked. "I'm cooking shank of lamb the way you like it."

"What?"

"I'm sorry, it's ridiculous, isn't it, me thinking of what to cook for dinner and—"

"Eight thirty will be about right," he said.

"Eight thirty it is, then," Christina said softly. "Had you seen David since Royal Ascot?"

"It must be a couple months since we've spoken," he told her. "I wanted to sell off some shares."

"How did he sound then?" she asked.

"I don't know. He was . . ." De Jersey frowned.

"He was what?"

"I don't know . . . a bit short with me."

In his office, de Jersey poured himself a small whiskey, added soda and ice, then sat down at his computer. He decided to start with the documents and tackle the disks later. He perched his half-moon glasses on his nose and peered at the first wad of papers. It was six thirty-five.

Two hours later he was still flicking through the documents. His wife popped her head in the door. "You almost done, darling?"

He swiveled round in his leather chair. "Almost."

"Dinner's ready and I've lit a fire."

"Good. Just let me close down my computer."

"Did you find out what David's problems were?"

"He'd got himself into rather deep financial trouble—not worth topping himself for, though."

"Too late to do anything about it now," she said sadly.

"I'll be right with you."

David had actually been in deeper water than de Jersey said, and it looked as if de Jersey was about to plunge into it too. An Internet company in which they had both invested had gone bankrupt, and David had lost all of his savings. All he had ever implied to de Jersey was that there were "problems" with the Web site. He had said, "Just leave it to me," and foolishly, that was exactly what de Jersey had done. Arranging for the horses to race abroad during the winter had forced him to leave London for weeks on end.

David's suggestion to invest in the Internet company had come at the right time. The stables and stud farm were in trouble, and with just over 2 million pounds left in various accounts, de Jersey had taken a risk and released that money to David to invest. Within six months de Jersey was worth 32 million on paper. His shares continued to rise faster in value than either man had anticipated, so eager to make more, de Jersey had remortgaged the stud farm and invested another 40 million. Now he was about to lose everything. No wonder David had attached the garden hose to his new Mercedes' exhaust pipe and rammed it through the window.

Christina placed a large platter of crisp lamb on the candlelit table. The air was permeated with the scent of rosemary. De Jersey sat down as she poured him a glass of California red wine. He sipped and let it roll around his mouth before he swallowed. "Oh, it's so good."

"Especially with the lamb." Christina handed him his plate. He leaned back, flipping his starched white napkin across his knee.

Christina raised her glass. "I want to make a toast," she said. "To David."

"To David, God rest him."

There was a moment's silence as they began to eat.

"Is everything all right?" she asked.

"Perfect." He felt the warmth of the fire on his back as he broke off a piece of bread and buttered it.

"I wasn't referring to the dinner. Tell me about David's financial troubles."

"He's made some foolish investments. Not sure exactly how much he's frittered away of mine."

"Yours? What do you mean?" Christina asked anxiously.

"Oh, nothing I can't take care of. Don't worry about it."

"But is it going to be a worry for you? Did Helen know anything about this?"

"I don't think so."

"Was he already in trouble when he came to Ascot?"

"I don't know. I haven't had time to review all the records yet." He was two people: one quietly enjoying his meal with his beloved wife, the other white with rage. He had trusted David and his judgment. He was not prepared to lose all of this, but he had never felt so impotent in his life.

With dinner over and Christina clearing the table, he sat preoccupied, tapping a dessertspoon.

"Should I call her?" asked Christina.

"Up to you," de Jersey said offhandedly.

"Well, do you think it would be appropriate?"

"How should I know?" he said and stood.

"I hate it when you behave like this." She pulled off the tablecloth.

"How am I behaving?"

She glared at him. "Like that! Shutting me out and snapping at me. I'm only trying to find out what's happened. David has killed himself, for

God's sake, and you say he frittered money away. Well, I would just like to know—"

"Sweetheart, I don't know the full extent of what David has or hasn't done," de Jersey said, softening his tone. "It's difficult. Twenty-five years is a long time to know and trust someone. Now, I'm sorry I've been abrupt, but I really must go try to sort out the facts."

Back in his office, de Jersey was forced to accept the reality of what had occurred. He had a terrible feeling that the gamble he had taken with David might now cause him to lose everything. He would not be the only loser: he had drawn in Wilcox and Driscoll, his two oldest friends. Earlier in the year, when de Jersey's share had trebled in value, he'd called them both and advised them to invest. He knew that he should contact them but couldn't bring himself to do it yet.

Someone would pay for this.

De Jersey's chest was tight with anger. Christina had lit the fire and left a bottle of port with some cheese and crackers on the table. In the dark, womblike room, with its heavy oak furniture and dark red velvet curtains, he sucked tensely at a cigar as he slotted a disk into the computer. Why had he been so foolish as to invest so much money in an Internet company? "Never get involved in anything you don't understand," his father had always told him.

De Jersey closed his eyes. He had not just got into something he didn't understand; he had walked blindly into a nightmare. Then he had become greedy and poured in more money and, even worse, had encouraged his friends to do the same.

Driscoll and Wilcox were the only living souls who knew how de Jersey had acquired his original wealth. Together the three men had staged some of the greatest robberies in British history, and they had never been caught. After their final heist they had agreed to a strict set of rules, which included not contacting each other again. But when David Lyons had started the investment bonanza, de Jersey couldn't resist breaking their agreement to encourage his old friends to jump onto the gravy train. He just hoped they had not acted as rashly as he had.

The snow that had been forecast was not yet falling, though the ground was hardened with frost. De Jersey, his hands deep in his coat pockets, his breath steaming out in front of him, had walked for miles.

He leaned against the white fence round the paddock. Christmas was always financially draining, and without liquid funds de Jersey knew he was in dire trouble. If he did not come up with a lucrative solution, he would soon be forced to start selling off his horses. He had to find a way of recouping his losses—fast. He tossed his cigar down and ground it out with his heel. He knew he was going to have to contact Driscoll and Wilcox, and it wouldn't be to wish them a happy new year.

"I'm going to see a specialist, maybe try this Viagra stuff," Tony Driscoll said in a depressed tone as he switched off the bedside lamp.

"Don't worry about it." Liz tried to pretend it wasn't important.

"That's the fourth time this month. Something's *got* to be wrong—I've never not been able to get it up."

Liz sighed.

"I've put on weight too." Driscoll rubbed his hairy chest, then let his hand slip down to the rolls of his belly. "You think it's something to do with my liver?" he asked.

"More likely it's just the traveling or the heat."

"We've been to Florida five times, so why should it suddenly affect me now?"

Liz sat up and bashed her pillow; he was not going to let her sleep. She snapped on the bedside lamp, got out of bed, and slipped a silk robe around her shoulders. At forty-seven she was in good shape, much better than her husband. But then the only thing she had to fill her time was exercise.

"Do you want a cup of tea or something?"

"Maybe a glass of water," he muttered.

Liz padded across the wide expanse of oyster-pink carpet to the fridge and poured some Perrier water into a tumbler. "I'll have to call down for some ice."

"Don't bother." Driscoll leaned back on the pillows. The hair on his chest was flecked with gray, as was the thick, bushy thatch on his head. At least there were no signs of baldness.

Liz returned to his side of the bed with the water. "I think I might spend the day at the hotel spa tomorrow. Have you got anything arranged?"

"Golf," he muttered.

"Shall I meet you at the clubhouse when I'm through?"

"Yeah, we'll have a drive around, then book somewhere nice for dinner. What do you think of the restaurant here?"

"I've not even looked at it yet, just read the leaflets. After that long plane trip, I could do with a stretch and a massage. I might have my hair and nails done too. Shall we meet up at about five?"

"I'm not playing golf all bloody day."

"Well, why don't you meet me back here, then? And don't get so shirty. It's not my fault you're impotent."

"I'm not fucking impotent," he snapped.

Her smirk turned into a laugh; he knew she was teasing him.

"Get off," he said as she tickled him but couldn't help smiling. She cuddled him and kissed his chest.

"I think I'll go to sleep now." He turned away before she could make another attempt. He couldn't stand the thought of failure twice in the same night.

Liz walked over to the dressing table and gave her long blond tresses a flick. She admired herself for a moment, then leaned closer to check her face. "I hate this light," she muttered, tracing the lines at the sides of her mouth. They seemed deeper, even though they had been injected recently. She pursed her lips; they too had been "fluffed up" with collagen injections.

"Are you coming back to bed?" Driscoll asked.

Liz was now studying the lines between her eyes. She was not supposed to be able to frown; her brow should have been frozen. "I don't think these Botox injections work, Tony."

"Well, I think you're crazy to have anything done, let alone stick poison into your face."

Liz pouted. At least her new lips looked great. She went into the bathroom.

"What are you doing?" he shouted.

"Having a tiddle. Is that all right with you?" She shut the door and gave herself the satisfaction her husband had been unable to provide.

They were both in deep sleep when the phone rang. Driscoll sat up like a shot. "What the hell? . . . What time is it?"

Liz moaned. "It might be one of the kids."

"If it is I'll give 'em a mouthful. It's only four o'clock." He wrapped a robe around himself.

"Well, answer it, then," Liz said, worried now.

"All right, all right." He snatched up the phone. "Hello?"

"It's the Colonel," came the soft voice at the other end of the line. Driscoll pressed hold and put down the receiver. He glanced at Liz and said, "It's okay, business. I'll take it in the lounge." He walked out.

"Business?" She flopped back, relieved that her children were not in trouble. They were in the south of France, staying with friends. They had grown out of accompanying their parents on holiday, even to Florida for Christmas. She wondered if they liked their gifts—they wouldn't have waited until Christmas Day to open them. Michelle had a gold necklace with her name picked out in diamonds, a matching bracelet, and her own credit card with five thousand pounds' spending money; she was seventeen years old and stunningly pretty, taking after her mother. Michael was the spitting image of his father, stocky, with dark eyes and thick, curly hair; he had been given the keys to a Lotus in a gold box; the car had been delivered to their home. He was nineteen and a first-year student of business studies at the University of Liverpool. He was very intelligent, and Liz doubted that a Lotus was the right kind of car for him; unlike his sister, he was quiet and studious. She worried about him much more than she did about her outgoing daughter, whose only real ambition was to be at the forefront of fashion and who was almost as obsessive about clothes as her mother. She could spend money just as fast too.

Liz knew that Michelle was spoiled, especially by her father, who doted on her. A good marriage with a nice, respectable boy was what they both wanted for her. At the moment, Michelle had a constant stream of boyfriends, all from wealthy families. Liz was determined, though, that her daughter wasn't going to get pregnant and ensured that she took sensible precautions. This was their mother-daughter secret; she knew her husband would not approve of his princess being on the pill. She yawned and looked at the bedside clock. The red light on the phone was still lit, and Tony was supposed to be semiretired.

"Tony? What's going on? Tony?"

"With you in a minute, sweetheart," he called.

The phone pressed to his ear, Driscoll listened to the soft, clipped tone of de Jersey's voice. The Colonel was the nickname he and Wilcox had given him, and only they used it. Driscoll's heart was beating rapidly, and he had broken out in a sweat. He did not interrupt, just gave the occasional grunt to let de Jersey know he was still on the line.

"There's nothing to be done before the Christmas break is over, but we'll meet up after you get back," said de Jersey. "The usual place, at the Ritz, but I'll call again as soon as I have more details. Tony?"

"We're due back mid-January."

"Fine. I'll contact James and pass on the news."

"He's in Aspen."

"I know."

Driscoll's mouth was dry. "There couldn't have been some fuckup, could there? I mean, are you sure?"

"Afraid so. David killed himself, that's proof enough. It's bad. I'll need time to sort through everything. I am truly sorry, Tony. I feel it's down to me, and I'll try to think of some way to make good our losses."

Driscoll closed his eyes. "I put all my eggs in."

"We all did, but like I said, I feel responsible."

"Hell, we're all grown men. You never twisted my arm, but I would like to know exactly what's gone down. We're talking millions."

"Try not to think about it. I'll work this one out for us, and that's a promise."

The phone went dead, and Driscoll sat cradling the receiver in his hands. He was still unable to take it in. He had just lost his life savings.

Tony Driscoll had started out as a runner in Ronnie Jersey's betting shops, but he was clever with his money. With the initial payoff from the Colonel, he had moved into the rubbish-collection industry, opening up big waste-disposal dumps and buying a fleet of trucks. In the mid-seventies he had married Liz, his secretary, and in the early eighties they had moved their children into a massive mock Tudor mansion just outside Guildford. Recently Driscoll had begun to play a big part in the local Labour Party, donating funds and attending functions. Driscoll glanced to the closed bedroom door. He still felt numb. He knew he couldn't take part in another caper, not after all these years. His hand was shaking as he poured a shot of whiskey. He felt fear when he considered his agreement to meet up with the others. Whatever the Colonel suggested to get them out of trouble, he would refuse. He kept looking at the bedroom door, wondering how he could explain his financial predicament to Liz. He'd have to get rid of the girlfriend, sell the flat he'd provided her with. He reckoned he'd have to sell off property fast, including his villa in Spain. He returned to the bedroom. Thinking about the life of crime he used to lead made the adrenaline pump into his tired veins.

Liz woke to her husband stroking her breasts, and suddenly he was on top of her, like a man possessed. He went for her with a passion that made her climax with a scream.

"Well, that must have been some phone call," she said, wide awake and smiling. "Whoever it was, you get him to call you just once a week. I couldn't take this every night! Tony? Was it good news?"

He closed his eyes. "Yes. And now I'm knackered." He turned over and fell almost immediately into a deep sleep.

Liz had no notion of her husband's life before their marriage. None of his business associates had an air of being less than 100 percent legitimate. If anyone had hinted to Liz that her husband had been involved with some of the most daring robberies ever committed in England she would have laughed. Not her Tony. Tony had a fixation on honesty; he'd even had arguments with his accountant over a few offshore tax-dodging schemes the man had suggested. He was paranoid if they were late paying the milkman. She loved and trusted him totally and had never been unfaithful, though recently she'd been fantasizing about her new personal trainer, Kevin. Just like Christina, Liz had been cosseted and adored but kept in ignorance of her husband's past activities. The three men had agreed: the less anyone knew about their past, the safer they would be. So their secrets were buried deep and covered with well-rehearsed lies. Liz had never heard her husband mention Edward de Jersey, just as Christina knew nothing about Tony Driscoll or James Wilcox.

The snowcapped mountains with the mellow light of sunrise streaming across their peaks made a wonderful sight. Aspen was not just great skiing country; its scenery was breathtaking. It also offered a fantastic social life, which was why James Wilcox and his present girlfriend, Rika, had booked their Christmas break there for two years in a row.

Rika had been the nanny. She'd arrived from the Ukraine hardly able to speak two words of English, a raw-boned, handsome blonde with a voluptuous figure. After six months, she moved into the master bedroom. Rika knew a good catch when she saw one, and born into poverty, she was determined to become Wilcox's wife number five.

At fifty-nine, Wilcox was slender and muscular from his daily workouts. He ran about fifty miles every week, cycled, and played tennis in the summer. He was still handsome and had only recently taken on the slight puffiness associated with age and high living. Rika was only twenty-eight. He could hardly ever understand what she said as her English was still appalling, but he had no desire for meaningful conversations. She was a great fuck, kept the kids in order and his homes clean.

Wilcox had stupendous energy and required only five hours' sleep a night. He practically rattled with the vitamin pills he swallowed in handfuls every morning. He ate sparingly, drank little, and smoked only the occasional cigar. His one vice was cocaine; he snorted mountains of it and depended on it to kick him into gear every day.

Wilcox was not as wealthy as Driscoll or de Jersey, but through wise deals in the car trade he had turned his earnings from the robberies into a lucrative business. At one time he had owned restaurants and garages, but he had recently liquidated the majority of his holdings in favor of a semi-retirement plan: he planned to pack up and live abroad. He had stayed on in England all these years only to educate his six kids. Since all of the older teenagers now either boarded at school or were heading for university, and only the twins still lived at home, it would be simple now to send them to boarding school, move to Geneva, and keep just a small house in England.

Wilcox and de Jersey had left Sandhurst at around the same time. Wilcox, though, had been thrown out for punching an officer. He had been enjoying his semiretirement, content to buy and sell expensive cars. The last robbery the three had pulled off had set him up for life. Like his hero de Jersey, Wilcox was legitimate now, but over the past few years he had overstretched his finances, unable to resist women and top-of-the-range motors. So when de Jersey had suggested the Internet venture, he had agreed to join in. At first, Wilcox had been uneasy about what de Jersey was going to propose. He discovered that Driscoll too was loath to get involved in any further criminal activity. But de Jersey had soon eased their worries. In fact he had laughed. He wasn't in any way going to suggest another robbery, far from it. "The Colonel's retired, my friends," de Jersey said. "I am about to offer you the chance to double your savings, no risk, nothing illegal."

He explained in detail. The investment was a new Internet company with its main base in the United States. He had inside information that, if they invested now, they would become billionaires within six months. De Jersey had seen his investment treble. So the three of them had become the main investors in leadingleisurewear.com. They released millions, and their shares doubled, then trebled, then skyrocketed. The company's Web site became one of the most popular in the country, and the press heralded the enterprise as a major success. Wilcox even remortgaged his house to invest more.

He was leaning back drenched in sweat in the chalet sauna when Rika opened the door. She was wearing a silk wrap, her long blond hair was in a braid, and her face was taut with anger. "I fund dis inda luggage!" she snapped.

"What?" He wrapped a small towel round his waist.

"I'm nut stupid, Jimmy," she shouted. "I bring ta Aspen da Christmas presents you give me, the ones from you to me and to da children. So who is diss for?" She wafted a ring box in front of his nose.

He stood up, towering over her, then walked out.

"Don't turn da back on me. I hate you!" she screamed.

He sighed, taking the box and flicking it open. "Don't you recognize it, Rika?"

"No, I do not."

"Well, you should. Go back to last Christmas, to that charity dinner. Sylvester Stallone was there. We were at the same table as Goldie Hawn."

"Vat about it?" she said, her hands on her hips.

"Well, this ring is identical to the one Goldie Hawn was wearing, which you admired. She said it was from a local jeweler, so I ordered one for you last year but it wasn't ready in time. I paid for it and asked them to keep it for me. Yesterday I picked it up. It's three diamonds on platinum and yellow gold. You don't want it? Fine, I'll chuck it out of the god-damned window!"

He strode to the window, and she ran after him. "No, don't! I am sorry."

"Yeah, well, you ruined the surprise. I'm getting sick of this, Rika."

She started to cry, and he wrapped his arms around her. After they kissed, she slipped on the ring.

"Can I finish my sauna now?" he asked.

"Yes, I make breakfast. I so sorry. I just love you so much."

He walked into the sauna and closed the door. It was all a lie, of course. He'd bought it for Cameron, his mistress in England. He had just poured pine essence over the coals when the door opened again. "A call for you."

"Who?" he snapped.

"I not know. You want me to bring it in here?"

"Yeah."

She returned a minute later and passed him the cell phone, then backed out and closed the door.

"Wilcox," he said.

"Hello, Jimmy," came the soft reply. "It's the Colonel."

His stomach lurched.

"Listen, this isn't a social call, it's bad news, so I'll give it to you straight."

Wilcox listened without interruption as de Jersey outlined the Internet crash. "But I don't understand. Can't David Lyons sort this out?"

" 'Fraid not, Jimmy. He's dead. He topped himself."

Wilcox was meticulous about how his food should be served, and Rika had it down to a fine art. Fresh white linen napkins lay next to the fine bone-china plates and coffee cups. She had changed into a navy ski suit. "I'm meeting the boys on da slopes. Will you see later?"

"I have a few things to do. Maybe we could meet for lunch, take the boys to the hamburger joint."

"But you no like dat place."

"I know, but they love it. Tonight I'll arrange a nice place for us to go and eat, maybe dance. What do you think?"

She curled her arms around him. "Vatever you vant. I love you."

"I love you too."

She cupped his chin in her hands. "You vould tell Rika somethink happen if it's not good, yes?" she asked.

"Of course. Go on, now, see you later."

She paused at the door. She was seeing something in Wilcox that she had never seen before. Something was weighing him down.

He smiled. "Now, go on, go meet the kids."

This time she left, and he closed his eyes. His entire fortune, bar a few hundred thousand, had gone. David Lyons had killed himself and, as he sliced the top off his egg, Wilcox wished he had done it for him. He did not blame de Jersey; it had been his own decision to bankroll the Internet company. And he still trusted de Jersey to get them out of the mess. Deep down, though, he was afraid. He wondered if de Jersey would have to res-urrect the Colonel.

3

De Jersey sat at his desk jotting notes. An opened newspaper had an article ringed in red about the falling prices of Internet stocks. Some compared it to the Wall Street crash. The headline screamed, TYCOONS WHO LOST A BILLION OVERNIGHT and THE STARS WHO SAW THEIR INTERNET FORTUNES CRASH. Five British investors had lost a billion in less than a year; five others had lost more than half a billion. The only compensation for de Jersey was that his name was not mentioned in any of the press reports.

Leadingleisurewear.com had grown into one of Europe's largest Internet retailers as well, but it had now been confirmed that they had brought in liquidators. The company had spent nearly 230 million pounds since its inception eighteen months previously. Staff at its New York headquarters learned that the fledgling enterprise had collapsed, taking with it the entire backing of its investors. The founder, Alex Moreno, admitted that the company had failed to control costs.

De Jersey wrote and underlined the man's name on his pad. He turned back to his computer, took out one disk, and slotted in another. He continued scrolling through David's reports, which detailed previous companies started by Moreno. Apparently, he had successfully launched four companies on the Internet over the past six years. In a lengthy article, Moreno expressed his deep regret but said he still believed leadingleisurewear had been on the right track in aiming to become the largest Internet retail clothing business in the world. He admitted they had spent money too freely opening lavish foreign offices in Britain, Germany, and Sweden, and offering perks to lure the best employees.

De Jersey almost bit through his cigar. Management had purchased fleets of cars and enjoyed first-class hotel accommodations as well as luxurious apartments and houses. The article identified the big losers in leadingleisurewear as "an English aristocrat and two other British businessmen." As the controlling shareholder, de Jersey had suffered the biggest loss: nearly a hundred million pounds.

It was almost five o'clock in the morning when he finished assessing the documentation David had compiled for him. His losses were far greater than he had at first anticipated. All that remained was the three million he had stashed in his offshore account in the Caymans, and with David gone, he would now have to gain access to this money personally.

He shut down his computer, then unlocked a drawer, slipping into it his notepad, which by now contained the names of the leadingleisurewear founders, their last known addresses, and details of their attempts to sell off what was left of the company. Moreno had already formed another company under a different name. This meant he could be traced, and de Jersey had every intention of doing just that.

It had snowed heavily during the night, and on Christmas Day the de Jersey home resembled a picture postcard of idyllic country life. Christina adored Christmas. She had decorated with bunting and arrangements of silver holly and fir branches. The tree in the hall reached the ceiling and was trimmed with silver ribbons and baubles. Under it the piles of gifts were wrapped in exquisite paper and ribbons. She loved the smells that wafted through the house. She'd baked for days, making baskets of Christmas puddings, cakes, and mince pies for the staff and the local church. Natasha and Leonie had arrived home yesterday after spending a few nights with classmates at their Swiss chalet. At seventeen and fifteen, the girls both enjoyed skiing. They were stunning, with their mother's crystal blue eyes and long, blond hair. De Jersey spoiled his daughters, but he was quite a strict father. Their friends were welcome to stay, as long as plenty of notice had been given. People were not encouraged to drop in; his family knew that he valued his privacy.

The annual Christmas Day party was in full swing. Christina distributed gifts to the staff and their families, and there was always a white envelope from the Boss, which contained a bonus.

De Jersey stood at the front door looking out with a lump in his throat. Royal Flush was walking sedately through the snow, carrying two baskets loaded with gifts from the staff to their employer. The horse was draped in a red velvet blanket with a sprig of holly in his forelock, and his breath steamed out in front of him. They surrounded de Jersey and sang "For He's a Jolly Good Fellow." He approached his champion and stroked his nose. He was not about to lose all this, he thought. It was everything he had dreamed of possessing.

After receiving the gifts, de Jersey slipped away and was not missed for some time. Eventually, Christina sought him out in their bedroom and was surprised to find him changing into his jodhpurs. "Darling, what are you doing?"

"I need a ride. I won't be long."

"But lunch is soon. You said you wanted to sit down at four."

"I'll be back by then. Please, I'm sorry, I just need some air."

He saddled up Royal Flush himself and rode toward the track on the outskirts of the farm, unmarked except for the footprints of foxes and birds. His lungs filled with the icy air as his thoughts turned to the problems he faced. He decided to leave first thing the following morning. He'd have his pilot arrange permission to fly into Heathrow's private heliport and then take a flight to New York.

After lunch Christina carried in the blazing pudding and received great applause. Around her wrist was the delicate diamond bracelet that had been her husband's present. He had given each of his daughters a special piece of jewelry too, as tasteful as their mother's. He had received cigars, socks, and a flamboyant embroidered waistcoat from the girls. And Christina gave him a small oil painting of the stud farm circa 1910 that she had found.

They had coffee in the dining room and played word games in front of the roaring fire. At seven Natasha and Leonie went to change to go to a party. Christina curled up beside her husband, her arms loosely wrapped round his knees.

"I have to go to London tomorrow," he told her. "I'm sorry, it's business."

"But it's Boxing Day," she exclaimed.

"I shouldn't be more than a couple of days."

She looked up into his face. "It's to do with David, isn't it?"

"No. Why do you ask?"

"Oh, don't do this. Since David's death you've been acting so strangely. Please talk to me. Is it to do with him?"

"Yes," he admitted. "I'm meeting a banker who's going to help me unravel the mess. I need to deal with it right away."

"Okay. Do you want me to come with you?"

"You stay with the girls. The sooner I leave the sooner I can come home, but it might be three or four days."

Christina threw a log onto the fire, then glanced at the mantelpiece; a Christmas card from the Queen was in pride of place. Her husband had been so pleased when he saw the crest on the envelope. He had always coveted acceptance in high-society circles, though she did not understand why. He had told her little of his past, and, not long before they met, his last relative, his mother, Florence, had died.

"Penny for them." He kissed her neck.

"I was admiring the Queen's Christmas card."

De Jersey laughed.

"Why do you never talk about your family?" she asked suddenly.

"What brought this on?"

"You go away sometimes—inside yourself, I mean. I know this David business is on your mind, but you told me it's not that serious. Then you have to go to see a banker on Boxing Day. It doesn't make sense to me. If it *is* serious, why don't you tell me, let me share it with you?"

"I've told you all I know." De Jersey had to control his temper. "And my family—you know that my parents died a long time ago, sweetheart. You know all there is to know."

"No, I don't," Christina persisted.

"Yes, you do," he snapped. "And you've had too much champagne."

"No, I haven't." She leaned against the mantelpiece watching her husband. "What was your home like, Edward?" she asked stubbornly.

He blinked rapidly. "Clean, neat, and tidy. My mother always said you could eat your dinner off her kitchen floor. We always had a Christmas tree in the front room window and paper chains all over the hall. There was usually a big fire—well, it seemed big, but the fireplace was small. It had pinkish tiles and two brass animals on either side."

Christina stared at him. "You make it sound . . ."

"Clean, neat, and tidy," he said.

"No, friendly," she said.

"Yes, it was. Everyone loved my father and mother. Now, as I'm leaving tomorrow, I thought maybe we could retire early," he said, cupping her breasts with his hands. They kissed passionately until he picked her up in his arms and carried her toward the stairs.

As Christina lay sleeping peacefully beside him, de Jersey moved a wisp of hair from her cheek. Their marriage had been so happy; his previous one seemed a lifetime ago. He had met Gail at a nightclub. She was the worst kind of spoiled "daddy's girl." Her father was a wealthy real estate agent with offices all over London. She was educated at Roedean, a top British private school, and attended finishing school in Switzerland. De Jersey was not a man who frequented nightclubs. Wilcox, a regular at every West End club, had cajoled him into going. This was before their last robbery. Wilcox seemed to have an endless string of women. In fact, it was he who had first known Gail Raynor and introduced them.

When de Jersey saw her dancing in the dim lights of the Piccadilly Blue Elephant Club, she had looked like a tempting angel. The Blue Elephant was the in place to be and be seen, always full of celebrities and famous socialites. Gail was waiflike, with auburn hair down to her waist. She wore miniskirts that showed off her beautiful legs and high, white Courrèges boots. She had an annoying nasal twang and haughty manner worse than that of her aristocratic "debby" friends.

"Can't you sleep?" Christina murmured, interrupting his thoughts.

"No, just thinking."

"About what?" She sat up, leaning on her elbow.

"Gail," he said.

"Do you think about her often?"

"No. Maybe it's David's death. I've been reflecting about a lot of things."

"Like what?"

"Why I ever got involved with Gail. To be honest, I think I was more impressed by her successful father than by her."

"Why?"

He wished he had not started the conversation. "Maybe because my own father was dead. I was not sure what to do with my life, and he gave me direction."

"By marrying his daughter," Christina said, yawning.

"Whatever. She was a mistake, but my friendship with her father wasn't. He was a good man."

She snuggled. "You hate talking about her."

"I just don't like wasting time thinking of her. She isn't worth it. Hate has nothing to do with it. It was a mistake, and I got out as fast as I could." He made no mention of divorcing Gail once her father had died, leaving him to run the business. It was also Gail's father who had suggested that if he was selling property to top-level clients he might think about dropping the overly familiar Eddy. Raynor felt that Eddie Jersey wasn't classy enough. But his son-in-law went one better, not only referring to himself as Edward but inserting the de. So it was that he became Edward de Jersey, and Gail's father would never know the many other names his son-in-law would use by the end of his criminal career.

"What happened to her?" Christina asked.

He shrugged his shoulders. "I don't know. When the firm went bust I sold up and . . ." He was moving into dangerous territory now. It was after the company fell apart that he'd started planning his final robbery. "I never saw her again," he said, leaning on his elbow and smiling. "I met this woman, well, she was just a young slip of a thing, and I saw her photograph in a magazine and . . ."

Christina giggled. She always loved hearing him tell how he had cut out her picture and traced her through the model agency. He had even traveled to Sweden to find her when she was already living in London.

"She who made up for all the tedious years I'd been with Gail. And she is now my wife, the mother of my daughters, and . . ." He kissed her, trying to prevent a return to the subject of his ex-wife and, more important, not wanting to approach the time in his life when he, Wilcox, and Driscoll had pulled off the robbery that had been the foundation of their wealthy lifestyles.

What troubled de Jersey was that when he met Christina he had been immensely rich and had used his wealth to court her obsessively. "Do you regret anything?" he asked stroking her cheek.

"No. Well, yes there is one thing," she said softly.

"What's that?" he asked, kissing her neck.

"I would like to have given you a son."

After a moment he raised his arm and drew her close to him. "I do not have a second of regret, not one second," he said. "We have two perfect daughters and"—he looked down into her face—"Royal Flush."

"I know," Christina said, "but it's not the same."

He gripped her tightly. "I don't want anything to change." His manner frightened her, but then he tucked the pillow beneath his head and closed his eyes, murmuring, "Good night, sweetheart."

"Happy Christmas," she whispered. She remained curled by his side, lying in the crook of his arm.

"Happy Christmas, sweetheart." He would not allow anything to harm their idyllic life.

By the end of Christmas dinner, he had to undo the button on his trousers. The Driscolls were in a booth in the main restaurant. He had ordered Krug champagne, as had most of the other guests. He had drunk more than usual, but he felt stone cold sober.

"Do you like this color?" Liz paraded her pearly false nails.

"Yes, very nice."

"Oyster pink shimmer," she said. "It's a perfect match for the dress I bought for New Year's Eve. I was just testing the colors out. Do you remember the dress? From Chanel in Knightsbridge." Driscoll recalled the floating chiffon with an embroidered vest top and ribbon straps. It looked like a nightdress, but he'd told her he loved it—he loved anything that made her happy. Suddenly he was overcome by emotion.

"Tone, what's the matter?" she asked, alarmed.

Driscoll was crying now. How could he tell her he was broke? That he'd been a bloody idiot and lost his life savings. A few thousand here or there wasn't going to keep this pretty little soul in the manner to which she was accustomed. "I've had too much to drink," he muttered.

She reached for his hand. "Let's go to the room. They've got the porno channel. We could order more champagne, get into the Jacuzzi, and have dirty sex." She giggled.

Dear God, he thought, how am I going to keep this up until New Year's Eve? All he wanted was to get back to London, meet de Jersey, and hear his plan. Just thinking about it, he got another erection. "Yes, darling," he said. "Let's go up to the suite."

They didn't make it into the Jacuzzi, and he didn't need to watch any porno film. To Liz's delight, Driscoll didn't even take off his dinner jacket, he was so desperate. They screwed against the bathroom wall, in the bedroom on the carpet, and then in their bed until he passed out. She wished their sex life was always this good.

Wilcox had never been money-conscious. He lived life on the edge in Aspen, keeping his mind off his financial crisis with excessive amounts of cocaine. Rika worried about his recklessness. Wilcox had more innate class than de Jersey, but he lacked prudence. This man liked taking risks. Over and over again Rika tried to stop him going out late at night to ski, but she always backed down at the first hint of anger. Fury lay dormant in Wilcox, and she did not want to provoke it against herself. So when he left the house on Christmas night, she didn't try to stop him.

The loss of his fortune had left Wilcox balancing on a precipice. When he got off the ski lift at the level for experienced skiers, he positioned himself, checked his skis, adjusted his goggles, then eased forward. In the five-minute descent, he made a near-perfect run. Upon reaching the lower slopes, however, he felt a tightening in his chest. He gasped for breath, and by the time he was at a standstill he was bending almost double. Lately these pains had been occurring more frequently. Added to chest pain, he'd been experiencing dizzy spells, and a couple of times during this holiday his nose had bled profusely. Even now, as he pulled off his goggles, there were spots of blood on the snow.

He removed gloves, then skis, which he carried to his truck. Once inside he leaned back until the dizziness subsided. Then he adjusted the rearview mirror; his nostrils were encrusted with dried blood. He took a tissue and wiped it away. When he got back to the chalet, every light was on. The kids would be listening to music, playing table tennis, or watching videos, and Rika was probably waiting to have another go at him for disappearing. He told himself he was too old to be indulging a serious drug habit—if he caught any of his kids using the same substance, he'd thrash them—but he could feel the itch starting. He dumped the skis on the ground by Rika's car and hurried up the stairs.

He locked the bathroom door, unfolded the wrap, chopped three lines of cocaine, rolled a dollar bill, and snorted. He was rubbing the residue on his gums when the door handle turned. "James, are you all right?"

He unlocked the door, smiling. "I'm great. Just got caught short coming up the drive."

"I vas vorried vhen I saw you just throw your skis inside the garage. You haven't viped dem clean."

"Yeah, yeah, I'll do it later."

"You do it now, James. You shout at the kids for doing just the same thing."

"Get off my back, Rika."

"I'm not on it." She stormed out.

Wilcox locked the door, then sat on the toilet. One more hit, he thought, then he'd dry off his skis. He snorted two lines, then reached for the phone. He knew it was against the rules, but he couldn't stop himself. A little later he went into the bedroom, packed a bag, and went downstairs to Rika. "I've got to go away for a day. I'll be back tomorrow."

She gripped his arm. "Vhere you going?"

He pushed her aside. "I've got a business problem. Just leave me alone!"

"I von't be 'ere ven you get back," she screamed after him.

Wilcox drove erratically down the drive, then reversed, almost skidding into the garage. Rika ran from the house and banged on the windscreen, but her anger turned to worry when she saw the look on his face.

"I'm sorry," he said. She opened the car door and got in beside him. "I've got big problems."

She put an arm around him; he rested his head against her. "Maybe I'll go tomorrow," he said. Then she helped him out of the Jeep and into the house. He told her that he had lost some money and needed to talk to someone about it. The following morning she drove him to the airport.

Wilcox flew to Florida. He had to talk to someone, and it could only be Driscoll. He had calmed down since the previous night, but he was cold— the air-conditioning made him feel as if he was still on the ski run. He was sitting at a booth in the bar, behind a massive aquarium with exotic fish diving around elaborate fake rocks. He'd had two diet Cokes.

Driscoll—white golfing cap, white T-shirt and shorts—entered the bar and saw Wilcox slouched at the table. He headed over and sat down.

"How did you find me?"

"Simple. Phoned all the top-notch hotels. Got to the tenth and they said you were there." Wilcox cast a bleary eye over his friend. "Christ, Tony, you look like a right arsehole! What have you got on your feet?"

"Gucci sandals. You look as if you've had a night on the tiles."

"Still a label man, are you?" Wilcox asked.

"The wife buys it all. I don't give a shit, but if it doesn't carry a designer name she won't buy it."

Wilcox slurped his Coke, and Driscoll ordered a decaf coffee from a waitress in a pink uniform. Eventually Driscoll said, "How much did you lose?"

"My shirt," Wilcox said flatly.

"Me too. I mean, I've still got a few thousand here and there, some property, but . . . He called you, did he?"

"Yeah." Wilcox rubbed his arms. "Bloody cold in here."

"Yeah, the hotel dining room's like a fridge, gotta wear a jumper to breakfast."

"What are we gonna do?" Wilcox finally asked.

"I dunno. The Colonel said he was trying to sort it all but not to hold out much hope. We may be able to salvage something."

"That prick David Lyons didn't top himself for nothing, and we're in a long line of losers. The Internet bonanza's screwed thousands like us." Wilcox twisted his glass. "Gonna meet us at the Ritz again, right?"

"He's arranged the meeting for when I get back from here, mid-January." Driscoll was staring at the fish.

"What do you think he's doing in the meantime?"

"I dunno." One tiny fish was swimming like quicksilver.

"I'd say he's up to his old tricks again. Nosing out some hit. What if he suggests we get involved in something? Are we up for it?"

Driscoll burped. "Thing is, Jimmy, I owe him. His dad took care of my mother. If it hadn't been for him she'd have been in a right mess. Paid for my school uniform. Like a surrogate father to me was Ronnie."

"I know."

Driscoll closed his eyes. "He used to look after a lot of people, did Ronnie, but when the shit hit the fan . . ."

Wilcox leaned back against the booth.

"Those villains, Jimmy, were something else. They came in the bookies with fucking sledgehammers, terrifying! I didn't know Eddy that well then. Seen him around, but he was at the grammar school so we didn't mix. And after he got into Sandhurst I hardly ever saw him. It was hard to believe they were father and son. I mean Ronnie wasn't a big fella, and

Eddy was always head and shoulders above him. My mother said it was from Florence's side he got the height. She was a big woman. Always knitting. She got him elocution lessons so's he wouldn't feel out of place at Sandhurst. But when I saw him at Ronnie's funeral limping on a crutch after he'd busted his knee, I said to myself, 'He's not gonna be able to deal with these villains coming into the shop, extortin' cash, smashing the place up.' I said to him that, as much as I respected his dad, I wasn't gonna stay around to get my head kicked in. And do you know what he said?" Driscoll asked rhetorically. " 'They've offered to buy me out.' I said to him, 'Sell. If you don't, they'll go after your mother.' You don't want to get in the middle of bastards like the Krays and the Richardsons fighting it out. 'Sell up and get out,' but he said he was going to the police."

Wilcox was looking around the bar, bored. He'd heard the story a thousand times, albeit many years ago.

"Offered him peanuts, the bastards did," Driscoll continued, "and those two betting shops were gold mines. Cops were no help. I said to him, 'Eddy, they're probably getting back-handers,' and I'll never forget his face. When they came back, pushing and shoving him around, he just stood there like a wimp. They threw the money at him and made him pick it up off the floor."

"I was there, Tony."

"I mean, if you'd told me then what he'd go on to do, I'd have laughed in your face," said Driscoll.

Suddenly Wilcox got up.

"Where you going?"

"To take a leak, then I want out of this place. We can go back to my hotel, have a sandwich."

"Oh, okay, I'll settle this." Driscoll took the check.

Wilcox gave a soft laugh. "That's generous."

Wilcox's hotel was evidently not a five-star establishment, and Driscoll balked. "Gawd almighty, Jimmy, why did you book into a place like this?"

"Anonymity," Wilcox snapped, and they went into the threadbare foyer, then up to his room, where Wilcox opened a miniature vodka from the minibar.

"I was thinking about you moving in with Eddy after Sandhurst," Driscoll remarked. "I bet his mother didn't like it."

Wilcox flopped back onto the bed. "You sound like a record that's got stuck. You don't owe Eddy. If you hadn't helped us out we'd never have got away with robbing the shops."

"I know," said Driscoll.

Wilcox recalled the way de Jersey had laid the plans after selling out to rob his father's old betting shops. They wore balaclavas and carried shotguns as they systematically cleaned out the takings. De Jersey became the Colonel because of the way he barked out orders when they rehearsed their attacks on the shops. They hit them on every big race meeting, de Jersey working out the details like a military maneuver. As a result of their robberies, the two big rival East End gangs started a war that eventually saw the shops firebombed and burned to the ground. Each believed the other was the perpetrator.

"How much do you reckon in today's money we got away with?" Driscoll asked.

Wilcox shrugged. "Maybe a quarter of a million, not a lot."

"To me it was. When he shared it out three ways I couldn't believe it. I thought I'd get a cut but not that much. You see that's another reason I owe him. I was able to set my mum up for the rest of her life, God rest her soul."

Driscoll called room service and ordered two hamburgers and french fries.

"You ever think, Tony, that he owes us?" Wilcox asked quietly.

"No way. He even split it three ways for the train robbery. He didn't have to do that."

"He couldn't have robbed his dad's shops without our help, and on the train job, all he did was suss out how to stop the train."

"And I was the only one with a car. Remember that Morris Minor? You two were havin' to schlep all over the place to check out the trains. You guys were catching trains to stop one!"

"We spent hours up at that railway bridge too. And it wasn't Eddy's idea about fixing the signals, it was mine." Wilcox lit a cigarette.

"But he worked out how to move the mail train into a siding."

This annoyed Wilcox. "You owe me just as much. I agreed to split that cash three ways as well. Look, you just did the route for that. Anyway, I don't call twenty grand in cash a big deal or any reason to feel you owe him for the rest of your life."

"All I'm saying is, he didn't always have to cut it three ways."

"Just think about his reasons. The others got thirty years apiece, right? And when they questioned us we could have put him in the frame with them. We were lucky they thought we were just dumb kids."

"Not that dumb. We got away with it."

"Yeah, yeah, yeah. And here you are, Christ knows how many years later, bleating on about how much you owe him. That's why he always did a three-way cut."

"What do you mean?"

"So we'd feel indebted to him," Wilcox snapped.

"So you do feel you owe him, then?" Driscoll asked, surprised.

Wilcox sighed with exasperation. "No. We all took the risks. It was only fair to cut three ways."

Driscoll opened a bottle of gin from the minibar and yanked out the ice tray. "Not the same on the last caper, though, was it?"

Wilcox tensed and opened another bottle. "I was up for it," he said shortly.

"Yeah, but the last time it was a big number."

"All right, I hear you."

"Yeah, stealing fucking gold bullion, Jimmy. If we'd been copped that would have been thirty years. Without Eddy we'd never have got away with it. It wasn't you or me that found out how to launder the cash."

"And it was almost a fuckup. He didn't have any idea how much there was."

Driscoll laughed. "Three tonnes of gold. Worth twenty-five million pounds. Damn right we owe him."

Wilcox reclined, his eyes drifted upward. Most of the gold had been melted down and moved abroad fast with the assistance of de Jersey's friend's helicopter and yacht. The robbery had been almost effortless, but moving that volume of gold had been a nightmare. De Jersey had deployed everyone he could think of to melt, move, carry, and shift the bars. Some were melted in a private kiln in a jeweler's garden; others were buried around London, carried out to Spain in suitcases, or even left in safety-deposit boxes. De Jersey shipped some to Africa, then brought it back into England after purchasing a smelting plant; there he altered the hallmarks and later sold it on the open market. The largest amount, however, had been stored in a small jeweler's workshop in France.

There was a rap at the door, and Driscoll got up to take in the hamburgers. He handed one to Wilcox and unwrapped the other.

"He moved those gold bars around," Driscoll said. "Turned them into cash."

"I don't know how he bloody did it," Wilcox said.

"He used assumed names and identities. He told me he'd worked out a system of depositing cash into high-street banks, in amounts as large as eight hundred grand."

Wilcox unwrapped his hamburger.

"It wasn't just us he took care of. Those 'soldiers' who were picked up, he looked after them. They never put any of us in the frame." Driscoll tried to open his ketchup packet; he swore as the ketchup spurted over his T-shirt.

Wilcox remained unimpressed by the argument. "Well, they wanted their payoff when they came out of the nick."

Driscoll peered at his hamburger. "You know Scotland Yard officers recovered eleven melted-down bars in 1985. None of the remaining stolen ingots has ever been found. Have you got a raw one? This is like old leather." Wilcox passed over his untouched hamburger, opening another miniature vodka instead.

The two men fell silent, Wilcox drinking, Driscoll stuffing french fries into his mouth.

Under de Jersey's orders, Wilcox and Driscoll had split up and moved to Canada, then to Los Angeles. De Jersey covered their tracks; he had given them fake passports and instructed them to be constantly on the move—and apart—until all was quiet. They were not due to receive the big payoff for another few years. They showed how much they trusted their "colonel" by their patience. The laundered money eventually ensured that all three men could lead a life of luxury. By now they had growing families and flourishing businesses. De Jersey himself emerged as a race-horse and stud-farm owner.

Driscoll looked up suddenly. "Why did you come here, Jimmy?"

"Thinking of writing my memoirs," Wilcox replied.

"You're here because you're worried about what he's gonna suggest, right?"

"Well, you keep saying how much you're in debt to him, so I guess whatever he suggests, you'll be up for it."

"And you don't feel like you owe him?"

"Like fuck I do. It was his idea to back that Internet company."

Driscoll opened a half bottle of white wine.

"Okay, let's be honest with each other." He sat back, watching Wilcox open another miniature. "Reason you're here is that you're scared shitless."

"Listen, I'm not scared of anything; I'm just being realistic. No way do I want to spend the rest of my life in some nick."

"Yeah. I've got a wife and two kids. I feel the same way."

"You do?"

"I can get by, like I said. I'll have to sell off everything. Liz will go ba-nanas, but hell. Ain't gonna starve."

"When we meet what are you gonna say? We should get it worked out between us."

"I know."

"But whatever he suggests we both walk away from, and this time we don't let him wear us down. If we stand up to him together . . . Tony?"

Driscoll took a gulp of wine, then another, draining the bottle. "I agree," he said. "I hope they serve better stuff than this at the Ritz, because I know I'm gonna need a few drinks to face him."

"Yeah, but if we do it together it'll be better."

"It's agreed, then?"

"Yeah." They shook hands, but neither could meet the other's eyes. They felt as if they were somehow betraying de Jersey.

Liz sat, surrounded by boutique bags, when her husband reeled in. "Do you know what time it is?" she asked, buffing her nails.

"I do, my love. I've been out on the golf course."

"No, you haven't. Your golfing shoes are still in the wardrobe."

"Well, I lied. I've been at the Pink Flamingo bar," he said as he tottered off to their bathroom.

"Who with?"

"Brad Pitt, and if you think I'm plastered you should see him."

"Tony!" she yelled, but he slammed the door behind him.

Driscoll knew it was going to be very hard for him to say no to the Colonel. It would be even harder for Wilcox. He remembered Wilcox's face when de Jersey had insisted they all have no further contact with each other. Since leaving Sandhurst, Wilcox and de Jersey had hardly been apart. Wilcox could not believe that his friend really meant it. He'd joked that maybe they could at least have a drink sometime.

"No, Jimmy," de Jersey had said. "When I walk away, that is it. You don't know me, we never meet up again. It's the only way we will protect each other." Then de Jersey had hugged Jimmy tightly. After he'd gone, Wilcox was in tears. "I feel like I just lost my brother," he said.

Driscoll had felt sorry for him. "He's just looking out for us Jimmy, like he's always done."

"Yeah, yeah, good-bye then."

"Good-bye, Jimmy. You take care now."

So they had all gone their separate ways. They had each been lucky and enjoyed a good life.

He sighed, sitting on the toilet looking down at his feet and his leather sandals. They reminded him of the ones he had worn when he was a kid. Outside the bathroom his wife was dripping with diamonds, and she had no doubt spent a fortune at the boutiques. The good life had softened both men, and Wilcox was obviously as afraid as he was of being drawn into another robbery. They would have to say no.

CHAPTER

4

De Jersey needed a big injection of cash to keep his estate afloat and to fund a follow-up to the bullion robbery. His first target was Alex Moreno. He had set the wheels in motion by hiring a private investigator from an advertisement in *The New York Times*. The man had a lead on Moreno, and de Jersey would fly to New York to confront him. In his study, as his wife slept, de Jersey removed the top right-hand drawer of his antique desk, then reached over to the side of the desk and pulled a section of the edge toward him. A hidden compartment slid open. He walked round the desk to the front false drawers and opened a four-shelved cupboard. First, he removed an envelope and put it on the desk. Next came a large, square makeup box, and last a plastic bag containing two wigs and a false mustache and eyebrows.

He settled back in his chair and shook out four passports from the envelope, all in different names. He laid them side by side, then shredded the one that carried an out-of-date photograph he could never match. The other three were in the names of Philip Simmons, Edward Cummings, and Michael Shaughnessy. He returned the last passport to the envelope and put the other two into his briefcase. Though he had bank accounts and credit cards in all three names, none of them held a substantial amount of money, just enough for emergencies.

De Jersey selected a few items from the makeup box, then placed them in a wooden pencil box. The wigs smelled musty but were in good condition. The glue and cleaning fluids were usable and the wig meshing clean, so these he placed in his suitcase, locking it afterward. He'd always traveled in disguise using his aliases with confidence, but now he'd have to be extra careful. Since the September 11 terrorist attacks in the United States, security at the airports, especially in and out of New York, had been stringent.

On December 26 de Jersey left home and booked into a small hotel close to Heathrow airport as Edward Cummings, an art dealer. The following day, using his British passport, he traveled Virgin, economy class, to New York. When he landed at JFK and booked into the Hotel Carlyle, he looked nothing like Edward de Jersey. His wig was dark and curly with flecks of gray, and de Jersey winced as he eased it off. He used a Pan-Stik suntan makeup base to darken his face and hands, then switched his watch, which had belonged to his father, for a flashy Rolex. He added a thick gold chain, a large diamond ring, and a gold bracelet. His suit was expensive but a shiny, light gray silk. The shirt was white with a pearl gray tie under the stiff collar. Adjusting the pale blue silk handkerchief in the top pocket, he stared at his reflection. The suit was now a little tight, but this added to the persona he wanted to create. Now he took out the other wig: a reddish color, with matching mustache and eyebrows, which had been made for him many years ago by a theatrical costumier. He trimmed the sides of his own hair so the wig would fit tightly and show no gauze. He had arrived as Edward Cummings, but now he was Philip Simmons, and he called the Ritz-Carlton hotel to arrange his first meeting.

"I'd like to speak to a Mr. Donny Baron, please," de Jersey said.

"One moment, sir. Who shall I say is calling?"

"Philip Simmons."

There was a short wait; then Baron was on the line. "Mr. Simmons, did you have a good flight?" he asked.

"I did—came out on the red-eye from Los Angeles. Can we meet up?"

"Sure thing. Come for breakfast. I think I have what you need."

"Good. How will I recognize you?"

"I'll be in a back booth of the Jockey restaurant. Just look for a short, bald guy."

"Be there in about fifteen."

De Jersey stared at himself in the mirror over the small telephone table. The game had begun.

He left by the side entrance to the hotel. Shortly afterward he entered the Jockey restaurant at the Ritz-Carlton. Most of the diners were young and rowdy, dressed in an odd assortment of designer clothes—the hotel was a known haunt of rock stars and their managers. So it was relatively easy to find the only short, balding man in the room. Donny Baron provided security for a mediocre band that was usually the support act for bigger names. As de Jersey approached he tried to stand, wipe his mouth, and hail the waiter at the same time, but de Jersey gestured for him to remain seated. "I've had breakfast, but please, carry on eating."

"Mr. Simmons" had spoken to Baron numerous times after seeing the advertisement the detective had placed in *The New York Times* upon leaving the NYPD. Private investigation work did not yet provide a steady income, so he had recently taken on the job with the rock group.

De Jersey placed an envelope on the table. "You track him?"

"I've got a few pals still in the game, you know, guys I was in uniform with. These days, with computers, tracing's a hell of a lot simpler."

De Jersey glanced around covertly. Then he patted the envelope, impatient to get his five hundred dollars' worth.

"He's here in New York," Baron said, chewing a mouthful of omelet. He took a slip of paper from the breast pocket of his crumpled, navy blue suit. "Phone number . . . An address not far from here. Doorman. Prewar building facing the park. Second floor. Pretty impressive. Must have cost a couple. He's got a place in the Hamptons under renovation: new pool, guesthouse. He goes out there most weekends to walk around the site, check it out. Frequent resident of the Maidstone Arms hotel." Baron handed de Jersey the slip of paper. "These are my extras: gas receipts, phone, and a couple a meal tabs, and here's a recent photo—our man's a sharp dresser."

De Jersey glanced at the photograph and slipped the paper into his wallet.

"I think you'll find that'll cover anything extra." He smiled and pushed the envelope across to Baron. "I'm glad you were available."

"Yeah, well, the band I take care of has been doing a recording here before we go on a twenty-city tour." He smiled ruefully.

"Nice to meet you, Donny. Thanks." And with that, de Jersey left him.

He walked to Moreno's apartment building, then stood in the shadows cast by the trees in Central Park, watching the comings and goings. A uniformed doorman stood outside the entrance, leaping to the curb when any of the residents or their guests drew up.

Then suddenly he was tipping his cap and holding open the glass-fronted door. De Jersey's eyes narrowed when Alex Moreno walked out. He was smaller than he'd expected, about five eight, and wore a full-length navy overcoat with a yellow scarf loose around his neck. He smiled at the doorman, who accompanied him to a gleaming black Lexus sedan and opened the door. Moreno tipped him and drove off. De Jersey checked his watch: ten fifteen. At ten thirty a white stretch limo pulled up. The doorman was kept busy carrying parcels and luggage back and forth as two women and a small child entered the complex. De Jersey moved fast; he crossed the road behind the doorman, entered the complex unseen, and headed upstairs.

He rang the bell of Moreno's apartment and waited in case a housekeeper or someone else was at home, but no one answered.

At the end of the corridor, a large window with heavy curtains opened onto a ledge, less than a foot and a half wide. The window looked down on a small, square garden; de Jersey noticed that, further along the ledge, which ran the length of the building, there was an open window in Moreno's apartment. He climbed out and moved sideways along the ledge until he reached the window.

He slipped through it, turning to face the reception room. It was a high-tech space with high ceilings and a minimalist feel: stripped pine floors, brown leather furniture, leather-and-chrome reclining chairs around a large plate-glass table, and a wide-screen TV. On the table was a heavy glass ashtray filled with cigarette stubs, the open window no doubt an attempt to air the smoky room.

The Bang & Olufsen stereo units had chrome cases holding hundreds of CDs, but they were dwarfed by a couple of huge oil paintings, both depicting a full-frontal nude man. The fireplace had been sandblasted and treated to resemble rough red stone; fake logs were stacked in the grate. De Jersey took it all in. Moreno was a man of undeniable wealth but questionable taste. In the hallway more paintings and large photographs of handsome men adorned the walls. Beyond, he located a shining state-of-the-art kitchen with a black-and-white checkered marble floor, a large island, and a restaurant-sized sink unit and fridge-freezer. It all looked as if it had never been used.

De Jersey moved into the office, where a bank of computers lined one wall and massive television screens hung from the ceiling. The leather swivel chair was well worn, the waste bins overflowed, and a large shredder basket was full. The desk, running the length of the room, was stacked with documents, loose papers, notebooks, more dirty ashtrays, and used coffee cups.

De Jersey examined everything, then went through the filing cabinets, gathering as much information as possible. He failed to open the computer files, which were protected by a personal password. His wristwatch alarm went off at twelve, as he had set it, and by one fifteen de Jersey was back in his suite at the Carlyle.

He sat down at the small antique desk and read the hurried notes he had made. When he felt that he had a pretty good assessment of Alex

Moreno's personal life, he went to shower. On his return he began to familiarize himself with Moreno's business activities. His bank statements made obvious the soaring costs of developing the Hamptons property but not where the money was coming from to pay for it.

At 11:00 A.M. Edward Cummings checked out of the hotel by phone. At eleven ten he left and, as Philip Simmons, caught the twelve o'clock jitney bus to the Hamptons, sitting in the back, where he read *The New York Times* and spoke to no one. At two thirty he arrived in East Hampton. He hired a car from Pam's Autos and booked into The Huntting Inn, a B and B. From his room he made an appointment to see Moreno's contractor at the site at 5:00 P.M. As "business adviser" to Moreno, he had spoken of the need to oversee the progress on the renovations. He learned that Moreno had an outstanding invoice for $155,000.

Moreno's property stood on a plot of land off the Montauk highway toward the luxurious and most sought-after district of Georgica. As he drove, he looked for Hedges Lane, finally locating it off Baiting Hollow Road.

De Jersey drove past the guesthouse, nearly complete. The main house was partially built. Massive plumbing pipes and air-conditioning vents were stacked beside it. Nearby stood a line of trucks, and on the far side of the skeleton building, he noticed a digger removing earth for the pool. It was freezing cold; the rain puddles were covered with ice, and the winter sun didn't even begin to warm the air.

No one paid much attention as De Jersey parked the car. His anger grew. The pool alone was costing a hundred thousand dollars and the guesthouse $2 million. The final budget had to be around $7 or $8 million. By the time he returned to London, the property would belong to him.

"Mr. Simmons?"

De Jersey was confronted by a muscular, rather stocky man in his late thirties. "I'm Brett Donnelly." They shook hands. "This is my team. The architect was around earlier. Did you want to see him? They're all running from one deal to the next. It's like a property bonanza. You live out here? Know the area?" Donnelly fired off questions seemingly without wanting answers. He pointed to various areas of potholes and planks as they made their way to his trailer. He banged his boots clean at the door; de Jersey entered close behind him. The heat was overpowering. Donnelly took off his padded jacket and hard hat and picked up a coffeepot. "Cream?" he asked, fetching mugs.

"Just milk," replied de Jersey.

Donnelly unhooked his phone, put down the coffee, then sat in his office chair, rocking back and forth.

De Jersey said coolly, "I think it all looks very impressive here."

"Yeah, it's been a big job. The East Hampton Village Zoning Board has been driving us crazy. We waited three months due to a variance with the land on the west side, and a further two weeks for the pool permits."

De Jersey sipped the bitter coffee as Donnelly talked. It was fifteen minutes before the man finally fell silent, leaning back in his chair with a blue cloud of cigar smoke above his head.

"When do you fill the pool?" de Jersey asked.

"Any day now, it's almost dug." Donnelly gave de Jersey a quizzical look. "Are you Canadian?" he asked.

De Jersey smiled. He had never thought of the accent he was using as Canadian, but he nodded.

"How can I help you?" Donnelly asked.

De Jersey opened his wallet and proffered a card; he'd had the forethought to have it printed. "As I said, I'm Mr. Moreno's business adviser."

"Nothing wrong, is there?"

"We need to discuss my client's financial situation."

Donnelly opened a drawer. "You know we have an interim payment due?"

"Yes. It's why I'm here."

"That's good. I'm just a local contractor, and I can't afford to keep all these men on without the payments being met on schedule. I've got a few other projects, but this is the most substantial."

"Mr. Moreno is broke."

"What?" Donnelly was stunned.

"I have to tell you to halt the rebuilding until we have released certain funds. At the moment, Mr. Moreno cannot pay your last invoice."

"What?" Donnelly repeated.

"I'll see that it is paid, but you must stop work until further notice."

"Jesus, God, I've got twenty-four men on this contract. I've gotta pay them a weekly wage. It'll bankrupt me. I mean, are you saying the guy's *totally broke*?"

"I am saying that there will be difficulties in meeting your last invoice. We could probably sell the property at a substantial loss, of course, but you would be paid eventually. The buyer might even retain you to complete the work."

"Oh, my God, I don't believe this!"

"This is an excellent piece of land in a prime position and with building permits already in place. I'm confident this is just a short-term situation, but you'll want to get Mr. Moreno down here fast to sort it all out as quickly as possible. I'm sorry."

Donnelly hesitated. "Am I missing something here? You say you're Mr. Moreno's business adviser, but you don't sound like you're employed by him, more like you're . . ."

"Handling a tricky situation. I refer to myself as his business adviser, but it's rather more complicated. I'm taking over his business because of his mounting debts, some of which are owed to me. I am making sure this development is completed, so I also get what is owed to me."

"You want me to get Moreno here?"

"Correct, and I suggest you do not mention I'm here. We don't want to make him feel like he's being ganged up on."

Donnelly punched the buttons on his phone and spoke briefly to Moreno, who said he would be at the site the next morning at nine. He hung up and told de Jersey what had been said.

They shook hands, and de Jersey, returning to his car, watched Donnelly instruct the workers to quit for the day.

De Jersey dined at a sushi bar in Sag Harbor. It was almost seven when he returned to his room and placed a call to the Maidstone Arms, which was virtually opposite his hotel. He was told that they were expecting Mr. Moreno to check in after ten.

At close to 11:00 P.M., de Jersey called the Maidstone Arms again; Mr. Moreno had just checked in. He identified himself as Mr. Donnelly and left a message asking to move the morning meeting up two hours, to 7:00 A.M.

De Jersey woke at five and, refreshed, checked out at six fifteen. He was on the site at six thirty and used a crowbar to open Donnelly's Portakabin. He was confident no workers would show up now that Donnelly knew Moreno's money had run dry. At seven on the dot the Lexus turned into the drive, and the immaculate Alex Moreno stepped out. He walked toward the cabin, stepping gingerly over the debris, afraid for his Gucci loafers. He entered, surprised to see de Jersey.

"Donnelly's not here. Sit down, Alex, we need to talk."

"Excuse me, do I know you?"

"No, you don't, but I know you."

Something about de Jersey's manner, his strangely soft voice and steely eyes, made Moreno hesitate about leaving. "What's this all about?" he asked.

"How many people did you take down when the company liquidated?" de Jersey asked.

Moreno shrugged. "Oh, this is about leadingleisurewear. I don't know. Investors are investors. Sometimes they win and sometimes they lose."

"Not everyone is a good loser, Alex," de Jersey said quietly.

"If this is some kind of scam, then screw you! I don't know you, and whatever you lost is not my problem."

De Jersey reached out and gripped the collar of Moreno's cashmere coat. "It *is* your problem, and I won't go away until you solve it."

"I dunno what you're talking about," Moreno stammered.

"I work for someone who invested millions in your company, and he is not a happy man. He wants compensation."

Moreno pushed away de Jersey's hands. "I'm cleaned out. We went into liquidation and there's nothing to be done."

"Wrong. My friend wants this house, plus the lease on the Central Park apartment."

"*What?*" Moreno asked.

"You heard. I have some agreements that will transfer your rights in those properties. Just sign here."

"Fuck you," Moreno said.

De Jersey walked to the door, blocking Moreno's exit. "It's you that will be fucked if you don't agree. Sign the papers and you walk out of here intact."

Moreno hesitated. He glanced at them. "My, my, you've done your homework," he said.

De Jersey picked up a pen and handed it to Moreno. "Just sign and no one will get hurt."

Moreno's hand was shaking. "I don't understand all this," he said.

"It merely instructs funds to go into the necessary numbered accounts."

"You work for the guy with these accounts?"

"Yeah."

Moreno bit his lip. "Why don't you and me do some private business? I can cut you in. When this place is finished, I'm gonna ask fifteen million. You'd get a nice bonus and walk away from"—he glanced at the document—"this guy, whoever he is. Screw him and you'll be a rich man. You could just say you never found me."

"Sign the papers," de Jersey said.

"He pays you that well, huh?" Smirking, Moreno tapped the desktop with the pen.

"Sign the papers."

Moreno took a deep breath but still toyed with the pen.

"Sign the papers," de Jersey snapped. "Now."

Moreno dropped the pen. "This is fraud," he said.

"It's called paying off your debts."

"I don't have to pay a fucking dime. There were a lot of investors. It was a new business. The investors knew the risks. It wasn't my fault they plowed in more funds."

De Jersey pushed Moreno's face roughly into the desk. "Sign the papers!" he thundered.

"No need to get nasty. I'll do it, okay? I'll do it," Moreno said. When de Jersey released his grip, Moreno put up his hands in a gesture of defeat. "You've won, okay? You get this place and the apartment."

Moreno signed each document de Jersey placed in front of him, flicking glances at him. "All signed. Okay? You wanna try on my suit for size?" he asked sarcastically.

De Jersey inspected each signature calmly, then placed the documents in an envelope.

Finding his way clear to the door, Moreno crossed the room. He yanked the door open, turned, laughing. "Listen, you son of a bitch, if you think those papers would stand up in any court of law, you're wrong. My attorney will have them laughed out of court, and I'll have you fucked over for kidnap and extortion."

In his eagerness to make a quick exit, he caught his sleeve on the door handle. He tripped and fell down the iron steps, cracking his head against the side of the railing. After he rolled onto the ground, his body jerked for a few seconds; then he lay ominously still.

Coming rapidly behind him, de Jersey felt for a pulse but without success. His mind raced. This wasn't the outcome he had intended.

He dragged Moreno back into the cabin, where he unbuttoned his coat and rolled up his shirtsleeves. He walked outside, picking up a spade on his way, and jumped into the half-finished swimming pool. He dug feverishly in the deep end until he had a hole big enough for the body. Then he returned to the Portakabin and emptied Moreno's pockets. In one he found a wad of cash in an envelope addressed to Donnelly. De Jersey quickly counted the money and discovered that it would cover the outstanding invoice. He removed Moreno's personal effects, dragged him from the cabin, and rolled him into the pool. Jumping down, he pushed the body into the newly dug grave and was filling it in when his watch alarm sounded. He climbed out of the pool. Next he drove Moreno's Lexus into a nearby lane out of sight, then returned to the pool. To be extra sure no one discovered the body, he used the compressor machine to level off the ground. He finished cleaning himself up and was double-checking that the gauze of the wig was in place when Donnelly drove up.

De Jersey immediately crossed to his car, smiling. "I want to take you to breakfast," he said. "There have been some new developments. Moreno isn't coming. Where do you suggest?"

*   *   *

At Marty's Diner, Donnelly had eggs over easy and a side of pancakes, while, opposite him, de Jersey sipped black coffee. He handed over the envelope. "That should cover your last invoice. You will see that it includes a bonus for the problems you've had to deal with."

Donnelly's face showed his relief.

"As of now," de Jersey went on, "I am monitoring the project and controlling the payments. I have here postdated checks to cover work for the next two months, and I assure you that I have funds to cover them. You are to complete the house, and I want the gardens landscaped. You know a good company?"

"Yes, I do. I've worked with them before."

"Good. So I can leave that with you to arrange?"

"Sure."

"We want the estate finished, if possible, by early summer."

"We were scheduled for completion by June."

"Good. I'll have someone, if not myself, come to the site at various times, but I've also hired a solicitor to take care of all payments due. It's a local firm called Edward and Maybury. They will deal directly with you and liaise with me. I require photographs and reports of work in progress to be sent to the solicitor, who will subsequently pass them on to me."

"So what's happened to Moreno? Will he be coming around?"

"He's gone to South America—keep that to yourself—and he's turned over the day-to-day running of his finances to me. I will be handling the sale of the property. As I mentioned, Mr. Moreno owes me a substantial amount, and this way neither of us suffers an adverse loss."

"He's not going to live here?"

"He can't afford it, and I will arrange a real estate agent to view the property when it is near completion."

Donnelly drained his coffee, then put out his hand to shake de Jersey's. "Thank God. I didn't sleep last night with worry. I'll get the men back working today."

De Jersey signaled for the bill, then opened his wallet. "I saw they had begun work on the pool. When do they pour in the cement?"

"They'll probably finish it today."

"That's good." De Jersey paid for breakfast and left.

In East Hampton, he discussed property values with a real estate agent. They were eager to help: a property in such a prestigious area would sell quickly. Once development was complete, they assured him, they could start with an asking price of fifteen million. That sum, with the proceeds from the sale of Moreno's apartment, meant that one small part of de Jersey's, Wilcox's, and Driscoll's fortunes would be salvaged.

After returning his rental car, de Jersey ordered a taxi and went to pick up the Lexus, which he drove into Manhattan. With Moreno's keys in his pocket, he was able to let himself into the apartment. Quickly, he packed most of Moreno's clothes into suitcases and made appointments with three real estate agents to discuss selling the lease of the fully furnished apartment. He phoned the doorman to arrange transfer of the bags to the Lexus.

When the first agent arrived, de Jersey explained his asking price was way below the market value in order to ensure a fast sale. By the afternoon, thanks to the legally binding letters and the lease reversal with Moreno's signature, a cash deal had been struck. Before he left the apartment, de Jersey unscrewed the back of Moreno's computer and, producing an electric drill he'd found in a kitchen cabinet, drilled several holes through the hard drive. If he was unable to gain access to the files, he didn't want anyone else to do so.

At 7:00 P.M., de Jersey parked the Lexus in the long-stay car park at JFK, leaving it unlocked with Moreno's suitcases in full view, thus assuring their quick disappearance. At the Virgin Atlantic desk he used Philip Simmons's passport and upgraded himself into first class. After boarding the plane, he changed into the courtesy tracksuit and slept for the entire flight. Once again, he spoke to no one. He was woken for breakfast shortly before landing.

After clearing customs at Heathrow, he returned to the men's room, where he removed the wig and mustache, and combed his hair. He left the airport as Edward de Jersey.

He was home in time for New Year celebrations. He was confident it would be a long while before anyone started to ask questions about Moreno's disappearance, and he was pretty sure that the body would never be found. The car would turn up, but it would be hard to prove that there had been foul play. It would be near impossible to trace de Jersey's own movements in and out of New York. Once Moreno's finances had been properly investigated, it would be surmised that he had done a runner.

The money from Moreno's properties was a drop in the ocean compared to the losses the trio had suffered. But de Jersey calculated his share of the cash from the sale of the apartment alone would be enough to keep his estate running for the time being. It was almost a week since he'd left for New York, but in that time he had felt the adrenaline pumping, the old excitement at being on the wrong side of the law. It was a different enjoyment than his horses brought: more like the thrill of walking a tightrope. He was forced to use wits and cunning, and he liked that. He felt no regret for Moreno's death. He was happy to use the accident to his advantage. The Colonel was back in business.

5

The New Year celebrations were over, and Wilcox and Driscoll were due to return to London, but de Jersey had still not formed a plan. He had been spending much of his time learning about the Internet, a vast world of which he had known so little.

After surfing the Web, he realized that his criminal expertise was outdated. A modern criminal needed only a computer and a modem to carry out a lucrative heist. He also realized that nothing was secure in cyberspace. De Jersey was intrigued by the way information could be appropriated by criminal organizations. The May Day riots, which gathered protesters and support worldwide, had been almost exclusively organized on the Internet. Even the Mafia carried out cyber-meetings these days. Crime was committed behind a hidden web of corruption and orchestrated from a simple keyboard. A teenage hacker had broken into the U.S. defense system and another into the Bank of England. De Jersey was astonished that American institutions were so vulnerable and so accessible. In the aftermath of the recent terrorist attacks, there was more security everywhere, but the dangers in cyberspace continued unabated.

Restricted information could be accessed through password-sniffing programs. Hackers disguised their computers rather than themselves to acquire sensitive information. Computer credit-card fraud was big business. De Jersey was concentrating so hard that he didn't hear Christina walk in. She was carrying a shirt. "What on earth is this on your cuffs?" she asked. "It's on the collar too." She held up the shirt he had used as Philip Simmons, and he couldn't think what to say.

"It looks like makeup to me," she said suspiciously.

"You've caught me out," he said.

"What do you mean?"

He grinned sheepishly. "It's fake tan."

"What?" she said, taken aback.

"Well, I looked so bloody pale I tried it out, but it turned me orange so I washed it off."

"Well, it's ruined the shirt."

"Chuck it out, then."

She flicked it toward him. "You silly old sod—wait till I tell the girls how you were trying to impress this banker. No, don't tell me, he was a woman!"

"No, but he was twenty years younger than me." He laughed.

"You *will* be pale and feeble if you keep yourself holed up in here," she said. "What on earth are you doing?"

"Moving into the high-tech world. It'll cut down on all that paperwork."

"Will it? But you don't know what you're doing, do you?"

"I'm learning," he said.

"You should get Tom to help you, he's doing a computer course."

"Tom who?"

"The vicar's son—Tom Knowles."

De Jersey looked at his computer. "Maybe you should get him to come over—sooner rather than later."

"I'll do it now, then," she said and left the room. De Jersey tapped the desk. He should have dumped the shirt before he came home. He would never have made a mistake like that in the past.

A few moments later Christina was back. "Tom is ready, willing, and able. I said you'd pay him per hour."

Tom Knowles was training as an information technology tutor at a local college. He was small and skinny, and wore thick-rimmed glasses. He arrived promptly each morning at nine o'clock and stayed for two hours.

One day he opened his laptop as usual and said to de Jersey, "Right, sir, last session you wanted to look into Web privacy. The best way to keep your personal data personal is by not giving it out in the first place. So, if I wanted total electronic privacy, I'd start with a made-up name or nickname for my e-mail account, using Hotmail or Yahoo!, for example. They'll ask you for personal information, but there is nothing to say that you have to tell them the truth. Always skip any optional fields. If, however, you want to order things off the Net, you'll have to give your address. If this is a concern, you can get a post-office box."

De Jersey nodded.

"You may think that surfing the Net is an anonymous activity, but every Web site you contact keeps a record of your computer IP address. Combine that with your ISP's logs, and you're right in the spotlight."

De Jersey pursed his lips. "Are there ways to cover your tracks when you're on-line?" he asked, staring at Tom's small screen.

"There are ways to hide behind someone else's IP address, but I don't know much about that. You'd have to talk to someone who's more knowledgeable in that area."

"And what about these ISP logs? Can't you just delete those from your computer?"

"Yes, but it's not as simple as deleting. Many people think that when they send documents to the recycle bin they're gone, but they're not. And even if you take the next step and delete the contents of your recycle bin, they're still on your database. Private detectives and police investigators could still use programs such as EnCase and FRED to recover evidence from parts of your drive."

"So you're telling me that if I, for example, had something sensitive, let's say illegal, and pressed delete, or put it in the recycling bin, it's always going be on the hard drive?"

Tom nodded. "Exactly. Which is why the police have been able to arrest so many pedophiles. The evidence of their illegal activities has been retained on their hard drives, even when they thought they had deleted it."

"Is there anything you can do to remove something completely from your computer?"

"There's something called Evidence Eliminator. It's the equivalent to a government-level wipe that people say can deep-clean your computer of sensitive material. I have never used the program myself, though, so I don't really know how efficient it is."

"Interesting," de Jersey said. "What about e-mail?"

"Well, an e-mail travels through several servers on its way to its destination. This means it can be intercepted and read. You never know who might be reading your e-mail. At the moment, police are monitoring the Net for terrorist communications. Numerous people have been arrested here that way."

De Jersey's mind was racing with ways to use the new technology to his advantage. "I read an article about hacking recently. How does that work?"

"What do you want to know?"

"Well, if someone wanted to hack into a company's files, how would they do it?"

Tom shrugged his shoulders. "I have a basic understanding of what's involved, but I've never done it myself so I couldn't tell you. Some of the things hackers have done are pretty funny, though."

"Like what?" de Jersey asked, not very interested.

"A few years back, two hackers rigged a radio station's phone system during a phone-in show to let only their calls through." He laughed. "They won two cars, trips all round the world, and twenty thousand pounds!" Tom noticed that his pupil's attention was wandering.

"You know what, Mr. de Jersey; the best place to get hold of this information is the Net itself. You should start using the chat rooms, get on-line with some guys who know what they're talking about." Tom checked his watch.

"Could you show me again how to get into the chat rooms? Then we'll call it quits for the day," de Jersey said. "Why don't we use your computer?"

Tom began tapping away. De Jersey didn't want to take any risk, however small, that someone might trace anything back to his computer. He thought it prudent from then on to use Tom's laptop exclusively.

"Okeydokey," Tom said. "Anything in particular you'd like to chat about or discuss?"

De Jersey gave it a second's thought. "Yeah, how about something like those kids that hacked into the radio show?"

Tom tapped away for a few seconds. "If we get someone on-line who doesn't have the information we want, he can direct us to a more specialized chat room. Here we go."

Tom typed away in search of information about hacking, then asked what de Jersey wanted to call himself.

"Erm, how about Bill Haley?" he said. Tom did not react—he was probably too young to remember the old rock-and-roller. He simply typed in the name. Then they watched the screen. Within moments they had received a message. "Good God, that was quick," de Jersey said, fascinated.

"Well, some of these guys spend all day on there."

A short message on the screen told them that its author didn't know anything about hacking but that he had lost the password to his Toshiba and did anyone know the break-in starter password for this computer?

Tom tapped the screen with his pencil. "Get out of this one. I'd say this guy has a stolen computer, that's why he doesn't have the password."

"My God, I've got a lot to learn," de Jersey said, intrigued.

Just then they heard Natasha return from riding. De Jersey glanced at Tom, who looked flustered.

"Excuse me," he said, "may I use your toilet?"

De Jersey nodded. "Say hello to Natasha before you come back," he teased. Every morning when his daughter came in, the boy needed to use the bathroom.

Tom slipped out of the room, so he missed the next message that flashed across the screen.

It was from someone calling himself Elvis who suggested that Bill Haley attend a public course on the Internet and thoughtfully listed numerous lectures taking place in colleges across London.

De Jersey asked which Elvis thought would be best.

"I hear St. Catherine's Church Hall, Lisson Grove, Notting Hill, Tuesday, eight fifteen P.M. is pretty good" came the response.

"Thank you," de Jersey replied.

Tom returned just as his watch alarm rang to herald the end of the session. He watched as de Jersey closed down his laptop for him, then delved into his rucksack. "I got you this. It's a novel by a guy called Douglas Coupland. It's a terrific read."

"*Microserfs*. Thank you."

De Jersey walked Tom to the door and, as an afterthought, said for the next few weeks he would be abroad on business. Tom looked disappointed but perked up when de Jersey handed him an envelope containing two hundred fifty pounds. "That's for all your help. I'll get in touch when I need you again."

De Jersey had enough knowledge now to come to grips with identity protection. If he was going to plan a robbery utilizing the Internet, he had to know how to avoid being traced. He would prefer not to involve anyone else, so he'd start by attending the lecture Elvis had recommended.

He spent the rest of the day in chat rooms. He used various names— on the Internet he could be whoever he wanted without the need for a disguise. Physical attributes, age, and gender were irrelevant; the only truth was what he chose to write on the electronic page.

De Jersey was amazed how easily he could contact other criminals on the Web. Many even had their own Web sites, paying homage to their crimes. He looked up the Metropolitan Police's list of Most Wanted criminals and allowed himself a satisfied smile; none of his many pseudonyms were mentioned.

He had not yet formed a plan but was storing away information. As he became more proficient, he ordered a higher-powered computer and arranged for it to be delivered and installed. As he completed the order form on-line, he noted with interest how many personal details he was asked to provide. Edward de Jersey was now a known entity in cyberspace.

*   *   *

Christina became increasingly frustrated. Her husband worked all day at the stables and then shut himself in his study every evening after dinner.

At breakfast she asked him what had happened when he was in London just after Christmas.

"Why do you ask?" He was reading the Internet novel Tom had left with him while he ate.

"Since you came back, you're always in front of a computer. You've stopped talking to me, you pay no attention to the girls."

He shut the book and sighed. "I'm sorry."

"I won't have my parents stay if you're going to continue."

"What?"

"Don't you remember? They're coming for a week's holiday. They only come once a year, and they want to see the girls before they go back to school."

De Jersey was upset by her anger. "I'm sorry. Why don't we go for a walk?"

"No, I'm going to do some baking."

"I guess I just got caught up in my new toys, and I've been working a lot too." He slipped his arms around her. "Let me make it up to you."

But she moved away. "They'll want to do all the touristy things. I know you hate anything like that, but it means a lot to them to be here."

"I'll drive them, fly them, and entertain them twenty-four hours a day, I promise," de Jersey said.

"You don't have to go that far, but they look forward to coming."

"I'll make it a trip for them to remember. I'll arrange tickets for shows, guided tours, Windsor Castle, you name it."

"They went to Windsor Castle last year," she said. "They said they'd like to go to the Tower of London this time and maybe see London Zoo. Perhaps we can go by barge up the Regent's Canal."

He slipped his arms around her again. "When do they arrive?"

"In a week's time."

"That gives me time to get it all sorted out. You sure you don't want to come for a walk?"

"Okay, then," she said, turning in his arms to kiss him.

Later that afternoon de Jersey made his presence felt, talking, as he always had, to each member of staff in the yard. He leaned against Royal Flush's stable door as the sweating horse was hosed down after his exercise and wrapped in a thick blanket.

De Jersey walked from stable to stable with the trainers and lads, examining all the working horses and the brood mares, the foals and year-lings. It had taken twenty-five years to build up a stable of such caliber, and Moreno's money would not last long. He needed a vast injection of hard cash to keep going, and de Jersey was not prepared to fire one em-ployee or send one horse to auction. He had coveted and created this life, and no one was going to take it from him.

He entered the kitchen from the yard. Christina was cooking dinner. As he passed her she caught his arm. "Are you going into your study again?" she said.

"Just to book some theater and the tourist attractions. I'll join you for dinner the moment you call me."

In his study he logged on to the Internet. When he had bought more theater tickets to West End shows than he had evenings to fill, he started to book London tours, ending up at the Tower of London's Web site. He was not really paying attention as he printed off the information, but articles about the spectacular jewels on display captured his interest. The gems in-cluded the Second Star of Africa, part of the Cullinan Diamond, the Koh-i-noor Diamond, St. Edward's Sapphire, and the Black Prince's Ruby. He leaned closer to the screen as the page went on to describe the magnificent pearls worn by Elizabeth I and the Stuart Sapphire from the time of Charles II. Over the years the regalia had been altered to suit various mon-archs. Queen Victoria's hand had been too small for the coronation ring, so a copy had been made. Edward VII had not worn the St. Edward's Crown as he was ill at the time of his coronation and it was deemed too heavy. Likewise, the arches on the Imperial State Crown had been lowered for Queen Elizabeth II's coronation as she was so tiny and the crown such a weight.

De Jersey became immersed in the Crown Jewels. He printed off some photographs. The article stated that the gold for the magnificent St. Edward's Crown might have come from the Confessor's crown. It was set with 444 semiprecious stones. The breathtaking Imperial State Crown was set with over 3,000 precious stones. Then he stared at the Koh-i-noor, set in the Queen Mother's platinum crown. Last he looked at the little crown made for Queen Victoria, studded with over 1,500 diamonds. A response to a letter in the Web page's mailbox stated that the last attempted robbery of the Crown Jewels had been foiled in 1671. These gems were kept closely guarded in the Tower of London and were seen by millions of tourists every year. A crown jeweler was responsible for their maintenance and cleaning. The Queen had last seen them in 1994, when the new Jewel House was opened.

De Jersey was so deep in thought that Christina called him numerous times for dinner. He appeared at last, smiling, and produced the printed information about theater and attractions, assuring her that he would come to everything with them.

"Darling, just a few dinners. I know you hate theater."

"Well, in return for you letting me off theater dates, I will personally take them to the Tower of London to see the Crown Jewels."

Once Christina had fallen asleep, he returned to his study and accessed more sites about the spectacular jewels. Their history was fascinating. Edward the Confessor and his successors had accumulated most of the regalia, but much had been sold off or melted down by Oliver Cromwell between 1649 and 1658. The current hoard dated from Charles II's coronation in 1661. The foiled attempt to steal the gems had been instigated by a Colonel Blood, who had almost got away but was trapped at the East Gate of the Tower. De Jersey remained in his study until dawn. He went back to bed, tired but elated.

He woke feeling well rested, then changed into riding clothes. He rode hard for a good hour on an old favorite, a big eighteen-hand gray called Cute Queenie. At fourteen she was no longer racing but, having produced some good colts, she was kept for de Jersey's personal use. He brought her to a halt, snorting and tossing her head. They looked across the downs.

"Good girl," he whispered affectionately, and he pushed her to trot, then canter, finally coaxing her into a full gallop. It was like opening the throttle of a fine old racing car. The big gray tore up the wet morning grass, her breath steaming. He had not felt so alive for years. The adrenaline buzz stimulated every part of his body—confronting danger had always been his preferred drug, and after the Moreno business he craved more of it. As the next audacious heist formed in his mind, he felt as he had on receiving the tip-off about the gold bullion at Heathrow. And now he was contemplating stealing the Crown Jewels. But contemplating it and pulling it off were worlds apart.

6

Tony Driscoll arrived home from his holiday, tanned, jet-lagged, and exhausted. He contacted David Lyons's office straightaway and spent two hours on the phone. He was sitting in a stupor, staring at the walls, when Liz barged in.

"Tony, have you unpacked?" she asked.

"You know I haven't," he snapped.

"Well, you can't skive in here. You have to put out your dirty laundry for Mrs. Fuller. I'm not going to do it."

"I've got a few business problems to take care of."

"Can't they wait? We only just got home."

"I guess they can," he said, standing, but when she left the room he sat down again. Until now he had maintained a positive attitude, sure that some money could be salvaged. Having been told bluntly by Lyons's assistant that there was no hope of recouping a cent, he felt sick.

James Wilcox had discovered the same thing. The family had arrived home in Henley only to learn that his basement was flooded. Now he stared at the mounting bills. His numerous maintenance checks to his ex-wives were months overdue. Rika, irritable from the long journey, kept asking him to arrange a grocery delivery from Tesco, but he couldn't think straight. One minute he had been worth millions, the next peanuts. He had not anticipated it would be this bad.

Rika slapped the grocery list down in front of him.

"This is gonna cost a fucking fortune, Rika. We've got eight different types of cereal here!"

"Vell, that is vat they eat!"

"From now on they're all gonna eat the same one."

Rika glared at him and slammed out of the room.

He was in real trouble. He had even remortgaged the house to throw more money into leadingleisurewear. He began to contemplate how he would react if de Jersey suggested another heist. It had been easy to agree with Driscoll to walk away, but now—with six kids, four ex-wives, a Ukrainian mistress, and only a garage full of vintage cars as collateral—he was heading for bankruptcy. If things got any worse, he would be hard-pressed to say no to anything de Jersey suggested.

De Jersey told his wife he would be away for a couple of days on business, staying at his club. Soon he would have to make his plans from a new location; it was too dangerous to work at home. He flew by helicopter to London, and by midmorning he was seated in a student lecture hall attending a computer-programming seminar. Afterward he approached the young lecturer and asked him to list some books that would assist in his training.

Armed with two bulging carrier bags, de Jersey went to the St. James's Club and sat in the lounge reading the complex manuals. Realizing that he still needed assistance, he hurried off to St. Catherine's Church for the lecture suggested by Elvis in the chat room.

The hall was small and freezing, inhabited by a clutch of nerdy figures with plastic coffee cups and cling-wrapped sandwiches. A plump blond girl munching on a Mars bar collected five pounds from each of them and handed out a computer printout of the evening's agenda; the session was to be conducted by someone called Raymond Marsh. "You been here before?" the blonde asked de Jersey.

"No."

"You got a contact who got you here?"

"Yes."

"The name? I've got to fill in the attendance list."

"Elvis," De Jersey said, feeling rather foolish.

"Okay, then. Sit down. He won't be long—baby-sitter didn't show up. What's your name?" She was ready with her pen.

"Philip Simmons," he said.

By eight thirty, sixteen people were hunched in thick coats over tiny laptops as they waited on plastic chairs. De Jersey glanced to the rear of the hall; he saw a strange apparition. This was Raymond Marsh, but it was clear he was known otherwise as Elvis. As Marsh reached into the cardboard box and pocketed the cash, de Jersey deduced that the blonde was his wife.

It was hard not to stare at Marsh's thin, pointy face, with its protruding chin and slanted cheeks. The hair, combed in from both sides to form a quiff, was held in place by thick layers of lacquer. He wore a worn black leather jacket, skintight drainpipe trousers, and winklepickers. He checked that the computer was running correctly through the overhead projector. "Right. We're all set. I've done some printouts that should answer yer queries from last week, right? I gorra bit worried about last session, so any questions needin' going over like, now's the time to do it." He had a thick Liverpudlian accent.

A tall, thin man in the front row put up his hand. "We were talking last week about hacking techniques being employed to protect computer systems rather than for criminal purposes. Could viruses ever be used for protection?"

Marsh swept a hand over one side of his head. "Well, there has been talk of creating good viruses in the future that, as with human diseases, will increase the host's immune system."

When a large, jolly-looking woman asked a question about the approaching DEFCON conference in America, Marsh launched into an enthusiastic description of the underground hacking convention. Much of what was being discussed was alien to de Jersey. He paid close attention to Marsh; he obviously had a high IQ, but his manner of speaking and delivery seemed to suggest low social skills. De Jersey wondered if the man worked in the information technology industry.

Raymond Marsh was employed as a telephone engineer but hacked and explored the Internet in his spare time, so de Jersey hadn't been too far off the mark. He was so deeply immersed in his analysis of the man that he jumped when he heard another audience member asking about identity protection and creating fake identities on the Net.

"Of course, mate, it's stupid to use your own details," said Marsh. "You can build up all kinds of identities in loads of countries and create plausible histories for all of 'em. One of my own Net IDs is an Australian schoolboy. He gets up to all sorts! This morning I hacked into a school in Adelaide, registered him, and created school reports for him. Gave him straight A's. I've traveled all around the world under dozens of different names, but I've never even left the country. I'm a grandmother of five in Russia, an S & M enthusiast in Ireland, and a fish farmer in Alaska. And there's no way they can catch me because I have a satellite linkup courtesy of work, which I use whenever I'm on the Net so I can easily break the link.

Working for a telecommunications company comes in handy when you've got this hobby!"

Everyone in the audience chuckled, but de Jersey sat mesmerized. This was perfect for his needs. He had to draft Raymond Marsh to help. The question was, Could he trust him?

At the meeting's end, de Jersey slipped out, mind reeling. It was pouring, and he caught a taxi. Back in the club, he sat in the reading room going over the handouts from the meeting, which included Marsh's e-mail address, home phone number, and address.

The next morning, when he phoned, a rather laconic female voice replied, "He's at work."

"Is there a number I can contact him on? It's important."

"His work don't like him taking personal calls. If you gimme your number, I'll get him to call you, or he'll be home about six."

"I'll call later, thanks."

It was almost six o'clock when de Jersey took the Tube to Marsh's home in Clapham. It was a small semidetached house with a bright pink Cortina, sporting two large, fluffy dice in the windscreen, parked outside. De Jersey walked up the path and rang the doorbell. The blond woman from St. Catherine's Church answered.

"Is he back yet?"

"You the bloke what called earlier?" she asked, glancing back to where a baby was screeching.

"Yes. I'm sorry if this is inconvenient."

"Well, it is a bit, he's not home yet." Suddenly she looked past de Jersey and waved. "Tell a lie, he's behind you."

De Jersey turned as Marsh, wearing an overall under a thick tweed coat, walked up the path. "Who's this?" he asked.

"Dunno, come to see you." He kissed his wife before she ran to the baby.

De Jersey passed him one of his Philip Simmons's "Computer Electronics Inc." business cards.

"What's this about then?" he asked de Jersey.

"A job you may be interested in."

"Already got one, mate."

"I need information and help with a project I'm working on."

"Information? I got plenty of that. My mind's full of it, but dunno if it's the stuff you're looking for."

"It would be helpful to know your experience," de Jersey said.

Marsh settled himself on the doorstep. "I work as a phone engineer now. Got into phone hacking in the early eighties, phoning everywhere long distance for free. Then I progressed to computers. This company hired me out to local firms to set up their networks, but the job bored me rigid. So me and my wife packed up, came to London, and I went back to phones—all legit now, of course. It's all computerized anyhow. Like to keep the computer hacking for my spare time. Is this the kind of stuff you want to know?"

"Yes. Go on."

Marsh was obviously not going to invite him in. "You wanna sit with me in me car?" he asked.

Marsh leaned back in his seat, stroking the Cortina's white leather steering wheel. The more he talked about himself, the more arrogant he became. An undercurrent of danger hung about him, an anger whose source de Jersey couldn't determine.

"So, Mr. Simmons, what is it you're after, then?" he asked.

"You," de Jersey said.

"Well, I don't come cheap."

"I didn't think you would."

Marsh took another look at the business card.

"I was there last night at St. Catherine's. I'd like you to help me build a fake identity and make it seem as real as possible."

"Anything's possible, mate."

Acting on Marsh's detailed instructions, de Jersey withdrew 130,000 pounds from his depleted accounts. He set up a post-office box and topped up the account in the name of Philip Simmons. From now on he would carry out all his financial transactions on-line.

While the bank assessed his details, de Jersey waited, and when everything was cleared, he rented a flat in Kilburn on-line. The company sent his keys to his post-office box, and de Jersey arranged for the domestic bills to be paid via the Net.

Two days later he returned to London, collected the keys, and traveled by bus, an experience he hadn't had in years, to Philip Simmons's new abode. The flat was two flights up and as seedy as he had expected for the price he was paying. It had that stale-food smell and orange-colored, foam-filled furniture. At least the bathroom and kitchen were clean and in working order. He had purchased two mobile phones in the name of Simmons, via the Internet, and another computer. The deliveries arrived within half an hour of each other. Now all de Jersey needed was a link to his own computer that could be destroyed at a moment's notice. For this he would have to have more help from Raymond Marsh.

* * *

By the time de Jersey returned home, Christina was in bed. He got in and nuzzled her neck. "Sorry I'm so late. It's been another day of meetings. David Lyons certainly left me in a mess."

She turned sleepily. "Tell me about it in the morning."

"I love you," he whispered.

CHAPTER

7

De Jersey played the perfect host to his in-laws. At the Tower of London, when they followed the guide into the main chamber where the jewels were on display, de Jersey was so eager to hear the guide's description that he kept stepping on the man's heels. Then he stopped dead. There, in all its glory, was the Queen Mother's platinum crown with the dazzling Koh-i-noor Diamond. Ahead, he noticed an empty case and a small plaque stating "In Use." A thought struck him: the jewels were occasionally taken out of the Tower. He hurried to ask the guide.

"The empty display back there, what's the crown being used for?" he asked.

"The Queen has gone to Norway and will be wearing some of the jewels."

"Could there be an occasion when they are all in use?"

"I doubt it. There'll be a few cases empty for the Golden Jubilee celebrations, but if there's not a good enough selection, we offer reductions."

"What crown will Her Majesty be wearing for the Jubilee?"

The guide shuffled impatiently. "One of the smaller ones. That one"— he pointed to the crown with the Koh-i-noor Diamond—"weighs a ton. There's over a hundred carats' worth of diamond in that one big stone alone. Would you mind moving on now, sir? The next tour is coming through." He moved on toward a display case. De Jersey barely glanced at the sumptuous crown as he walked away.

James Wilcox arrived at the Ritz early. He was wearing one of his designer suits. Over the years he had become fastidious about his clothes and accessories. He ordered a vodka martini at the bar. De Jersey had booked a suite on the second floor under the name of Simmons, as usual. Wilcox ate the cashew nuts provided and unwrapped a cigar.

"How you doing, my old son?" Driscoll said, plonking himself down on a stool next to him.

"I've been better. I've been over it all with that assistant at Lyons's office."

"Tell me about it." Driscoll ordered a chilled glass of Chablis.

"I'm skint. You able to salvage anything?"

"I've got a few thousand here and there, own some property, but . . . yeah, bulk went into the leading fucking leisurewear."

"Fuck me. Pair of us must have been crazy. I remember Ronnie Jersey saying to me once, 'Tony, learn from these punters coming in day after day. You might get lucky once, but you'll have ten nonrunners and it's not worth throwing hard-earned money away.' I kept on pouring everything I had into that damn company."

"Schmucks the pair of us." Wilcox drained his martini.

"I remember one day at Ronnie's, we'd got a surefire winner. In those days there was none of the TV sets in the betting shops, and we listened to the radio."

"Don't start the Ronnie Jersey stories again," Wilcox moaned.

"I'm not, I'm not, I am just saying—"

"I'm not in the mood." Wilcox sucked on his olive.

"Oh, excuse me for living."

They sat in silence a moment.

Driscoll looked at Wilcox's suit. "What's with the satin lining?"

"I like it."

"Bit bright, isn't it? Suit's a good cut, though. Pity to ruin it with the cuffs turned back like that."

"I ordered the cuffs that way!" Wilcox snapped.

"How much that suit set you back then? Go on."

"With thirty-odd million, I wasn't quibbling over how much a friggin' suit was going to set me back. Change the subject."

Driscoll took out a slim cigar. "You want one of these?"

"No. You want another drink?"

Driscoll nodded. Wilcox signaled the barman.

"You see that race then . . ."

"Tony, I don't wanna hear about fucking Ronnie and—"

"I'm not talking about the old days. I'm talking about Ascot; the Colonel's horse romped home. Royal Flush. It's called Royal Flush."

"You know something that you do," Wilcox said. "You've always done it. You repeat things twice."

"I do not. I don't."

"Yes you do, you just did it then."

"I didn't. No, I did not."

"You just did it again!"

Driscoll then leaned in close. "He's here. Shit, he looks good. See him talking to the doorman?"

De Jersey was a hard man to miss, in his brown trilby and a brown tweed suit. He looked very much the racing gentleman, right down to his checked shirt and brown brogues. He made his way to the restaurant and disappeared.

"What's he doing? Isn't he goin' up to the suite?"

"Looks like he's gonna have lunch."

At the entrance to the Ritz restaurant, de Jersey was chatting with the maître d'. Then he returned to the lobby as if to leave the hotel. But instead of going toward the front door, he turned sharply and headed for the stairs.

"He's putting himself about a bit, isn't he?" Driscoll said softly.

"I reckon it's time we went. Split up as usual, okay?"

Wilcox tapped on the door and entered. The spacious suite was furnished with elegant, Regency-style furniture and thick gold curtains. A polished mahogany table displayed salmon, cheese, and a large bowl of fruit salad with cream. De Jersey was opening a bottle of champagne.

"Tony's coming up via the stairs," Wilcox said, closing the door. "You look fit—all that riding, I suppose."

"You're in pretty good shape yourself," de Jersey said. "I'm sorry about all this."

"So am I."

De Jersey popped the cork and placed the bottle in the ice bucket. "Good to see you, Jimmy."

"Yeah, we go back a long way, you and me." Wilcox crossed the room to hug him.

Driscoll came into the room as Wilcox was accepting a glass of champagne.

"Christ, my knees. I tell you, I'm falling apart. I got to the second floor and thought I was having a heart attack." He shook hands with de Jersey. "Still holding up well. How do you think the years have treated me, then?" Of the three men, Driscoll showed his age the most.

De Jersey poured him a glass of champagne, then made a toast. "To meeting under better circumstances next time."

When de Jersey sat down, they followed suit, chatting relaxedly about their families, then enjoying their meal. Driscoll remembered to congratulate de Jersey on his win at Royal Ascot.

"It's the Derby next," de Jersey enthused. "He'll do it. He's the best colt I've ever had. Oh, I meant to ask. Did you ever know someone called Harry Smedley? He came up to me at the racetrack. Said we were at school together, but I can't for the life of me remember him."

Driscoll was wiping his mouth with a napkin. "Yeah, I remember him. He was at the comprehensive with us—well, with me. He'd have been in the class below me. Little kid with a big head."

"I still don't remember him," de Jersey said.

"You might remember his mother, Margie, though. Gawd, she was a case. She'd go an' collect her social dosh in the morning and lose it by the afternoon. Ronnie tried to stop her gambling, but every day she'd be in the shop, soon as the doors opened, shilling each way. She was a tough old boiler." Driscoll waved his fork. "She was there when those heavies came in with the sledgehammer. Got herself under a table when it was all going down. All the while, the racing commentary was coming out over the Tannoy. As soon as they left the shop, up she pops and tells Ronnie he's got to pay out on the bet she was about to place. She says it was a pound on the nose, a twenty-to-one outsider called Danny Daly."

Wilcox got up. "Which is the bathroom?"

De Jersey pointed to a door close by. "There's that one, or another one off the bedroom."

Wilcox went into the bedroom and closed the door.

"What did my father say?"

"He says, 'Mrs. Smedley, you haven't put paper on a runner in here ever, but just for your bottle, I'll pay out,' and he did. He was some fella, your old man."

De Jersey still had no recollection of mother or son.

Wilcox returned. "Has he finished, or is he just drawing breath?"

Driscoll gave him the finger.

De Jersey passed the cheese board. Wilcox poured more champagne and returned to his seat. They continued to chat about old times. Finally Driscoll pushed aside his plate. "Our luck ran out, though. This latest venture has done me over good."

De Jersey started to clear the dishes. "Let me explain how we lost our cash. You must know by now that the Internet crash has affected a lot of people even worse than us. Lots of companies have gone down. Ours was just one of many."

"I spoke to that bloke at Lyons's office, and he said that if we could contact this fella Alex Moreno he might be able to salvage something," said Driscoll.

"Not a hope in hell," de Jersey replied. "Leadingleisurewear has been liquidated, and Alex Moreno, the managing director, has disappeared."

Driscoll banged the table with the flat of his hand. "I'd like to get him by his scrawny neck and throttle him."

"He's been trying to form another company."

"The little shit," Wilcox blurted out while de Jersey opened another bottle of champagne.

"I've done what I could," de Jersey replied.

"You've been over there and seen this Moreno guy?" Wilcox asked, surprised. De Jersey remained silent. "I'm not bleating, Colonel, but I'm only just keeping my head above water right now. I'm going to have to sell my homes, my cars . . . I've got six kids, four bloody ex-wives. I'd like some kind of retribution from this arrogant son of a bitch."

De Jersey blew a smoke ring above his head. "Moreno is taken care of. He had property in East Hampton. We should get at least twelve million for it, hopefully more, and he had a lease on an apartment worth a couple of million. I'll split it three ways as usual, but it can't be touched until we're sure it can't be traced, maybe in six to eight months' time. Moreno himself is not a factor anymore." De Jersey gave each man a cold-eyed stare. "He's out of the loop. I've taken care of him. Understand me?"

They knew then that Moreno was dead, and not to press for details. After a strange, depressed silence, de Jersey went to the bathroom to wash and comb his hair. He was leaving shortly to collect his in-laws from their shopping expedition at Harrods, but he needed at least another hour with Wilcox and Driscoll.

He returned to his guests. "I've been thinking of something we could do. It's—"

Driscoll was the first to interrupt. "Eddy, listen, I don't want to hear. I'm too old. I've got responsibilities. I can't go back to what I was like in the old days. I almost didn't show up here this afternoon, because I reckoned you'd have arranged some kind of business to get us out of this mess—but nothing illegal, not for me. I can't, I'm sorry."

De Jersey reached out and touched his hand. "That's okay." Wilcox was staring at the table. "What about you, Jimmy?"

"Same goes for me. I reckon I've lost my nerve. I just don't have the bottle for it anymore, and if, like you said, we're in line for a few mill from the sale of the Moreno property, that's . . . that's enough for me."

"I forget how old I am sometimes, and it was a crazy idea anyway," de

Jersey said. "You're right. We'll leave our separate ways, see each other again when we're on walkers."

De Jersey started to count. He reckoned that when he got to ten Wilcox would want to know more, but he was wrong: it was Driscoll.

"So come on, then. Just 'cause we're not players doesn't mean we're not curious. What caper were you gonna line up for us?"

De Jersey faced them. "No, you're right. Better if we just walk away now."

Wilcox couldn't meet his eyes. De Jersey continued, "No hard feelings. Now or ever. They broke the mold when they made you two."

Driscoll said, "If we don't come in, will you go it alone, whatever it is?"

"Maybe, I don't know. But now I have to go collect my in-laws."

"It's not as if you can't trust us. Why don't you just run it by us?" Driscoll said stubbornly. "You know whatever you say to us won't go any further."

De Jersey put on his hat. "Not this time."

"Come on, you can't bullshit a bullshitter," Driscoll said, smiling.

"There's a first time for everything, Tony," de Jersey said.

Wilcox glanced at Driscoll, and their eyes met. They both wanted to know what deal they had just turned down.

"You let us decide, Colonel, that's fair, isn't it?" Driscoll said.

After a long pause, de Jersey returned to the table. He took off his hat. "You forced my hand."

Both men waited, and de Jersey seemed to relish the moment. "I want to steal the Crown Jewels."

"Not the ones in the Tower of London?" Driscoll asked, incredulously.

"The very same."

"The fucking Crown Jewels!" Wilcox let out a loud laugh.

"He's having us on." Driscoll grinned.

De Jersey twisted his hat around on his hand. "It'll take months of preparation. I've not formulated the details as yet, or picked out the people I'll need."

"You're gonna break into the Tower of London?" Wilcox said.

De Jersey put on his hat and pulled the rim to the angle he liked. He walked to the door and unlocked it. "I can't say I'm not disappointed, considering our past connections. See you."

"Edward!" Wilcox flew to the door. "Don't do this. I've been grateful to you more times than I can remember, but this . . . You can't expect us to take you seriously! This isn't a serious gig, is it?"

Driscoll joined them at the door. "Like James just said, I owe you for everything and I won't ever forget what you or your old man did for me, but no way am I going to feel guilty for turning this caper down. So come clean. Admit it's a big joke."

"No joke," de Jersey said. "When I get the money from Moreno's properties, you'll get your cut." He gave them a long, cold stare. They moved away from the door, and he opened it again.

"I have to go—I'm taking the in-laws for dinner at San Lorenzo. They'll be waiting for me outside Harrods." He closed the door silently behind him and walked down the thickly carpeted corridor. He passed the elevator and headed down the stairs. He didn't feel let down, just foolish for believing that the three could pick up where they had left off. That was his mistake. Too many years had passed.

Still in the hotel room, Wilcox chopped a line on the table. He offered one to Driscoll.

"Not for me. Gives me a runny nose."

Wilcox sniffed, then tapped the rolled banknote on the table.

"You feel as bad as me?" asked Driscoll.

"Yeah."

"But we agreed, right? I mean, no way. Not at our age."

"Yeah."

"You think he was serious?"

"The Crown Jewels—it's insanity."

They looked at each other.

De Jersey had arranged to meet Christina and her parents at Walton Street. The entrance to the streets was busy; Harrods was holding its January sale. The Rolls-Royce was waiting in line, his chauffeur was inside, and once he was seated in the car, de Jersey closed his eyes and tilted his hat over his face. Thirty minutes later Christina came out with her parents and they drove toward Beauchamp Place. He had booked a table for an early dinner, and he became the charming host, making polite conversation about their visit to the Tower of London. He had even purchased a video of the tour and bought many of the books on sale at the kiosk, maps, and numerous large color photographs of the crowns.

Wilcox left the Ritz feeling depressed. He made his way to Bond Street, irritated that he could not get a taxi. He passed Asprey & Garrard and paused to stare at the diamonds in the window. The cocaine was wearing off. It was raining and his suit was damp. His knees were a constant source of pain after so many skiing accidents. Did de Jersey still suffer from his knee injury? Memories flooded back. It had actually been Wilcox's idea to rob the shops for de Jersey to take back what was rightly his. Wilcox was all for using the same violent tactics the villains had, but de Jersey had refused and a few weeks later contacted him with a plan. Wilcox pictured the three of them as young bloods, daring robbers. Those had been thrilling times. But even de Jersey couldn't steal the Crown Jewels. Could he?

Driscoll had parked his new Jaguar not far from Piccadilly Circus. His dismay changed to frustration as traffic inched along toward Haymarket. When he turned into the Mall, the magnificent sight of Buckingham Palace confronted him. He thought of de Jersey's insane suggestion of stealing the Crown Jewels. He drove past the Palace, remembering the crazy guy who had broken in. Despite all those guards on duty, alarms, and security devices, he had slipped into the Queen's bedroom and sat on her bed.

Liz was waiting outside Victoria Station, soaked to the skin. She shot into the road from the bus depot when she spotted the car. Driscoll loaded the bags filled with bargains into the trunk.

"Why are you so late? I said seven fifteen. I've been standing there for over three-quarters of an hour. Did you buy the golf clubs you wanted? I went to Harvey Nicks. . . ."

He never listened to her monologues, which didn't seem to require answers to the questions or views on her many purchases. He felt tired, old, and bored.

"You're very quiet," she said. "How's your stomach?"

"Fine."

"You take your antacid tablets?"

"Yeah." He sighed; ahead was another traffic jam at Vauxhall Bridge.

"If you'd gone over Chelsea Bridge it'd have been better, or you could have gone over Wandsworth Bridge."

"Shut it, Liz."

"What the hell's the matter with you, Tony? All you do lately is moan. Half the holiday in Florida was ruined by your bad moods."

Tony didn't reply. How was he going to tell her that forty-five million pounds had gone missing in cyberspace?

De Jersey felt drained when he got home, but he had to maintain his good humor for that evening, and the following morning, walking round the estate with his in-laws. However, his mind was only half there. He had decided to go ahead, even without Wilcox and Driscoll. Their refusal to join him had not dampened his spirits; it had made him even more determined.

8

Christina and her parents had been delighted with the surprise gift of a trip on the Orient Express. Planning a robbery would be easier without marital commitments, he reasoned. He needed space to work and to gather a new team. The following Wednesday, de Jersey's helicopter landed at the heliport beside Heathrow. The pilot's orders were to refuel and return to the estate within the hour.

Meanwhile, de Jersey traveled by bus to Kilburn; at almost twelve he arrived at the flat. He spent some time arranging the orange nightmare into what looked like a lived-in home, with newspapers and magazines on the coffee table, books on the shelf, and some clothes in the wardrobe.

Raymond Marsh had arranged a meeting for two thirty and arrived promptly to set up the computer. He had brought with him various antivirus programs and other systems to protect de Jersey's files. He also brought a satellite dish. This, he explained, would enable de Jersey to use the Internet by connecting through a satellite rather than a phone line. The beauty of the system, in hacking terms, was that it was much more difficult to trace, and the link could be broken in seconds. When he had finished, he accepted a cup of coffee and sat down on the orange settee. "Fire hazard these, you know," he said, tapping the cushion and slurping his coffee. "Against the law to sell them, catch light faster than a match. My missus won't have anything flammable around."

"It serves its purpose," de Jersey said, bringing out a thick wad of cash. He peeled off notes, and Marsh stashed them in a zip-up wallet, which he tucked into his overalls. He glanced at the remaining wad of money, which de Jersey had set on the arm of his chair. "Anything else you need from me?"

De Jersey nodded. "Show me how it all works."

Raymond stood up to check his watch. "Not got long."

"How about we arrange some private lessons? I need to get more familiar with chat rooms and retrieving information from the Net."

"I'm not cheap. One-on-one will cost you a hundred an hour." Marsh sat down at the computer. "Let's open her up and play," he said. His fingers flashed over the keyboard. "If you want to be a player in this community, you got to earn respect from them. So familiarize yourself with the geek-speak. There's a lot of goodwill around. Hackers don't work for money, they work for intelligence. The value system of a hacker, pirate or cracker, the good or the bad, is different from normal consumer society. If you want to be recognized as a good citizen in the Net community, you've got to contribute, and that means sharing material or information for free. Since I'm getting paid, I won't ask any questions about what you're up to." Marsh laughed.

"Get me up something on anyone who's worked in the Royal household recently. Someone who was on security," de Jersey said.

De Jersey hated to be at his mercy, but Marsh gave no indication that he was surprised by the request. He gestured for de Jersey to sit beside him. They worked together, pulling down newspaper reports, logging into various sites until Marsh had downloaded sheets of articles from numerous newspapers dating back about eight months. Exactly an hour later he said he had to leave. He put out his hand for his payment, and they arranged for the next session.

Alone, de Jersey read the news articles. One man's case stood out from the others. Gregory Jones had been convicted of murdering his wife and was presently serving life at Franklyn Prison. He was a former palace security guard who had discovered his wife in bed with another member of the Queen's household. It was imperative to find out about the security setup at the Palace and the procedures surrounding the Royals when they appeared in public, how many security men and ladies-in-waiting would accompany Her Majesty. De Jersey hoped Gregory Jones could provide this information.

He logged on to Web sites about the Royal Family. He was even side-tracked into reading about the Queen's love of horses. There were pictures of her at Ascot when her horse Enharmonic won the Diamond Stakes. The jockey, Frankie Dettori, stood beside her, wearing her racing colors. Then de Jersey scrolled through pictures of the Crown Jewels, pausing when the screen filled with the Queen Mother's crown. It was the only one mounted in platinum, and there, set in the front, was the magnificent Koh-i-noor

Diamond, which drew him like a magnet. He touched the screen with his hand. Right now, it was so far out of his reach.

De Jersey planned to fabricate a plausible reason for occasional trips to London after Christina returned. Raymond Marsh was a frequent visitor to the apartment now, guiding his experiments. As de Jersey got to know the odd man, he admired him more. Marsh was not only a top cracker but a phacker. He was adept at disrupting and illegally tapping into phone systems via his computer. De Jersey felt sure all his experience would come in handy. When Marsh left, de Jersey would set timers on the lights to make it appear that the flat was constantly occupied, then travel back to his estate to carry on his work there.

Slowly he began to formulate a plan for the robbery. In order to visit the ex-security guard in Franklyn Prison, he had to acquire fake documents. He researched Hunting and Letheby, the firm of solicitors who had dealt with Jones's case and printed out an imitation of their headed notepaper, then wrote to the prison requesting a visitor's pass for the solicitor handling the man's appeal.

Next he had to hunt down another ex-employee of the Royal household, someone who could provide inside information on protocol. He placed a message on various electronic bulletin boards: "U.K. novelist wishes to contact any employees (or recent ex-employees) of Royal household for confidential information." He was astonished at the number of replies. He knew that a vast percentage would be from idiots messing around, but after a while it became easy to assess them, and he made lists of those he would contact. It was time-consuming work, though, and the pressure was on.

De Jersey had been occupied at the stables virtually all morning. He discussed forthcoming racing events with his trainers, the twelve mares in foal, and various veterinary matters. A three-year-old colt that had cost him almost three-quarters of a million pounds had not been fit enough to race yet, and the strangles bacteria had struck a wing of the yard that stabled eighteen horses. Veterinary bills were always high, but this winter they were astronomical. And foot-and-mouth restrictions still held up traveling. The good news, however, was that his pride and joy, Royal Flush, was in fine health and training for the season, which, de Jersey hoped, would place him on track for the Derby.

De Jersey had only just returned to his office when he received a call from David Lyons's widow. Helen asked if he would see her that afternoon, on a personal matter that she preferred not to discuss over the phone. De Jersey agreed.

Helen waited outside her house for him. Her face was white and drawn, and she was not wearing any makeup. Usually an immaculate dresser, she was wrapped in a drab brown coat with a fur hat pulled down roughly over her hair. "Thank you for coming, Edward," she said, her eyes brimming with tears. "I had no one else to turn to." She led him inside the house, poured coffee, and they sat down at the kitchen table, where she fiddled with a teaspoon. Her eyes had the lost look of the recently bereaved. "I don't know where to begin. It's to do with David's death." She reached for a tissue and blew her nose. "He left everything to me. I'd always believed we were comfortably off, but . . ." She stopped.

"Go on, Helen," he prompted quietly.

"David borrowed on the house. He liquidated almost everything we possessed, and I don't know what trouble he had got himself into, but the savings accounts . . ." She took a deep breath. "David withdrew every penny we had. My sister, who's been overseeing everything for me, says he took out almost two million pounds. It's all gone." De Jersey said nothing. "I'm not asking you for money, please don't think that. I've still got a few thousand in my own account. I'll be all right." She twisted the sodden tissue. "I don't know what he was doing, I really don't. His assistant is devastated, and they're closing the office. My sister took a week off work to help sort everything out."

De Jersey was feeling edgy, but he gave nothing away.

"She is an accountant too. In fact, David and I met through her. She's gone through all of his business accounts. It seems he had invested in an Internet company based in New York, leadingleisurewear. Many of his clients also invested in this company." She glanced toward de Jersey. Although he didn't show it, de Jersey was furious at David's indiscretion. "My sister was stunned at the amount of money you and David put in, and those others, a man called Wilcox, and I think Driscoll."

De Jersey's mind was racing. This was probably the only time that their names had been linked. He smiled. "I had presumed I was the only unfortunate gambler."

"I am so very sorry," she said, patting his hand. "The reason I asked to see you was because Sylvia—"

"Your sister."

"Yes. She works for an international investment company. This company had invested in a similar venture and lost a considerable amount as well. So she did some checking for me; she's thinking of hiring an investi-gator over there to help."

"Checking into what exactly?"

"Into leadingleisurewear. It was started by a young man called Alex Moreno. Now he and another leadingleisurewear ex-employee have been trying to set up another Internet deal. Sylvia couldn't believe their audac-ity. I said to her that if I told you this you'd want to do something about it. Sylvia said if there was a possibility of getting some of the money back, then I or you or the other men should contact this Alex Moreno and find out what's going on."

De Jersey leaned forward. "My new financial adviser has told me there is no possible recourse and that I simply have to accept I made a poor judgment."

"But you can't just accept it!" she exclaimed.

"I am afraid, Helen, that that is what I have to do. We are a part of a worldwide Internet collapse. There are not just a few losers but thousands. Many Internet companies have gone bust."

"You could find Moreno."

"I've accepted my losses."

"You're just going to walk away?" she asked, aghast.

"I've been advised that I have little or no hope of recouping them."

She looked at her hands. "Sylvia has consulted a private investigator in New York to try to trace Moreno."

De Jersey felt his gut tighten. "Has she succeeded in finding him?"

"No. It would seem he's disappeared. She thinks he has probably stolen a lot of the funds. She found a letter from the auditor dated shortly before leadingleisurewear collapsed, questioning the figures of the annual audit.

"And Sylvia found out that he sold his apartment in New York. The doorman said it went to a German. But Moreno has a house in the Hamptons too."

De Jersey was seething inside but reached across the table for Helen's hand. She gripped his, and the tears started again. "I feel so bad about what happened," she said. "I should try to trace the other men involved."

He released her hand. "The investors have never publicly admitted their losses, as I have not. It is highly confidential information. I can't ad-vise you, Helen."

"But don't you think they would want to know what my sister has dis-covered?"

"I can't speak for them," he said quietly.

"Don't *you* want to find out about Alex Moreno?"

He chose his words carefully. "Hiring an investigator in another country is not something I have considered doing. I am sure if David believed he could retrieve any of the money, he would not have taken such a drastic way out."

"Would you look over some of the documents I found?"

"Of course. But I want my involvement with this company kept from the press. This could all blow up if the investigator's discoveries were ever made public."

"I thought perhaps you'd help me."

"I doubt I can be of any assistance. And I'm confused as to how you gained access to my personal files."

"They were in the safe in David's study upstairs."

"Are the other investors' details there too?"

"Yes."

"Then I would like mine returned, and I advise you to return theirs as well."

"I'll tell my sister," she said, flushing.

David Lyons's study was in disarray. Boxes and files were stacked against the wall, and papers were heaped on every available surface. Helen gestured to the paperwork. "I've been sent these from his office." She crossed to the fireplace and lit the fake-coal gas fire. "It's cold in here. I've not had the heating on." She looked at the mound of files. "David kept all his files on his computer but always made hard copies for reference. Mostly they're quite old. These are the most recent ones." She looked around, puzzled. "Oh, I think I took your files to the kitchen," she remembered and hurried out. A few moments later, she returned with a large, square box. She handed it to de Jersey and moved aside some papers for him to place it on the desk.

De Jersey spent almost an hour in the study. Helen hovered for a while, then left him to answer the door to the removal men. They carried out the items of furniture and ornaments she had earmarked to sell. Flustered, she directed them around the house and frequently appeared to apologize to de Jersey. Eventually he walked into the hall. "I'm taking all my personal papers and details of transactions relating to my business, Helen."

"Oh, yes, yes, of course."

De Jersey ordered a local minicab and returned to the study to await its arrival. As he was going through the desk drawers one last time, he found an extra set of house keys, which he slipped into his pocket. He would have to warn both Driscoll and Wilcox about the new developments.

As soon as he arrived home, de Jersey started to thumb through a stack of documents with his name underlined at the top and a thick wedge of accounting ledgers. His head began to throb as he realized David had systematically plundered all of his accounts in a desperate attempt to salvage leadingleisurewear. To meet Moreno's requests for more funds, he had thrown good money after bad. Had de Jersey just lost his original investment, he could have kept running the stables, but this was far worse: he was heading for bankruptcy.

Although he welcomed her home warmly, Christina knew something was wrong. Her husband was deeply distracted and quickly retreated to his study. After unpacking she went to join him, but when he dismissed her concerns, she became angry.

"Please, darling, don't fend me off as if I was a child. I know something has happened. Stop hiding things from me. What is it?"

He sighed. Now that Helen and her interfering sister had details of his private affairs, he could no longer keep the situation from Christina.

"David Lyons lost millions of my money. He invested badly, then tried to salvage the investment by throwing more money at it. He lost his own savings too and a few other people's."

"Oh, my God, that's dreadful. Can you do anything about it?"

"No, it's all gone."

"Is that why Helen wanted to see you?"

"Her sister's thinking of hiring a private investigator to try to retrieve some of her losses."

"What can an investigator do?"

He shrugged. "I doubt he can do anything. The money has gone. The Internet company went bankrupt."

"What is this investigator looking for?" Christina asked.

"Some Internet whiz kid."

"If they find him, will they arrest him?"

"Even if they did they couldn't prove embezzlement. He kept the money he made from selling the company's software, but as he designed it, he owned it. The investment stank, and David was a fool. I have only myself to blame . . . and him, of course."

"But what about that banker you met up with? Can he help?"

"I hoped he might but he can't."

Christina looked shocked. "How bad is it, Edward? Tell me."

"Nothing I can't fix." He forced a reassuring smile.

"Oh, thank goodness," she said, holding him tightly. "I know how much you love this place."

"We're not going to lose this." He kissed her.

He walked across the yard and let himself into the office, shutting the door behind him. He took out the cell phone he'd bought in Simmons's name and called Driscoll and Wilcox, informing them about Helen's intervention. Then he locked away the phone and returned to the house. Christina was curled up in bed watching TV and laughing.

"What are you watching?"

"An advert," she said, pointing to the TV. "It's for royal jelly, and she's so like her it's unbelievable. For a moment I looked, and I thought, It can't be, surely she wouldn't, but it's . . . Look, she's identical!"

De Jersey stared at the TV. A look-alike playing the Queen was sitting on a throne wearing a fake diamond crown and holding up a pot of royal jelly. On the screen she mimicked Her Majesty's voice to perfection.

De Jersey pulled his tie loose, laughing. Another piece of the jigsaw had just fallen into place. It was the first piece of good news he'd had all day.

The following morning de Jersey was up early and went riding alone. He returned to the house for breakfast. He suggested to Christina that she invite Helen Lyons for lunch to show her there were no hard feelings. He said he felt guilty for having been so brisk with Helen yesterday and for not attending David's funeral. Christina slipped her arms around her husband's neck. "I'll call her if it's what you want, but I hardly know what to say to her, considering how David has treated us."

"Thank you, my love. Can you ring her now?" he asked.

"But it's too early."

"No, it isn't." He continued with his breakfast as he heard Christina arrange lunch for the following day.

Christina left in a chauffeur-driven car to collect Helen from the station. After watching her go, de Jersey took the helicopter to a small airport close to the Lyonses' home. He hoped the house would be empty. He had called ahead twice to make sure no one picked up the phone. He let himself in with the keys from David's desk, waited for the sound of an alarm; when nothing happened, he went straight to the study. He turned on the fake-coal fire and kicked some files closer to the grate, then he gathered all the documents he could find relating to Wilcox and Driscoll.

* * *

After de Jersey landed the helicopter, he went directly to the stables. One of the stable girls was waiting for him in his golf cart, and they drove toward the east wing.

"I didn't know for sure they'd reached you."

"How in God's name did it happen?"

"We don't know. He just stumbled on the way to the gallops, but when he returned, he was lame," she said. "It's quite badly swollen, but we don't think there's any bone damage."

In the center of the yard, his trainer and a couple of lads hovered around Royal Flush. The vet had instructed he be walked about; Royal Flush dropped his shoulder, showing a pronounced limp. De Jersey was on his knees beside the vet when Christina and Helen walked across the yard.

"We'd given up on you," Christina said, then fell silent as her husband looked up at her.

"We don't think anything's broken, but it's badly swollen," he said. "Helen, I'm sorry, but as you can see this is a bit of an emergency."

"Will you be joining us for lunch?" Christina asked.

"Start without me, darling. I won't be too long, I hope."

To Christina's annoyance, de Jersey never made it to lunch. After a rather tedious and tearful meal, she saw Helen on her way, making promises to stay in touch.

When Helen arrived home, the house was blazing and the fire brigade struggled for control. The study, hall, and part of the staircase had been gutted. David Lyons's papers had fed the fire, and charred documents fluttered in the chilly afternoon air. Helen, now faced with the destruction of her home, became so hysterical that her doctor had to sedate her.

Christina put down the phone, stunned.

"Who was that?" de Jersey asked.

"It was Helen. Said that the house was on fire when she got home. Started in the study. All of David's papers were destroyed. Does that matter to you?"

"I don't suppose so. Whatever documents he had I'll have copies of."

"She asked me if I knew these other investors, Driscoll and Wilcox."

"She asked me the same thing. I've never heard of them. I wish she'd just leave it alone."

Sylvia helped Helen into her car. "You'll stay with me until it's all sorted out."

"I'm never going back to that house."

"You won't have to. I'll get all your clothes and anything you want to put into storage. The estate agents aren't worried—you could repair the house to sell, or sell it as it is."

A couple of hours later they were in London. Sylvia Hewitt had a large flat in St. John's Wood, overlooking Regent's Park. Eight years Helen's junior, she had never married. The apartment was spacious, with three bedrooms, and tastefully furnished. Sylvia hurried around, making up a bed, then setting a tray with tea, scrambled egg, and smoked salmon for Helen.

Helen leaned back on her pillows. She was simply too devastated to talk.

"Eat up. You're going to fall down a crack in the pavement you're so thin," Sylvia said, puffing on a cigarette as she wandered restlessly around the room. "Bit odd that the fire started in David's office," she remarked. She started hanging her sister's discarded clothes in the wardrobe.

"I think the window was open, and I must have left the fire on and some papers blew onto it."

Sylvia stubbed out her cigarette. "Suppose there was information in David's files that someone wanted to keep secret?"

"What do you mean?"

Sylvia folded her arms. "This Alex Moreno guy seems very dodgy. My detective, Matheson, can't find him anywhere. All that money poured into leadingleisurewear and he just disappears? Matheson thinks something smells."

Helen sighed. "I don't know, Sylvia. I'm so tired."

Sylvia removed the tray. Her sister had hardly touched the food.

"You'll feel differently when you can think straight. I won't let it go. You've lost a lot of money."

"It wasn't just me, you know. Edward de Jersey lost millions too, but he isn't interested in doing anything about it. Didn't want to hear about the private detective."

"Maybe he can afford to lose the odd million."

Helen sat up. "He lost a lot more than a few million, and it was mostly David's fault. He could have advised them to get out when he knew it was heading for a fall. Instead he encouraged them to put up more money and . . ." She hesitated. "Edward had been his friend for twenty-odd years, and he trusted him implicitly. I think David made some illegal transactions. I found correspondence between David and this man Moreno and some documents from a private account. I think David took some of that money and was encouraging Edward to keep investing more and—"

"Helen, what if Alex Moreno didn't want those papers floating around?

What if he started the fire? I think we should contact all the people who lost their fortunes. I mean, maybe de Jersey has so much money he doesn't need what he lost, but the others might."

"Oh, I don't know."

"Get some sleep. Don't think about any of it—leave it to me. Daniel from David's office is coming by to talk about a few things."

Once Sylvia left the room, she called Victor Matheson, the private investigator, and informed him about the fire and her suspicions.

"You could be right, ma'am. Here's what I've got so far: Alex Moreno left the hotel in the Hamptons early on the morning after his arrival. He was driving the Lexus, which I'm also trying to track down. The building contractors say Moreno's business adviser was a Philip Simmons. Ring any bells?"

"I don't think so."

"Canadian? Tall, over six feet, red hair and a mustache?"

"Still no. My sister met with one of the investors, Edward de Jersey. He lost millions. His details are in the file I sent you. He didn't seem interested in discovering Moreno's whereabouts."

"He must be stinking rich if he doesn't give a shit about finding where all the money's disappeared to."

"Continue your inquiries for now," Sylvia said. "I'll be in touch again shortly. I plan to contact the other investors. If Mr. de Jersey isn't interested in taking this matter further, maybe one of them will be. I'm determined to salvage my brother-in-law's savings."

The doorbell rang almost immediately after she hung up. She let in Daniel Gatley, David's assistant, who held a briefcase.

"I have the information you asked for."

"Thank you," she said. "Helen doesn't know I've lost money as well. It may not seem like a lot in comparison, but it was my life savings—two hundred and fifty thousand."

"Yes, I know. I'm sorry."

"I don't believe that fire was an accident. It's odd that it started in David's study and that his papers fueled it. Helen says she might have left the fire on and a window open, but that doesn't make sense."

Daniel opened his briefcase. He looked uncomfortable. "This is all I could find on the main investors, but I shouldn't let these documents out of the office. They're confidential."

"Oh, for goodness' sake, Daniel, there *is* no office now. But if anyone asks I'll say David left them here."

He took out the files and placed them on the table. "Does Helen know?" he asked.

She shook her head. "Nobody knows, apart from you," she said. She covered her face with her hands for what seemed a long period. "I miss him so much. I've had to look after Helen when all I wanted to do was curl up and cry."

"I know David cared deeply for you," Daniel said awkwardly.

"Yes, I know he did too. But he lost my life savings and I've got to do something about it. Do you think Moreno could have had anything to do with the fire at the house? It's all very convenient, isn't it?"

"Well," Daniel said, "I've got the files here for the other investors, apart from Edward de Jersey. After David's death, he came and took everything out of the office. David had put everything on disk for him."

Sylvia opened a drawer. "I have some disks too, which David left here, so I know just how much de Jersey lost."

Daniel nodded to the files he had brought. "Details of the small investors plus the other two main ones."

She snatched the top sheet of notes from him. "Driscoll and Wilcox," she read. "I'll concentrate on them."

Daniel stood up to leave. He pulled a Jiffy bag out of his briefcase and handed it to her. "Just a few personal items from David's desk that I thought Helen or you might like to keep."

"Thank you for coming over. And for keeping my secret. Helen hasn't the slightest idea about David and me. I don't know what it would do to her if she did find out."

Daniel nodded. At the door, he paused and turned. "Sylvia, I wouldn't bring this arson thing to anyone's attention. The police will be looking into the fire because of David's suicide, and if there is any hint that it wasn't an accident, the insurance won't pay out. As you said, Helen has been through enough already."

9

Sylvia contacted James Wilcox first—his unlisted telephone number had been in David's file. "I'm David Lyons's sister-in-law," she told him. "My sister Helen has asked me to help her sort out David's financial problems in connection with the Internet company leadingleisurewear. I believe you were one of the main investors and suffered considerable losses."

"That is correct," Wilcox said. "My business adviser is looking into the matter."

"I have hired a private investigator to try to track down Alex Moreno."

"My advisers are handling my interests, and I am loath to confuse the issue by becoming involved with any other backers. I would appreciate it if you did not press this matter further on my behalf or call again."

"But you lost a fortune!"

"That's my business." Wilcox sounded annoyed.

"Do you know Edward de Jersey?"

"No."

"Mr. de Jersey was the largest investor and will lose everything he has—" Wilcox had hung up. Sylvia was astonished that he didn't want to know any more.

Undeterred, she called Anthony Driscoll. He was not as brusque as Wilcox, but he made it clear that his own advisers were investigating the company's downfall. "Please feel free to call again if you acquire any information you think I would be interested in," Driscoll said.

"I am contacting all the investors," Sylvia persisted. "Are you aware that a Mr. Edward de Jersey lost nearly a hundred million pounds?"

Driscoll was taken aback momentarily. "No, I am not. Listen, are you asking for me to assist this investigator?"

"Only if you wish to do so. I am quite happy to continue paying him until I get results."

"Well, I admire your tenacity, Miss Hewitt, but I am quite perturbed that you have called an unlisted number and that you seem to have access to very personal details."

"I explained who I was," Sylvia replied rather petulantly.

"That in itself does not give you, or anyone close to Mr. Lyons, the right to access my private and highly confidential transactions. I want my losses to remain my own business."

"Well, I apologize," she said, embarrassed. "I am really doing this for my sister."

"Frankly, Miss Hewitt, I am not interested in who you are doing this for. While his suicide was tragic, David Lyons made some extremely ill-advised business moves. I blame myself for making the investments; nevertheless I was under Mr. Lyons's guidance. That I had a disastrous loss is my business, and I would appreciate it if you did not call again or use my name in reference to any private investigation you may instigate."

Sylvia interrupted before he could hang up on her, like Wilcox. "May I just ask if you know any of the other investors? A Mr. James Wilcox."

"No, I've never met any of the others."

"Did you ever meet Alex Moreno, the man who ran leading-leisurewear?"

"No. Furthermore, I have no interest in meeting him. I wish you success, but I have no time to discuss this further. Good-bye." He hung up abruptly.

Sylvia was aware that big investors did not like their losses known. However, she was infuriated that these three men could accept losing millions. She had lost a pittance in comparison, but it had been her life savings. She had no intention of letting the matter be swept under the carpet.

Liz Driscoll had answered Sylvia's call, and after he hung up, she waited for her husband to explain it.

"So who is this Sylvia woman then?" she asked eventually.

"The sister-in-law of an old business adviser."

"So what's she calling you for?"

"He topped himself," he said irritably.

"Who did?"

"David Lyons, the business adviser."

"Do I know him?"

"No, but he handled an investment of mine."

"Oh, I see," she said, pouring some power juice ingredients into the mixer.

"Do you?" he snapped.

"Yes, anything concerning money is a mood swinger with you. Bad news was it?" The mixer whirred noisily.

"Yeah, but nothing I can't take care of."

"I know, darling, but what's she doing calling you at home? Was it an emergency?"

"No."

"So was it about this guy topping himself?"

"Yes," he hissed.

"Why did he do it?"

He hesitated, then prepared to face the music. He rested both hands on the marble worktop. "I just lost a bundle on what I was told was a sure-fire investment."

"Oh, Tony. How much?" she said sipping her drink.

He simply shrugged. When he avoided eye contact with her, she became worried.

"Tony, answer me. How much did you lose?"

"I don't want to talk about it."

"Why not?"

"Cos I hate fucking losing, all right?"

"Don't you swear at me. I knew something was up. I just knew it. It started in Florida, didn't it? You were told about this then." He nodded. "Why don't you talk to me, Tony? Worried myself sick wondering, is it me? Isn't he enjoying his holiday or is something up with the kids? Tony, all these things go through my mind when you get this way. I was worried all holiday. Look at me. Do you know what I'm talking about?"

When he walked out of the room, she followed. "Tony, tell me. Have you got yourself into real financial difficulty with this? I need to know, especially now."

"What do you mean especially now?"

"I was going to tell you tonight. It's Michelle. She wants to marry that Hamilton boy, you know the one who plays polo with Prince Charles?"

"What?"

"She's been keen on him for months. Blond with nice blue eyes. He's been around here, Tony, loads of times. They met at the Dunhill polo match at Windsor last summer, and she was with him over Christmas in France."

"She's only seventeen!" he blustered.

"So? I was only eighteen when we married."

"That's different. She's my daughter."

"He's coming over with his family for dinner Thursday."

"Thursday? I might have to go into town to get this stuff ironed out."

"What stuff?"

"I told you. I done a bad investment, got to catch up on the finances." Under pressure he always lost his grasp of grammar, even his old accent returned.

"How much have you lost then?" she asked, frightened. She had already started planning a sumptuous wedding. What they lacked in class she intended to make up for in expenditure.

"Not enough for you to worry about."

"I hope not. He's a sweetheart, you know, and his family are all titled. It'll take me three months to plan and prepare, and they want to do it as soon as possible. Where are we going to hold the reception? What about her dress? I was going to see about getting Stella McCartney to do it. You know, have a real fairy-tale wedding."

"Sweetheart, if my baby wants to get married in a palace I'll arrange it, you know that. She'll have the wedding of her dreams, that's a promise. But why the rush? She's not up the spout, is she?"

"No, she bloody isn't! Oh, Tony, you've got me all worried now."

"When have I ever let you down?" He kissed her.

"Never. I love you, Tony," she said.

Driscoll plodded across the bedroom and fell flat on the bed. "Oh, Jesus Christ," he muttered. He stuffed two antacid tablets in his mouth and chewed them like peppermints. A fucking wedding was all he needed. Then there was the call from Sylvia Hewitt to worry about. The three men had never been linked together like that, and he didn't like it one bit. Finally, he was really concerned about de Jersey's financial situation. He could never recall feeling sorry for de Jersey before, but though Driscoll had lost most of his own savings, he could still find nearly a quarter of a million, while, if what Sylvia said was true, de Jersey had lost everything. Driscoll, probably more than anyone, knew what the stud farm meant to de Jersey. He could remember old Ronnie Jersey's words: "I once owned a leg in a horse. I cried when he won a little race at Plumpton. I loved that horse, Tony." Sometimes Ronnie had fantasized about owning his own racing stables. "It's a mugs' game for the rich nobs, though," he'd said. "You can't win. It's all payout. Gotta have more money than sense." His son had achieved all Ronnie had ever dreamed of, and it made Driscoll sad that the old man had never known of Edward's success. Truth be told, he'd been a bit overawed by it himself. In many ways Driscoll was more like Ronnie than his own son was.

The wind eased in his belly, but that didn't make Driscoll feel better. He wandered slowly around the vast upstairs part of his home, from the children's bedrooms to the gym, where his wife was working out with a young instructor in tight Lycra shorts, then down the wide staircase to the baronial-size hall, where antique side tables and oil paintings decorated the circular, oak-paneled reception. The spacious drawing room had been copied from a *Homes and Garden's* picture his wife had liked. Sitting at the grand piano, he lifted the lid, revealing the ivory keys in perfect condition. No one had ever played it. He looked over the array of large, silver-framed photographs of his family and their various dogs, his daughter's horse and his son's aviary.

He loved his family. He was proud of his own achievements. He reckoned that he was a good man. He'd certainly given enough to charities over the years. He had never been a violent person. He'd seen violence at close quarters, but he had never taken up a gun or taken a life. He drummed his fingers on the polished lid of the piano. The villa would have to go, plus the Chelsea Wharf apartment. All the trappings of wealth would need to be sold off, and this just as he had a massive tax bill coming in. Though he didn't know what de Jersey's scheme was, he knew that it would be planned down to the last detail. He slapped the piano lid hard with the flat of his hand and swore out loud at David Lyons. He should have refused to invest; he was almost bloody well retired. As he shook his head at his own stupidity, the pit of his stomach started to rumble again.

Wearing an oil-stained overall, Wilcox was leaning over the Ferrari Testarossa. His young mechanic was sitting inside the old car, revving it up. Wilcox spent hours in his garage, tinkering with his eight vintage sports cars. They were like much-beloved toys. He would race round and round the small racetrack he had built in his grounds, testing and reworking the engines. These were the only times he was totally content. His domestic life was clouded. He had always searched for the perfect union, but the reality was he had found it and it had four wheels. Today, however, he was unable to concentrate. The call from Sylvia Hewitt was nagging him like a hungry, mangy dog. He hated the fact that she knew so much about him and knew that she could be trouble. He was also rattled that de Jersey had not brought him or Driscoll into his plans to get rid of Moreno. It was, after all, very much their business. It was also very unlike de Jersey. He had never advocated violence, so why had he murdered the guy? It should not have been his decision alone.

Wilcox sat wiping the oil from his hands, perched on the bumper of a Silver Cloud Rolls-Royce. He had let the mechanic go for a spin on the track. His financial situation had proven even worse than he had at first anticipated. He had left himself short, and he had various outstanding debts that needed to be paid. His drug dealer for one was screaming for his due. Wilcox had been shocked at how much he owed—two hundred thousand pounds to be exact. He couldn't believe how much he was using. He had planned to cut back, though under this recent pressure he'd needed more. If de Jersey found out, he might consider him a security risk.

Wilcox tossed the oily rag into the bin. What if he trashed the entire garage and hangar and claimed on the cars' insurance? He couldn't bring himself to do it, even though the premiums were another vast expense. The days of running twenty garages were certainly over. He'd begun buying and selling cars at the age of forty, flush with the proceeds of the gold bullion robbery. Later, he had blithely and irrationally continued buying vintage vehicles without reselling them. By then he had grown tired of the business side and just wanted to race his cars and enjoy life. He truly did not want to be drawn back into crime, but he knew that he would feel obliged to go along with whatever the Colonel was putting together. The prospect scared and excited him, prompting him to take more cocaine. He needed the drug from the moment he opened his eyes in the morning and used it all day. That was more worrying than anything else. What had started out as a release from boredom had slowly taken over his life.

"I've got to kick the habit," he muttered as he chopped four lines up in the back of the garage. After snorting all four of them, he called Driscoll.

"It's me."

"Yeah, I recognized your voice. You heard from the Colonel?"

"Only to warn me about that woman."

"Oh, right, well that's why I'm calling you."

"We're not supposed to make contact."

"Yeah, well, I just did, all right? I am really worried about this woman, Tony."

"She called me at the house."

"Yeah, me too."

"I didn't like it," Driscoll said. "Are you on something?" Driscoll could tell Wilcox was unusually wired.

"I'm just looking out for us. Is that a bad thing? What's got into you?"

Driscoll cut across the potential argument. "He's lost the lot. Did she tell you? Reckons his stud will go down the tubes."

Wilcox let out a long sigh. "Yeah, she said he'd lost his shirt. You know what that means, don't you?"

"Yeah, he's more broke than we reckoned."

After a pause, Wilcox's voice came back over the line sounding slightly muffled. "No, Tony, it means whatever he wants from me, he's got."

There was a long silence. "Me too, I suppose," Driscoll said, resigned. Wilcox slapped the cell phone off and turned to see the young mechanic standing close enough to have overheard every word.

"What's with you?" he snapped.

"Sorry, James. We broke down on the S bend, pouring smoke and oil. You wanna take a look?"

"Don't go sneaking up on me like that," Wilcox said angrily.

"Sorry, I did knock."

Wilcox stared at the kid's young, concerned face. He relaxed. "That's okay, Dan, no problem. Let's go check out the car."

Rika was looking for Wilcox. She headed into the garage and, finding it empty, walked into his back room, where she found the mirror. She licked her finger and tasted the cocaine. She shook her head. It was bad enough him using it, but to leave it out in the open for the children to find was something she would not tolerate. Rika found him with his mechanic, leaning over the open bonnet of the smoking Ferrari on the track. She marched straight up to Wilcox and pushed him away from the car. "Ve got to talk."

"Not right now, I'm busy."

"You have to collect the twins from school. I told you diz morning, you are late for them now."

"Why can't you do it?"

"Because I have an appointment wid my dentist. I tell you diz."

"Okay, okay, I'll get them."

"No you von't."

"What?"

She faced him, hands on her hips. "You look at yourself in the mirror you leave in ze garage?" she asked. She threw the mirror at his feet. "I'll get them, but I von't have diz near to de kids. You should be ashamed of yourself, a man of your age. Vat you think you are playing at? And vipe your nose, it's running. You sicken me."

Wilcox gripped her arm and frog-marched her to the side of the track. "You never speak to me that way, you hear me? Especially not in front of someone like Dan."

"Why? Because he'd lose respect for you? Don't kid yourself, James. Everyone around you knows vat you are doing; ve can't miss it! You vant to kill yourself, I no watch you do it! I am leaving you and your kids."

Rika stormed back across the field, and Wilcox wiped his nose with the sleeve of his overall. If he had felt shame before, he now felt it doubly, and upon his return he could not meet the eyes of the young mechanic, who tried hard to appear as if nothing had happened.

Wilcox patted the boy's shoulder. "Can I leave you to finish up here?"

"Yes, sir," he replied shyly.

Wilcox let himself into the house through the mudroom, which was cluttered with kids' skates, Wellington boots, fishing rods, and skateboards. Racks of kids' clothes hung in various sizes and lengths, along with overcoats, raincoats, riding hats. Wilcox kicked off his muddy shoes and stripped off his overall, adding it to the pile of clothes discarded in a corner. The phone rang as he passed the big pine table in the kitchen already set for tea. Four of the six kids were expected, and that meant their friends too. His house was always jammed with kids of every shape and size. They had an entire floor to themselves, with a big games room full of equipment, computers, and computer games, but seemed to prefer running wild, wrecking the place.

He snorted another couple of lines in the en suite bathroom upstairs, then lay down on the quilted bedspread. Deep down he knew the cause of his anguish; with de Jersey having lost so much money, his plans to regain it would be illegal. Wilcox knew he was already involved. Loyalty and need ran too deep to say no.

The swelling had gone down, but Royal Flush was still lame. The vet was observing him in the indoor exercise arena.

"What the hell is the matter with him?" De Jersey was beside himself with anxiety.

The vet was at a loss. "I've X-rayed him, checked and double-checked, but I can find nothing that would stop him putting weight on that leg. It might be psychosomatic—he avoids using the leg because he remembers the pain it caused."

"So what do we do?"

"Encourage him until he forgets. Next time he does a good run, make a fuss of him."

De Jersey stroked the horse's head. "You old so-and-so. Need a bit of love, do you?"

The horse pushed his head into de Jersey's chest. He was after peppermints, and de Jersey slipped him one.

De Jersey went to Fleming's office in a darkened mood. The vet had apologetically requested that he cover his quarterly bill; the usual check had bounced.

When de Jersey expressed his indignation to the bank manager, inquiring why he had not been contacted about this refusal of payment, the man suggested they discuss the matter in his office. De Jersey persisted and was horrified to hear how far his account was into the red. Of course all he had to do was transfer funds from his other major account, but the incident demonstrated just how quickly money was draining away.

He still had his account in the Caymans, and he could keep the yard running, with a few cost-cutting exercises, for another six to eight months, but he would have to prepare for the money running dry altogether.

When Fleming came back to the office, de Jersey dropped the bombshell. "Sell off the east wing," he said. "Contact Tattersalls and add our entries to the next catalog. I'd like you to contact some bloodstock agents about selling privately. I made a bad investment, but I should recoup my losses shortly," he said, feigning confidence.

"Is there anything I can do?" Fleming asked tentatively. "I've got a few thousand saved, and if it's just a short-term problem . . ."

De Jersey put his arm around him. "It is, but I want to be careful. I don't want to get into real financial difficulties. We just have to ease the strain for a few months until I can release some more investments."

"When you said to sell off the east wing," Fleming said, "you didn't mean that Cute Queenie should go too, did you?" He was referring to the old gray mare de Jersey always rode himself.

"Yes, let her go. Get whatever you can for her." He clenched his fist, wanting to punch something, anything.

"Whatever you say."

Christina had hardly seen her husband recently; he spent more and more time in the City. So she was happy when he suggested they go to Monaco for a week. For de Jersey, the trip meant they would be away when the east wing horses were led away. Christina would not be privy to what was going on. While in Monaco he planned to attend a race meeting, check on the state of his offshore accounts, and touch base with Paul Dulay, alias Philip Christian, alias Gérard Laroque, alias Jay Marriot, alias Fredrik Marceau.

De Jersey and Christina flew to Monaco in a private plane. A suite at the Hôtel de Paris had been booked. De Jersey had been a regular customer over the years, and champagne, caviar, fresh fruit, and large bowls of glorious flowers welcomed them.

They hoped the weather would be mild, but it was almost as cold and wet as London. Christina had to unpack. They were going to the casinos that evening, so she needed to press her evening wear. She had also booked hair and manicure appointments and a massage. She felt like being cosseted, and de Jersey encouraged her to enjoy herself.

Telling her he would take a walk, he headed straight for the exclusive shopping malls not a hundred yards from the hotel. He carried an umbrella and, in his immaculate gray pin-striped suit and brogues, looked every inch the wealthy Englishman. He paused by Paul Dulay's small, elegant jewelry shop in a corner of the arcade. The main window displayed a diamond tiara and matching necklace. A smaller display at the side boasted an array of emerald rings and earrings.

There was a camera positioned to observe the arrival of each customer at the entrance to the shop. De Jersey pressed the bell once, and the door buzzed open. The sales assistant asked if she could help him.

"Is Paul Dulay here?"

"*Oui*, Monsieur. May I ask who wishes to see him?"

"Philip Simmons."

The assistant disappeared through a mahogany-paneled door. De Jersey wandered around the reception area. A velvet-covered chair stood close to a Louis XIV table on which lay a black leather visitors' book, a white telephone, and a credit-card machine. A few display cases were visible, exhibiting even more opulent jewels than were in the window. De Jersey took note of the security cameras swiveling to keep him in focus.

In the back room, Dulay was selecting diamonds from a black velvet cloth. He used a jeweler's magnifying glass and a pair of long, delicate tweezers.

"Monsieur, there is a gentleman to see you."

He looked up, irritated.

"A Mr. Philip Simmons."

Dulay removed the eyeglass. "Show him—" His breath caught in his chest. He found his voice and told her to take Mr. Simmons into the private showroom.

Sweat had broken out over his entire body. He packed away the stones, then gritted his teeth. He could not stop shaking. Approaching the inner door, he looked through the two-way glass and saw that it was indeed Simmons. His heart rate increased. Dulay took a deep breath and went in.

10

Paul Dulay, though no more than five foot nine, was broad-shouldered and had a large face. He had aged considerably since their last meeting in South Africa, where Dulay was buying stones for a top French jewelry design company. He had been at De Beers to negotiate for them. He and de Jersey had stayed at the same hotel in Pretoria. De Jersey was already using the name Philip Simmons and traveling on a fake passport. They had formed a loose friendship over a misunderstanding about their rooms. De Jersey's purpose in South Africa was to make a contact who could move the stock of gold bullion he intended to steal. The confusion, however, benefited him.

One evening Dulay was in the hotel bar quite drunk, having just been fired by the Paris-based company. He refused to divulge reasons, just ranted at the bastards who would steal his designs. He rambled on morosely about his prowess with gold. Finally, gazing into his drink he said that, with a bad reputation, it would be hard for him to get into another legitimate company.

A few days later de Jersey introduced the idea of setting up Dulay with a store of gold that would make him a wealthy man. He knew by now that the jeweler had been sacked for switching real diamonds and fakes, and pocketing the proceeds. Dulay had protested his innocence, maintaining that most people wouldn't know a real diamond from a zircon.

They had both made fortunes since that meeting and agreed never to make contact again. As he closed the door behind him, Dulay's face showed clearly that he was very wary, if not afraid, to see Philip Simmons again. Dulay wore well-fitting black trousers and black shoes with white socks. His thinning hair fell to the shoulders of his collarless black shirt.

Now he ran his stubby fingers through it. "Well, Philip, it's been a long time," he said.

Smiling, de Jersey shook hands. "Maybe fifteen years."

"More. Can I offer you a glass of champagne?"

"No, thank you. Can we be overheard here?"

"No." Dulay bent down behind the desk and opened a small fridge that was hidden behind it. "Do you mind if I do?" He took out a half bottle of champagne, then replaced it with vodka. As he poured, his hands shook so much the glass rattled against the bottle. After the Frenchman gulped down his drink, he poured himself more vodka. "To . . . old times," he said softly. "Please, take a seat. Why are you here?"

"Possible business deal," de Jersey said.

"I am legitimate now, Philip. I have a good business and a good life here, and I don't want to lose it."

De Jersey shifted his weight. "You married?"

"Again? Yes, I am, we have three kids. We live in a wonderful old farmhouse on the outskirts of town, which we've spent years renovating. You?"

"I have my lady friends."

Dulay cocked his head to one side. "Apart from the other business, you were in real estate when we first met."

"You have a good memory."

"Well, I am not likely to forget you." Dulay unscrewed the top of the vodka bottle again. "Please don't draw me into anything."

"I have never forced anyone into doing anything," de Jersey said.

Dulay opened a leather cigar box. De Jersey refused, watching Dulay's shaking hands pick up a long panatela, cut off the end, and light it. The blue haze of smoke circled his head like a halo.

"Have you ever seen the Koh-i-noor Diamond?" de Jersey asked.

"Yes."

"What do you know about it?"

"It's the biggest in the world."

De Jersey's hands indicated the size of the diamond. "When it arrived in England it weighed 186.1 carats and was set in a kind of armlet. It was recut in Prince Albert's time. At that point it went down in weight to 105.6 carats."

"I didn't know that," Dulay said quietly.

"You ever seen the Imperial State Crown? It contains over three thousand precious stones—sapphires and rubies that would make a joke out of your display windows. Costs almost twelve quid nowadays just to see them. I've been a frequent visitor over these past few weeks."

Dulay said nothing. When de Jersey stared at the man, he smiled weakly back. "It's a massive operation, but I know it's possible."

"You're insane!" Dulay said hoarsely.

"You would not be involved in the insane part, just the aftermath. Just think about having access to those stones. Surely it must excite you."

"It scares the living daylights out of me. Even to contemplate it is insanity. I won't get involved. Even at the so-called safe end. It took years of planning and dealing and living on a knife's edge to melt down that gold bullion and distribute it."

"Yes, and you were fucking brilliant. You designed some spectacular pieces in eighteen-carat gold—bracelets, necklaces, earrings, rings."

Dulay's brow poured with sweat.

"And you were never found out. Even with the larger items: hubcaps and other motor vehicle accessories. You're expert with gems, and cutting is your specialty."

Dulay nodded. He had spent many months in South Africa before they met, being taught by the old De Beers masters.

"I look around, Paul, and see that you are doing very well." De Jersey gestured expansively. "With all that gold and your knowledge of diamonds, you produced some of the finest exhibitions in Europe, and now this chic little shop right next to the Ritz. Great location. I congratulate you."

"Thank you. But it's taken hard work, Philip. My name—"

"Your name. Yes. For the last fifteen years your name has been synonymous with class and beauty. Your work is featured in *Vogue* and *Elle*; your jewels are worn by the rich and famous. See? I have followed your career with interest, my friend."

"I've opened a Paris shop, in the Avenue des Beaux-Arts."

"Close to Chanel, YSL, Christian Dior, and Cartier. Very good position again. Is it doing well?"

"The usual teething problems."

De Jersey plucked at the crease in his trouser leg. "Any way you look at it, though, Paul, the gold bullion, used sparingly over the years, has made all of this possible."

"I am legitimate now, Philip. I want to stay that way."

"But you weren't always so straight. You laundered tons of gold bullion for me," de Jersey said.

"It aged me ten years. If I got involved in this jewel heist, it would kill me."

De Jersey collected his thoughts. "If it aged you then, you're looking good now. Must be the great lifestyle."

"I don't need any more, Philip. I'm looking to retire in a few years. I've got responsibilities."

"Understood. No hard feelings." De Jersey stood abruptly and offered Dulay his hand. "I protected you. You would have nothing if the Colonel hadn't taken care of you. You never had to live life looking over your shoulder because there was never so much as a hint of your involvement in the bullion robbery. That is what the Colonel promised you. That was his deal."

"Philip, I have always appreciated it. I mean, I would do anything within reason, but what you are asking is—"

"Just a possibility at the moment," de Jersey interrupted. "Until I have more details. But, as in the old days, I like to be prepared, and you were top of my list. You weren't the only fence for the gold bullion. And you are not the only craftsman I'd trust with gems of this size and value, but as we had a good relationship, I came to you first, to give you this chance."

"Thank you. It goes without saying you can trust me."

"I always have."

"Good. No hard feelings, then?"

"No hard feelings."

Dulay crossed to buzz open the security lock on the side door.

"Do you have a workroom here?"

"Yes, at the back. Would you like to look around it?"

"I think I would, thank you."

Feeling less pressure, Dulay was quite animated as he led de Jersey down a narrow corridor into a large back room. There were two steel vaults, which held all of the gems, and at the rear was a small kiln for melting down gold, silver, and platinum. A white-coated lapidary was hard at work at a long trestle table on which equipment for cutting the stones was laid out. He was shaping a magnificent pink diamond.

"This is my pride and joy. It's a piece that's been commissioned by Prince Rainier." Dulay crossed to the table. "The tiara had been in their family for generations, but the band was bent and the stones loose, so we're resetting and replacing a few missing ones." He held up the work in progress. "It's a beautiful piece but intricate work. The filigree between the stones is so old and fine it's very easily broken off. To match the design and make it sturdier is not as easy as it sounds. I'm making platinum bars first, then coating them in eighteen-carat gold so it'll have more strength and durability. The fire in the diamond is astounding."

De Jersey bent over the table. "Never ceases to amaze me that a man with such big hands can do such fiddly work."

Dulay nudged him in an overfamiliar way. "You know what they say about big hands?"

De Jersey laughed. "But earlier you were shaking badly. Shaping these tiny stones into settings must take a steady hand."

Dulay blushed. "I admit I was nervous to see you again."

De Jersey looked at his watch. "I'd better go. You can call me on this number, should you change your mind."

"Thank you. You must come to dinner and meet my family," he said.

"Another time perhaps."

Dulay watched Simmons on the surveillance camera monitors. He saw him exit the building, then pause a moment to glance at the window. Then Simmons suddenly looked up, virtually into the eye of the camera.

"Who was that?" the shop assistant inquired.

"Just a buyer," said Dulay, unnerved. "Wanted a birthday gift for his wife."

"What did he buy?"

"Nothing."

"Will he be coming back?"

"No." He hoped to God it was true.

The bank manager laid a thick file in front of de Jersey. "A deposit was made recently from a U.S. bank account for one point five million dollars." He uncapped his fountain pen. "The transaction was cleared two days ago."

De Jersey studied the documents. This was the money from the sale of the lease of Moreno's apartment.

"I will need to make a substantial withdrawal," he said.

"No problem. We can have the money transferred within the hour."

De Jersey looked up. "Now, I'd like the details of my discretionary trust."

The manager turned to the relevant pages, and de Jersey was stunned to see that the balance of the offshore account in the Caymans stood at only a few hundred pounds. He flicked back through the pages, checking the transactions as the truth dawned on him. David Lyons had abused his position as a named trustee in the discretionary trust to withdraw nearly every penny from the account. All de Jersey had left was the money he had taken from Alex Moreno.

"That seems to be in order," he said without emotion as he stood up and shook the bank manager's hand. "Thank you very much."

*   *   *

De Jersey tilted up his head, and jets of ice-cold water from the shower pummeled his face. He was angry that he had so misjudged David Lyons, angry that he had not retained more control over his finances. He made himself focus on Dulay. He had presumed that a man with such a passion for the profession could not resist the lure of the Koh-i-noor Diamond. But Dulay had turned him down. Wilcox and Driscoll had turned him down too.

De Jersey dried himself, then lay down on the bed. His whole fortune was gone. Worst of all, he was unable to do anything about it. But he refused to allow himself to dwell on such disastrous events. He closed his eyes. He adored Christina and his daughters. He loved his life and his champion, Royal Flush.

He opened his eyes to stare at the ceiling. "All or nothing," he whispered. That was what made him different from the others. He would take the risk, with or without them.

The extensive gardens were lined with olive trees; they forged avenues bordered with thick clumps of lavender. Tall, pointed conifers like slim sentries towered above the old stone walls. The vine-covered terraces were winter bare. Dulay parked his Jeep outside his villa and hurried inside. The kids were playing in the sprawling back garden. His wife, Vibekka, was gardening, wearing old jeans and a sweater.

"Hi, you're home early," she said, stretching her arms wide for a hug. Her silky black hair was twisted into a thick braid down her back. Even at forty she had a taut body and was naturally beautiful without a trace of makeup. "I've had a really lazy day. The kids and I just hung out here all afternoon. Then when it rained we watched TV." She was six inches taller than her husband and hooked her arm around his square, solid shoulders. "We have that big party tonight," she reminded him. "You want me to fix you a sandwich or something?"

"No, I need a shower. I'll eat later. Do we have to go?"

"A lot of your customers will be there, and it'll be good for business." She ruffled his hair.

"Don't do that."

"You're in a nasty mood."

Dulay walked to the house, stepping over the steel straps of the pool cover. All he could think of was Philip Simmons. Your past always catches up with you, no matter how many years go by, he thought.

After dinner Christina and de Jersey had decided to have a quick flutter at the tables. They didn't do well, so they returned to the hotel. The following morning de Jersey could muster little enthusiasm for shopping and returned to the hotel alone. By the time they met for lunch, Christina was carrying several boxes and two suit carriers.

"Did you enjoy yourself?" he asked, smiling.

"I met a girlfriend I haven't seen for years, not since I was a model, and she lives here. We're invited to a big charity function this evening," she told him. "So I decided to buy something new to wear."

"I thought we might go to Longchamp," he said. "I want to meet up with a breeder who's been recommended to me and see his yard."

"We can go another day," she said. "Vibekka's lovely, and she's very high up in society here. All the Monaco Royals will be at the ball."

"In that case we'll go to the stables another day," he said, feeling frustrated; he did not have the time for frivolous charity events.

"It's just that we haven't seen each other in so long, and besides, I'd like to meet Vibekka's husband. She said I could borrow some jewelry from her as I've brought so little with me, and since her husband is Paul Dulay, I'll have quite a choice."

The waiter interrupted them to take their order, and de Jersey went on automatic pilot, hardly aware of what he ordered.

"So it'll be a stuffy dinner-jacket evening?" he asked eventually.

"Yes, darling, but Vibekka is so looking forward to meeting you. They have three children, they've converted a farmhouse, and they have a huge yacht in the harbor. Maybe we should think about it for summer."

De Jersey's mind was turning somersaults; this was a potentially dangerous situation.

On returning to their suite, Christina promptly called Vibekka. De Jersey watched her, almost girlish with excitement as she discussed her evening attire and arranged to meet up later at Vibekka's husband's shop. Afterward she unwrapped her purchases, showing de Jersey a sleek emerald green silk dress, and another in ice blue chiffon with a tight bodice and multilayered skirt.

De Jersey said quietly, "It's warm in here. I think I'll take a shower."

When he returned, he lay down on the bed. "My head hurts," he murmured.

Christina walked over to him. "You should never order oysters out of season. I'm always telling you this. Let me feel your head."

She laid a hand across his brow. He was hot—he had showered in almost boiling water. "Darling, I think you have a temperature."

He jumped up and hurried to the bathroom. "I'm going to throw up." He remained in the bathroom, making retching sounds and flushing the toilet, then came out and slumped onto the bed. "It must be those oysters." He moaned.

Christina wanted to call the hotel doctor, but he wouldn't hear of it, insisting that she leave him to sleep, that he would feel better by the evening, and she should go to meet Vibekka as she had arranged.

When his wife had gone, he threw back the sheets and began to pace the suite. This situation with Paul Dulay would never have happened in the past. Then again, he was a bit out of practice. He sat at the writing desk, picked up a pen, and began to doodle on the hotel notepaper. In the old days he would not have risked meeting up with Paul Dulay without being certain he would bite. He should not have mentioned the Koh-i-noor Diamond. When the robbery hit the press, Dulay would know the identity of the thief. The Colonel was losing hands down, and he had to do something about it fast.

CHAPTER

11

Sylvia Hewitt received the call from Victor Matheson in her office at twelve. Alex Moreno's car had been found in the long-stay car park at JFK Airport. A police informant friend of Matheson's had tipped him off that the Lexus was discovered unlocked and empty, the stereo missing, wires hanging loose. Moreno, however, had not been listed on any flight leaving or arriving at the airport at the time the car had been parked.

Inquiring at the Maidstone Arms, East Hampton, Matheson gained another possible lead. Moreno had indeed checked into the hotel. After dining there, he had left and not returned until later in the evening, when he went straight to his room. Early the next morning he left, after settling his account. There had been an incoming call on his arrival and an outgoing call, which Matheson had traced to a local gay club called the Swamp. Since then the club had been sold and was closed for refurbishing.

"Did you find anyone who talked to Moreno that night?" Sylvia asked.

"Not yet. I'll go back and find who was running the place at the time. There might be someone he spoke to at the club." Matheson had also talked to Brett Donnelly, a local contractor. He had found Donnelly still at work on Moreno's property, which had now progressed considerably since de Jersey's visit. Donnelly was evasive at first, but after Matheson told him he was investigating a fraud, Donnelly became more helpful; he discussed Moreno freely and ventured information about a certain man, Mr. Simmons, who had showed up on-site. "How I figured it," Matheson said, "this guy, Philip Simmons, was owed cash by Moreno, and they did a deal. Now it looks like Simmons is completely running the show. He's ordered the renovations to continue, and when the job is done, he told Donnelly he's selling the property."

"Do you have a contact number for Simmons?"

"Just a mailbox number. Perhaps when he invoices Simmons, Donnelly will get further information."

"I hope so. In the meantime, I'll check if he was an investor. His name's not familiar, though. Did he say he was English?"

"I didn't ask."

"Doesn't matter." But Sylvia was disappointed not to have more to go on.

Matheson cleared his throat. "If I'm to keep looking for Moreno, I'm going to need an additional retainer."

"Do you think he's just upped and done a runner with my money?"

"Could be. Finding that car abandoned at the airport is suspicious. And I have yet to take a look at Moreno's apartment. No telling what I might find there. There's always the possibility one of the investors got to him. You should check if one was called Simmons," Matheson said.

"Even if it was one of the investors, he might have been using a false name." Sylvia was starting to get into this detective work.

"True. Are the other investors Brits?"

"The main ones are. There are others scattered all over the world, but their losses were not as great."

"Well, let me see what I can come up with. If Simmons comes into the U.S., maybe I can track him down. I've got a lot of contacts at the airport."

"Don't do anything yet. Let me get back to you," she said.

"Whatever you say—but somebody has just got themselves a fifteen-million-dollar property, maybe as a payoff," Matheson said.

Sylvia thought for a moment. "Okay. Keep on trying to track down this Simmons man. I'll discuss your findings with the other main investors and get back to you."

"You're the boss. I'll send on my accounts and carry on the work."

"Keep in touch."

Sylvia hung up and dialed de Jersey's number. The housekeeper informed her that both Mr. and Mrs. de Jersey were in Monte Carlo. Sylvia hung up and called James Wilcox, but he refused to speak to her. She hung up, frustrated, then called Tony Driscoll. At first he was rather short with her, but he became intrigued by her discoveries.

"So this private investigator believes that someone received a nice payoff?"

"Moreno signed over the property, and it was all organized by a business adviser named Philip Simmons. Do you know him?"

"No, I don't."

"All I have is a mailbox number for him in New York, and Moreno seems to have disappeared without trace."

"I see."

"What I was wondering, Mr. Driscoll, is if we couldn't, all four of us, pay Matheson's accounts. You see, if Simmons is taking over Moreno's property, by rights we should benefit too."

"Let me think about it," Driscoll said and promised to get back to her.

A few minutes later he was talking to Wilcox.

"Whatever he's done, we don't want to know," Wilcox snapped. "The less we know the better. But he's got careless. The stakes are higher for him, and he's not handling it well."

"He's never been violent before."

"And I hope he's covered his tracks well, because it's not going to be too hard to figure out who he is."

"Yeah. How're your finances?" Driscoll asked.

"Fucked, but I'm not getting involved in murder."

"Same here. But we should be careful. You know what he's like. If he finds out we've been talking behind his back—"

"But we haven't really known him for a long time, Tony," Wilcox interrupted. "We can't keep harking back to the old days. A lot of water's run under the bridge since then. Sometimes I wonder if we ever really knew him at all."

Wilcox's words hit a nerve in Driscoll. "We shouldn't be talking like this."

There was a pause and then they hung up, as uneasy as they had been before their conversation.

De Jersey had only just got back into bed when Christina returned. She had obviously been shopping again, and a porter was struggling with her purchases.

"How are you feeling, darling?" she whispered and sat on the edge of the bed.

"Not too good. Did you have a happy reunion with your friend?"

"I went to her husband's little jewelry store. I just looked, but Vibekka was choosing a diamond necklace to wear tonight with matching earrings. It must have been worth at least half a million pounds, but I'd be afraid to wear anything so valuable. She told me she likes to advertise his work! She showed me the most unbelievable Russian tiara. The owner's grandfather got out of the country with the diamonds sewn into the hem of his coat."

De Jersey leaned back on the pillows. No wonder Dulay wasn't interested in working for him—he was hobnobbing with high-society Euro-trash.

Christina yawned. "You are coming tonight, aren't you?"

"I'm not sure. I still feel as if I have a temperature."

She touched his head. "No, you don't. You can't get out of it either. I decided your old dinner jacket wasn't smart enough, so I've got a new one for you, plus shoes, a shirt, and a tie. You have no excuse, darling." She gave him a wonderfully seductive smile. "Anyway, I want to show you off. I can't wait to see her face when you tell them who you are. I didn't mention the estate or the stud."

He sighed, as if he was still feeling unwell. Maybe he should rob Dulay's shop and not bother with the Crown Jewels.

De Jersey admired himself in the full-length mirror. The white tuxedo was a perfect fit, as were the shoes and the shirt. Christina wore a pale pink beaded dress that fishtailed out in a slight train behind her.

"I returned the other dresses and replaced them with this. You know, for a man who was at death's door only hours ago, you have improved vastly." She smiled at him in the mirror. They made a handsome couple.

De Jersey's mood had lifted because Vibekka had called to say that her husband was ill and had taken to his bed. Instead she was bringing Julian, a family friend who owned a restaurant and had shares in their yacht. She suggested they might walk down to the harbor to see the *Hortensia Princess.*

"What *did* you tell her about me?" de Jersey asked.

"I could hardly get a word in edgeways. She never stops talking, especially about the yacht. Never even got a chance to tell her your name."

"Did you tell her I was almost as old as your father?"

"All I said was that you were rich and handsome and I loved you." She kissed him, then held him at arm's length. "Because you are the best thing that ever happened to me."

"Thank you," he said.

"We're having a glass of champagne in the bar before the car takes us to the palace," Christina told him.

"You make me feel old," he whispered.

"You are the reason I stay young," she said and slipped into his arms to kiss his lips. Then she gently traced his mouth with her little finger to remove signs of her lipstick before she took his hand and drew him toward the door.

He'd forced all thoughts of his financial situation out of his mind, and now he was looking forward to their evening out.

* * *

Vibekka approached them with a handsome, swarthy companion. De Jersey kissed her on both cheeks then shook Julian's hand. Vibekka was wearing a black sequined bias-cut dress that showed off her perfectly toned body. She had a full-length sable coat draped over one arm and clutched a tiny gold lamé purse. They went into the hotel bar, and as de Jersey ordered a bottle of champagne, the two women chatted about fashion shows they had worked on together. De Jersey called over the waiter and chose a small Havana for himself. As he puffed on the cigar, he watched Julian and wondered why he looked so on edge. He gestured toward Vibekka's diamonds. "They are very beautiful," he said.

Vibekka paused for breath. She touched the necklace, then drew back her hair to show off the large drop earrings. "Aren't they gorgeous? And look . . ." She held out her slender wrist to show off the matching bracelet, two diamond-encrusted bands linked by emeralds in the style of a daisy chain.

"Oh, that is just *beautiful*," Christina said.

De Jersey glanced at his wife, who wore only a wedding ring and a thin gold chain with a pear-shaped five-carat diamond. It was simple but had cost fifty-five thousand pounds. The diamond was a yellow stone and had been auctioned at Sotheby's. It had been his first gift to her after they met.

When they had drunk the champagne, their car arrived.

"I hope you've brought a lot of money," Vibekka whispered to de Jersey. "It's a charity ball Princess Caroline throws annually. Everyone always feels obliged to buy raffle tickets and bid for silly things in the auction after dinner. It's all in aid of a children's charity. In the past a number of guests bought items in the auction and their checks bounced! So now it's cash only."

The venue for the ball was the Salle des Étoiles, a vast space with a roof that slid back in summer. There were wondrous views across the bay, and it was often used as a concert hall by stars such as Whitney Houston and Barry White. Tonight, however, the room was a sea of white tables and waiters. Everyone important from the glittering world of Euro-trash was there. At the head table sat Prince Albert, surrounded by an array of models and raffish young men. Wherever the eye fell there were glorious gowns and sparkling jewels, and a high-pitched babble of women greeted each other in various languages.

Among the other guests at their table de Jersey saw, with interest, was Michael Maloney, a well-known British financier who owned twenty-five racehorses stabled in France. De Jersey had met him once fleetingly at an auction. At thirty-eight, he was a City whiz kid turned tax exile. Tonight his companion was a nubile blonde who had already drunk too much champagne and kept falling off the seat next to him. There was also an Italian prince with his fourth wife, an American heiress. Her face-lift made her look about the same age as Christina, but de Jersey thought she was closer to his. She described in amusing detail the extent of her operations and the number of surgeons she had checked out beforehand. Recently she'd had cheek and chin implants and, as she gaily informed everyone, more implants in her lips and a full laser treatment on her skin. While she was totally unconcerned about everyone knowing, her husband cringed with embarrassment.

"If you want the best lip-line lady, you gotta visit this woman in Paris. She is just the best!" She loudly gave the name of her surgeon to Vibekka and passed the card to Christina with a flourish.

Talking to Maloney proved difficult with the tittering blonde demanding his complete attention. Julian hardly spoke a word during dinner and looked impatiently at his watch. De Jersey asked him if he was expecting someone.

"No, I just hate these balls. I don't drink much, and the smoke gets in my eyes." He shrugged and turned away.

Two hours later, when it was time for the raffle, the prize giving, and the charity auction, De Jersey excused himself. "I'm going for a breath of air," he whispered to Christina. "I'm still feeling a bit fuzzy."

He walked out to the balcony, threading his way through palms and flower beds, and sat on a thickly cushioned chair to look out at the sea. He lit a cigar and watched as the blue smoke drifted into the night air.

A voice startled him. "You mind if I join you?" It was Norma, the American woman, carrying a tumbler of Scotch and her cigarettes.

"Please do," he said.

"I hate these charity balls. They expect you to throw thousands around, but I leave that to my husband. He's gay, you know."

"Really?" de Jersey said, amused.

"I married him for his title, and he married me for my dough. I like being a princess. Here they're two a penny, but in the States it always gets you the best table!" She gave a throaty laugh and perched beside him. In the soft candlelight she was rather beautiful, her cheek implants giving her a Marlene Dietrich look.

"Your wife is exquisite," she said.

"I think so too."

"Nice stone round her neck." She leaned forward as he lit her cigarette. "Bet that didn't come from the creepy Paul Dulay. His wife has a lump of Moissanite round her neck."

He laughed. "I think you're mistaken."

"Honey, I have one of the finest collections in the States. I bought up a lot of the Duchess of Windsor's pieces. Now *there* was some high-class junk, but with her name attached it retains its value."

"Are you in the jewelry business?" he inquired.

"Only the business of buying the stuff. I have no other investments. Daddy was a Russian Jew. He arrived in the States with a couple of rubles to his name and opened a hardware store. When Wall Street crashed, he made his fortune because he had hard cash. Lesson in life, that. He was always paranoid that he would lose his fortune, so he invested in things like this." She lifted her thin, freckled hand with its red-painted nails and withdrew a fine platinum chain from beneath her gown. Attached to it was a pendant with a single, stunning diamond. "Liz Taylor owns one just like it. What do you think?"

"I'm awestruck," he said softly. "Aren't you taking a risk wearing it?"

"Nope, I've got my protection." She turned and pointed to a small square-chested man in an ill-fitting evening suit. "He's never far from me. He'd spring into action if you tried to rip it from my neck." She opened her top to let the stone drop back between her silicone-enhanced breasts and laughed. "I had them lifted so they could carry the weight of it." She picked up her tumbler and sipped. "I can spot a fake. Vibekka's is Moissanite. It might glitter like the real McCoy, but it wouldn't pass a double refractive test."

"What's that?" De Jersey asked.

"Well, honey, when you look at a diamond, tilt it. Look for the light that's refracted through it, and if it's a real diamond it'll shine in one straight line. Now, with a fake or a Moissanite you tilt it and it's got two lines. It's something every gem dealer does without thinking. Vibekka is saying to me that this necklace she's wearing is worth a fortune, so she hands it to me in the ladies' room!" She laughed. "The bracelet she's wearing is a nice piece, and real stones—but I've never been an emerald woman." Norma downed her drink and stood up. "She's working the room trying to sell her husband's wares. She took that necklace off faster than a whippet the minute I showed some interest, but I won't be buying it."

Her bodyguard swayed in her direction.

"Nice talking to you, Edgar," she said and strolled away, her minder dogging her heels.

De Jersey didn't care that she had forgotten his name. What she said was swirling around in his brain. Could Dulay still be replacing diamonds with fakes?

De Jersey surprised Christina by insisting they stay to dance, although he didn't spend much time on the floor with her. He chose instead to part-ner Norma, listening intently to her as they danced. She was delighted that she amused the handsome man and leaned closer to him. When she started to discuss Paul Dulay, de Jersey listened even more intently.

"Dulay's the darling of society out here, but I wouldn't trust him as far as I could throw him. My sister, God rest her soul, was at his Paris store. He tried to sell her a diamond and black pearl ring. That black pearl wasn't out of any oyster. But he does do beautiful settings, and that wife of his is a pretty little thing. Costs a lot to keep but not as much as that floating gin palace she talked him into buying. Believe you me that thing costs!" Norma didn't stop to draw breath, and de Jersey didn't try to halt the flow.

"You got on well with that awful American woman," Christina said as she cleansed her face.

"She was delightfully crude," de Jersey said.

"What on earth did you two have so much to talk about?"

"Horses," he said flippantly.

"She looked like one," Christina replied testily.

De Jersey washed his face.

"I had to listen to Vibekka for hours. I'd forgotten how self-centered she is. Her guest hardly said a word. Then you danced more than I've ever known you to dance before with that raddled old woman."

"She's not that old, sweetheart. She's probably my age."

"She's seventy-two!" Christina exclaimed. "What are you laughing at?" she snapped.

"That she's seventy-two, and if I didn't know you better, I'd say you were jealous!"

"No, darling, I am not jealous. But I hate to be left sitting like a fool."

"You wanted to go, not me."

"Maybe I'm just fed up because you had such a good time and I didn't. I didn't win anything, and I paid a fortune for those tickets. I noticed Vibekka and Julian never opened their wallets. I just don't understand her. They're obviously not short of cash. I don't like people taking advantage."

"What's a few raffle tickets?" he said.

"It's more. When we went shopping Vibekka said she'd lost her card and I ended up putting all the things she bought on my credit card."

"Christ, not that sable coat?"

"No, that belongs to a friend, but she bought the dress, shoes, and some other things, and tonight when I asked her if she'd found her card, she changed the subject. Even though I told her we're leaving in the morn-ing."

"You think they're in financial difficulty?"

"It seems like it."

He drew her close. "I can drop by the shop in the morning and sort it out. How would that be?"

"I'm sorry. It was nice to see her, but she did get a lot of money out of me. I don't like feeling a fool." She nuzzled his neck. "And with you chatting up a seventy-two-year-old crone with a plastic face and her dreadful prince checking out all the waiters, it's no wonder I'm in a bad mood."

Her foot stroked his; he turned to face her. "I'm exhausted. The last tango did me in."

De Jersey felt her warmth as she slid down his body and started to kiss his thighs. He abandoned thoughts of Moissanite diamonds and Paul Dulay's scams as he concentrated on making love to his wife.

Dulay was having a heated conversation on the phone with Vibekka, who had returned late after the ball. He had left for work the next morning before she was awake, so she had called him at the shop about repaying Christina. He had been happy to do so until she told him the amount owing.

"You're kidding! After we just discussed cutting back?"

"I wanted to make an impression."

"Well, forget it. You said they were loaded."

"But they might be good customers. I'll go to the bank and get some cash out. Which account should I use?"

"The mortgage one. I'll sort it out later. But this has got to stop, sweetheart. Vibekka? Hello?"

She'd already hung up. He slammed down the phone just as the door buzzer sounded. He pressed the entry release without looking up.

"Trouble?" de Jersey inquired.

Dulay recognized his visitor and, paling, tried to avoid de Jersey's eyes, busying himself with selections for the window display. "Is there anything you wanted to see?"

"Cut the bullshit," de Jersey said softly.

Dulay's lips tightened. "You won't get me to change my mind." He switched on the low lights for both displays, then locked the window. As he turned back, de Jersey flicked the switch to lock the front entrance.

"What do you think you're doing?" Dulay stuttered.

"Ensuring some privacy." De Jersey strolled past the counter to the door of the small showroom. Dulay followed him in.

"Listen, if you're worried about me opening my mouth to anyone, then you must know you can trust me one hundred percent. I mean, I wouldn't be so foolish as to drop you in it, not after all you've done for me in the past." Dulay was nervous now.

De Jersey sat down. "I'm interested in a bracelet for my girlfriend. She likes emeralds."

Dulay began to relax. "I've got a beauty. It's expensive, but high-quality stones, matching diamonds, beautiful emerald links. I designed it myself. Or there's a ruby link with sapphires and pearls."

"Can I see the first?"

Dulay left the room, returning soon with a large, flat leather case, which he laid on the desk.

De Jersey opened it and lifted out the bracelet. Dulay passed him a jeweler's eyeglass and turned on a high-beam spotlight. De Jersey studied it. "Very nice." He glanced at the necklace and earrings also in the leather case.

"What about the necklace?"

"That's not for sale. It belongs to an Italian couple, ditto the earrings. The pieces are in for an evaluation. Only the bracelet's for sale."

"They're fakes, aren't they? Unlike this piece," said de Jersey.

"You are mistaken!"

De Jersey sat down. "I met someone last night who is on to you. I know you're switching stones. I wanted to tip you off to be careful."

Dulay rubbed his head.

"You don't need to be doing that kind of shit. Why are you getting so greedy? I've got to look out for myself here too. I mean, they pick you up on one thing and they might dig backwards."

Dulay opened a pack of Gauloises cigarettes. "It was just a couple of times. Some of these rich bitches don't know what they've got on. But you're right, it's stupid to take that kind of risk."

"Must be easy pickings," de Jersey said. "Come on, though, it's not just the odd one, is it, Paul? Is that how you work your business? You value the piece and replace a stone or two. Then, because of your reputation, the owner is unlikely to have it revalued and is therefore none the wiser. Correct?"

"Listen to me," Dulay said. "I run a legitimate business. Like I said, it's just the odd stone here and there."

"You must have built up a lot of trust to be so popular. But that's what it's all about, isn't it? Trust."

Dulay remained silent as de Jersey continued. "I won't meddle in your private deals, but I could cause you a lot of trouble."

"And I could do the same for you," Dulay said angrily. He had found the courage to stand up to the man he still knew only as Philip Simmons.

De Jersey sighed. "How?" he said coolly.

"You know damned well, so stop this bullshit. I will not be drawn into this robbery by your threats because, although you may have something on me, I've got just as much on you. The gold bullion is only the beginning."

De Jersey sat back in the swivel chair. "Are you threatening me?"

"No more than you are me."

"Don't take me on. You'll lose. I'll make sure of it."

"Try it and see," Dulay said, blustering now.

"No, but you have to straighten out, Paul. I'm not pressuring you to do anything. All I am doing is making sure I feel one hundred percent certain you'll keep your mouth shut. Stop what you're doing with these fake jewels, because I can't afford any worries where you're concerned."

"My financial difficulties are not going to make me blab about your criminal activities."

"Oh, so it's money problems, not just greed?"

"Things are a bit tight," Dulay said, "and I don't want to lose this buyer I've got, a billionaire Japanese gem dealer. He's too big and lucrative a fish not to provide the goods for."

"Asks no questions, huh?"

"Precisely." Dulay sucked on his cigarette. "Don't get me wrong, though, I'm still not interested in your proposal. I've just got into a bit of difficulty, that's all. It's called divorce, and my new wife, the one I'm crazy about, spends money like it grows on trees. She also talked me into buying that fucking boat with that French twat Julian. It's the size of Versailles, and it took every franc I had to refurbish it. Now we can't sell it because we still owe the shipbuilders, and nobody wants to charter it." He sighed, then shrugged his wide shoulders and stood up. "Maybe things will pick up in the summer. I hope to God they do." He was pacing up and down.

"Sit down, Paul."

Flushed with anger, Dulay reminded himself that he was not going to be cajoled into something as risky as Simmons was proposing. He remained silent as his old partner in crime toyed with a gold Cartier pen that was lying on the desk. Then he twirled the bracelet on his index finger and slipped it into his top pocket. "I'll take this in lieu of all the worry you've caused me," he said. "No hard feelings. And don't worry, your secret's safe with me. Like you said, we're bound to each other in many ways. Love me or hate me, we're shackled together for life."

Dulay didn't say anything about the bracelet. "Why are you attempting this robbery? It's insane."

"Because, like you, I'm hurting for cash, and after years of legitimate work I'm not prepared to go under. It goes without saying that I won't take any foolish risks. And since I do not intend to be caught, I will take every precaution to ensure the safety of everyone involved."

Dulay interlocked his fingers. "You always did take great care. You using the same team again?"

"Yes. No one will take any undue risks, and everyone will be paid handsomely. After all, the Colonel has always been fair."

"I know all that," Dulay said, flushing. "I didn't mean some of the stuff I just said. You know I'd never put you or Driscoll—" Dulay stopped.

De Jersey leaned forward, so close that Dulay flinched. "You had better forget that name, Paul, but you can give me one. Who's this Japanese buyer? Tell me more about him."

"No way."

"If he's buying anything you throw his way, he may be interested in what I might have to offer."

"I don't want to risk getting on the wrong side of him. I don't ask him too many questions, and he isn't interested in the finer details of what I sell. If I start passing his name around, he's not gonna like it, and I don't want to end up in the river with my hands cut off."

De Jersey raised an eyebrow.

"I mean it," Dulay said. "He comes to Paris a couple of times a year, that's it."

"What about London?"

"I don't know." Dulay closed his eyes, and his voice dropped to a low, hoarse whisper. "Don't do this to me. Please don't draw me in." Beads of sweat were forming at the edge of his receding hairline. Then he licked his lips. "Look, I can't promise, but when I see him next—"

"Not good enough," de Jersey said. "I need his name and a contact number."

Dulay sighed. He opened his desk drawer and took out a crocodile leather box edged in gold. He pulled out a card and passed it over. "He's a computer giant. His company's worth billions."

"He buy any of your gold items?" de Jersey asked softly.

Dulay flushed, then nodded. "That's his box number and e-mail address. I don't have a direct phone number."

De Jersey glanced at the card. He slipped it into his wallet and took out one of his own before he stood up. "Good. Now I know I can trust you. And I'm sure you don't have to worry about Mr. Kitamo. You've been dealing with him for long enough. Did he approach you, or the other way round?"

"He came into my shop as a straight customer, but over the years, after I'd built up his trust, he would ask if I could get this or that for him."

"Legitimate stuff?"

"Some of it, and once he had some gems he needed me to disguise."

"Disguise?"

"Cheap settings, a few glass beads mixed in with the emeralds and diamonds. After that he started buying the gold items."

"I see."

"I hope you do, Philip. This guy has been my lifeline, and I wouldn't want anything to jeopardize my relationship with him."

"Not with that boat round your neck." De Jersey smiled. "If you need me, you can always contact me on this mobile number and also my e-mail address." He placed Philip Simmons's card on the desk.

"You really believe it can be done?"

"I wouldn't be here if I didn't. Nor would I approach anyone I couldn't trust to do his part. It's been good to see you again. No hard feelings?"

"No hard feelings," Dulay said, and de Jersey shook his hand.

Dulay watched him walk away from his shop with a diamond and emerald bracelet worth thousands, but no way did he feel like stopping him. After all, he owed him. The bullion had got him started. Dulay picked up the small white card with "Philip Simmons, Consultant" printed on it. He didn't rip it up, just stared at it, then went into the rear office. He opened the small fridge and took out the vodka bottle, poured himself half a tumbler, and gulped it down as if it were water. He placed the glass on top of Philip Simmons's card.

"The Koh-i-noor Diamond," he whispered. Now there was a stone he'd like to get his hands on.

Christina loved the bracelet—it was the only piece of jewelry Vibekka had worn that she had admired. She told de Jersey that Vibekka had also contacted her at the hotel and returned the money. During the helicopter flight back from the airport he said little. When his phone rang, he turned to see if Christina was paying any attention. She wasn't, so he checked the message screen and saw, to his amusement, that Paul Dulay was calling. His pilot glanced at him—it was always foolish to use cell phones in flight.

"Two minutes and I'll turn it off," de Jersey reassured him.

"That's okay, sir. More of a risk when landing and taking off."

De Jersey answered the phone and listened to Dulay. He arranged to meet the jeweler in London in a week's time. He smiled. Dulay had bitten faster than he'd thought he would.

CHAPTER

12

The next morning de Jersey left the farm. Several hours later, at the Kilburn flat, he was working on his files. He had made lists of the Royal household interviewees by name and background.

Even so, when he opened up his e-mail account he was surprised at the number of messages. He printed them out and sifted through the answers to his inquiries. One message in particular interested him: a Lord Henry Westbrook, who said he had in-depth knowledge of the Royals and the running of their households, gained first as a page and later as an equerry. He added that he had recently been a "guest of Her Majesty."

De Jersey printed out a series of questions he had sent to an infamous computer hacker with their answers. To one question, the hacker had responded that companies should be far more worried about an insider than an outsider, due to the insider's easy access and increased capability of infiltrating the company's systems. Nine times out of ten, security breaches were caused by an employee, and rarely were they reported. De Jersey made himself a cup of coffee. He needed an insider in place to deal with aspects relating to the Royal Family. He would need access to Her Majesty's diary and, most important, to the security that surrounded her.

The coffee tasted rancid—he'd forgotten to buy fresh milk. He threw it away and went back to the message from Lord Westbrook; he had been an equerry to the Queen from 1984 to 1986. Soon after the termination of his employment he was sentenced to seven years in jail for "taxation fraud," for setting fire to his ancestral home, then claiming the insurance for art treasures he had already sold. Now, eight years later, he was still broke, living in a small studio apartment in Mayfair that belonged to an elderly relative. It seemed to de Jersey that he would be a perfect candidate.

Despite debts and a checkered past, Lord Westbrook was sought after socially, and not for his title alone. At fifty-four he was still a handsome, charming escort and a witty companion. Since his release from prison he had been the life and soul of every dinner party. Lord Westbrook knew that his next bride had to be wealthy. He was an outrageous flirt and adored pretty society girls as much as they adored him, but securing a young bride was proving difficult since his reputation always preceded him. Middle-aged widows or divorcées were his best bet. The title helped; some woman was always eager to be seen on his arm, even if it meant taking on his mounting debts.

De Jersey remembered seeing Westbrook at various charity events although they had never met. He made phone calls to the exclusive gentlemen's clubs in London, then tried fashionable restaurants and, finally, the Jockey Club without success. Ultimately he called what had once been Westbrook's estate, fully aware that his lordship no longer lived there, and was eventually put through to a manager. De Jersey said that he was unable to keep a luncheon appointment with Lord Westbrook and had misplaced his telephone number. He was provided with both number and address.

Westbrook answered the phone abruptly. His drawling voice had the husky quality of a chain smoker.

"My name is Philip Simmons. I'm a novelist. You replied to the query I posted on the Net—"

"Yes. How did you get my number?"

"I asked around. It wasn't that difficult."

"Right. Well then, you said you wanted some research done. How can I help you?"

"I wonder if we could discuss it over a drink. I have a deadline, so earlier rather than later would be appreciated."

"Of course. Where do you suggest?"

A cigarette dangling from his lips, Westbrook strolled into Brown's Hotel. It was dark and located in Kensington, where there was less risk of de Jersey running into someone he knew than in the West End.

"Lord Westbrook?" The man gave a cursory glance around the almost empty bar.

"Yes," he said bluntly.

"I'm Philip Simmons. Please sit down. What will you drink?"

"Vodka martini." He drew up a high stool and sat beside de Jersey, then stubbed out his cigarette and immediately lit a fresh one. The Silk Cut packet was almost empty.

"Vodka martini, twenty Silk Cut, and a Bloody Mary," de Jersey said. The barman nodded, placing two small bowls of peanuts in front of them. De Jersey had no intention of being overheard and motioned Westbrook to a small table in the darkest recess of the room.

"Well, this is all very cloak and daggerish," Westbrook said. The waiter put down their drinks and more peanuts. "Cheers!" He gave a lopsided smile, and they drank. "You never know with this Internet stuff. A pal recommended that I hunt around on it to find work. I went to one of those Internet cafés, awful places." Westbrook's dark eyes roamed the bar. "Not been here for years. Odd place. Perhaps you could enlighten me about your project. Not another book on the Princess of Wales, I hope."

"No, it's not, but it will be worth your while."

"Well, if you're hoping to use me as a social entrée, I'm afraid my name won't do you much good. It would have, when I was first released from prison, but now I don't generate much excitement. Am I talking myself out of a job?"

"Not at all."

"Well, as I was saying, my best days are behind me."

De Jersey smiled. His lordship was very self-effacing. After two more martinis, his tongue was even looser. He talked endlessly about his days in prison and the cons with whom he'd been cooped up. Eventually he wound down. "So, let's cut the small talk. What you up to? I've got a feeling that, whatever it is, it's not kosher."

De Jersey began to like him. "You could say that."

"What do you want?"

"You."

Westbrook looked perplexed.

"And particularly your past experiences."

"In prison?"

"No, before that."

"What for?"

"The book I'm writing."

" 'Blue blood gets arrested for fraud, ends up serving time,' that kind of thing?"

"Further back. Your contact with the Royal Family. Your knowledge of the Royal household and the Queen's routines. Protocol. To be more specific, I need to know more about Her Majesty's ladies-in-waiting: where they stand, how they dress, how they address her. Also, how many security men travel with a Royal cavalcade, what they wear, how many per vehicle, and so on."

Westbrook frowned into his empty martini glass. "What kind of money are we talking about?"

"That would depend, but I am prepared to pay a high price for the information. I need to be able to trust you. The more details you can give me, the higher the bonus. Can I get you another drink?"

"I don't think so. Coffee maybe."

De Jersey patted Westbrook's arm. "Good move. I don't work with drunks. Excuse me." He ordered coffee and sandwiches at the bar, then went to the restroom. He was giving his lordship time to think, to get hungry for the money being dangled in front of him, hungry enough to become part of the team.

The sandwiches were consumed rapidly, but after de Jersey ordered a second pot of coffee, Westbrook's manner changed. He sat back, lit his sixth cigarette, and sucked in the smoke. He had sobered up.

"Now, cards on the table. Who the fuck are you? This novel doesn't ring true to me. Not when you're coming on like some James Bond figure. I can't figure you out."

De Jersey hesitated, then began. "Okay, my name is Philip Simmons, and I'm a nobody. I have lived mostly in the U.S. for the past decade, got a nice little nest egg and was about to retire when I lost it on some bloody useless Internet company that was supposed to make me more than secure for the rest of my life. It bankrupted me."

"I know the feeling," said Westbrook, with a detectable undercurrent of anger.

"I need to make a quick kill," de Jersey said.

"I gather that. But from what you've just said, how are you going to pay me for what you want to know?"

"There's bankrupt and there's bankrupt. I can still lay my hands on a few bob."

"I see, but this information isn't for some coffee-table book, is it? So, get a bit clearer, Mr. Simmons, and stop wasting my time."

"It's a nice earner."

"How much of a nice earner?"

"Enough."

"So the sum is just what size?"

"If you produce the goods, your cut will be in the region of five or six million."

There was a long pause. His lordship lit another cigarette.

"It's not on the square, that's for sure. You want information regarding the Royals and their household. What are you going to do? Let's see. Break into Kensington Palace? If that's your idea, forget it. It's been broken into countless times, and everyone always gets caught."

"It's not that."

"Shame. I know the place like the back of my hand."

De Jersey watched him like a hawk.

"If it's the Crown Jewels, there's not a hope in hell. Total waste of time. Only one chap ever broke in, sixteen something. He failed."

"I know."

"So it could be the Crown Jewels?" There was another long pause. "They come out now and again, for the State Opening of Parliament, coronations. . . . Ma'am's Golden Jubilee is this year. She'll need a fitting—Royal heads have swelled a bit since Edward the Confessor's time . . ."

They left the hotel together and took a taxi the short distance to Westbrook's home, where they continued their discussion.

De Jersey grew more confident about Westbrook's help. A single room in Pimlico, very shabby. The Persian carpets were beyond threadbare, and the single bed was draped with a tatty paisley throw. Even the few elegant oil paintings were damaged. The small kitchen was filthy, and the cabinet doors were falling off their hinges. "I just use this pad to doss down in. It's not even mine—belongs to an old and distant cousin. I seem to be out of instant coffee. What about a chilled vodka?"

They drank from chipped glasses. Westbrook showed off his most prized possessions: a row of silver-framed photographs of his children, a son and twin daughters. The pictures also showed an austere blond woman. "My ex-wife," he said sourly. "She has custody. They all live in South Africa now. I'd see them, but the plane fare is a bit of a problem." He sat down cross-legged on the couch and gulped his vodka. De Jersey left his untouched.

His lordship lit a cigarette. "There's an added problem."

De Jersey remained silent.

"I have cancer."

"I'm sorry," de Jersey said, with sincerity.

"So am I sometimes, when I look at the photos and remember such happy days. But the old man left me with a nightmare of death duties. I loved that place with a passion. It's my heritage and by right my son's. I'd like to own it again, pass it on to William."

He passed one of the silver frames to de Jersey. "My ancestors have lived there since seventeen eighty. Now it's owned by a group of bloody salesmen in gray suits. Tragic. All my family looking down the baronial staircase while the imbeciles ruin the place. I can't even visit." He replaced the photograph. "Now you know all there is to know."

De Jersey remained silent.

"I have told you all this for one reason, to make you understand that this little . . . "flutter" could not have come at a better time, and I'm up for it *if* there's enough lolly in it for me."

De Jersey drained his vodka. "You were on to it."

"What?"

"You were on to what I have in mind," de Jersey said.

"Not the bloody Crown Jewels?"

De Jersey laughed. "Yes."

"You're out of your mind."

"Not really. What do you know about the jewel fittings, the one for the Queen's Golden Jubilee?"

Lord Westbrook poured himself some more vodka. "My God, are you serious?"

"Yes."

"I see. Well, my cut would certainly get me the ancestral home back. How many will be in on it?"

De Jersey hesitated, then went for it. "Eight, I think, including you. I may need a few more heavies. Not everyone will get the same amount. It depends on how important they are to the heist."

"I see."

"Do you?" de Jersey asked seriously.

"I spent seven years in jail, so I can see quite clearly that it's a hare-brained idea. Why decide to trust me?" Westbrook asked.

De Jersey gestured to the squalid room. "To die in this place isn't what you want, is it?"

Westbrook drained his glass. The bottle was empty.

"I'd say you are an embittered man. You've lost your self-respect, your children, and your home. Spending years in prison gave you plenty of time to review your future and reflect on your past. I'm willing to pay you, starting this week, to work for me. I can't say at this stage if it will go ahead. And it won't until I'm satisfied we can do it with the least risk to all concerned."

"What's the downside?"

"There isn't one. If I think it's impossible and call it off, then it's just been an experience. However, if I think it's a viable project, the only downside would be if one of us opened his mouth, because that would ruin any chance of our survival."

De Jersey stood up straight, like a colonel, his massive frame dominating the small studio. "So I demand total loyalty."

"Demand?" Westbrook smiled.

"Yep. We cannot afford a weak link, and if one did arise it would be erased."

"How would you know?"

"I would know, and I would see personally that it was taken care of. You come on board, you obey the rules." De Jersey picked up the empty vodka bottle and tossed it into the fireplace. It smashed to pieces on the empty grate. "No boozing, no drugs, and this"—he moved close to Westbrook, took his jaw in one hand, and ran his fingers over the man's mouth with the other—"one word leaked and everyone goes down." He released his hold and picked up one of the photographs of Westbrook's children. "Every man involved is hungry. They have families, children. So if a blabbing mouth hurts them they will want retribution. Do you understand?" He set down the photograph carefully.

"I resent the threats."

"I hope you do, Harry. That *is* what your friends call you, isn't it?"

"And we're friends now, are we?" Westbrook asked.

"No. But I will be more of a friend to you than any other man you know. If this is going to work, you will have to trust me one hundred percent, and trust is what makes a friendship."

Westbrook watched as de Jersey picked up his cashmere overcoat. "If you decide not to go ahead, will you still pay me?"

"Of course, per week for however long it takes to accomplish your part of the heist."

"How much?"

"One thousand cash every week and a cut of the jewels once they've been broken up."

Westbrook took another cigarette.

De Jersey struck the match to light it. Their eyes met. "You should get enough to leave your son and heir his rightful inheritance."

Westbrook stared into de Jersey's cold blue eyes. He did not flinch; de Jersey was impressed.

Westbrook said, "I put my trust in you. God only knows why—it's a gut feeling. This morning I really didn't care how long I had to live, but now I do. I want to live long enough to pull this bloody thing off, and if I die in the process it doesn't matter. But if we do it, I'll leave my son more than an empty title. I'd like that."

* * *

Back at the flat in Kilburn, de Jersey logged onto the computer and began to search. When "The Golden Jubilee Program Pages" came up, he scanned them for details of the Royal calendar. Since the festivities would begin in early May and continue through June and July, he reasoned that the crown and the jewels which were to be in use would have to be removed from the Tower some time before then. But where would they be held for safekeeping? With the jeweler appointed to the Queen? A plan was finally forming. He closed down his computer and leaned back in his chair, smiling. Just then his cell phone rang.

"It's me, Eddy," Driscoll said. "Me and Jimmy. We want to meet up again, the sooner the better."

"Tomorrow," de Jersey said calmly. "There's a pub by Robin Hood Gate in Richmond Park. See you both there at twelve." He hung up confident. His team was coming together.

CHAPTER

13

The public house chosen for the meeting was in Kingston, far enough from their homes for them not to be recognized, and full enough for them not to stand out. A large family-style dining room was next to the bar. The pub meals were home-cooked and cheap, the atmosphere friendly. Driscoll's dog had accompanied the threesome.

They sat in a booth and ordered beer and sandwiches. They exchanged pleasantries as the drinks and food were put before them, then got down to business.

"It's this fucking Sylvia Hewitt," Wilcox said.

"She's called us both at home." Driscoll peered at his sandwich. He'd had stomach trouble for days and was apprehensive about eating.

"What's she on about now?" de Jersey asked, sipping his pint. She hadn't called him.

"Well, for one thing, I don't like her having my private number," Driscoll said.

"Goes for me too," Wilcox said. "Rika's on edge now. She thinks I'm having an affair with any woman who calls the house." He gestured to de Jersey's untouched plate. "You want yours?"

"No." He pushed his plate forward. "Change your numbers."

"The wife's in the middle of organizing our daughter's wedding; she'd go apeshit if we changed the number now. And this Hewitt bitch having my phone number is the least of our worries. She's on to Philip Simmons," Driscoll said.

This caught de Jersey off guard. "What?"

"She'll be on to you. Any second."

De Jersey placed his beer on the mat. "Shit."

Wilcox took over. "You need to be careful. What if she discovers you went to New York? Airport security is tighter than it's ever been. Do you think you can be identified?"

"I should be okay. Simmons only facilitated the house sale. When she can't get hold of him, she'll start pursuing other avenues to track down Moreno." De Jersey tried to make light of a difficult situation, but he recognized a major headache in the works. "All anyone over there knows is that Simmons is a redheaded Canadian business adviser."

"Listen," Wilcox interjected. He stared at the beer mat in front of him, as if afraid to face de Jersey. "Tony and I still have some collateral. This Hewitt woman told us how much you lost, and we know how much cash those horses of yours eat up. Why don't you get shot of the Hampton property and use the money until you get something worked out?"

"You can pay us later," Driscoll chipped in.

"I have something worked out."

There was a pause. Wilcox didn't look up from the beer mat. Driscoll chewed a nail.

"A plan?" Driscoll said at last.

Wilcox wiped his mouth. "You're not still on about the Crown Jewels. I mean, that was a gag, right?"

"It was no joke."

"Sweet Jesus, he's serious!" Driscoll said incredulously.

"It can work. It'll take a lot of time and preparation. We can't afford to make any mistakes."

"Oh, *we* can't, huh?"

"Just listen. The items we're going to take will not be in the Tower. We're going after the jewels the Queen wears for the Golden Jubilee. They'll be taken off-site for preparation, and that's where we'll pick them up."

"Where will they go?" asked Driscoll.

"Possibly to one of the jewelers in Hatton Garden," de Jersey replied. "I'll find out soon enough. I've been gathering the people we'll need on our side. There's an equerry, who was close to the Royal Family for years and knows the protocol. We need a substitute for the Queen, some motors, a lady-in-waiting, and two more heavies."

Driscoll and Wilcox stared at him, speechless.

"We'll need to get into the Royal household's diary of events to figure out the security measures, and I'll need to find myself a computer hacker."

Driscoll's dog yawned and shifted position under the table.

Wilcox broke the silence. "Say you get this organized and pull it off. How much do you think we're looking at?"

"The Koh-i-noor Diamond should fetch us millions. Then there's diamonds, rubies, pearls. . . ."

"Fuck me," Wilcox said, frowning.

"But until it's firmed up, it's just work in progress."

Driscoll drained his beer. "What do you want from me?" he asked quietly.

"The name and address of the actress who does the TV ad for royal jelly."

"What?" Wilcox was unsure he had heard right.

"Why not?" Driscoll said. "It's just a few phone calls."

"You line up the vehicles," de Jersey said to Wilcox. "We need two Daimlers spruced up. Copy the badges, Royal coat of arms. But don't leave traces. Spread the work. The automobiles must never be connected to any of us." De Jersey drained his glass. "Another drink?" he asked casually.

Driscoll asked for tonic water.

"I'll get this round, you paid for the last." Wilcox headed for the bar.

"You feeling all right?" de Jersey asked Driscoll.

"My nerves are shot. I can't take this all in. I didn't come here to discuss a fucking heist, Eddy. I told you I wasn't up for it. Him neither." Driscoll jerked his head toward the bar.

De Jersey ignored what he had said. "Wait till you see the commercial. Then you'll understand why I want the actress."

"Fine, right, I'll check it out."

As Wilcox was returning with the drinks, Driscoll leaned in close to de Jersey. "What's the time span we're looking at?"

"It'll be May. According to my contact, the crown fittings will be held three or four weeks before the Jubilee celebrations, which take place on the fourth of June," de Jersey said, lighting a cigar. "So it looks like early May. From now on, contact me only on my cell phone—no calls to the house."

"Hang on!" Wilcox said. "I only went to get a round and now you're talking as if this is all agreed to. Good job I didn't go for a slash too or I'd have no idea what was going on."

De Jersey gave him a half smile. "It's work in progress. Decision time is still way off. Right now I just need the pair of you to help me with the setting up. That's all."

Wilcox raised his glass to de Jersey. "It looks like early May then," he said.

De Jersey glanced at them. "So it's agreed. You'll help me set it up?"

They nodded, and de Jersey raised his glass to both.

* * *

De Jersey and Driscoll walked into the park with the dog. They headed for a Toyota Estate belonging to Driscoll's wife. After Driscoll opened the door for the dog to hop in, De Jersey watched him swing the door back and forth absentmindedly. "What's up with you?" he asked. "You worried?"

"Well, for starters, you're not on your toes. Not like you used to be. And this Hewitt woman could be trouble." Driscoll closed the door. "Also, I worry about Jimmy. He's doing too much coke. I've told him that to his face but—"

De Jersey put his arm around Driscoll's shoulders. "I've never taken unnecessary risks with you or James and I'm not going to start now. If this caper looks like a no-win situation, or if one of you isn't up to the job, I'll be the first to pull out."

Driscoll nodded, unconvinced.

De Jersey went on. "It means a lot to me that you've both offered to help."

Driscoll sighed. "You're worth it."

"I'll talk to James," de Jersey said. "He won't know it came from you. It's obvious to me, too, when he's high."

Driscoll drove away, the dog staring out of the rear window. De Jersey watched the car go. He had suspected Wilcox of doing coke. He would have to keep an eye on him. Wilcox had always been a bit on the wild side, but in the end he delivered.

This time he would deliver even faster than de Jersey expected. That afternoon he got a call from Wilcox saying he might have located the vehicles. He'd seen an ad in *Motor News*, and he was going to check it out.

The following morning, Wilcox walked along the cobbled mews behind Leicester city center and paused outside a double garage. A peeling "Hudson's Weddings and Funerals" plaque hung precariously from a rusty nail on the garage door. He had parked his Ferrari a good distance away, outside a large petrol station. He'd asked the proprietor to check the oil and fuel, telling him he would return soon.

The double garage appeared to be locked, and Wilcox stepped back, annoyed. But when he gave a really hard knock, there was the sound of footsteps. The door creaked open, and a short, wiry man with bifocal glasses peered out. He had iron gray hair in a spiky crew cut and was wearing oil-stained overalls. Ken Hudson was seventy and suffered from glaucoma. He gestured for Wilcox to follow him into the gloomy garage.

It was larger than it had appeared from the outside, with four covered vehicles parked in a square. Hudson switched on a yellowish light and launched into a monologue on his now defunct wedding and funeral business. He was selling everything, including the tools, the paint-spraying and car-cleaning equipment, the four vehicles. Wilcox poked around the small back office, which was home to a kettle and a small camping stove.

Hudson squinted at him through his thick glasses. "You wanna look at the vehicles?"

Wilcox smiled and shrugged. "Eh, Pops, I can shift the hearses, but they're not what I'm after. I want to make this a paint shop, respray cars, stuff like that. I'll take 'em, but it's the premises I'm primarily interested in. What's your asking price? It'll be cash, so don't play silly buggers." Wilcox lifted a tarpaulin and discovered a Daimler.

"Ten thousand," Hudson said.

"I'll give you eight, cash."

Hudson paused. "All right, but that's a damn good price."

The deal done, Hudson brought out the grubby documents, signed everything over to "Tom Hall," and gave him a receipt for the cash. After another fifteen minutes of small talk, the old boy handed over the keys and left. When he was alone Wilcox dragged the tarpaulin off each of the Daimlers. They were exactly what de Jersey had requested. Two were hearses and two had been used for weddings, but not for some time. Mildew and cobwebs threaded across the seats. Wilcox inspected each vehicle's engine. He would use two for parts, and it would take a lot of elbow grease to get that bodywork gleaming again.

Before driving back to London, he purchased a book on the Royals and, using a magnifying glass, checked out their Daimlers. He would need to make a copy of the mascot fitted to the Queen's car. He also had to match the seat colors. It would take time, but he was in no hurry. It was still early days. In some ways it was good to have something to take his mind off his financial problems, and as the Colonel had said, if it didn't work out and he wanted to walk away, he could. He was just carrying out orders, as he had in the past.

Later that day de Jersey arrived outside Sylvia Hewitt's apartment block in St. John's Wood. He had telephoned from a small café along the high street. Helen answered and told him that Sylvia was not at home but that she expected her at any moment.

"Would you like her to call you at home?"

"No, I'm in London. In fact, I'm not far from St. John's Wood. May I come round tonight?"

"Of course," Helen gushed.

"Good. I'll see you shortly then."

He snapped his cell phone shut and sat with his cappuccino, wondering how to approach the matter. He had to find out the private investigator's name and, more important, if the PI had discovered anything that would lead Sylvia to him.

Helen opened the front door. She looked dreadful, even thinner than before. "Sylvia's on her way. I called her office and she was just leaving." She gestured for him to follow her into the drawing room. "Would you like some tea?"

"That would be nice," he said. "I've had a long day."

Helen clasped her hands. "I'll just slip out to the high street. There's a very good deli, wonderful cakes, unless . . ."

"I don't want to put you to any trouble but I'm a sucker for chocolate éclairs."

Helen tucked a wisp of hair behind her ear. "I'll be two minutes. Would you like the television on?"

"No, thanks. It'll be nice to sit here and relax."

As soon as he heard the front door close, de Jersey was on his feet. He searched the room, then looked through the rest of the apartment, walking past the immaculate kitchen and bathroom to Sylvia's bedroom. He was fast and careful, first her wardrobe, then her dressing table. Last he searched her bedside table and, in one of the drawers, discovered a photograph of her with David Lyons, several letters, and Sylvia's birth certificate and driving license. He hurried from the bedroom into a small adjoining room she used as her office, where he uncovered the mail from Matheson in New York, his carefully listed expenses and updates of his investigation. Then he heard the front door open and was caught near the bedroom door. He smiled apologetically. "I'm sorry, where's the bathroom?"

Helen pointed to a door opposite as she made her way into the kitchen.

He went in and closed the door. Then he read one of the letters he'd taken from the bedroom. It was a love letter from David to Sylvia.

It was almost five thirty when Sylvia arrived. De Jersey stood up to shake her hand. Helen seemed as relieved as he was to see her. "If you two will excuse me, I think I'll just go and have a lie-down. I hardly sleep at all these days," she said.

"I'll wake you for dinner," Sylvia said.

She took off her coat and gestured for de Jersey to sit down. "I suppose you've heard all about her depression. I have to listen to it day and night, and it's becoming a strain." She tossed her coat over a chair and sat primly opposite him. "After everything is settled I think she'll have enough to buy a small place of her own. These things take so much time, though. We've sold the house, or what was left of it after the fire, but poor David was in a dreadful mess. The house was in both their names, but he'd even remortgaged that. Helen just signed whatever he put in front of her." She sipped her tea. "For a while the police and the fire specialist were suspicious of the way the fire had started, but in the end they couldn't find anything, so the insurance company was forced to pay up. At least Helen has salvaged something from this mess."

"Unlike you," he said quietly.

"What?"

"I understand that you also invested money in the Internet company."

"How did you find that out?" Sylvia asked, surprised.

"You aren't the only one with access to information, Miss Hewitt."

"Helen still doesn't know I was one of the unlucky investors," she said. "I'd prefer to keep it that way, at least for now. It has been a very sad business all round." She took another sip of tea. "I have contacted the two other main investors, and they are surprisingly reticent about the matter. Although I haven't lost as much as them or you, I'm not prepared to sit back and accept it."

De Jersey was angry. "So, contrary to my request that you keep my financial documents confidential, it seems you have been using them."

"Well, David often stopped off with me to do some homework. He left a few files and I looked through them," she admitted.

"Homework?" de Jersey asked, feigning surprise.

"It was such a long journey home that he often waited here until the rush hour was over."

"You should tread carefully. If you are privy to my private transactions—"

"Not all of them," she interjected.

"That is beside the point. As I have told you, I am distressed to think that my financial documents are being discussed without my permission. It is highly irregular, not to mention illegal."

"I am aware of that. But under the circumstances with his suicide—"

"The manner of his death has little to do with me, Miss Hewitt. If you continue to search through my private papers, I will be forced to consult a lawyer to—"

"I haven't shown them to anyone else. In fact, I'd have thought you'd be pleased that I'm making progress in trying to trace the man responsible for the losses you have incurred."

"I am here to request again that you cease doing this."

"But why? You have lost a substantial fortune, Mr. de Jersey. Don't you want it back?"

"I am more than aware of what I have lost—"

"But I have some information. My private investigator has discovered that a man called Philip Simmons has been acting on Alex Moreno's behalf in financial matters, and I am determined to track him down. I think they made some kind of deal that enables Moreno to benefit from the sale of his property without having to worry about creditors seizing the funds."

De Jersey clenched his teeth.

"I'll get the details for you." Sylvia scurried from the room and returned with a bulging file. She sat down at the table and began to take out documents. She handed them to de Jersey with a flourish. "The same man, Philip Simmons, organized the continued refurbishment of the East Hampton property and apparently intends selling it as soon as it is completed. He also sold Moreno's apartment. I have searched through file after file, and I can find no one of that name in David's records. I've asked his assistant, Daniel Gatley, and he cannot recall meeting him. So who is he? Is he in partnership with Moreno? At the very least this Mr. Simmons must know how to contact him. Or maybe it's something more sinister."

"Sinister?" de Jersey repeated.

"Moreno has disappeared without a trace. Maybe Simmons is using an assumed name. I'm sure we're on to something because Mr. Matheson has confirmed via some contact he has in Immigration that no one by that name ever arrived in the U.S. from Canada. In fact, they have no record of him entering the U.S. at all."

De Jersey thanked God he had used his Cummings passport to enter the United States. "Is Simmons among the investors?" he asked.

"No, he isn't. He might be Canadian, but I assume he lives in the States, because why would Alex Moreno use a Canada-based financial adviser? It doesn't make sense. I have a list of the other investors if you would like to see it. None suffered the losses you, Mr. Driscoll, or Mr. Wilcox did."

Every time she mentioned their names together he cringed inwardly.

"I have paid this detective a substantial amount already, so to just let it go would be silly," she went on. "I have therefore asked him to continue. I think it would be sensible to pool our resources, split the cost of hiring Mr. Matheson. I'm sure he will get us results."

"How much do you believe the house and the apartment in America are worth?" de Jersey asked.

"You mean, what has Simmons got away with?" she asked.

"Didn't you say he was just a business adviser that Moreno employed?"

"Yes, but even if he isn't profiting himself from the sale, he will know who the money goes to when it's sold, won't he?"

"And if you trace that person, do you think he will just hand over the money?"

"Well, whether it's Simmons, Moreno, or someone else, they should be forced to split it with us. If we can't make them, we'll get the police and the courts involved."

De Jersey remained silent for a moment as she began to collect the papers. Then he asked, "These two other major investors, have you their permission to act on their behalf?"

"No, as I said earlier, they're rather dismissive. All the other investors I've spoken to are eager for results. I've also discovered David began to communicate with Moreno six months before the crash. He was e-mailing him daily. These are copies of the e-mails." She passed the printouts to de Jersey. "As you can see, around five months ago Moreno wasn't giving David any hint of the company's financial troubles and instead was suggesting that he bring in more financial backers. And he did. You yourself remortgaged your property, as did Mr. Wilcox."

"It seems suspicious to me that you have access to such sensitive information," de Jersey remarked, in a cold but even tone.

"What do you mean?" Sylvia said, unnerved.

"I'm not sure if you want me to discuss this here," de Jersey said and glanced toward Helen's bedroom.

"Is it to do with Helen?"

"Yes. You see, David was an old and trusted friend. He often confided in me."

"Really?" Now it was her turn to tense.

"I have said that my business with your brother-in-law was highly confidential. The fact that he embezzled substantial amounts of my money is shocking, and I was not prepared when my solicitors informed me of another perplexing and deeply worrying discovery."

Her face took on a puzzled expression.

"Perhaps David had a partner assisting him in the fraud. Someone with access to his papers, to his clients, someone to whom he was very close."

Sylvia sat back nervously. "I don't follow."

"I think I should make it clear, then. I'm presently taking legal advice, and we have been discussing action against you, as we believe you assisted

David in embezzling money from my accounts which I had not authorized to be invested."

Sylvia sat in shocked silence.

"There is also a trust fund that David stole from me, and we believe he must have had an accomplice."

"That is ridiculous." Sylvia bristled.

"Is it? Well, then, perhaps you should know we are aware that you and David were involved sexually. We have photographs of the two of you together in—"

"That isn't true!"

"I'm afraid it is." He knew he'd got her. "I know that you were his mistress."

Sylvia stood up, her face drained of color.

"I'm sure poor Helen has no idea that you and David had been having an affair for years. You may have hired a private investigator, Miss Hewitt, but so did I. I can assure you that my information regarding your connections to David could have you charged with conspiracy."

"No, no! I swear before God it's not true."

"Isn't it? Maybe you're pretending to pay for a detective when what you're really doing is attempting to squeeze even more money out of the investors."

"You're wrong."

De Jersey stood up and stared at her. "I'm warning you, Miss Hewitt. You will return my financial documents and everything else in your possession that concerns me or I shall proceed with legal action."

Sylvia began to weep. "I admit that David and I were lovers, but I did nothing illegal. Nothing."

"Well, I would like to believe you, but my solicitors do not agree. I came here today to warn you. I care for Helen and don't want to see her hurt any more than she already is."

"Please don't tell her this, she'll have a breakdown."

De Jersey ran his fingers through his hair. "Then you had better call off this chap in America. My financial situation is not your problem. My people do research on my behalf. If they prove to me without a doubt you had no involvement—"

"But I didn't!" She started to sob. "I loved him, but whatever I say won't help. I know how it must look, but I had no idea he was involved in such terrible frauds. I'm sure most of it was unintentional. He always spoke so highly of you."

"Miss Hewitt, I am not interested in hearing sad stories about David," he snapped, and this time he moved very close to her. "I will not hesitate to make sure your sister knows the truth, and I won't be sorry to drag you through the courts if that's what it takes to stop you invading my privacy. Do you understand?"

Fifteen minutes later de Jersey left the St. John's Wood apartment, carrying disks and papers he had taken from Sylvia. She had called Matheson in New York and, in front of de Jersey, taken him off the case. She'd also signed a confidentiality agreement, promising not to divulge anything she had learned about his private affairs. She wept when he promised that he would reimburse her losses at some time in the future if she kept her word. He warned her against making any further calls to Wilcox or Driscoll or making his losses known to other investors.

It was after eleven when de Jersey arrived home. He went straight to his study and had just filed away the papers he had taken from Sylvia when Natasha walked in. "Daddy, we've been trying to contact you all day."

He whipped round, startled. "What's wrong?"

"It's Royal Flush. The vet's taken swabs from his throat. He's had a bad chest after his training session."

"Thanks for telling me. I'll go and have a look at him." He threw on an overcoat and walked out into the yard. He let himself into the manager's office and read the vet's reports with a sinking heart.

After tests it had been surmised that Royal Flush had nothing more than a cold. But the mere fact that the horse had been off color worried him. First the leg injury, now the chest infection. If Royal Flush had trouble with his breathing, it was a sure sign of problems to come. As soon as the weather cleared the horse would begin training for the Derby, but fortunately there was still considerable time before June. He put the reports back in their place.

He was so deeply in thought he was startled to find Natasha standing over him. She had on an overcoat over her nightdress, and Wellington boots.

"Is he all right, Daddy?"

He reached out his arm to draw her to his side. "He's doing fine." Then he stood up and ruffled her hair. She buried her face in his chest, and he chuckled. "Still my little girl. But you should be in bed."

"I was worried about Royal Flush."

"So am I, but the vet says he's just got a chest cold, and there's plenty of time for him to recover before the season starts."

He turned out the lights, and they walked out of the office past the back room. This was where the racing colors of his stable were kept. He switched the lights on and stood breathing in the smells he loved and touching the colors displayed on the wall alongside the plaques and pictures of past champions. So many races, so much of his life was here in this tack room. Next to his knee boots and weight cloth hung Royal Flush's bridle. Laid out on the table was the grooming kit that the lads used with such care to maintain his beautiful coat. Natasha slipped her arm through his as he touched Royal Flush's bridle.

"Your granddad, he would have been so proud. You missed a lot not knowing him and my mother. In fact, she looked a lot like you: tall, strong, knitting. Always knitting. And when I was a little boy she'd read to me. She could read and knit at the same time. Click click. She had a soft, warm voice. She read me all the classics. Sometimes I think she knew whole passages of them by heart. I owe her a lot. Shall we go and say good night to my boy, then?" he asked.

They went into the yard, and he opened the stable door. Royal Flush kicked out, then stared at de Jersey angrily.

"What's up with you, my old son?" he said quietly and approached him.

The magnificent horse snorted and allowed de Jersey to stroke his neck. From his glossy coat and impressive presence, it was hard to believe there was anything wrong with the stallion.

De Jersey rested his head against the big beast's neck and closed his eyes. Here was the jewel in his crown. Never before had he placed so much expectation in a horse. "Don't let me down," he whispered. He felt so close to Royal Flush that it was hard to drag himself away. As he shut the stable door, he took one last look.

"What is it, Daddy?"

He had almost forgotten Natasha was there. "Well, darling, I've never put my dreams on the line like this. Sometimes at night I close my eyes and I see him winning the Derby. I truly see every moment, and I feel the most extraordinary pride. That's my boy coming out of the starting gate, and I know he's going to win for me. Then, when he passes that winning post, I'm cheering and waving my hat in the air. . . . But then I wake up and realize it was only a dream."

She slipped her hand into his, and they walked back to the house in silence.

He had been thinking that he should come up with some kind of insurance in case the robbery was unsuccessful, whereupon not only would he lose the estate but any buyer for the yard would want Royal Flush. In the past he'd always had a backup plan in case a robbery failed. Now was the time to put in place a safety net.

14

The problems with Royal Flush continued, and it was decided that his throat should be scraped. Any inflammation caused by mucus might have repercussions. The next morning de Jersey gave the go-ahead for the operation and watched sadly as the horse was driven from the yard. It was not yet seven o'clock, so he had a lengthy workout in his gym. He pushed himself, first on the treadmill, then the rowing machine before moving on to the weights. By the time he was showered and changed, he felt clearheaded and hungry. Christina cooked him scrambled eggs and bacon.

He reached for her hand. "Got some business to do in London. If I have to stay over I'll call you."

"Say good-bye to the girls. They go back to school today."

He drained his coffee cup just as Natasha and Leonie came in. He hugged and kissed them both. When the phone rang, his body went rigid. It might be the vet. He nodded for Christina to answer it, which she did, then held out the receiver to him.

"Darling, it's the vet."

De Jersey took the phone with trepidation. Then his face broke into a wide smile. "You're kidding? Are you sure?"

"We're certain," the vet reassured him. "We don't think the operation's necessary after all. It was just a bit of a cold. His chest is clear, and although his throat is a bit rough, he's in terrific shape compared to when we last examined him. It must have been the antibiotics."

"Are you bringing him home?"

"We are. Give him a day or so, and then he can go back into training."

It was just what de Jersey needed. He rushed to Christina and lifted her off her feet. "My boy's coming home. They don't need to operate!" He kissed her lips and bounded out the door without a backward glance. Now he could get on with preparing for the robbery without worry about his "boy." Everything was back on track, and he knew he had to get moving. It was already late January.

De Jersey walked through the door of the Kilburn flat and straight to the computer. There was an e-mail from Elvis asking when he wanted his next tutoring session. Then checking the post he had brought in with him, he found a long-anticipated letter from Gregory Jones, responding to his fake solicitor's letter. The blue notepaper was stamped "Franklyn Prison."

Jones's handwriting was looped and slanted backward, but the letter was well constructed. It said that a visitor's pass would be allocated shortly, and he was looking forward to discussing the possibility of appeal. De Jersey wrote to confirm he would see Jones, signing himself Philip Simmons.

Later that day, Paul Dulay phoned. He had an appointment in London several days hence, so they arranged to meet. Things were starting to pick up pace.

Philip Simmons, Solicitor, pinned a visitor's pass to his jacket. His briefcase was searched but contained only documents from the firm of Hunting and Letheby. He was ushered into a booth next to the main visiting hall, security cameras monitoring his every move.

After ten minutes, the door opened and Gregory Jones, wearing a yellow striped bib, was led in by two officers. They stood by the door as he sat down in front of de Jersey, then moved outside.

Once the door was closed, Jones, a surly-faced man with an athletic build, took out his tobacco and cigarette papers. His face was pockmarked, with two fresh scars down one cheek, like thin tramlines, where he had been cut with a razor. It was a typical prison injury, no doubt caused by a pair of razor blades stuck so close together in a nailbrush that the wound would be difficult to stitch. Jones rolled a thin cigarette, took a box of matches from his pocket, and placed it on the table. Then he broke the silence. "You had no trouble getting in, then?"

"No. Thank you for agreeing to see me."

"You intrigued me." His voice was coarse with a trace of the West Country. His teeth were stained. "There's no hope of an appeal, so I know you aren't from my solicitors."

"Do they tape these meetings?" de Jersey asked.

"Invasion of privacy, pal." Jones leaned back in the chair. "They're supposed to monitor the odd phone call, but they don't bother. Too much aggravation. Imagine the fucking nonsense they'd have to wade through."

De Jersey looked down at the papers. "Your two daughters live with a relative in America?"

"California. One wrote for a while, then stopped. Why do—"

"You must want to see them again."

"They'll be married with kids of their own by the time I get out, if I ever do." He sighed. "I'd like to see them. It'd be a light at the end of the tunnel."

"How are your finances?"

"The savings I had disappeared with the legal costs. Like the wife." He sucked in his breath. De Jersey could feel the man's pent-up bitterness. "So, let's get to the point, Mr. Simmons. You got the visitor's pass. I'm here. What do you want?"

"Information."

"I thought as much. Who are you?"

De Jersey glanced at his watch. "I have a proposition for you."

Jones stared at the ceiling. "Well, I'm not going anywhere."

De Jersey took out a file. "I need certain information, and it is imperative that the details you supply are legit." He passed over a sheet of typed questions.

Jones took a long time reading it. He flicked ash from his roll-up a couple of times but did not look up until he slid the paper back to de Jersey. "What's the deal?"

"Fifty thousand. Any bank account, any name, any country."

"But I'm in here and you're out there, so how can I trust you to do what you say?"

De Jersey leaned forward. "You can't, but how about putting faith in the old saying 'My word is my bond'?"

"I suppose I've not got much to lose," Jones said.

De Jersey began to pack his briefcase. "You interested?"

"Maybe."

"Do you have the information?"

"You know I do. That was my job, but how do I know you're not setting me up?"

"Not much point. As you said, you're in here already."

"I need more information."

"The less you know the better. But I mean no harm to the Royal Family."

De Jersey clicked his briefcase shut.

"You want me to phone you with the info or what?"

"Too risky, even if they're too bored to tape calls. I think the best way is another face-to-face. Before then you can phone me with your account details. . . . I gather you *are* interested?"

Jones lit up. "Bet your arse—and I'll tell you something for nothing. I know a lot more than what's on that page. The security there is archaic."

A bell rang to indicate that time was up. De Jersey said, "I do not intend to break in. As I stated, I have no desire to harm the Royals or put them in jeopardy."

Jones's voice was hardly above a whisper. "You're not the fucking IRA, then? Cos I draw the line there, pal."

"I am not connected to them." De Jersey leaned close, his voice hardly audible. "I can give you the light at the end of the tunnel, but no more questions. I need answers, understand me?"

Jones nodded. Their eyes locked, then the door opened.

Jones stood up. "Mr. Simmons, can we shake on it?"

De Jersey grasped the prisoner's hand.

"I'll call you just to arrange payment, all right?" Jones said softly.

De Jersey felt Jones grip tightly. "Yes, but I don't want answers. Not then. After I hear from you, we'll organize another visit."

After Jones was led out, de Jersey waited for an officer to take him back to the gates. Next visit, Prisoner 445A should have all the answers he needed.

Raymond Marsh seemed even odder-looking than previously. His hair shimmered as if it had been sprayed with crystallized sugar. "Can't stay long. Taking the wife out. There's an Elvis at a pub that's shit-hot. He's Chinese, but he's got an amazing voice."

He sat in the chair in front of de Jersey's computer and swiveled toward him. "You've been spreading yourself around the chat rooms. You're getting quite good, but I was disappointed you were checking out other hackers when you've got the best right here."

De Jersey smiled. "Prove it. I need some information."

"What's it for this time?" When de Jersey didn't reply, Marsh gave him a sideways glance. "Novel, right? I read your messages. What do you want?"

"I need to know the Queen's diary movements. I am writing about the Golden Jubilee. Can you do that?"

"Do what exactly?"

"Gain access to the Royal household's computer and check out the Queen's diary dates, especially for her fitting of the Crown Jewels. I know it should be in May sometime, but I want the exact date and time. It should be listed."

Marsh chewed his lip. "That's a bit dodgy, mate."

"I'll pay you well."

Marsh nodded. "A grand?"

"Five hundred, cash."

"Okay, I'll have a go. It'd be easier to read it in *The Times.* They list her comings and goings next to the births, deaths, and marriages."

"By the time it's public, it'll be too late for what I have in mind."

"And you're writing a book." Marsh grinned. "I believe you. Thousands wouldn't."

De Jersey went into the kitchen and put the kettle on. He could hear the click of the keyboard as Marsh moved through cyberspace, inching closer to his destination. After about half an hour he laughed. "I'm in! I'm fucking in!"

De Jersey leaned against the table.

"You're in luck, pal," Marsh said.

De Jersey read over his shoulder while Marsh printed out the lists as they appeared on the screen. Finally, he passed the pages to de Jersey with a flourish. "Her Majesty's diary."

De Jersey glanced down the list of all the Royal Family's current engagements. He flicked to the May–June dates: June 1, Princess Royal takes salute at the Centenary Parade; June 3, Duke of Kent to open the Montgomery Exhibition; June 4, Duke of Edinburgh as Master of the Corporation of Trinity House attends the Outward Bound Charity Golf match; June 5, the Queen holds an Investiture at Buckingham Palace. There was no mention of the jewels fitting, no mention of Jubilee celebrations at all.

"This isn't any good. It's from the Royal Web site. I could have got it myself," he said frustratedly.

Marsh dangled two sheets of paper in front of him. "Not these, though. For an extra two hundred, they're yours."

"One hundred. And let me see them first."

Marsh threw the pages to him.

De Jersey studied them closely. This was made different from the engagements sites by the alterations, queries, and question marks. "TBC" was written beside numerous appointments. His heart jumped. There, on May 2, was the word "Fitting." Beside it was the name of the jewelers, D'Ancona, and the time, 10:30 A.M. De Jersey folded the pages.

"Is that what you wanted?" Marsh asked. "I couldn't come up with anything else."

"Not really," De Jersey lied. "I was hoping to find out about her portrait sittings, but it'll still be useful." He withdrew six hundred pounds from his wallet and handed the cash to Marsh.

"Ta. I'm gonna put it toward a holiday I've promised the wife. She's not seen her sister for eight years. They live in New Zealand."

As the door shut behind Marsh, de Jersey breathed a sigh of relief: he had found not only the date and time of the fitting but also its location. He reread the printout and laughed out loud. There was another piece of vital information on a February page: a D'Ancona representative was flying in from Antwerp for an appointment at the Palace. Since D'Ancona was a jeweler by appointment to the Queen, the alterations must be under way. By tailing the D'Ancona agent from the airport, perhaps he could discover the location of the "safe house" where the jewels were being kept. He needed Marsh again to find the list of passengers traveling on the nine fifteen from Antwerp to Heathrow.

The Daimlers had been stripped down. Wilcox had spent hours in the dank mews garage respraying and fixing them. As he expected, buffing the bodywork to gleaming Royal standard took time, but fitting the new carpets and replacing the leather seats would take even longer. Now Wilcox checked the engines. The cars would be taken to London in one of his own trailers. He didn't want them to be seen driving through the city. He had already made the Royal mascot, which would be attached to the front, a silver St. George on a horse, poised victoriously over a slain dragon.

He had just turned on the electric polisher when de Jersey paid a surprise visit.

"How's it going?"

"The engines are all tuned up, but the bodywork's a problem."

De Jersey inspected the cars. "Travel in style, don't they?"

"I guess so, but they don't make them like this anymore. We were lucky to find them. You wanna hear the engine?" He turned it on, and they listened to it purr.

"You here alone?"

"I get here early and leave late. I see no one."

"Got a place to brew up?"

"Sure, out the back," Wilcox said, wiping his hands on a rag.

As the two men sat with mugs of tea in the grimy back room, de Jersey updated Wilcox on the plan. Wilcox said little, smoking one cigarette after another.

"We've got a date, May second. Can the cars be ready by then?"

"Hell, yes. I'll work on the upholstery in London, but we need a place to store them."

"I'll find it," de Jersey said. "Gregory Jones is putting together the rest of the information, then I'll proceed with the Palace security research. Now we just need the D'Ancona rep to lead us straight to the jewels."

"What arrangements did you make for moving them on?" Wilcox asked.

De Jersey sipped his tea, and Wilcox repeated his question.

"You know, Jimmy, I still don't have it direct from you that you're not going to get cold feet—or Tony for that matter."

"Don't do this to me," Wilcox said.

"What am I doing, Jimmy?"

"My head in. Obviously I wouldn't be schleppin' up and down the motorway fixing up these motors if I wasn't in."

"But you haven't said it to me directly."

"I'm saying it now, all right? And I reckon Tony's in too."

De Jersey continued drinking his tea.

"Did you hear what I said?"

"Course I did."

De Jersey looked into his eyes. "Cut out the coke, James. Doesn't do you any good, and it worries me."

"I'm clean, Eddy," Wilcox protested.

"Keep it that way, because I need you beside me."

Wilcox's face broke into a smile.

"I think I've got a buyer, a Japanese guy."

"What about Dulay?"

De Jersey nodded. "The contact came through him. Dulay's not firmed up yet. He's coming for a meeting in three days' time, but I reckon he's onboard. I don't want him meeting you or Tony. Less he sees of any of us the better."

"Sure. I never met him anyway. Tony said he looks like that French actor Gérard somethin'. You went over to Monaco to see him, did you?"

"As Simmons. He doesn't know who I am. He just needs to produce a buyer and get the big cut he's after."

Wilcox stubbed out his cigarette. "Have you found out where the jewels are being held?"

De Jersey glanced at him. "I told you, the D'Ancona rep will lead us to the jewels. They'll be in a safe house somewhere, being prepared for the fitting." He stood up to leave.

Wilcox walked him to the garage door, where de Jersey patted his shoulder. "It's coming together. Don't worry." Then he stepped through the doorway and was gone.

Wilcox locked the door. He was shaking; the palms of his hands felt clammy and cold. He walked back to the annex, where he opened a silver snuffbox and performed his regular ritual. He was still shaky, but his head was clearer now. He went back to work.

De Jersey called Christina to say he would be going to Dublin for a few days, then spoke to Fleming about Royal Flush. He was informed that the horse had started training with no problems. They were pacing him with other horses, and that morning he'd passed them with ease on the gallops. Fleming asked which stallion he should put to the filly coming into season, and de Jersey said he would have to think about it. Calmly, he noticed that the date for the Derby was almost a month to the day after the heist. He hoped for enough cash to keep the estate going for the rest of his life.

A few days later, after a call from Jones, he arranged for his second visit to Franklyn Prison. The money had been deposited in Jones's account, and Jones was ready to talk. In fact, he provided more information than de Jersey had hoped for, such as the number and type of vehicles required per Royal, how many motorbike cavalcades would be allocated by the Metropolitan Police, how many police cars, and the number of their own security guards who would act as bodyguards.

"A complete Scotland Yard division is allocated to the Royals, so get your pencil out. With Her Majesty, we're talking about the full treatment. The number of guards and security officers goes down according to the rank of the Royal."

Jones had the contact numbers of every police officer working out of Scotland Yard assigned to the Royals. He also knew what police and security procedures were in place before the Royals stepped into their cars.

"Every vehicle is inspected for bombs, not to mention engine faults. So is the route they'll take—every inch, every possible sniper location—checked and cleared. You getting all this?" he asked.

"Keep going." De Jersey's pen flew across the page.

Jones leaned back in his chair. "Right. The Scotland Yard unit in charge of the Royals is called the Royalty and Diplomatic Protection Department. These guys, all skilled motorcyclists and car drivers, provide twenty-four-hour protection. They are recruited from the ranks of police officers experienced in operational street duty. I was part of this group for five years. There's nothing I don't know about all areas of Royal protection."

He lit a roll-up, heaving the smoke deep into his lungs, then let it out through his nose. He continued. The head of Palace security received a special code word from Scotland Yard daily. Scotland Yard would use this same code word to inform Palace security if an IRA threat had been issued. Then Royal visits planned for that day would halt, unless Scotland Yard gave the all clear.

"Only the head of Palace security and Scotland Yard officials know these code words. And, of course, the IRA."

"Wait a second. The code word comes from the IRA?"

"Yeah. The IRA gives Scotland Yard a code word that the IRA will use that day if they want to alert Scotland Yard to an impending terrorist attack."

The bell rang, ending visiting time. De Jersey collected his papers and placed them in his briefcase. The door opened, and two prison officers walked in. "Thank you, Mr. Simmons. I appreciate you comin' to see me. Good luck, then," Jones said.

De Jersey shook Jones's hand. The officers stood aside to allow him to pass, and he walked into the corridor, then left the prison.

Jones's information had been invaluable. He had also provided answers to de Jersey's questionnaire. De Jersey plotted his next step. While he needed Marsh, he was beginning to worry about the hacker's involvement. Did he have the expertise to carry out the work required? He was a dabbler. In order to get the job done, de Jersey would have to divulge the entire plan.

CHAPTER

15

As usual, Marsh arrived reeking of hair spray. His pointed boots tripped him as he headed up the narrow staircase. "Not got long. I've got another of my lectures tonight. Gotta make ends meet."

"What if I offered you something that could make you a millionaire?" de Jersey asked softly.

"Would I have to go down on you?" Marsh gave a high-pitched laugh. "I would."

"Let's not get carried away." De Jersey smiled. "What I'm suggesting would be illegal and dangerous."

"Wanna tell me about it?"

"It would mean a long prison sentence *if* you were caught."

"I have a job that feels like that!" Marsh wasn't laughing, though. His eyes were steady, beady and direct. "I always figured you were up to something."

"It's a robbery."

"Oh. Daylight, is it?"

"You could say that."

Marsh pointed to the window and the satellite dish. "That got something to do with it?"

"Yes."

"So I'm involved already, aren't I?"

"You can walk away right now, no hard feelings." De Jersey sat back. "There'd be no further involvement. You'll not encounter the other players."

"Apart from you," Marsh said softly. He stood up, squeezing his hands into his tight leather trouser pockets. "Well?" he asked.

"Well what?" asked de Jersey.

"What do you need from me?"

"I need you to get me information on communications between the Royalty and Diplomatic Protection Department at Scotland Yard and Buckingham Palace. I need to know the line on which IRA threats come into Scotland Yard, and the code word they use, the one that will alert Scotland Yard to a possible terrorist attack, and in turn halt all movements by Royals from the Palace."

Marsh considered. "That'll be tough. The Protection Department is bound to have more than one line. I'd have to monitor them all. It's risky, but I'm in the best position to do it."

"I know," de Jersey said.

"You're not IRA, right?"

"Correct."

"So why do you need this information?"

"I want to steal the Crown Jewels."

Marsh's reaction threw him. He collapsed on the floor and rolled around laughing. "The fuckin' Crown Jewels?" Eventually he lay flat, arms outstretched. "Man, you're something else!"

"You'll get a thousand pounds cash every week. Once we make the hit, you'll wait for the payoff. It could be weeks or months."

"What sort of payoff?"

"We don't know exactly, but it will be in the millions. In the end it's about trust. You and I have to trust each other."

"When's the job?" Marsh asked, sitting up.

"May second. Plenty of time to monitor the calls."

Marsh stretched out his hand to de Jersey. "You're on, pal. I can start tomorrow."

"Good, but tonight I need a little hacking job. There's a flight from Antwerp, day after tomorrow. Can you get me the passenger list?"

"Is the Pope Catholic? Just gimme a flight number, time, and date."

Before Marsh left, de Jersey had the passenger list of the flight taking in the D'Ancona representative. But out of the twenty-two names, who was their man? De Jersey decided that Dulay, due at the same airport shortly before the Antwerp flight, might be able to identify the man; he had once worked for the company. Also, on his arrival at Heathrow the representative was likely to be carrying gems, a briefcase chained to his wrist, and be accompanied by a security man. He should be fairly easy to identify.

Wherever it was, de Jersey still did not know what kind of security to expect inside the safe house, but he knew it had to be high tech. He needed information about modern security techniques, particularly those used by

D'Ancona. He surfed the Net, looking for sites dealing with high-tech security. Eventually he came across a company called Interlace Security,
which listed D'Ancona among its clients. De Jersey noted that Interlace
would be attending a security trade fair in Birmingham the next day.

Early the next morning de Jersey set off for Birmingham in a hire car. He
was used to luxurious cars, and this was a small, cheap vehicle. The seat
hurt his back, the gears kept jumping, and the brakes were uncertain.

The vast hall was crowded. He was astonished to see so many gadgets
on display. Electronic alarms for cars, houses, and businesses were pre-
dominant. Some stands were selling high-tech surveillance equipment.
Security guard companies were also represented, and some gave martial
arts and self-defense demonstrations. He wandered the aisles, sometimes
stopping to look over the goods for sale and watch demonstrations. The
section in which he was most interested displayed large safes and alarm
systems. He checked out three stands before he spotted Interlace Security.
He crossed the thick red carpet to pick up their brochure and was approached by a sales representative. "Can I be of assistance, sir?"

"I hope so. This is very impressive."

"Thank you. We are one of the top security consultants in England—
indeed, worldwide. We provide a complete range of services for business,
and real, workable solutions for risk management. It is our job to relieve
you of worry."

"Do you concentrate specifically on large companies?"

"No, not at all. Did you have something in mind?"

"I had a jewelry store close to Harrods, and we had two robberies
within months of each other. Now I'm opening another. It'll be close to
Theo Fennell's shop in London, Fulham, actually. It's a central location,
three floors."

The assistant handed de Jersey a steady stream of brochures, listing
top clients like British Aerospace, the National Criminal Intelligence
Service, Oracle, the Post Office, Railtrack, and of course . . .

"Good heavens, you do the D'Ancona security. What security do they
have?"

"Well, sir, we provide a virtually impenetrable surround with active
infrared beams and digital door-locking devices. Panic buttons and strips
are placed at strategic positions around the location and link to an alarm
receiving center, which is in direct contact with the police. We work closely
with our customers to ensure one hundred percent security. The grilles on
the vault act automatically if an infrared beam is broken or a panic button
is pressed."

"Expensive?" de Jersey mused.

"For D'Ancona we shipped in specially reinforced steel from Germany, which was fire- and bombproof. Since then, Asprey and Garrard's have ordered similar materials."

De Jersey, noting his cheap suit and tatty lace-up shoes, let the young man gabble through a few more sales pitches. "Would you oversee the installation?"

"Oh no, sir. I'm in sales." He spoke with a public-school accent.

"How long have you worked for the company?"

"Six months, sir. My father is one of their top consultants, though. He's been with them for eighteen years."

De Jersey took his card and glanced at the name: MALCOLM GRIDLEY, JUNIOR SALES EXECUTIVE. "Thank you, Mr. Gridley. I'll know who to contact when I've made up my mind."

De Jersey left with an armful of brochures and Malcolm Gridley's cell phone number. He also carried the firm's London, Birmingham, and factory addresses.

Though Gridley had twice asked his name, de Jersey had successfully distracted him with more questions and requests for leaflets. When de Jersey glanced back, the young man was being grilled by one of the older salesmen.

De Jersey spent a few more hours in the hall, waiting until he saw his salesman heading out for lunch. He watched as Gridley ordered a cheeseburger and chips from a stall. Just as de Jersey was about to join him, Gridley, unaware that he was being followed, headed for a bar on the far side of the hall. De Jersey watched him order a pint. After a moment he walked over. Sitting at the bar, Gridley was smoking. "On your lunch break?" he said.

"Yes," Gridley said, surprised.

"Can I buy you another drink?"

"No, thanks. I've got to get back. Erm, I didn't get your name before, and it's kind of company policy and—"

"I've gone over all the data you gave me, and I wanted to ask you if it would be possible to arrange a private showing of the D'Ancona installation. It's state of the art, isn't it?" De Jersey reached into his pocket and withdrew his wallet. "Here's my card."

"Thank you," said Gridley. "Unfortunately, I can't give you details of the D'Ancona facility; no one is allowed to view our clients' locations after the contract has been completed and the security measures installed. In fact, D'Ancona hired its own contractors to install the equipment."

De Jersey signaled to the barman.

Gridley swore under his breath. "Oh, Christ!"

A portly man in a navy pin-striped suit was striding toward them. He sat down next to Gridley. De Jersey moved off. The man spoke sternly to Gridley, pointed at the half-drunk beer. Then Gridley got up, his face tight with anger. "It was one drink, for God's sake!" he said, walking away.

"One too many, Malcolm. I warned you—Malcolm?"

The portly man took off after Gridley. De Jersey earmarked young Gridley as possibly useful to him.

Driscoll sat in an Italian restaurant waiting for de Jersey. After half an hour, he had eaten one roll and was half inclined to take the other when de Jersey walked in. They ordered their food with a bottle of house wine. "How are we doing?" de Jersey asked.

"There are these agencies that represent look-alikes, and I rang round until I found her. They said she was booked up, so I gave a lot of bull about needing to speak to her about a personal appearance. Anyway, I got her home address and phone number. She lives in Esher."

"Family?"

"She's married, husband's retired. No children. She makes a fortune doing special appearances. It's freaky. She's the Queen's absolute double."

"Have you checked out her home?"

"Not yet."

Their minestrone arrived, and they ate in silence.

"I had a few words with Jimmy," de Jersey said.

"How was he?"

"On good form. He assured me he wasn't using anymore. The vehicles look in great shape. We need to find a London base soon so he can do the final adjustments."

Driscoll nodded. "Is he in or out?"

"In."

"I see. Well, I expected he would be."

"What about you? Are you up for it?"

Driscoll licked his lips. "Course I am. I'm in. God help me."

"I couldn't go without you. It'll be the three of us again, right?"

"We must be out of our bloody minds."

"I'm working on the safe house location. Dulay is flying in, and so is a D'Ancona representative. We have to follow him to wherever they have the goods. Then I've got to work out how to get past the security system. It's very high tech, and they installed it themselves."

"How do you know?"

"Trust me. I've checked out the company that did the security. It sounds like a bloody big walk-in vault with lasers and panic buttons like you wouldn't believe."

Driscoll dribbled soup down his chin.

"But these vault doors are going to be open for our Queen," de Jersey assured him.

"You'll be keeping your eye on Wilcox, then?" Driscoll asked. "Maybe he is clean, but he was shoving a lot of snow up his nose not too long ago. He's got to be monitored. He's not the same, you know."

"None of us are, Tony. We're all a lot older now. That's why I am taking it slowly. We can't afford any mistakes, and if it's too risky we pull out, simple as that. But we'll keep an eye on him."

Driscoll changed the subject. "What about the Hewitt woman?"

"She's sorted. We may have to bung her a few thousand, but not until we've done the job."

Driscoll wiped his mouth. It made him uneasy that de Jersey was keeping the plans so close to his chest. It was not the way they had worked in the past. "I need to know our progress, Eddy."

"You will, as soon as I've moved on to the next stage." De Jersey sounded annoyed. "You've got to trust me, Tony, like in the past. Now, give me the photographs of our lady and the contact address. I'll get Wilcox to check it out."

Driscoll passed him a manila envelope.

"Maybe in three weeks' time I'll be ready for preliminary talks. You have your instructions until then." He handed him an envelope.

Driscoll put it into his inside pocket.

De Jersey had never used women in the past, but a lady-in-waiting would surely accompany the Queen to the safe house. He sighed. She would have to be right in on the action, perhaps even armed.

Tomorrow would be another busy day. He was to meet Dulay, and they would identify the D'Ancona representative and follow him to the safe house. If all went well.

16

Dulay was wearing a navy cashmere coat and an Armani suit. He held a small carry-on bag and a briefcase. De Jersey had waited for him at the arrivals barrier in Terminal Four. They had an hour before the flight from Antwerp was due. Dulay agreed to identify the man, though he declined to follow him. He and de Jersey agreed to meet later that day at Dulay's hotel, the Grosvenor House Hotel on Park Lane.

When the Antwerp flight landed, de Jersey was waiting in the car park. Dulay called him on his cell phone as soon as he had picked out the target. De Jersey drove into position outside Arrivals. Dulay called again to say the flight had coincided with two others. The Antwerp passengers had gone through customs and were coming onto the concourse, but now the departure lanes were full of trolleys and passengers, making it difficult to spot the D'Ancona representative. Then Dulay suddenly said, "I've got him. He's carrying a brown leather briefcase, raincoat, and *yes!* A tall blond man is right at his heels. That's his guard. I can just see the chain on the guy's briefcase—it's handcuffed to him."

"Describe him," de Jersey snapped.

Dulay spoke rapidly. "He's moving fast, heading for the middle exit. He's balding, wearing rimless glasses, a navy suit, white shirt, and tie, about five ten, slim build, and he's on a cell phone. He's heading out now!"

De Jersey couldn't see the man. A black Range Rover passed him with a uniformed driver at the wheel. Then de Jersey spotted the D'Ancona man. He and his bodyguard came out together. The driver was quickly out of the Range Rover and opened the passenger and rear doors. Both men got into the vehicle and closed the doors. They moved off quickly. De Jersey followed, right on their tail.

He had the Range Rover within easy viewing distance thanks to the heavy traffic. It was still backed up, even when they hit the A4. Twice when the traffic thinned out he almost lost them, but roadworks saved him and he was able to watch their progress four cars ahead. The distance lengthened as they drove into Cromwell Road, heading for Knightsbridge, then traffic was heavy again. Suddenly they headed toward Earl's Court, and he followed as they crossed the Fulham Road, then King's Road. The Range Rover continued toward the Victoria Embankment. Then it was driving toward Blackfriars Bridge, to Newgate Street, where they passed St. Paul's. De Jersey sensed they were taking a very roundabout route. They were just passing Montague Place when the Range Rover took a sharp left. It was impossible for de Jersey to stay close at their heels without being spotted, so he drove on, making the next left. He drove into Smithfield, but there was no sign of them. He had lost them! Frustrated, he circled the roundabout in West Smithfield and branched off down a narrow side street leading into Bartholomew Close, which came out at King Horn Street. The Range Rover was parked on the corner of Newbury Street. He was just in time to see the two men from D'Ancona enter a building together. A moment later, the Range Rover drove off.

De Jersey parked in a side street and walked back. The safe house was on the corner. A narrow road ran alongside the four-story building. Rubbish bins had been placed on the pavement. The place was unimpressive, painted black, and gave no indication of its function. There was no plaque outside, no bell, no letter box, and the double door leading into the property was made of reinforced steel. Although the upper windows looked innocent, they were not windows at all. The casements were built over shuttered protectors with tinted black glass. De Jersey could not risk spending any more time in the area and walked on.

Less than a hundred yards away, the road curved to the right and led into Aldersgate Street. He walked a little further, then stopped outside a large, two-story, flat-roofed warehouse for lease. Perfect, de Jersey thought, for their purposes. It appeared to back onto the street where the safe house was. By the time he reached his car, he had called the estate agents and arranged to view the property the following morning. Then he drove back to the West End to meet Dulay at his hotel.

Dulay had a pleasant room overlooking Hyde Park. De Jersey and he sat at a small table by the window.

"Pigeon went home to roost. It's a building in the Barbican, small back street, not far from Smithfield market, and it's smack on a corner," de

Jersey said, drawing the safe house on a square of paper from his note-book. "Getting into it won't be the problem. It's knowing what we'll be confronted with once we're inside." He passed the drawing to Dulay, who glanced at it, then jabbed with his stubby finger.

"D'Ancona will have it secured like Fort Knox. They'll have cameras on the outside. How the hell do you think you're gonna get in without being seen, especially on a corner?"

De Jersey repeated that that was not the problem. It was the layout in-side the house that he needed to know. "What would you say I'm up against?"

"Well, there are usually two reinforced doors as an external entry sys-tem, then another door leading into the foyer. I've been to a couple of their locations, and there were always several inches of bulletproof glass. They will have a sophisticated phone system to link the safes and selection rooms and even the fitting rooms. There may also be another set of doors, maybe three or four, to get into the inner sanctum. They have panic but-tons dotted around like M&M's. I doubt they'll have a walk-in safe in a safe house, but I could be wrong."

De Jersey ripped up the drawing. "I take it you're in."

Dulay nodded. "Yeah, I'm in."

"Okay, what about your Japanese buyer?"

"I've contacted him. All I said was that I might get my hands on one of the most famous and largest diamonds in existence. I said I'd be looking for around a million a carat."

De Jersey smiled. The Koh-i-noor was 105.6 carats.

"He said he'd be in the market for something of that price, and any other stones. I could get the Koh-i-noor cut by my lapidary, but if we sell to my Japanese buyer, he'd want it uncut. Buyers like him are interested in the stone's size and history."

"Maybe we don't touch the Koh-i-noor, but we're going to have other stones of immense size and value. Can you trust the lapidary?"

"I'd trust him with my life. We've worked together for twenty years. Even so, to move the stuff fast means he'll be working day and night alter-ing the stones and putting them into new settings so they'll be untrace-able. I need a nice cash incentive for him."

"How much are we looking at?"

"Maybe a quarter of a million. If we do end up cutting the Koh-i-noor, he's the right man for the job. It would take weeks to do, and we'd have to pay him extra to disguise it without dropping its value. We can transform it from an oval into a pear shape by tapering it at the back. I've listed gem dealers worldwide where we can spread the other stones. I've got contacts in New York, Antwerp, and India."

Occasionally the Frenchman would run his finger round the collar of his shirt. De Jersey listened, aware that Dulay was leading up to the subject of his cut.

"How honest are the D'Ancona employees?" de Jersey asked. "I think we might need an insider and wondered if it was a possibility."

"Well, I was one." Dulay shrugged. "I'd say the top brass would be un-bribable—you only get to the top at D'Ancona by being above suspicion. But there are always the underlings. It's all in the choosing. You get the wrong type and they'll blab."

"Could anyone in the safe house be skimming?" asked de Jersey.

Dulay looked doubtful. "If they're dealing with such top-quality gear, there's no way. These guys are working by appointment to the Queen. That rep you followed had to be carrying in some heavy-duty stones, with his briefcase chained to his wrist."

This wasn't what de Jersey wanted to hear, so he changed the subject. "How's the boat?"

"The fucking money pit?" Dulay said angrily. "That's partly why I'm here. It's costing me a fortune."

"If I needed to use it, would you be up for it?"

"If the price is right."

"Not for charter, for the pickup."

Dulay sucked in his breath. "Woooooh! This is drawing me in closer than I want to be."

"Not if it's, say, chartered to a company. We can use your crew. Can you trust them?"

"Sure, but it depends what they have to do—and they'll cost."

"They won't know what they're doing. You and I will."

Dulay tapped the table with his knuckle. "When would this company charter the floating palace?"

"I'll need it ready for the first week in May."

Dulay crossed to the minifridge. Suddenly he was not quite so confident. "So it's May, is it?"

"I haven't got the exact dates, nor have I worked out how I want to use the boat, but make sure it's crewed up and ready."

Dulay scooped a handful of ice into his vodka, then returned to the table. "I want a heavy slice, Philip. If I'm going in this deep, I want to be paid big bucks. I've brought you the buyer and now you want me to get the boat ready. So how do we work the payoff?"

"You'll get a split. Not a payoff, a split. We can't do it without you. How does that sound?"

Dulay drank thirstily. "Good, but I need cash up front to start getting the shop prepared for the work we'll have to do. Extra furnaces, a smelting kiln for the gold. It all costs."

De Jersey agreed to pay him ten thousand. "I'll also need some assurance from the buyer. All I have is your word that he's interested. Don't take this the wrong way, because I do trust you."

"That's big of you, considering how far I've gone already."

"Calm down. It makes sense, though, doesn't it? We need our buyer to put himself on the line with us. If he wants the Koh-i-noor, we want a cash incentive from him to know he's trustworthy."

"We can trust him. He's worth billions, and I'm vouching for him, for Chrissakes."

"Not good enough. We want a million per carat, and we want a million in cash up front as a down payment or we might sell to someone else."

"He's not gonna go for it." Dulay drained his glass.

"If he wants it, he's rich enough to make sure he gets it."

Dulay was pulling at his thinning hair. "Okay, I'll put it to him, but you can't mess him around. Like I told you before, I don't wanna turn up as chopped liver."

"Put it to him, or if you don't want to, I will."

Dulay hesitated. "Okay, let's see what he says."

"Is he still in Paris?"

"Yes. I'll fly out this afternoon."

As soon as Dulay was in his car, de Jersey called Wilcox. He wanted to check out Dulay and, more important, his buyer, so he needed Wilcox to tail him from the London hotel to Paris.

"You've never met Dulay, have you?"

"Tony did once, but I never have. What time have I got to be there?"

"Go straight to the airport and wait."

Wilcox sighed. "I've only just got in from Leicester, Eddy."

"So, make a trip of it. Take your woman."

De Jersey took the warehouse for a year and paid six months' rent in advance in the name of Philip Simmons. Also through the agents, he gained, with some financial persuasion, access to the drawings of the D'Ancona building. For security reasons, no single party ever held a complete layout of a safe house, so all he found out was the size of the building, the rear door area, and small backyard. The drawings showed that the building had four floors and a basement. He could not discover anything about the work inside, though four years previously the owners had been granted planning permission by the council for the installation of undisclosed security measures. D'Ancona had covered their tracks; any attempt to find out details of these "undisclosed security measures" would alert the company to a possible problem. De Jersey had to find another way of gaining an interior plan of the safe house.

Driving through Aldgate into the East End, he called Driscoll and told him to monitor the D'Ancona safe house. He had spied the perfect observation post. The warehouse had a flat roof, and from there Driscoll could watch the safe house without being seen.

"I got a lot going on right now," Driscoll said, sounding tired.

"And I haven't?" snapped de Jersey.

"Why can't Jimmy do it?"

"He's tailing Dulay, who's meeting up with our buyer. I just want to make sure he's on the level."

"The buyer or Dulay?"

"Both."

"So I got to schlep over to this warehouse now? The wife is gonna have a fit."

De Jersey was impatient to get on. He told Driscoll where he would find the keys to the warehouse and hung up.

When he got home de Jersey was unprepared for Christina's concern. She had contacted the horse breeders in Ireland, only to hear they were not expecting him. Her concern quickly turned to anger, though. Every time she had tried his cell phone, it was turned off. It was irresponsible to go off without leaving a contact number. She told him that her mother was ill and she had to leave for Sweden.

"You should have just gone, darling," he said.

"*You* should have called home."

"I didn't think."

"No, you didn't. I want to know why you lied about going to Dublin."

"I didn't."

"Freddy said you weren't even expected."

"I wasn't with him."

"I don't understand."

"I don't buy all my horses from Freddy. Sometimes I want it kept under wraps exactly what I'm thinking of buying. I'm sorry. It won't happen again."

"You've always got such good excuses for disappearing." She sighed. "I've been so worried about my mother. You've not been fair." Christina hesitated to voice her suspicions, but she couldn't help blurting out, "Are you seeing someone?"

De Jersey was genuinely shocked that she could even consider it a possibility. "Of course not! No woman could ever—"

"Well, why have you been taking so many clothes from your wardrobe then? You take them each trip and they never come back. I checked because I wondered if anything needed to go to the cleaners. Two suits are missing and several shirts." She folded her arms.

De Jersey had left the clothes at his Kilburn flat but came up with an excuse fast. "I gave them to a couple of the trainers. Ask them if you want proof, but this is so unlike you, Christina. I've never given you any reason to think I might be having an affair."

She burst into tears. He held her close. "Get your things packed. We'll put you on the first plane out to see your family. There's not another woman in the world I would so much as look at."

He arranged for his pilot to fly her to the airport. He knew he must take greater precautions from now on, especially since he would need to spend more time away from the estate. It was already early February, and if they were to go ahead on the second of May, they had to work fast.

Wilcox called from Paris just after four o'clock. He and Rika had caught the same plane as Dulay and had followed him to the Ritz.

"I had to book in, Eddy, just for a night. Anyway, it got Rika out of my hair. Dulay didn't check in. He went straight to the desk. They handed him the house phone, he spoke briefly, then went into the coffee bar. About ten minutes later this huge guy appeared. Looked like Odd Job man in the James Bond movie. He had a few words with Dulay, then they went out to the foyer." Wilcox explained how he had followed Dulay out of the hotel, where he had had a conversation inside a parked Mercedes with another man, presumably their buyer.

"He's tall for a Jap," Wilcox said. " 'Bout five eleven, well built, snappy dresser. Odd Job was hovering around, so he's got to be the bodyguard."

"Jimmy, did you get his address? Who the fuck is this guy?"

"I got it from the porter. He's a regular guest. Comes over five or six times a year. He's a computer giant. His company's worth billions, and he's based in Tokyo. His name is Mr. Kitamo—"

"That's all I need to know right now."

"That's what we should have put our money into, computer software."

"Well, we didn't! Talk to you later—"

"He'll probably have a Web site—"

"Jimmy, get off the phone."

"Try searching the Web for Kitamo triple K computer software and—"

"Jimmy, go screw your girlfriend!" de Jersey snapped, ending the call.

De Jersey spent the rest of the day with his jockeys, trainers, and managers. The cost of the heist so far was straining his resources. It would be paid back by the Moreno sale, but that was still not liquid. He gave instructions for two more horses to be sold, which hurt him and perplexed the managers and trainers. Looking over the accounts later, he saw that even with the sale of another eight racehorses and two brood mares, he could not keep the estate going for more than four months. It was imperative that he pull off the heist.

That afternoon Fleming took Royal Flush out on the gallops for de Jersey to watch. He was in stunning form. However, that night de Jersey couldn't sleep. He was overtired, with a head full of plans. He went to his study for some brandy. Eventually he walked outside.

It was a clear, cold night, and his breath steamed. He was jolted out of his dark reverie by Fleming, who was hunched in his overcoat.

"Can't sleep?"

De Jersey shook his head.

"Me neither," Fleming said.

They walked in silence for a while, then stood against the fence that surrounded the grazing paddock.

"You have problems, haven't you?"

De Jersey nodded.

"It's obvious with the pick of your crop being sold off. It's breaking my heart."

"Mine too, but I'm in a deep hole." He paused. "I have a friend in Ireland, Michael Shaughnessy, not a big breeder but a good man."

"I don't think I know him," said Fleming.

"He keeps a low profile," de Jersey said. He wondered how Fleming would react to what he was about to propose. He guessed that he'd have to make it worth his while with cash. It usually came down to that.

When he quietly suggested to the trainer what he had in mind, Fleming was so shocked he could hardly speak.

"We'd get a nice kickback—in fact, a blinding one. She's the best filly I've ever had."

"Sweet Jesus! He's the best too. You know what this could do, sir. Illegally covering a mare is a terrible risk to take."

"We keep him separated directly afterward, then push his training up."

"It could be disastrous."

De Jersey kicked at the ground. "You're right, forget it."

But Fleming put his hand on de Jersey's arm. "We'll need three of us. My son'll help, but we have to keep this quiet. We'll do it at night, when the yard's silent. If it ever got out . . ."

De Jersey put his arm round Fleming's shoulders. "Well, we hope something will come out, and I guarantee Shaughnessy will most definitely want something out of it."

It was almost one in the morning. The two men talked for another half hour, then shook hands. Fleming would receive ten thousand in cash, but the mare had to be in foal or there was no deal. They would ship the filly out to Dublin for Shaughnessy to collect and stable, de Jersey said. No one would know. They shook hands a second time. Both men knew that what they were doing might spoil the chances of the greatest horse de Jersey had ever possessed. They returned to their beds, depressed.

Driscoll and Wilcox were now taking turns monitoring the safe house. Wilcox found it tedious, irritating work, but Driscoll didn't mind; it gave him something other than the escalating wedding costs to think about.

When Wilcox was not on surveillance he had been scouting out other locations for the vehicles to be parked. They would not be placed in the Aldersgate warehouse until the day before the heist. He eventually found a disused barn in the Surrey countryside. This was also where the team would gather to complete preparations for the raid.

Wilcox had discovered various costumiers around the country where he could hire authentic police-motorcyclist uniforms. He would pretend to be employed by a film company when he needed them. He had also acquired two motorbikes, which he was respraying to match the Metropolitan Police ones. Driscoll was assigned to find two shotguns and several small handguns. As he had a personal arsenal, he decided he'd remove the numbers from some of his own licensed guns so they could not be traced back to him.

Raymond Marsh arrived at the Scotland Yard telephone exchange at eight forty-five, as he had every morning that week. He had arranged to do the regular maintenance check on the exchange's telephone lines. He would spend the next two weeks there, checking the main systems, and return at regular intervals to do spot checks. Scotland Yard's telephone exchange handled the lines for the Yard exclusively. Marsh had been provided with the password, security code, and an electronic card to allow him access to all areas of the building.

The basement held the batteries and the equipment, the middle floor housed the computer systems, and the administration was on the top floor. The day after his last meeting with de Jersey, Marsh had gained access to the master computer and had quickly located the twenty-four lines responsible for all incoming and outgoing calls to Royalty and Diplomatic Protection. Today would be the first opportunity for him to set up a tail on these lines; all calls made and received by the department would be logged, with incoming and outgoing numbers.

Once he had set up the tail, Marsh began to monitor and record the calls. If he was caught he would be fired, or worse. By the start of his second week at the exchange, Marsh had worked out who was responsible for liaising with the Palace and confirming that security measures were in place.

When de Jersey received an e-mail from Marsh informing him of his progress, he had an adrenaline rush. They were a step closer to executing the robbery, and it was time for his second meeting with Lord Westbrook. His lordship answered the phone and gave an audible sigh of relief. "Thank God. I was beginning to think you'd got cold feet."

"You received payment, though, didn't you?"

"Yes. Thank you."

"We need to meet. Do you know Shepperton?"

"Yes."

"Go to Church Square. There's a bench in front of a small waterfront mooring. We'll meet there, then go to the pub for lunch."

"Fine. When?"

"Tomorrow, midday."

When de Jersey called, Wilcox was in bed with a bad cold. "I've got something I need checked out."

"I'm sick."

De Jersey continued as if he hadn't heard him. "I want you to check out an address in Esher, but don't approach the property, just monitor who's coming and going. Mark it out, front and back, and ascertain if only the woman and her husband are living there. Then report back to me."

"You want it done tonight, then?"

"Yes." He gave the address.

"I've got a terrible cold. I'm in bed."

"Then wrap up," de Jersey snapped. Both Driscoll and Wilcox worried him, but he said no more and hung up. Then he went over his meticulous lists, ticking off each item he had dealt with. They still had no lady-in-waiting.

Wilcox was freezing. Number 23 was a neat house with a large pond in the front garden. A garage stood to one side with a clean red Toyota parked on the pink-and-white-squared drive. Wilcox walked past on the far side of the road first, making it look as if he was searching for a specific address. As he crossed the road to make his way back, the door opened at 23. A bald man was wrapping a scarf around his neck, shrugging on a camel coat, his car keys in his hand. Then a small woman, wearing a blue coat and a woolen hat, came out.

"Eric, did you lock the back door?" she called.

"Yes."

She shut the front door and headed for the passenger door of the Toyota, which her husband held open for her. "I don't want to stay too long," she said. As she got into the car, her face was lit clearly by the streetlights. Wilcox's jaw dropped, but he did not stop.

Eric started the engine, and they drove out past him. The woman was talking, looking ahead. He could hardly believe it; she was the Queen's exact double.

Now, with the occupants gone, Wilcox was able to have a good look round. He headed up the path and rang the front doorbell, peering inside as if he expected someone to be at home. He even called, "Eric?" Then he went round to the back and did the same, checking the path, the kitchen, and the windows. He saw no one, so he returned to his car and called de Jersey.

De Jersey was alone, smoking, when his cell phone vibrated. He knew it was Wilcox from the hacking cough.

"It's easy access both back and front, and I had a good look as the occupants left. Only the two of them live there. The back door's hidden from the other houses by a big hedgerow. The front is visible to the neighbors."

"Mmm, good. You still there?"

"On my way home."

"You see her, then?"

Wilcox sneezed. "It's freaky. She's the image of her, identical."

"She makes her living as her double."

"We kidnap her, then?" Wilcox asked.

"No. We offer her a job first," de Jersey said.

"I don't understand." Wilcox sniffed.

"She's our way in, Jimmy, that's all you need to know right now."

De Jersey was exhausted, but before he went to bed he called Christina. She told him she'd have to remain in Sweden for some time as her mother had been diagnosed with a severe form of cancer and was undergoing chemotherapy. De Jersey offered to join her, but she refused. Although he wasn't glad her mother was sick, his wife's absence would leave him free to focus on the robbery.

17

Lord Westbrook was already waiting in Church Square at Shepperton. De Jersey was taken aback by the change in him: he was gray with fatigue. He sat on the iron bench by the riverbank, hunched in his coat, a cigarette dangling from his bluish lips.

"You all right?" de Jersey asked and sat next to him.

"Been burning the candle at both ends," Westbrook joked, but his eyes—dull with exhaustion—betrayed him.

"I have a list of queries," de Jersey said crisply.

Westbrook reached beneath the bench for his briefcase. "I have tried to ascertain all that you want to know."

"Look, why don't we go over to the George? They've a comfortable lounge there. We can order coffee."

"Thank God, I'm freezing." Westbrook stood up and dropped his case. De Jersey scooped it up under his arm. "Thank you," said Westbrook.

In the pub de Jersey chose a window seat away from the bar.

"Shall I order some coffee, something to eat?" Westbrook asked.

"I'll just have a coffee."

De Jersey spread out Westbrook's notes and studied them while Westbrook ordered coffee, cigarettes, and chicken sandwiches from the friendly bar staff, but de Jersey was watching him out of the corner of his eye as Westbrook went into the men's restroom.

When he returned, his eyes were red-rimmed. He sat down heavily. "Fire away," he said laconically, his face shiny from sweat. He had a coughing fit as their order was brought to the table. De Jersey poured coffee for them both and passed a cup to Westbrook. He took a few sips then bit hungrily into a sandwich, all the time holding his cigarette.

"Right, let's get started," de Jersey said.

Westbrook swung his legs onto the cushioned window seat. He continued to eat at an alarming rate. He then gulped at his coffee and lit another cigarette. "We do have a deal, correct?" he asked.

"Yes, of course."

"I've been thinking. I'd hate to snuff it and not get what's due to me if you pull it off. I was wondering if you could draw up something for me in the name of my son. We are talking about big money here, aren't we?"

"Yes, but as you just said, it depends on whether we pull it off. So making out a contract is impossible. All I can give you is the agreed amount for the preparation. If we're successful, you will get your cut."

"You're asking a lot on the old trust market."

"Not really. We're all protecting each other's identities, so you're not likely to be swindled."

"All right. But if I snuff it, who will make sure my son gets my share?"

"I will." De Jersey stared hard at him.

"Okay." Westbrook swung down his feet. De Jersey drew his pages of questions toward him and unscrewed the top of his gold Cartier pen. "Who would accompany the Queen on such a visit?"

"An equerry. He's a member of the small but select team responsible for the detailed planning and execution of the daily program. They support H.M. in her official duties and private life."

"You can carry that off, be this equerry?"

"Oh, yes, that's my background, absolutely. Good family connections and all that stuff. Equerries are seconded from the armed forces after three years. They wear a uniform during H.M.'s daytime engagements when they're in personal attendance. I still have my uniform, so no worries there. Though often it's not necessary. H.M. will say, "No medals today," that sort of thing, so then it's just a smart suit. Did I mention I was based in the Royal Mews at Buck House? I co-coordinated transport for H.M. Now, if it's a state occasion, the ponies and traps are out, but for something like this, a fitting, it'll just be her in a Daimler and another following."

"And she would use a Daimler. You're sure?"

"Oh, yes."

"The mascot—" de Jersey began.

Westbrook slapped the table with the flat of his hand. "Very important. The Queen's vehicle has to have her silver St. George and the dragon on it."

"I believe one of my team has already copied it. Who else besides the equerry would be with her?"

"Well, she'd have a lady-in-waiting, who deals with the handbag and flowers and acts as a part-time secretary, answering letters and so on."

"Would she be around the same age as the Queen?"

"Usually. She'll be well-dressed, pleasant, nothing that sticks out. A fade-into-the-background type."

They continued discussing the lineup, which became tedious as Westbrook went off on irrelevant tangents. However, sick or not, he was indispensable.

Later that day de Jersey called Christina to see how her mother was. The news was not good.

"She's dying. I'm going to talk to my father about stopping the treatment altogether. She's in such pain, and as the doctors don't hold out much hope, it seems wrong to subject her to it."

"It must be terrible for you. I wish I could do something to help."

He hung up feeling depressed and went for a walk. His thoughts wandered to Lord Westbrook. He hadn't looked good that morning. Just how sick was he? The equerry had to be fit and well to be convincing.

He headed for a public telephone kiosk and rang Raymond Marsh. His wife answered, and then Marsh spoke.

"Who is this? Mr. Simmons, right? About time. We gonna meet?"

"I hope so. You free tonight?"

"Yep, and have I got news for you! Can you come to my place?"

De Jersey followed Marsh down a hallway with carpet so thick he felt as if he was wading through soft mud. Marsh was wearing skintight drainpipe trousers with thick-soled suede shoes in a shocking pink. They matched his shirt, which he wore with a skinny strip of leather as a tie.

"Come upstairs." He led the way up the stairs, past posters from all of Elvis's films. At the end of the landing Marsh opened a door and gestured for de Jersey to walk in. Inside there were banks of computers, a mass of cables, overflowing ashtrays, and pizza boxes.

Marsh said, "This is my office. As you can see, it's all state-of-the-art equipment, worth thousands."

"How have you been getting on at the exchange?"

Marsh produced a cheap canvas bag and dumped it on his desk. "Good. I've made printouts for you to take away, plus tape recordings. The IRA call in every morning at a designated time. They have ten lines, which they use in a certain pattern. They call the first line one day, the second the next, and when they get up to the tenth they go into reverse. I think I've predicted which line will be used on the day of the heist as long as they don't change their pattern—but we've got plenty of time to see if they do."

"Good work. What about the link between Scotland Yard and the safe house? What conversations have already taken place? Who has placed calls and to whom?"

"No contact yet concerning security for the fitting, but the date's still a long way off. I expect something soon."

De Jersey was impressed that so far Marsh was coming up aces at every meeting. Marsh wouldn't let go of the canvas bag, though, and said determinedly, "It looks to me like I've got a pretty hefty role in this, and I'm not doing it for the joy of hacking. We need to talk about my cut."

"Okay. We now know that the main piece we'll get our hands on will be sold for close to sixty million, and we'll get more for the rest of the jewels," de Jersey lied, knowing it would be considerably more.

Marsh wanted to be assured of at least ten million, plus the thousand a week, which de Jersey agreed to. Then Marsh tossed over the canvas bag, saying, "Closer to the day of the fitting, the commander of the RDPD will liaise with D'Ancona about security procedures. I can identify the line to the safe house, and I'll be intercepting the call to notify them that the Queen's visit has been canceled."

The two continued working through the plan. Once Marsh secured the code word for the second of May, he would pass it on to de Jersey. De Jersey, posing as an IRA informant, would call the police using the code word and make a bomb threat that would be deemed genuine. Scotland Yard would call the Palace, and all Royal proceedings would halt immediately. Marsh would be waiting for the commander to call the safe house to cancel the visit, and when the call was placed, he would break into the line and answer it himself. The head of security at the safe house would still be expecting the Queen.

"I'll get to the exchange before six A.M., and I'll stay there until about ten thirty, when you'll be taking care of matters," Marsh said. "I'll keep a check on the lines just in case anyone has noticed anything dodgy." He sucked in his breath. "Get out of the safe house as fast as you can; they won't take long to figure it out. Palace security are gonna keep checking for clearance. You'll have ten to fifteen minutes to pull this off."

De Jersey knew Marsh's physical presence in the exchange would be risky. "We'll be as quick as possible," he said. "Straight in and out. Any way you can get a layout of inside the safe house?"

"You're telling me you've made all these plans and you still don't know what the interior is like? That's fucking nuts! It's imperative you know what the layout is."

"Why? We're going in through the front door. There's no problem. We just need to know where the vault is."

Marsh pointed a finger at de Jersey and said angrily, "This is an amateur's night out, mate."

De Jersey's mouth tightened. "Not necessarily."

"I just hope to God the other guys know what the fuck they're doing. You can't seriously contemplate busting into this place if you don't know what's gonna be waiting for you. Can you get to someone on the inside?" Marsh paused. "Listen, I might be able to help you out, but I can't promise nothing. Maybe I'll find something that shows their security system layout. If it's on a computer somewhere, I can get to it."

"How long do you need?" de Jersey asked, worried. Marsh's remarks had hit home.

Marsh grinned. "How much are you prepared to pay?"

De Jersey sat pondering the plans. He didn't feel much better after a good night's rest. The interaction with Marsh had unnerved him. "Amateur?" His wallet was also hurting. He'd better come up with the goods after that last payment. De Jersey still had to find a suitable woman to assume the role of the lady-in-waiting and persuade the Queen's look-alike to take part. He was also short of the two bikers. Perhaps he should use the Internet again. He sighed.

De Jersey caught a train back to his estate. He needed to unwind; the tranquillity of the house soothed him as he wandered from room to room.

He was sitting at his desk when Christina called. Her mother had died that afternoon. She spoke incoherently through her tears. Her mother had been only sixty-two. De Jersey was gentle and understanding. After he hung up, he contacted Driscoll to say the plans would be halted for a few days. Driscoll seemed relieved that the funeral would take place over the same weekend as his daughter's wedding. Then de Jersey phoned Wilcox, now really sick with flu and unable to move. He too was relieved that de Jersey was taking time away. Neither man mentioned the heist, and de Jersey wondered if they were still having doubts.

The truth was, he had lost confidence that they would be able to pull this off. After his meeting with Marsh, all he could see were the holes, and what a weird mix his team members were: Driscoll, the cocaine addict Wilcox, the cancer-riddled Lord Westbrook, the pockmarked Gregory Jones, the egotistical Raymond Marsh, and the nervous Paul Dulay. Add to that the cost to date, and he felt sick.

*　*　*

Throughout the flight to Sweden the next day, de Jersey sat with his eyes closed, going over details that were now so familiar it was like turning the pages of a book he knew by heart. He was interrupted by the flight attendant offering refreshments and the newspapers. He took *The Times,* the *Express,* and the *Daily Mail.* In the *Express,* an article caught his eye. Two elderly spinsters had conned the equestrian circuit out of thousands of pounds. A picture showing them beaming into the camera, holding a winner's cup and rosette, triggered a memory. He tried to calculate how old Pamela Kenworthy-Wright must be now. They had met in the seventies through a mutual friend. Pamela had been a RADA-trained actress and married a wealthy stockbroker, whom she had later divorced for his infidelity with a manservant. Afterward she had tried to resurrect her acting career and appeared in a couple of TV series, but in the late eighties she was arrested for shoplifting in Harrods, which resulted in a stint in Holloway women's prison for credit-card fraud. He smiled to himself. Pamela might be just the woman he needed, but first he had to find her.

The funeral was a small affair with just the widower, Christina's siblings, and their children in attendance. Though Christina was pale, she maintained her composure, apart from shedding a few tears. De Jersey was attentive and caring, and father and daughter were grateful for his support. When de Jersey proposed that Christina stay on to deal with her mother's belongings and to help settle her father in a smaller house, both deemed it a thoughtful suggestion. He even offered to remain with her, but she knew he had pressing business in London and, as de Jersey had hoped, refused his offer. He loved Christina, but time was moving on. His team was still incomplete, and most important, he still did not have the layout for the safe house.

It was after midnight. Driscoll's daughter was safely on her way to her honeymoon while her father sat by one of the specially installed outdoor heaters near his lily pond. It was full of streamers, confetti, and cigarette stubs, but he could have cared less. His head throbbed—he'd had too much to drink, though he didn't feel drunk—and his gut was on fire.

"It's Tony, isn't it?" said the burly figure in the green security uniform.

"Do I know you?"

"Been twenty years, maybe more. I'm Brian Hall."

Driscoll didn't recognize the guy.

"Used to work for you, long time ago, when you had that waste-disposal company. You did me a big favor. I was on parole, needed work; you gave me a job, even though you knew I had a criminal record."

"Sure. So, how're things?" Driscoll asked, not really caring.

"I get a bit of work here and there. Been with this company for a few years, but I'm a reserve. They pull me in when they need extra hands, like for this kind of gig." He gestured to the wedding remnants around him.

"Did you stay clean?" Driscoll asked.

Hall shook his head, laughing softly. "I tried for a while, but when you've got a wife and three kids, you've gotta do what you've gotta do, know what I mean? I got my fingers burnt a few times more. I've only been out ten months."

Driscoll reached into his pocket for his wallet, but Hall laid a hand on his arm. "Oh, no, I'm not looking for a handout. I just wanted to thank you."

"Fancy a drink?" Driscoll asked.

"Not while I'm on duty."

"Who's to see you? Besides, I hired you."

They walked back to the bar in the marquee. Driscoll found a half-full bottle of brandy, picked up two glasses, and made his way to the corner of the patio. "Brandy suit you?"

"Yeah."

Driscoll divided the bottle between them, then proffered a cigar, and they lit up, sitting in the darkness with the music still banging away.

"I don't suppose you've got any work going?" Hall asked.

"Not really. I'm semiretired," Driscoll said, then gestured to the gardens and the house. "But don't think all this is safe and secure. I'm skint. I made a bad business deal and got screwed out of all my savings."

"I'm sorry," Hall said. "I've got a little sideline, though, if you need any heavy work—know what I mean? If these people that screwed you on this business deal need sorting, me and my pal Kenny Short, we do contracts. Not the really heavy stuff, but we certainly put some pressure on."

Driscoll remained silent.

"Hope you don't mind me asking. It was just a thought."

An idea slipped into Driscoll's mind. It sat there for a while before he said quietly, "You know, I just might have a nice earner for you. Can this Kenny geezer be trusted?"

"With my life!" Hall said.

"Gimme a contact number and maybe I'll be in touch. I'll have to talk it over with a pal first, all right?"

Back in England after the funeral, de Jersey turned his attention to tracking Pamela Kenworthy-Wright. He quickly established that she was no longer a member of Equity, then discovered in the telephone directory that three people had the same last name and initials. When he called the first, the phone was answered by an upper-crust military type: "Peter Kenworthy-Wright speaking." De Jersey hung up and tried the second number. This time he spoke to an elderly lady, who said Miss Petal Kenworthy-Wright was out walking her dog. The third time, the phone rang twice.

"Hello?"

"Miss Pamela Kenworthy-Wright?"

"For my sins, yes, it is. Who is this?"

"I'm doing a census inquiry for the government with regard to people living in your area and claiming unemployment benefits."

"Oh, God, this really is an invasion of one's privacy."

"Do you own a computer?"

"Yes, I do. I also vote Conservative, I smoke, and I'm divorced. Now piss off."

"Were you an actress?"

"I still am."

"Thank you very much."

He hung up before she could start asking questions.

De Jersey thought his run-down flat in Kilburn was a palace compared to Pamela's bedsit in a converted fort in Plymouth. To gain access to the apartments you had to cross a drawbridge. The main courtyard was filled with boarded-up huts. Stray dogs and cats scuttled around stinking trash bags. Broken sinks, lavatories, and fridges littered the cold, damp corridors. The stench of urine pervaded the stairs and the second-floor corridor leading to number 20. There was a sign that read, "Do not disturb before eleven A.M., thank you." De Jersey smiled and rapped on the door.

"Who is it?" demanded an authoritative, aristocratic voice.

"Philip Simmons." De Jersey heard the lock slide back, and the door was edged open.

"Are you from Social Services?"

"No."

"So what do you want?"

"To talk to you. I met you a long time ago." He smiled pleasantly.

"Well, I don't recognize you and I'm very busy right now."

"Please, Miss Kenworthy-Wright, this may prove lucrative for us both."

"Do you have identification?"

He produced a driving license in the name of Simmons.

"Come in. I need my reading glasses."

He followed her into the flat, which was better furnished than he had expected. There was a good-quality rug and comfortable leather armchairs, a computer, a large TV set, and a gas fire, which made the room very warm. A few large oil paintings of men in wigs and a dour-faced woman dominated the walls. A sofa bed with an orange duvet was dangerously close to the fire.

Pamela was wearing a velvet dressing gown over her skinny frame with rabbit-fur slippers. She delved into a cloth bag for her glasses, held them to her nose, glanced at the license, and passed it back. "What do you want?"

"May I sit down?"

She shrugged, sitting in the chair opposite him. Her face was heavily wrinkled, and lipstick rivulets ran from her thin lips in rows of tiny red lines. Only her eyes, a wonderful china blue, retained a spark of brightness. Her hair, various shades of dark auburn tinged with gray, was dyed, probably by herself.

"I can't for the life of me think what I could have that would be of any interest to a nice strapping man like you. I like your shoes."

"You're a technological lady?"

"Yes. I had computer training in prison," she said, without embarrassment. "I'm quite proficient. I'm writing a book about my life. It would be so nice if you were here about that. I did send off a first chapter to all and sundry, but I've not heard a squeak back." She lit a cigarette.

"I'm not here about your book."

"Pity, that was really why I let you in, but we all have these fantasies. You know, dreams of overnight success. Couple of small parts in *The Avengers* wasn't going to take me to Hollywood, but at the time I believed it might. I was in it with Honor Blackman."

"I met you with Victor Markham, back in the seventies," de Jersey said.

"Did you? He's been dead for years. Of course, after my problems I lost touch with a lot of the old crowd. You said something about . . . lucrative—was that the word you used? I'm running out of pleasantries, Mr. Simmons. I'm waiting with bated breath."

"I may have a proposition for you."

She laughed a smoker's throaty laugh, revealing coffee-stained teeth. "Well, talk, dear boy. I'm in need of anything that'll make me a bob or two." She gave a sly smile. "It's not legal, is it?"

"No."

"Anyone who knew Victor Markham was bent. So why are you here, Mr. Simmons?"

"I need you to impersonate someone."

"And what would it be worth to me?"

"More than you would get from any publishing deal. I'll need you to stay in London. I have a place—it's not very comfortable, but it would only be for a short time."

"Mmmm. I think I'd rather like a gin. Can I offer you one?"

On his return to Kilburn, de Jersey rented a small studio in Maida Vale and arranged for the keys to be sent to his Kilburn address. His cell phone rang. It was Driscoll.

"How are you doing?" de Jersey asked.

"I think I've got your motorbike riders," Driscoll said thickly.

"You don't sound like yourself," de Jersey said warily.

"Got a hangover, but I'd say these guys are the real thing. You wanna check them out?"

"Yes."

"I'll arrange a meet. Tomorrow morning?"

"Fine, what time?"

"Lemme get back to you."

De Jersey switched off the phone.

It rang again. This time it was Wilcox. "How we doing?" he asked, sounding perky.

"I'm fine, and you sound a lot better."

"I am. Few days in bed sorted me out. I think we should meet at the barn so I can show you what I've been up to."

"Fine. Tomorrow?"

"Let's say seven, make it really early."

"Seven it is. See you there."

Driscoll and Wilcox were both moving things forward just like the old days. De Jersey liked that. They were starting to be more of a team.

Just after seven the next morning, de Jersey met with Wilcox. He parked by a thick hedgerow and walked toward the large barn, which had huge double doors. Wilcox opened them and came out. "I saw you drawing up. It's freezing in here, but we're pretty secure."

De Jersey followed him in and closed the door. The vehicles, shrouded in big white sheets, were parked in the center of the barn. Beside them were the two bikes, also draped in sheets. Next to them was a trestle table with the weapons, the mascot for the Queen's car, and so on.

"This looks good. And the nearest farm is, what? Two miles north?" de Jersey queried.

"The two houses at the top of the drive are empty, so we can come and go. Nobody's gonna be around."

Wilcox pulled the sheet off one of the Daimlers, which gleamed. "I'm almost finished with the upholstery. I've got a guy making up the seats. He has no idea what they're for, and I can collect them in a couple of weeks. The color is close enough. Dark maroon, right?"

De Jersey walked around the car. "Tony says he thinks he's got the bike riders. I'm going to meet them this morning."

They went to a small back room area, screened off from the main barn. Wilcox had collected a few chairs, a kettle, and coffee mugs.

"We'll need some heaters in here," de Jersey said.

"I'll get one of those big ones they use on film sets." Wilcox sniffed. His nose was running.

De Jersey wondered if this newfound energy was not a return to health but, in fact, chemically fueled.

"You want the surveillance details me and Tony have been working on?" Wilcox asked.

"Fire away."

"We've been taking turns monitoring the safe house, and we've got the following regular workers and visitors. Two females, one about twenty-five, the other middle-aged. Three males, mid-thirties, and two white-haired men. Four security guards. Two come on early morning, two at night. Four other men turned up, but they weren't regulars." Wilcox laid out photographs of each one. Even if he was still doing coke, de Jersey could not fault his preparations. If anything, he himself was lagging. He felt uneasy when Wilcox pressed him for details about the interior of the safe house.

"We'll discuss all that at the first big meet. I need a few days. Good work, James."

"Not got it together yet, then?"

"Almost, but it's taking more time than I thought. I'm getting there, though."

"I sincerely hope so, old chap. Time's moving on." They gave each other a brotherly hug. "So, what's next for me?" Wilcox asked.

"Just get the vehicles ready."

"We're on course, are we?"

De Jersey hesitated a beat before he answered. "Yeah, we're on course, James."

Later that morning, de Jersey met with Driscoll and Brian Hall and Kenny Short. De Jersey suggested they take a ride on an open-top bus, and the four men were the only occupants of the top deck. As they stared out at the sights of London, de Jersey—as Simmons—questioned Hall, then Short. When they parted, he tapped Driscoll's arm and said softly, "Nice work. They seem steady guys."

Driscoll nodded. "I reckon we'll have no problems. They agreed to the fee, and I trust them. I have to, cos Hall knows where I live."

"Right," de Jersey said. In the old days, Tony Driscoll would have moved house. Fortunately de Jersey did not have to. No one new coming into the team had the slightest notion who he was.

When de Jersey called to say he was arranging a meeting for the following week, Westbrook had been having migraines that left him so weak he could hardly lift a cigarette to his lips. De Jersey's call lifted the pain and cleared his head abruptly. He didn't know if it was terror or having something else to think about. He wasn't scared; there was nothing to be scared of. He was dying anyway.

Pamela Kenworthy-Wright agreed to travel to London. She didn't ask questions except where she would find the keys to the apartment she'd be staying in.

Just as de Jersey was beginning to feel he was making good progress, Raymond Marsh called and dropped a bombshell.

"This is hot off the Buck House telephone wires. She's snuffed it."

De Jersey took a deep breath. "What are you talking about?"

"She was rushed to hospital last night and died early this morning. It'll be front-page news by tonight, so—"

De Jersey clenched his teeth. "She's dead?"

"Yeah. Be a big funeral, they'll be lowering the flags and stuff."

"Dear God. Are you sure?"

"I'm certain. My gran always said she should have been allowed to marry Peter Townsend."

"Wait, you're talking about Princess Margaret?"

"Yeah. Who did you think? It means that H.M. might not be keeping to her diary."

De Jersey's heart rate dropped slightly. For a moment he had believed the Queen was dead. "How soon can you find out?"

"All I can do is keep you posted. I just thought you'd want to know."

"Yes, thank you." He hung up.

De Jersey sat stunned. This could throw a major spanner in the works. A few days later, however, after the media had run coverage of the

Princess's death virtually into the ground, Marsh called again. He said he needed to talk to de Jersey urgently.

"Is this about the funeral?"

"Nope. As far as I can tell that'll all be over soon. The diary hasn't changed for May. Busy this month, though. Not sure I'd fancy being cremated myself, but—"

"What did you call to talk about then?" de Jersey asked, cutting Marsh off.

Marsh refused to say over the phone, so they arranged to meet in a coffee shop a stone's throw from the entrance to Buckingham Palace. It was Marsh's morning break, and a long line of tourists was waiting for the Changing of the Guard, their umbrellas up against the cold February drizzle and their coats buffeted by the brisk wind.

"You've got real problems," Marsh told him. "I did some rooting around at work cos I figured the D'Ancona alarm system might work through their phone lines."

"And what did you find out?"

"They've got serious panic buttons—fifty-two of them—all wired up individually to the phone system with a direct link to an alarm receiving center, which contacts the police. I suspect they'll be set up so that if you deactivate one line the others will go off."

De Jersey's heart sank.

Marsh continued. "They'll be dotted around all over the place. I tried to get more information using the Web, but there's nothing on D'Ancona that we don't already know, and besides, they ain't gonna give details on the Web about their security. But it's logic that they'll have 'em on the walls and under the carpet so you won't even be able to tell if one's been set off until it's too late. Step on one an' you'll trigger the rest."

"So you got nothing on their security layout?"

Marsh shook his head. "The plans aren't stored on any computer network that I've dipped into. They're gonna protect themselves an' gotta be wise to hackers. One more thing I did find out, though. There's activity on those lines at precisely nine o'clock every morning. I assume that's when they check their system, so if you deactivate the phone lines connected to the panic buttons, it'll need to be done after that. But it's not all bad news."

"Go on."

Marsh wiped his mouth on a paper napkin. "I hacked into the Royal diary page again. Been keeping my eye on it for you, especially since the Princess died. The fitting's been confirmed. It's Thursday the second of May, ten thirty."

De Jersey stared at him. If the fitting was now confirmed, so was the date of the robbery.

"See? I said it wasn't all bad news. The party they've got listed for the fitting includes Her Majesty, a lady-in-waiting—Lady Camilla Harvey, the equerry, plus a detective, two bike riders, the chauffeurs, and some security geezers."

De Jersey gave Marsh a guarded smile and patted his arm. Then he got up and walked out. Marsh pocketed the fiver de Jersey had left for the waiter and substituted two pound coins.

Two steps forward and a bad one back. It was disappointing if not catastrophic not to know the layout of the security at the safe house. De Jersey knew how many people worked there, what time they came in and out. He knew how many telephones there were, but he did not know on which floor the main vault was and, most important, the locations of the panic buttons and security alarms.

He put up his umbrella and walked toward Victoria Station, where he caught a bus to Kilburn. He sat upstairs in a front seat, deep in thought, watching the rain pelting down. He calculated that, apart from the obvious, they were in good shape all round with more than eleven weeks to go. He stared out of the window at the traffic snarled up alongside Hyde Park. Just as the bus drew up by the Park Lane underground garage, he noticed the Eye Spy security company housed in an elegant corner shop across from the old Playboy Club. It was not the shop, however, that had caught de Jersey's interest but the figure of a young man leaving it. It was the salesman from the security exhibition in Birmingham. The bus jolted forward, and de Jersey watched him walk down Park Lane toward the Dorchester Hotel.

De Jersey jumped off the bus as it idled and made it safely to the pavement, just a few yards up from the Grosvenor House Hotel. He put up his umbrella and walked back briskly in the direction of the Dorchester.

"I am so sorry," he exclaimed, as he caught the young man with the edge of his umbrella.

"It's okay."

He was about to walk on when de Jersey said, "Wait a minute, we've met before, haven't we?"

"I don't think so."

"No, I never forget a face. You were on the Interlace Security stand at the Birmingham exhibition."

"You're right." But the puzzled expression on his face meant that he didn't recall de Jersey.

"Philip Simmons," he said.

"Oh, yes." He obviously still had no recollection.

"Are you working in London now?"

"Erm, not as yet."

He seemed eager to continue down Park Lane and was obviously uneasy as de Jersey walked alongside him.

"Is there an exhibition on? I still haven't contracted a security company for my new business."

"I'm just here for the day, going back on the four o'clock train."

"I'm going to have a bite to eat at the Grosvenor House's coffee shop. Do you have time to join me? We could perhaps continue our discussion."

The young man hesitated and glanced at his wristwatch. "No, thank you. I should get to the station."

"Nonsense. You have plenty of time. Join me, please. As I said, I really would like to continue our conversation."

Gridley looked at de Jersey. "Are you picking me up or something? If you are you've got it wrong. Excuse me."

"Dear God! I've never been accused of that before." De Jersey laughed. "I assure you, I simply wish to talk to you about my business, and I'm certain you have plenty of time to catch your train. We could have a glass of wine or coffee, whichever you prefer."

"Thank you," Gridley said. "I'm sorry if I seem crass, but . . . Oh, why not? My train isn't until four."

They sat at a window table, and de Jersey took charge, ordering a bottle of Merlot. The young man seemed awkward in the elegant surroundings. They had both removed their wet coats, and the cloakroom attendant had taken de Jersey's umbrella. Gridley was wearing the same cheap suit he'd had on the last time de Jersey met him.

"Mr. Simmons," he said, "I think I had better tell you that I'm not going to be working for the company for much longer. My father retired last week. After he'd gone they gave me a month's notice. I think they only kept me on because of him, so I came up here to look for work."

"Any success?"

"Not as yet. At the end of this week, when my notice is up, I'll come back and have a really good scout around."

"Well, I wish you every success. We never did get to finish the conversation we started in the bar at the exhibition. That man who interrupted us, he seemed to be giving you a bit of a dressing-down."

Gridley sipped his wine. "I don't remember. They've been daily occurrences, the dressing-downs." He drained his glass, and de Jersey refilled it.

"Thank you. This is part of my problem," he said, tapping the glass. "I have been a bit hungover a few times but . . ." He tailed off and stared into his glass.

De Jersey could feel the adrenaline pumping. He knew he had to take this opportunity very carefully. First he intended to lull Gridley into a false sense of security. He would then dangle a carrot the young man would be unable to refuse. He suggested they order lunch, his treat, and Gridley agreed.

They finished lunch, having discussed the progress of the building works on his fictional jewelery-shop premises. By this time Gridley had consumed most of the wine and de Jersey had ordered another bottle.

Then he went for it. "You know they had another robbery in Bond Street, and Gucci's warehouse was also done over? Did you read about it?"

"Yes." Gridley nodded. "They should have used Interlace. It would never have happened. I mean, although they're making me redundant, I reckon they really are the best company. You don't get contracts like we have for not being top of the ladder."

"Exactly, which is why I am so pleased to bump into you this morning."

"But I'll be an official job seeker next week, so if you decide to go with our security system, I won't get the salesman's bonus."

De Jersey topped up his own glass. "I don't think that's fair. You sold the company to me. I shall insist you get it. How's that?"

"Well, I obviously appreciate it, but as I won't be employed there I doubt if it could be arranged."

"Well, then, I'll do it on a personal basis. How about that?"

There ensued another fifteen minutes of discussion on how de Jersey could pay the bonus to Gridley directly. Then he went for the kill. "I would pay you more than the bonus if you could let me see how the D'Ancona security works. I don't think that company has ever been robbed. I know they lost a diamond recently, but that was just one stone."

"It was worth a couple of million, though." Gridley glanced at his watch.

"But their safe houses have never been breached, and it would be a major plus for me to have an insight into how they have been so successful. And since your company, or your ex-company, drew up their plans . . ."

"That would be impossible," Malcolm said.

"But not if they didn't know. Just make me a copy. Could you do that?"

"I really couldn't. Besides, they'd probably know it was me."

"All I want is to be sure my business is as well protected as possible, and Interlace would get the work. I could pay you five thousand for your trouble. I'd also make sure you got the bonus. I don't think they could possibly have any ill feelings toward you. On the contrary, they should offer you a better position instead of firing you."

He still had not bitten and was now checking for his train ticket. He had consumed almost the entire second bottle of wine.

"I might even be able to help you get another position. Are you planning to continue working for—"

"Mr. Simmons, I have to be honest with you. The type of work I was doing bored the pants off me. I was only working there because of my father, and I have no idea what I want to do next. I'm sort of looking around but . . . I've recently split up with my girlfriend. She's gone to live in Australia, and it's really cut me up. And when I said to you before that I had been rather hungover occasionally, that was putting it mildly. A couple of times I was three sheets to the wind, so I can't really blame them for firing me. I was probably a bit sozzled when you came to the exhibition."

He looked morose and fished in his suit pocket for a packet of cigarettes. "Can we smoke in here?"

"Go ahead, unless you'd prefer a cigar."

"I'll stick to these."

De Jersey ordered a brandy for himself, and Gridley flicked nervously at his cigarette ash. "I've had a series of job interviews. The old man has virtually given up on me, but I can't seem to find anything that, you know, interests me, and with Francesca leaving . . ."

"Why not go out to Australia? Maybe that's the place for you."

"I only had just enough dosh for the ticket to London, but I have thought about it."

"That bonus I spoke of would come at the right time, then, wouldn't it? Why don't I take you round my shop? I really do need some advice. We can be there in half an hour, and you could look over the premises." He knew he was on safe ground inviting Gridley to his nonexistent shop as the young man had said he was catching the four o'clock train. It was already five past three.

"I'm afraid I can't. I have to get to the station."

De Jersey wasn't sure his fish was on the line, but he had gone quiet, which was a good sign. De Jersey paid the bill, and they collected their coats and de Jersey his umbrella. Gridley remained silent as he watched de Jersey give the cloakroom attendant a heavy tip. They walked into Park Lane together. De Jersey was getting worried; perhaps he had overestimated his powers of persuasion. He wondered if he should have offered more money, but that would have made Gridley suspicious.

"I'm not a salesman anymore," Gridley said suddenly. "They have me doing menial tasks around the office." He hesitated. "It means I have access to the files, but while I would really like to help you out, and obviously the bonus you mentioned would come in handy, I don't think . . ." He was flushing.

"Really? Well, that makes it even easier for you." Relieved, de Jersey put up his umbrella, sheltering them both from the rain. "But I don't want this to get you into any trouble. It would help me cut corners, but if it's at all risky then I understand if you feel you can't help me."

Gridley looked relieved. "Thank you. And I'd like to help you out, but it's impossible, and I'm afraid you're rather out of touch."

"I'm sorry?" de Jersey was stunned by the young man's change of heart.

"I doubt that any reputable security company retains easily accessible blueprints of their customers' premises. Everything is computerized, and it's virtually impossible to gain access without permission. If you open up a file on the computer, you need the password, and the date and time will be recorded. So even if I attempted to do it, I'd be caught red-handed." But thank you so much for lunch," Gridley said. "It was really nice to meet you again. Now I should jump into a taxi or I'll miss my train."

De Jersey forced a smile. "Good luck. And here's some advice," he said, gritting his teeth. "You only live once. If you don't go after what you want, you'll watch it slip from your grasp." Then he turned and walked away, his face taut with anger. He had certainly misjudged the young man. In fact, he would have liked to ram his umbrella down his throat.

The meeting at which all the team would get together for the first time was set for two thirty at the barn on the following Monday. It was imperative that de Jersey show 100 percent confidence in his plan. But it would be difficult; so much still depended on him being able to secure the layout of the safe house. Once again he contacted Marsh. To date he had only attempted to gain access to D'Ancona records, but what if he could tap into the Interlace computer files? Marsh promised to "give it a whirl," but he warned de Jersey that they risked tipping off Interlace that someone was sniffing around.

"I need the layout," de Jersey said stubbornly.

"Listen, mate, it's not you that's doing the dodgy stuff. I got to watch my back. Like I said to you, I'll give it a go, but these top-notch companies have got all kinds of hidden traps, an' I don't want nothing zapping back to my gaff."

"Will you do it?"

"I'll see if I can break in tonight. All I'm saying is, it's a risk."

"Take it," de Jersey snapped, then drew a deep breath. "It's very important."

"I know, pal. Without it, you're walking into a minefield. Like I said, I'll do what I can."

De Jersey had a restless night waiting to hear back from Marsh. When he opened his e-mail the next morning it was not good news.

"Problems," the message said. "Attempted to do as requested. Gained password, entered, and then all hell broke loose. Pulled out fast, but the company will have been tipped off. Sorry! Elvis."

De Jersey stared at the screen with no idea of what his next move should be. As Marsh had so succinctly put it, entering the D'Ancona safe house without a floor plan would be like walking into a minefield.

18

As the meeting grew closer, de Jersey had still not overcome the heist's major problem. Then he received a small padded envelope in the mail, postmarked Birmingham. He did not recognize the handwriting. He opened it and caught his breath. It contained a single CD and a typewritten note from Malcolm Gridley:

Dear Mr. Simmons,

We recently had an electronic security alert, and all our computer files had to be checked as it was first presumed to be some kind of virus that would corrupt all the data. As I was working in the office, part of my duties was to assist the IT department to verify whether any of the data had been corrupted. I therefore had access to the enclosed. I am leaving for Australia to join my girlfriend, but if you do decide to use Interlace and perhaps see your way to paying me the bonus we spoke of, my address will be Apartment 4B West Street, North Sydney, NSW 2060. If, however, you decide otherwise, perhaps you would destroy the CD. Thank you for lunch.

Yours sincerely,
Malcolm Gridley

De Jersey could not believe his luck. He kept staring at the CD and rereading the letter. At his computer his jaw dropped. Then he started to laugh. He now had everything he could have hoped for—and all for the price of a cheap lunch.

The Interlace CD contained an interactive floor plan of every section of the D'Ancona safe house. It indicated where Interlace had recommended the panic buttons be placed. It also showed the security cameras, the grilles and electronic pulses required for each door, and the costing for the equipment. One incredibly useful feature was a virtual tour of the entire safe house, and de Jersey was able to visualize the route from the front door down to the basement, where the vast vault was located. If one panic button was pressed, the alarm receiving center would alert the police almost immediately, and a team would be dispatched with an estimated response time of two minutes. Once the alert was given, all access to the building would be secured.

De Jersey was aware that D'Ancona might have made changes from what was on the CD, but even so he now felt prepared for the meeting with his key team members.

In a pin-striped suit, brown brogues, and a blue shirt, de Jersey sat at the back of the Surrey barn. Wilcox had sectioned off the area with screens, and four calor-gas heaters were blasting out warmth. There were a few folding chairs, a folding picnic table, and an old armchair he'd found in the rubbish. A camping stove stood in the makeshift kitchen to brew tea and coffee.

The team had been instructed to leave their cars in the yard at the back of the barn, which was protected from view by the overgrown hedge. As soon as de Jersey heard the first car arrive, he stood at the door with a box of surgical gloves and handed a pair to each team member as they entered. A large drawing board had been set up, and he had brought his laptop.

Driscoll was the first to arrive and snapped on the gloves without a word. He was closely followed by Pamela Kenworthy-Wright and Lord Westbrook. The bike riders would not be privy to these early meetings. As de Jersey bolted the door behind them, Pamela complained about the rubber gloves. "Wear them at all times," de Jersey told her. "This box will be placed by the back door."

"Are we expected to do some kind of cleaning?" Pamela inquired.

De Jersey showed her that he too was wearing them. "You know how they identified Ronnie Biggs? He put a dish of milk out for a cat. One thumbprint, that's all it takes. When we move out of here to the second base, we must leave no record of any one of us ever having been here. Is that understood?"

The team all nodded in agreement, and Pamela made tea and coffee before taking her seat in the row of folding chairs facing the drawing board.

The team sat in awkward silence, avoiding each other's eyes. De Jersey leaned against the table. "From now on you refer to me only as the

Colonel, and you will refer to each other by Christian names only. First, Pamela."

She raised her beaker.

"James. That's Tony, and Henry." He nodded to each as he said the name. "From now on we protect our identities. The less we know about each other the better. I have put my utmost trust in each of you."

They remained silent as he picked up a black felt-tipped marker, crossed to the drawing board, and listed roles beside the names: the Colonel, main bodyguard; Henry, equerry; James, chauffeur; Her Majesty the Queen, not present; Pamela, lady-in-waiting; Tony, private secretary; two bike riders, not present.

Everyone listened as he gave the date and time they would be moving base to get ready for the hit. He detailed their jobs and explained how he and Marsh would stop the Royal convoy and how they would arrive at the safe house in place of the authentic party. By the time he told them how they would accomplish entry to the safe house, they were all ready for another round of tea and coffee. Everyone seemed tense; it was a lot to take in.

After the short break, de Jersey moved on to the last phase of the plan. "So far so good, but the most important element for all of us is getting away with it. I will use four helicopters to act as decoys. They will be ordered from various companies in the Southeast to pick up a passenger or package from various points in London. When they arrive and their assignment is not there, the helicopters will leave London to return to their bases, which will coincide with the time of the getaway. It will be mayhem after the hit, and the police will monitor the air traffic, so we want as much organized chaos and as many distractions as possible. We will split up and move across London separately. First, two boats will be taken from a mooring at Tower Bridge Marina and driven across the river by the two bike riders. They will both motor to Putney Bridge, put the boats in the boathouse, and take the Tube home."

"That all seems very . . . well, not what I expected," interrupted Westbrook.

"You expected fast cars, speedboats, and getaway drivers?"

Westbrook gave a shrug. "Well, I don't know about boats. That big diamond heist that fell foul of the Dome, they were going to make their getaway by the river."

De Jersey pinched his nose in irritation. The police, he pointed out, were already on to them, and they were not making their getaway via the river. "Anonymity is our best disguise. Just blend in with the commuters."

De Jersey pointed to Pamela and Westbrook. "The City Thameslink

Station is a five-minute walk from the safe house. You two will jump in a cab to the station. There's always a stream of them near the Barbican. You'll travel from there to Brighton. There's a train at just gone eleven, which if all goes to plan, you will make easily. The next one is fifteen minutes later. From Brighton you are to separate. Pamela will go by train to Plymouth. Henry will return to his studio in Pimlico." De Jersey knew that the only one of them that could possibly be recognized was Westbrook, but his life expectancy was so short, De Jersey didn't feel the risk of his discovery would endanger any of them as long as Westbrook and Pamela separated.

De Jersey then pointed to Driscoll and Wilcox. "Tony, James, and I will work out the best way to get the jewels to my helicopter for the drop." De Jersey flipped the pages on the board back to the beginning. "Any questions?"

No one said a word. Now de Jersey turned to an enlarged copy of the safe house layout. He gestured to the warehouse, which was to be their second base. "So, we move out from here and drive round the block. Now you all know the fundamentals, and I want us to begin to break it down into sections and allocate specific roles." De Jersey nodded to Westbrook and gestured for him to come to his side.

"Henry here will detail the lineup of the Royal party, how they behave, protocol, et cetera."

Westbrook opened a bottle of water and drank thirstily. His pale face shone with sweat. "The lady-in-waiting must, at all times, adhere to the Royal protocol. She will always be to the left side of the Queen, two or three paces behind, a small enough gap for Her Majesty to pass her her handbag or flowers without stretching. In the car, she must sit well back and not in any way hamper the view of Her Majesty. In public, she will speak only when spoken to."

Pamela asked a few questions about her dress, her demeanor, and whether or not she should also carry a handbag. De Jersey held up his hand. "As we all have a lot of work to do, I suggest Henry work with Pamela, and we can get on with other things."

Pamela and Westbrook disappeared into the main area of the barn. De Jersey took out a cigar and lit it. "So, what do you think?"

Wilcox glanced at Driscoll, then back to de Jersey. "What about the security measures in the safe house?" He pointed to the basic layout of the house. "This doesn't give any information about what we're going to be facing once we're in there."

De Jersey dismissed his concern. "We know there'll be top-of-the-line security measures. I'd say we can handle it, though."

"Yeah, well, saying and knowing are two different things. Christ only knows what could go wrong."

De Jersey looked to each of them. "Trust me, the security will be taken care of."

When Westbrook had finished with Pamela, he took Driscoll through his paces as the private secretary: where he would stand and how he would behave at each step of the way. By now, Wilcox was seated in the car acting as the chauffeur. The gray uniform was slightly too large, but this would not be noticed from his position behind the wheel. Westbrook instructed him to stare ahead, never look back at the passengers and never remove his cap.

De Jersey, playing a front-line role for the first time since the early raids on his father's shops, was the bodyguard. Although the Queen usually had more than one, Westbrook agreed that, as this was not a public event, they would be fine with just de Jersey. The two bikers would pose as Special Branch police officers. De Jersey would be the first to leave the safe house, and it was imperative that he move fast.

The meeting went on for four hours, and by the end the strain showed in them all, apart from de Jersey, who remained energetic and alert. Westbrook looked gray, almost matching the chauffeur's uniform. He took painkillers continually through the session. By the next meeting they should have done all the necessary shopping and any further research. He doled out cash to Pamela and Westbrook for their purchases. He agreed that Westbrook would assist Pamela in selecting the most suitable outfits for herself and for their Queen, including the correct type of handbag.

After the others had left, Wilcox, Driscoll, and de Jersey began a dissection of the meeting. Wilcox asked about the validity of their security information.

"For Christ's sake, Jimmy, we have the safe house plans, and they're authentic."

"That's not good enough, Eddy. I want to know *how* it's going to be done. We're risking a fucking lot out there."

De Jersey lit another cigar. "We walk in through the front door, James. We've discussed this."

"Yeah, okay, so what about this other unknown quantity? This guy that's gonna give us the IRA code word and intercept the call. We are dependent on him, but we've not even met him. How can you be so sure that he'll be okay on the day?"

"Marsh is an expert, not only in computers but also in telephone engineering. He's done fantastic work so far, and if it weren't for him, I'd never have worked out a way to stop the Royal party without the safe house knowing. He's handling the whole technical side of the operation, and it was at his request that he has no involvement in the physical side of the heist. I respect that because it's not necessary for him to take part."

This satisfied Wilcox and Driscoll to some extent but not completely.

"Look, Eddy," Wilcox said, "we've come this far, and it's just odd for us not to know the full details. I dunno how Tony feels, but we're putting a lot of responsibility on Marsh and also on Dulay. I think we should have had them here for a face-to-face. I mean, how much are we paying these guys?"

"I hear what you're saying, but look at it from my point of view," de Jersey said. "I've been laying out the cash for this. I haven't asked you two for anything." De Jersey picked up his black marker pen and began to write on the board. "Right now I'm paying Westbrook, Pamela, and Marsh full-time, plus one-offs to Gregory Jones and the security guy." He listed the payments, even down to the money he intended paying Malcolm Gridley. Next he listed the fees for the helicopters and the money put aside for them to secure the speedboats. "You calculating all this, Tony? Both of you start figuring it out, cos I'm the one who's thousands out of pocket. Then there are the costumes, the rent for this place and for the warehouse. Too damned right I've kept quiet about a lot of things, especially what it's costing me to set up this fucking robbery! So far you two have contributed a few grand between you. You hear me complaining? *No!* You don't hear me asking for the major slice when, as you can see, I've been working morning, noon, and night on this. But don't fucking thank me. Sit there and moan your arses off. The pair of you make me sick."

Driscoll and Wilcox were stunned by de Jersey's anger, and by the sum he had invested in the heist. Equal contributions would make deep holes in the funds they'd salvaged from their ruined fortunes.

"You got something to say, Tony?" de Jersey asked as he started putting away the drawing board. He ripped up the big sheets of paper with the lists of payments and folded up the safe house plans. He put the plans into his briefcase and tossed the other papers in a dustbin.

"You could say that." Driscoll was agitated.

"Well, say it," de Jersey snapped, struck a match, and lit the paper.

"I'm getting serious cold feet about the whole fucking thing."

De Jersey sat down, flicked the ash from his cigar, and stared at Driscoll. "Spit it all out now."

"Look, Eddy, we go back a long way, but we've never had such a big core team. This Westbrook character, he was stuffing himself with pills all bleeding afternoon. Come four o'clock he was spaced out of his head, and this was only the first meeting. What's he gonna be like on the day? Neither of us has met Marsh, so how do we know we can trust him? How do we know he's going to pull it off?"

De Jersey turned to Wilcox. "What about you?"

Wilcox shuffled his feet with embarrassment. "Well, what Tony's saying is true. That Pamela woman's a flake too. Thinks she's auditioning for the National Theatre the way she's carrying on. If we come in on the expenses you're paying out, we'll be paying her a grand a week like the others, more than she's ever earned in her life I reckon."

"She's worth it. She's going to be right in the thick of it," de Jersey snapped.

"You say so, but how do we know she won't cave in?"

"She's as tough as they come, plus she knows the consequences if we fail. She's worth her price."

"But, again, we only have your word and you only have the trust you've placed in them. Then you say we've got two speedboats and you've ordered four helicopters as decoys. Have you got all these extras lined up, or are you just making out lists of things you're thinking about doing but haven't got round to yet? Where are we gonna get these two boats from? Then there's got to be river moorings organized. It's still all up in the air."

De Jersey bit off the end of his cigar and spat it out.

Wilcox continued. "We've got to be tooled up, and I wouldn't trust that Westbrook character to carry a water pistol let alone a shooter. We've never used so many amateurs for a gig before." He took a deep breath. "It could all fall apart, and then I'll be in an even worse situation than when we started. You say you've laid out for everything, and you have, I can see that. But I've paid for the cars, and Tony sorted out the weapons. I can't pay out any more."

Driscoll started again. "I'm broke from this wedding. I mean, we've been lucky in the past, we all know that, but this is stretching it to the limit. We've not even got into how we're getting the gems to France."

De Jersey blew a smoke ring above his head as Wilcox took over where Driscoll left off.

"And this Dulay character. You say we can trust him, but you've had to squeeze his balls to get him to agree to be part of this, and that's always dodgy. Carrying that gear out of the country is impossible. The scream will be up so loud that every airport and dock will be surrounded. I know you've worked out decoys, and I'm sorry to sound so negative, but I just don't buy it."

"Dulay has a big yacht. I was planning to use it unless you want to use yours," de Jersey said to Wilcox.

He was taken aback when Wilcox shouted, "I bloody can't use mine! I had to sell it months ago. You see what I'm talking about? We're up shit creek on this one, and you are gonna have to admit it."

De Jersey was finding it hard to maintain his calm. "Things will go wrong if you don't keep your cool. Dulay is picking up the jewels from the south coast. It's all taken care of."

Wilcox bowed his head. "All taken care of! I hope bloody Sylvia Hewitt's also taken care of. That's more cash you'll likely have to pay out to keep her quiet. So if you've got it all planned, why the fuck don't you tell us about it and take care of our worries?"

Driscoll put up his hand, like a schoolkid. "There's another thing, Eddy. I see what you've paid out and I know I've not come in with much, but you've never discussed what you expect to get from the sale of the jewels. Can you give us an idea?"

Wilcox interrupted. "Hang on a minute. We're depending on Dulay for this Japanese buyer. Dulay says he's got him, but that's just his word. If he doesn't pull off the sale, we're gonna be left with the hottest gear around. Nobody'll touch it, no matter what it's worth. We'll all be left with fuck-all. And another thing—"

Driscoll put up his hand again. "Have you met the buyer?"

"No," de Jersey said, and he flushed with anger because he knew they were right. He was not being as professional as he had been in the past, and he was depending heavily on Dulay and Marsh.

"Shit, this is a mess. Admit it, Eddy, it's just not working." Wilcox heaved himself out of the worn, old armchair.

"It is, and it will work. I trust Dulay. If he says this Japanese guy is good for it, he is, and you checked him out in Paris."

"I don't call that checking out," snapped Wilcox. He was pacing up and down now in fury. "All I did was tail Dulay to the Ritz and see him meet up with the guy. What they said and how far we can trust them is another matter."

"He's agreed to pay an excellent price for the Koh-i-noor Diamond alone," de Jersey said, opening his briefcase.

"How much?" asked Driscoll.

"One million per carat. It's over a hundred carats," de Jersey said, tight-lipped. He took out his notebook.

Driscoll's jaw dropped.

"He wants the Koh-i-noor for starters, but selling him the other gems will be no problem."

"But who is this guy?" Driscoll asked.

"He's a contact of Dulay," said de Jersey defensively.

Wilcox looked at Driscoll. "But how can we trust Dulay? How do we know he's not going to just disappear? And now you tell us this buyer *knows* about the diamond already. Jesus Christ! We're leaving ourselves wide open. What if this fucking Jap raps to someone?"

Now it was back to Driscoll. "He's right, Eddy. And, thinking about it, I have big worries. If the worst comes to the worst, I can sell my properties and go back to work full-time. At least I'd still have something. I'm getting too old to take such risks. I'm really sorry to sound off at you this way, but—"

"You want out?" de Jersey asked coldly.

"The way things are right now, yes, cos I just don't think we can do it. It all depends on people trusting one another, and with so many parties involved we could get screwed from any angle. Right, Jimmy?"

Wilcox nodded.

"I've never let you down before." De Jersey sounded bitter.

Wilcox gave an impatient sigh. "We both know that. But the plan isn't right yet, and all this farting around today wasn't good enough. We've not got that much time to get it together."

De Jersey flicked the ash from his cigar. "Fine. Walk away. I won't hold you to anything. I never did before and I won't now. That's not to say I'm not disappointed. Of course I am, because I'm down a lot of cash already. You two don't want to come in and help me out, fine. But I've always made sure that whoever worked alongside me got a fair share and I'm not about to change that. The fair share is the reason we can trust the people I've brought in. It is that element of the deal that binds us all together. It worked for us in the past and it will work for us this time."

"Come on, Eddy, we know that," Driscoll said. "And don't think I'm not grateful for our past deals, but they were a long time ago. We were younger then, more prepared for the risks."

Wilcox nodded. "Yeah, I've got six kids."

"And a habit to feed," de Jersey snapped.

"I'm clean," Wilcox said defensively.

"So you say." De Jersey knew that he had to steer them back on course and, worse, that without them he could never pull it off. He pointed to Driscoll. "You think you and Wilcox here are the best I could get for this? I brought you in on this to ease my guilt for the bad investment advice I gave you. I'm not prepared to lose what I've spent the best part of my life building up. Neither do I want to lose my wife or my daughters by spending the rest of my life banged up in prison. I will ensure there's as little risk as possible for all of us. I've taken on board what you've said, but when in the past did you ever know all the details and every member of the team? Never! You trusted my judgment. If you no longer trust me, then get the hell out."

Driscoll put his hands up. "Come on now, no need for this. You said it yourself, Eddy. You said if it didn't look kosher you'd call it quits and there'd be no hard feelings."

"What do you say, James?" de Jersey asked.

"I am not doing drugs! I've worked my arse off getting these two cars and the bikes ready. I just think the plan's not up to your usual standard, that's all. Maybe if we thrash out the details a bit more, know exactly what you've planned, we'll feel happier."

"Come on, we've all done a good share," Driscoll said, angrily.

"Yeah, us three have, but the computer geek is getting a grand a week and a big cut!" Wilcox was still in a rage.

De Jersey stood up, his military bearing intimidating. "You two are getting greedy. Raymond Marsh is not going to betray us. He's already in too deep. He's hacked into the private Royal diaries, intercepted Scotland Yard calls, and made sure there won't be any links between him and me when this is all over."

Wilcox sucked in his breath. "Leaving yourself out in the open, aren't you? You may be using Philip Simmons as a cover, but something this big will have every cop in the U.K. after you."

"It's more than a cover," de Jersey interjected brusquely. "In cyberspace, Philip Simmons is almost as good as flesh and blood. As soon as this is over, he disappears into thin air and all the leads and clues disappear with him. There is no connection back to me because Philip Simmons organized the whole thing."

Neither man understood what he was talking about, but his confidence in the alias was a bonus. After all, de Jersey himself was a direct link to both of them.

He continued, "Marsh is worth every cent we pay him because we couldn't pull this off without him. He's a genius."

Wilcox and Driscoll fell silent. Then de Jersey's bravado slipped. He gave a long sigh. "All I can say is this, I'm not just protecting myself. I have to look out for all of you. I've been working on how all of us move out when the scream goes up, just as I always did in the past. It takes time and planning down to the last second. If there are loopholes then we have to rethink, or I do. So, ask me what you need to know." He picked up the black marker pen and crossed to the board. "List every loophole. We'll go through them one at a time."

Driscoll rested his head in his hands. Wilcox slumped into the old chair. "I can't fucking think straight now."

De Jersey looked from one to the other. He tossed aside the marker pen. "Sleep on it, then, but I need to know what the two of you decide by tomorrow."

He picked up his briefcase, took out the CD, and opened his laptop. "Take a look at this. When you're through close it down and remove the CD. Don't let it out of your sight. This is for our eyes only." He snapped his briefcase shut and collected his coat. "Good night." A moment later they heard the side door slam shut.

Both men remained silent for quite a while. Eventually Wilcox stood up. "Did you tell him I had a drug problem?"

"No way!"

"Did you understand any of that stuff about the alias?"

"Nope, but he seemed to, and that's what counts."

Wilcox got up to look at de Jersey's laptop. Driscoll followed him and pushed in the CD.

"Fuck me!" he exclaimed. "Look, Jimmy." He pointed to the interactive floor plan of the D'Ancona safe house.

They sat close to the small screen, taking the virtual tour. When it ended Driscoll pressed eject and took out the CD. "Jesus Christ, do you know what we just watched?" They looked at each other and knew without saying it that they were back on board.

"Let's go for it! All or nothing!" Wilcox said.

"Yeah, give it our best shot. If we go down at least we'll be famous. This is gonna be the biggest robbery in history, right?" Driscoll was now determined to see the positive side.

Wilcox laughed. "Just one thing. You don't have any sort of moral issue over this, do you? I mean, they are the Crown Jewels, and breaking them up is sort of—"

"Unpatriotic?" Driscoll laughed. "Fuck 'em! The Royals have had 'em long enough." He clapped Wilcox on the shoulder, and the two of them packed up and left.

In the darkness, inside the main part of the barn, de Jersey moved silently from behind the screens. Neither man had seen or heard him return to listen to their conversation. He sat down in the armchair and went through the meeting, listing every gripe that had been raised. Each was valid; they were still a long way off. Could he trust Marsh? So much depended on him. He sighed. Bottom line, he could trust no one involved completely, but that was the risk in this game. He must check out the Japanese buyer for himself and contact Sylvia Hewitt to make sure she was behaving. It irritated him that he had promised to pay her off, but it would be worth his while to keep her silent.

David Lyons was still in Sylvia's thoughts, and her sister was still living with her. Helen had recovered somewhat from the trauma of losing her husband, but she talked about David all the time. Some nights Sylvia didn't want to return home and wished Helen would find her own place to live.

On the day de Jersey had brought together the key team, Sylvia had just got home, later than usual as she had dined with a client.

"I'm in here" came Helen's high-pitched voice. She sounded angry.

Sylvia felt annoyed that her sister would undoubtedly ask her where she had been. "Give me a minute," she called back and took off her coat. She hadn't had time to hang it up before Helen marched out of the drawing room carrying a bundle of photographs. "I wasn't prying. I was looking for a needle. I knew you used to keep a sewing kit in your bedside table drawer. I found these." Helen thrust the pictures at her. One showed Sylvia and David kissing.

"Oh, it was some office party," Sylvia said lamely.

"No, it wasn't. How do you explain the beach and palm trees? What was going on between you and my husband?"

"He's dead, Helen. What does it matter now?"

"It matters to me. I want to know the truth. Look at me, Sylvia. Tell me what was going on."

"Oh, for God's sake, Helen, it's obvious, isn't it?"

"No, it isn't. I want you to tell me."

Sylvia sighed. "I never wanted to hurt you."

"Tell me what was going on between you and my husband!" Helen shrieked.

"We were lovers," Sylvia said at last. It all came out: how long it had gone on, all the times they had been together. She felt wretched, and so sorry for Helen that she burst into tears.

"Sylvia, you disgust me. My own sister!"

Helen walked into her bedroom and shut the door.

The following morning Sylvia tried to speak to Helen again, but she remained in her locked room. When Sylvia returned that evening, two suitcases stood in the hall and Helen's coat lay over them. She was waiting, her face drawn and chalk white. "I'm leaving. I can't talk about it. I don't know if I ever want to speak to you again. I trusted you, and you went behind my back and took the only thing in my life I have ever felt proud of.

My marriage is now just some terrible sham, and you are despicable for letting me stay here with you. I was pleased to have you at my side at his funeral, and now I discover that all the time you've been lying to me."

"Did you really want me to tell you the truth? How would it have made a difference, you knowing once he was dead? You certainly never suspected when he was alive. And I let him use all my savings and he lost the lot! So much for good, dependable, honest David. He was a fool!"

"I don't believe you."

"I'm telling you the truth. I've lost over two hundred thousand, all my savings. That's something else I didn't tell you because I didn't want you to worry. Whatever happened between me and David is history now and—"

Helen didn't wait to hear any more. She picked up her coat and her suitcases and made for the door. She glanced back at her sister. "That explains the real reason why he went with you. He was using you for your money." With that, she slammed the door.

Sylvia was incensed by Helen's insult, which also reminded her of Edward de Jersey's accusation. How dare de Jersey suggest she had been involved with David's frauds? She walked around the flat kicking the furniture. Her bedroom was littered with torn photographs of her and David together. She picked them up, then let them fall from her hands like confetti and started to cry. She had loved David, and now she had lost everything—lover, money, sister. She wondered what had happened to de Jersey, whether he had held on to his estate. It had been weeks since she had spoken to him.

The phone rang and she picked it up. "Hello."

"Is this Sylvia Hewitt?"

"Speaking."

"This is Victor Matheson, Miss Hewitt, the private detective you hired. Remember me?"

"Yes, of course." She was puzzled: she'd told him weeks ago his services were no longer required.

"A strange coincidence has just happened. I think it would be worth us meeting up."

Sylvia listened as Matheson explained that he had met another private investigator and discovered that he had been hired to trace Alex Moreno by Philip Simmons. "I have to arrange time off from work," she told him, "but it shouldn't be a problem. I'll fly out as soon as I can and meet you in New York."

"Good." He hung up.

She gave no thought to the fact that she had promised de Jersey she would not take her inquiries any further. In fact, she was determined to prove that David Lyons did not commit any fraud. She called her boss and told him that urgent family business had cropped up and she needed to take the week off.

De Jersey outlined "rehearsal" days for the team to meet at the barn. They had moved another step closer to the plans being completed. Driscoll had booked "the Queen." She was to be collected at 8:00 A.M. for a day's commercial shoot. The agent did not query the name of the company but seemed more interested in the fee, which was substantially more than usual.

Far from being a big risk, Westbrook proved invaluable. He was getting sicker by the day, but he remained in good humor and the team admired his determination. Pamela was highly professional and a constant source of humorous stories during coffee breaks. She provided cakes and biscuits too, which they devoured hungrily. She was having a wonderful time. She had always enjoyed the company of men, and it had been a long time since she had been surrounded by so many. She adored Westbrook, and they swapped stories about their time in the nick while smoking their way through packets of cigarettes, their conversation interspersed with coughing fits and shrieks of laughter.

De Jersey rarely joined in the banter. He was constantly checking his notes and plans. Dulay's boat was now set to anchor six miles off the South Coast, near Brighton. The diversion helicopters were booked and false pickup points agreed on. De Jersey had arranged for one of his horses to be at the Brighton racetrack on the day of the raid. He had also marked in blue crosses on the floor of the barn the positions of the panic buttons in the safe house. Every one of the team was made to learn their exact locations.

"Darling, just a small point," Pamela said one day, cigarette dangling out of her mouth. "We know where these thingies are, but what if one of the D'Ancona employees throws caution to the wind and stamps on one? Will we get out fast enough before the police show up?"

"What?"

"Well, darling, do we know how long we've got if someone inadvertently or deliberately steps on one? There's going to be an awful lot of anxiety and"—she hopped from one blue cross to another—"they're all over the place."

De Jersey gave her a dismissive glance. "Hopefully we'll have discovered a way to deactivate them. In the meantime, however, we should know exactly where they're located."

"Yes, but do you know how long it takes for the boys in blue to arrive if one goes off?"

"Pamela, why don't you put the kettle on?" De Jersey crossed to Wilcox.

He kept his voice low. "We hit one and the lot of us will be in trouble. Steel trapdoors come down like a guillotine."

Wilcox turned away. "So, we've got to deactivate the buggers."

"I'll work on it."

The two bikers were scheduled to arrive that afternoon, and de Jersey wanted everyone out of the way except Driscoll, who knew them. Brian Hall arrived first. He parked his motorbike as instructed in the yard at the back of the barn. Kenny Short turned up in an old Mini five minutes later.

De Jersey had watched them arrive. He opened the door almost immediately and handed them pairs of surgical gloves. The two men followed him toward the table, and he gestured for them to sit. Driscoll sat to one side. De Jersey took them through their duties and the getaway details. They listened attentively, asking relevant questions, to which de Jersey always had answers. They knew the risks they were taking, but the authoritative manner of the Colonel eased their fears, and after the instructions were clarified both men tried on their uniforms and tested the bikes. If they had any doubts they did not voice them.

De Jersey took pains to ensure that the men realized their importance. They were all dependent on each other to pull it off, he told them. Every one of them was an essential part of the heist, and one mistake could bring the rest down. When the two left, he turned to Driscoll. "What do you think?"

"They'll do the business. It's just his lordship we've got to watch out for. He's very jittery and well drugged up."

"I know. If he gets to be too much of a liability, we might have to lose him."

Driscoll licked his lips and changed the subject. "What about deactivating those panic buttons?"

"Working on it."

"Want to look over the guns?"

They had been under pressure for a considerable time now, so de Jersey suggested they take a few days' break. Christina was expected home from Sweden, and he was worn out; they all needed time to recharge their batteries. It was March 15; they could stand back and review the plan for any weak spots they had missed—there was still time.

* * *

De Jersey returned home, but although he needed a rest he didn't take one. Things at the estate needed his supervision, for although his staff worked diligently when he was absent, some issues had to be solved by the boss. There was a stack of paperwork that needed his attention, but the financial pressure was uppermost. He wondered if he could sell the Moreno house yet. He was still in the office after midnight when Fleming tapped and entered.

"Brandy?" de Jersey asked.

Fleming shook his head no. "You owe me the cash we agreed on," he said softly, not meeting de Jersey's eyes.

There was a long pause. De Jersey unscrewed the top from the brandy bottle, opened a drawer, and took out a glass.

"My son and an old lad helped me out. They're both trustworthy. My son won't say anything, and if the lad had a notion of what we were up to, he didn't let on. I gave him a couple hundred quid."

De Jersey gulped the brandy. "How did my boy do?"

"Fine. So now we wait. I've put him in the far stall. We'll push his training up and see how he behaves, but we've risked a hell of a lot."

"I know." De Jersey was hardly able to speak.

Fleming changed his mind about the brandy, and the two men sat drinking quietly. They were both ashamed of the subterfuge and worried that they might have damaged Royal Flush's concentration and thus his chance of winning the biggest race of his life. Eventually Fleming stood up and buttoned his coat. He nodded to the racing diary displayed on the office wall. "We'll see what effect it's had when he races at Lingfield."

Two days later Christina arrived home, and de Jersey took her in his arms. "I've missed you so much," she said, as they hugged.

"I've missed you too, darling. Let me carry your cases upstairs."

"No, they can wait but I can't. Let's just go upstairs," she said coyly.

He smiled. "Whatever you say."

"How's everything been?" she asked.

"Not too bad. I've had to sell a few more horses, but Royal Flush is in great shape. It's been very quiet here without you," he said.

"It's such a comfort to be back here with you. This place is so precious to me," Christina said.

De Jersey didn't reply as he followed her up the stairs. So much was riding on him pulling off the heist.

CHAPTER

19

Sylvia had taken a taxi straight from JFK Airport to the InterContinental Hotel because of its proximity to Central Park and easy walking distance to Moreno's apartment block. She had decided that since she had time to kill before her appointment with Matheson, she would do some research of her own. She'd taken Matheson off the case before he had had a chance to check out Moreno's apartment. Maybe she could discover something there that would help them. She had slept badly on the plane, so she decided to have a nap until midday, but she was still sound asleep when the chambermaid woke her at three. She showered and changed, and left the hotel at four.

The doorman at Moreno's apartment was none too friendly until Sylvia slipped him twenty dollars. Then he told her he remembered Moreno well, a pleasant enough man, but he'd kept to himself.

"Did he warn you that he was leaving?"

"No. One minute he lived here, the next he didn't."

"But did you see him leave?"

"No. He might have gone when I wasn't on duty. All I know is, the apartment changed hands. You need to talk to the agents. They handle the leases. The guy living there now is German, but I don't see much of him either."

"Is he at home?"

"No. Leaves early, comes back late. Days can go by and I don't see him, but he uses a limo company." He passed her a card. "They're good. I know one of the drivers. Mr. Goldberg is a regular customer, like I said."

"You've been most helpful, but I really did need to speak to Mr. Moreno. It looks like I'm out of luck, though."

"Afraid so."

"Thank you."

"Have a nice evening." He hovered for another twenty dollars, but she pulled her collar up around her face and walked off.

She had gone no more than twenty yards when she saw a limousine draw up. An immaculate gentleman climbed out of the backseat. He was wearing dark glasses and carried a slim briefcase. She heard the doorman address him. As he headed into the apartments, she hurried after him. "Mr. Goldberg! Excuse me." He turned and stared at her. "I wonder if I could possibly have a few moments of your time?"

"Do I know you?"

"I'm trying to trace Mr. Moreno. He lived in your apartment before you."

"I'm sorry I cannot help. I did not know him. He has nothing to do with me. Excuse me."

"Please—if I could just ask you a few things?" she persisted.

"I did not know Mr. Moreno. If you want any details about him, I suggest you contact the agents for the property. Excuse me."

She stood helplessly as the door swung closed after him and the doorman took up his position outside again. "If you want the agents, they've got an office in the next block up across Eighty-sixth Street. Dugdale and Martin. Mr. Dugdale handles this place." Sylvia handed him another twenty-dollar bill and headed for the Gothic-style block he had indicated.

Dugdale and Martin had a small office on the ground floor of the plush apartment block. The thickset doorman said he thought she might be too late; their office closed at four thirty. He hovered at her side as she tapped on the door and waited. She was about to walk away when it opened.

"Good evening, my name is Sylvia Hewitt. I wondered if I could speak to someone concerning Mr. Moreno's apartment?"

"He's no longer a tenant there," said a stern, white-haired man.

"Yes, I know, but perhaps I could tell you my reasons for contacting you. I've come all the way from England."

"Come in." He opened the door wider. He was already wearing his overcoat. "I'm off home, Jacob. Can I leave this with you?" he said to another man, then walked out and closed the door.

Sylvia took out one of her business cards as the man at the window turned. "Sylvia Hewitt. I'm an accountant. I'm inquiring about a Mr. Moreno, who lived in—"

"Come in and sit down. I'm Jacob Martin. So, you are Mr. Moreno's accountant?" he asked.

"No," she said. "He had various interests in London but I've not been able to contact him since before Christmas."

"Well, he just disappeared, and we have no forwarding address."

"But you must have arranged the changeover of his apartment. There's a new owner, a German gentleman."

"Yes, he purchased the lease."

"From you?"

"Yes, we handle the property, but we did the transaction with a lawyer acting on behalf of Mr. Moreno. All the documents were in order, so we had no reason to query the sale."

"So Mr. Moreno never discussed leaving the apartment with you?"

"No. He left without notice, but that's not unusual. The only thing unusual was . . ." He hesitated. Sylvia waited. "He left a lot of personal items, which we removed before the next tenant moved in. He seemed to have departed in quite a hurry."

"Can you tell me what he left?"

"Clothing, stuff like that. We kept it weeks in storage. The new owner bought all the furniture and fittings."

"He just bought everything?"

"Well, not everything. There were items like videos, books. He didn't want those."

"Who took all that?"

Martin gave an embarrassed shrug. There had actually been a hell of a lot that Mr. Goldberg had not purchased: the paintings, mirrors, ornaments, and so on. But after keeping them in storage for a short while, Martin and Dugdale had done a little filching for themselves. In fact, they had stripped the place of anything remotely valuable. Sylvia suspected this, but it was not why she was there. "Do you have the name of the lawyer who handled the transactions?" she asked.

Martin walked to a cabinet, flicked through a row of files, and withdrew the one with Moreno's apartment number written on the front. "Mr. Philip Simmons. We have a phone number and"—he turned a page—"just a box number, which is unusual, and a further contact number for an address in the Hamptons."

"Could you give me the number? I really would like to speak to him."

Martin took one of his cards, copied down the number, and passed it to Sylvia. Then he walked back to the cabinet, still reading the file. He paused, frowning and turning pages. "I doubt you'll have much luck. Seems we've attempted to contact him as various maintenance charges were left unpaid and we wanted to get the accounts settled. It was not a large amount, but our letters went unanswered." He rested his elbow on top of the filing cabinet.

"Did you meet the lawyer?"

"No, I didn't. This was all handled by the boss, Mr. Dugdale. You saw him as you left. . . . Ah, forgive me, I did meet him just once, when he came to sign over the lease to Mr. Goldberg. He went into Mr. Dugdale's office."

"Could you describe him?"

"He was well dressed, elegant, I'd say, and tall. A big man, much taller than me and I'm almost six feet. He had reddish hair, and a mustache."

Sylvia stood up and shook his hand. "Thank you so much for your time. I really do appreciate it."

Sylvia returned to her hotel and called the number for Simmons. As she expected, it was no longer in use. Later she called Matheson, who agreed to meet her in the hotel bar at nine. She asked what he looked like.

"I'm small, nothing special. I'll have a big red and black scarf round my neck, glasses and thinning hair."

"I'm dark-haired, and I'm wearing a tweed suit with a white blouse and pearls," she said primly.

Sylvia entered the reasonably full bar and peered around until she spotted the investigator. Then she threaded her way through the low tables to join him. "How do you do?"

"Miss Hewitt, it's nice to put a face to the voice. Can I get you a drink?"

"White wine, please."

He signaled to a waiter as she sat down on one of the low seats opposite him. The man came over, and Matheson ordered a beer for himself and a chilled Chablis for her.

"It's so noisy here," Sylvia said. "They even have music in the lifts."

"You get used to it," he said and drew his chair closer to her. "Can I just get something straight? I mean, I don't wanna sound pushy, but this is my livelihood and I'll charge my hourly rate for tonight's meeting. How's that suit you?"

She nodded. "Fine."

He sat back as the waiter put down a bowl of nuts and their drinks. She raised her glass and sipped. "Well, I'm here, Mr. Matheson. You did say you had some developments, and I've come a long way to hear them in person, as you suggested."

"Like I said on the phone, I met up with an old friend. I want you to know straight up, I wasn't being unethical in discussing your business with him. It just came up in conversation. I never mentioned your name."

"Who is he?"

"An ex-cop, like me, from way back. He's about the same age, works mostly on security now. Been on tour with this rock group. In fact, he's with them now."

"What's his name?"

"Donny Baron. Nice guy. He says to me that he's fed up with schlepping all over the country. I ask him if he's doing any private work, and he says he had an interesting gig a few months ago. He ran an ad in *The New York Times* and this guy made contact, wanted him to do a bit of ducking and diving around town, checking out a guy that had done a little Internet fraud. And I said to him, 'That's a coincidence. Guy's not called Moreno, is he?' So he looks at me and he laughs and says he is. Said he'd been checking out Moreno's apartment for his client."

"When was this?"

"Just after Christmas. So I ask him about his client and he tells me he was a Canadian, flew from Los Angeles on the red-eye. Paid him a nice whack and that was it."

"Did he say what this man's name was?"

"Well, he was a bit edgy about that, but in the end he said it was Philip Simmons. Same guy we discovered. Donny's met him."

"So he was an investor?"

"Could have been. He's obviously more than just Moreno's financial adviser. I mean, if he was Moreno's financial adviser, why did he need to hire Donny to find him?"

Sylvia sipped her wine again, then placed it carefully on the table. "He's been posing as his solicitor too."

"Really? Well, Donny told me that this guy's accent was strange, said he sounded more like a Brit, so that was why I contacted you. The contractor in the Hamptons, he said he thought he was Canadian. There's obviously something funny going on with this guy."

Sylvia sighed. "I was a small investor in Moreno's company. I was told not to interfere by someone who had lost a considerable amount more than myself. In fact, three people I know of lost millions, and they all said they were handling it. They also refused to help me pay your wages. I thought that when I told them about your investigation they would have been eager for you to continue, but they weren't."

"Maybe they're getting a cut from Simmons. Who knows what's going on? I just reckoned you'd want to know about him cropping up again." He toyed with his empty beer glass. "I reckon you should go out to the Hamptons and check it out."

"How far is it?"

"Train would be about two hours. If you drive it's around the same; out of season there won't be much traffic. I can go out there with you if you want me to." Matheson was pushing to be rehired, but Sylvia was not prepared to pay out any more than she had to. He wrote down the address and passed it to her, then suggested she stay at the Maidstone Arms Hotel.

"I'll go alone tomorrow." She looked at the address and slipped it into her purse.

Matheson went on. "You mind if I say something? This Philip Simmons is, by my reckoning, somebody you should tread carefully with. If, as you say, that property in the Hamptons is worth millions, he might just have . . ." He took a deep breath.

"What?"

"Murdered for it."

She was not taken aback. Quite the contrary, she was very calm. She leaned forward and conspiratorially lowered her voice. "I thought about that, even more so if he lost his savings. It's a strong motive." The wine was making her giddy. "I feel like throttling him myself," she said.

"Yeah, well, feeling like doing something and actually doing it are two different things. This guy, whoever he is, seems like a real pro to me. He's covered his tracks too well not to be."

She beamed and gripped his shoulder. "But he *has* made mistakes. We can report this to the police and they can look for him. Or perhaps we can find this man, put pressure on him, and then I'm sure he'll pay us off. That's all I am interested in now, Mr. Matheson. I want my money back."

"You lost a lot, huh?"

"Yes, I lost my lover because Moreno used him. Moreno lost my life savings, and I intend on getting them or part of them back. And after what you have told me, I think there's a possibility of doing so." She hesitated. "I've not been able to discover if Philip Simmons was an investor. His name isn't on any of the documents I have, but he may have been investing in Moreno's company through someone else. There's something else I need to ask you, Mr. Matheson. During your inquiries, did you ever come across a David Lyons?"

"I don't think so. Was he in on this Internet deal? Did he lose out too?"

"He lost out completely. He committed suicide. He was very dear to me."

"He couldn't take the loss, huh?"

"No, he couldn't, but he was also responsible for encouraging people to invest with Moreno. He lost a lot of other people's savings as well."

"I see," Matheson said.

"He was my sister's husband." She had tears in her eyes.

"Oh dear. Tragic all around," he said.

"It was implied that he might have been involved in some kind of fraud with Moreno, but I know he wasn't." She took out a tissue and blew her nose. "I'm sorry." She picked up her handbag, took out a wad of cash, and paid what she owed him.

"I've got one final invoice for you covering some miscellaneous expenses, but I forgot to bring it with me," he said.

"Send it to me in London."

"Good luck, Ms. Hewitt. I hope you find him."

"I will," she said softly and left the bar.

When she got back to her room, Sylvia was exhausted, but she sat down at the desk and added up how much she had paid Matheson. At least she had made progress. It was looking more and more as if Simmons, whether acting for Moreno or representing one of the investors, was collecting a lot of money, and she felt that at least some of it should be hers. Could it be that Simmons had killed Moreno for the money invested in his properties? Certainly Simmons was not all he seemed. He had asked Donny Baron to check out Moreno's apartment. Why would a financial adviser use a PI to keep tabs on his own client?

Sylvia sighed and gathered her papers together. She opened her briefcase to put them away and saw a photo of herself and David at a Christmas party. She pulled it out. "It was you who got me into this mess," she said to David's smiling face. It was a group shot, but it was the only one she had of her lover now; Helen had destroyed all the others. As she looked at it, something caught her eye. One man in the shot stood head and shoulders above the rest. Edward de Jersey. The estate agent's and Matheson's words suddenly flooded back to her. "A big man . . . sounded more like a Brit . . ." Now if one man had lost out in the fall of leadingleisurewear, thought Sylvia, it was Edward de Jersey. Could he and Philip Simmons be the same person? The more she thought about it, the more convinced she became. She felt like a cat with the cream. She had to think carefully about how to handle Mr. Big Cheese de Jersey. She could either expose him or push him for a payoff, a lot more than she had lost. But first she needed proof.

Early the following morning Sylvia checked out and caught the jitney bus to East Hampton, where she checked in to the elegant Maidstone Arms. This was where Moreno had stayed, and she could see why: it was a charming, elegant hotel with blazing log fires in the stylish public rooms.

After unpacking she went down to the desk and asked to speak to the manager. He was charming too but not very helpful. Moreno had been there numerous times, he said, but he had no idea of his present where-abouts. Sylvia had coffee in a long room overlooking the street and located Moreno's property on the hotel's street map. Later she hired a taxi and asked to be driven around Georgica. To her annoyance she'd lost the piece of paper with the address on it that Matheson had given her the night before. All she knew was that it was a large piece of land not far from the ponds and under construction. The taxi driver was chatty, but Sylvia lost interest in what he was saying when they passed a large fenced property with construction in progress. "Could we drive in there?" she asked.

He reversed, and they passed the open drive, still not paved and muddy with tracks from the construction vehicles. They splashed and jolted along until the path widened and she could see the substantial house. It was almost as large as the Maidstone Arms, with a porch, gables, and massive pillars positioned at intervals along what would become a wide south-facing veranda. It was on the crest of a hill, overlooking a pond with willow trees trailing on the banks. There was an Olympic-size swimming pool covered with a dark green tarpaulin to protect it from the debris that littered the site, and a newly constructed pool house with a white stone patio. Then she saw the large Portakabin with the construction company's name written across it. "I won't be a moment," she said and got out.

"Excuse me. Could I see the person in charge?" she called as she approached the open door.

A burly man carrying a hard hat filled the small doorway. "Who do you want?"

"Whoever's in charge," she said sweetly.

"Can I ask what it's about? He's busy."

"I'm a friend of the owner, and I just wondered, as I'm here, if I could be shown the house. I'm from England," she added.

He disappeared, then returned and beckoned her inside.

"I'm the foreman," said a ruddy-faced man, who was sitting behind a desk.

"I'm Sylvia Hewitt, and I wondered if I could speak to whoever is in charge."

Sylvia waited in the cramped office as the men cleared up plans and went outside. The foreman said he would see if Mr. Donnelly was around. Ten minutes later Donnelly came in. "You wanted to see me?"

"I would really appreciate it if you could answer some questions for me."

"What about?"

Sylvia took a deep breath. "I believe a Mr. Moreno owns this property, and I'm eager to speak to him."

"Well, I can't help you. We never see him now. Our only dealings with him are through his financial adviser."

"Oh. I'll be honest with you," she said, "Mr. Moreno owes me a substantial amount of money. I was told he might be here. I've been trying to make contact with him."

"Aha," he said slowly, eyeing her up and down.

"I even hired a private detective. I think he might have spoken to you, a Mr. Matheson."

"Yeah, but I told him what I'm telling you. I don't know where Moreno is. He almost left me in a real hole too. He couldn't make the payments, but it was settled in the end by his financial adviser."

"Philip Simmons?" she asked.

"That's right. He's running the show. I get his orders from his architect and designers. They come down and check everything's to their specifications."

"Do you have a contact number for Mr. Simmons?"

The number he passed over was for a law firm in East Hampton. When she asked to be shown around, he said it was not possible.

"Did you ever meet someone called David Lyons?"

"Who?"

"David Lyons was a business associate of Alex Moreno's, and I wondered if you had ever met him here. Small, dark-haired, balding."

"I don't think so."

"Would you mind if I showed you a photograph? It will only take a minute."

She took it out and passed it to Donnelly. She pointed to David. "That's him."

He stared at the photograph, shook his head, and was about to pass it back when Sylvia stopped him. "Is that Philip Simmons with him? Just to the right." She pointed to de Jersey.

Donnelly stared at the picture. "It sort of looks like him. I dunno. Could be him."

"But you're not certain? Please, look at it closely. Is that Philip Simmons?" Her heart was pounding.

Donnelly stared at the photograph, then handed it back. "Like I said, it could be, but it's hard to tell. Mr. Simmons has a mustache and red hair."

"But you do think it looks like him?"

"Yes, sort of. What is all this about? Why are you here?"

She stood up, rather flustered. "I'm trying to trace Mr. Simmons."

"Then I suggest you talk to his lawyers. I gave you their number." He was obviously impatient for her to leave.

Sylvia walked out of the Portakabin, then decided to take matters into her own hands. She wanted to check out the property, and if anyone asked she would say she was just another English tourist. She inched back over the wooden planks, then onto the path to the house. She made her way to the pool house and peered inside. A white marble floor had already been laid, and ornate light fittings were being hung. A boy with paint-stained dungarees passed her. "Hi there," he said affably.

"This is going to be very nice."

"Yeah, it sure is. That marble was shipped in from Italy, and one of those lights cost more than my year's salary." He grinned.

"It's a very large swimming pool," she said.

"Yeah, it's one of the first things that was done out here. One end's more than ten feet. Diving board's gonna go at that end, and over there they're gonna lay a tennis court."

Sylvia thanked him and headed for the guesthouse. She peered inside. It looked fit for Royalty. Then she returned to the cab.

She had lunch in the hotel dining room. Her waiter was a young, rather handsome boy with dark, slanting eyes. He suggested the eggs Benedict, which were a specialty and served with home-cured ham. After she had finished he asked if she'd enjoyed it. "Delicious, thank you."

She decided to take a chance. "I wonder if you can help me. I'm trying to find someone who used to stay at this hotel, a friend. I'm desperate to get in touch with him. His name is Alex Moreno." She looked at him directly. "Did you ever meet him?"

"I met him," he said softly.

Sylvia flushed. Could she have struck lucky? "Oh, great! I can see you're working now, but could we talk later?"

"I'm off duty at two thirty, unless we get busy." He stepped back.

"I'm in room—"

He shook his head. "Staff are not allowed to go into guests' rooms, invited or not. House rules. I'll be in the hotel parking lot at two thirty."

"What's your name?" she asked.

"Ricky." He walked away but turned back briefly and gave her a dazzling smile.

Sylvia went to the coffee area, where she ordered a cappuccino, disappointed that Donnelly had not clearly identified Simmons and de Jersey as the same man. She wondered if she was being foolish. Then, at two fifteen she saw Ricky leave the hotel and meet a blond man on the pavement. They talked for a few moments, then walked out of sight. Promptly at two thirty she went into the hotel car park. It was almost empty, with no more than seven parked vehicles. A black, soft-topped Jeep headed toward her. The blond she had seen talking to Ricky was driving, and Ricky was sitting in the small backseat.

"Hi, you want to hop in?" he said. "We can drive to the beach." He was tanned with white teeth, bluer than blue eyes, and a whiter than white cap-sleeved T-shirt.

Sylvia climbed into the passenger seat.

"I'm Clint," said the driver. "What's your name?"

"Sylvia," she said. "Where are we going?" she asked nervously.

"Just to the beach. You want to talk, right?" All the way there, Clint chatted like a tour guide while Ricky remained silent.

When they arrived, Clint helped her out and suggested they take a walk. Sylvia looked at Ricky, who remained in the backseat. "Aren't you coming?" she asked.

"It's not me you need to talk to." He nodded to Clint, who was putting on a leather jacket.

Sylvia walked beside him. The wind was bitingly cold, so she pushed her hands into her coat pockets.

"So, is there some cash in this for me?" he asked, staring ahead.

"Well, I hadn't anticipated paying anyone, but I can go a couple of hundred. I don't know what you know that might help me."

"Maybe something, maybe nothing." He hunched his shoulders against the wind.

"You met Moreno?"

He nodded, and they walked in silence. After a moment she said she needed to know what he could tell her before she agreed to pay him.

He stopped. "Say five hundred?"

Sylvia sighed. She was really cold now. "Okay, but it's got to be worth it."

"Cash?"

"Yes," she said sharply.

They walked on, and he turned toward some sand dunes. She followed him, and as they reached the dunes he jumped into a hollow. "Out of the wind here," he said and sat down.

Sylvia joined him. "So, what do you know about Alex Moreno?"

Clint held out his hand. She opened her purse and counted out five hundred dollars. He pocketed them. "He was a real sharp dresser, designer labels, down to his socks. Never wore anything but the purest cashmere sweaters." She had not paid out five hundred bucks for a clothing catalog, but she said nothing. "I used to meet him when he came down looking for property over the summer. He always ended up at a place called the Swamp, real late, always alone. Sometimes he'd have way too much to drink. He liked the odd joint too, always asking around if anyone had any grass. I guess he was down there maybe four or five times over a few months, and then one night, it would be about the sixth time I'd seen him, he said he was celebrating and did I want to have a drink with him. I said yeah. We both worked there, you see, me and Ricky. That's how we met. Anyway, Moreno was sitting up at the bar, and he'd had a few already. He said he wanted to get blown, so after we closed he was waiting with his flash new Lexus. We went back to his hotel. He was drunk, and he told me he'd done this great deal, bought some property and got all the building permits agreed. He said it had taken months."

"When was this?"

"Oh, around July, maybe mid-August. Next time I met up with him would have been around mid-November. Ricky tipped me off that he was in town. He was staying at the Maidstone. I got a call from him. He wanted to see me, so I met up with him at the Blue Parrot—it's a bar on Main Street. We had a few drinks and went back to his hotel room. We were on the bed when he starts crying. He tells me he's got into real trouble financially. He rambled on and on, blubbering like a kid about how it was all falling apart. Then he passed out. I took my money and left. I could have taken a lot more, but I reckoned he was the type to cause trouble."

"When was the last time you saw him?"

"Okay, this would be just after Christmas and he came in real late. We met up again in the bar. He looked beat, needed a shave, but was all cashmered up as usual."

"December?"

"Yeah, said he'd come to sort out his property. He was having a hard time meeting payments. I thought he was just trying it on again, you know, not wanting to pay me, but then he says he's real serious about me, wants me to come to New York. He was drinking heavily, said he was staying at the Maidstone as usual but he was meeting someone real early the following morning. Said he was gonna check out of the hotel before breakfast. He said he'd take me to New York and told me to get a taxi to his place for eight. I live way out in Montauk, right? So, anyway, this time he was real edgy, like nervous all the time. Kept on about how much trouble he was in and that he was having a lot of pressure from some guy."

"Did he tell you his name?"

"Just that it was some builder."

"Donnelly?" she asked.

"I can't remember. I was real buzzy about him offering to take me to

New York and to travel with him. He was making me big promises and, you know, come winter out here, it's hard to make a living. Summer's when I make the dough."

"You get paid for sex?"

Clint's face tightened. "Moreno offered me a trip, lady. Whatever I get paid for is my own goddamned business."

"I'm sorry. Please go on. You agreed to accompany him to New York and then what?"

"That I'd see him after this meeting he had was over."

"Did he say who he was meeting?"

"No, but it was at his property. It's a huge place over in Georgica Ponds. I was to get there and we'd drive to New York together." Clint yawned and ruffled his hair. "So I'm packed and ready at seven. This guy was always going on about the place he had in New York just across from Central Park. He sort of made out that he was getting out of his problems, said something about his company crashing but that he might be doing some big deal and his finances would be in better shape and if I wanted we could go to Bermuda." He was staring at the ocean. "So one of my mates gives me a ride in to the gas station on the corner. I just had to walk across to Georgica Road and over to where Moreno's house was."

"Did you meet up with him?"

Clint shook his head. "No. There were trucks and stuff around, big diggers, so I reckoned it had to be the right place. It was still quite dark and there were lights on, but I couldn't see him or his car, so I took a walk around, and a few streets away I saw his Lexus parked, which I thought was odd. I hung around it for a while, maybe ten, fifteen minutes, then started walking back along the lane. I could hear machines turning over, so I reckoned the builders were starting work. I headed into the drive, and the noise was really loud. Then it stopped, so I kept walking, and what had been making all the noise was a machine to flatten down the earth in the bottom of the swimming pool."

"So work *had* started?"

"I dunno. There was just this one guy working the big compressor machine. There was no one else around. I wondered if maybe I'd got the wrong place. Like I said, Alex's car was some distance from the site."

"Did you go in?"

"No. I stood watching for a while, then I left to go back to the Lexus."

"Could you describe the man you say was using this machine?"

"Er, not really, he was a good distance away from me. But it wasn't Moreno. Too big for him."

Sylvia licked her lips. She opened her bag to look for the photograph. "What did you do next?"

"I hung around at the car, maybe another ten minutes or so, then I went back to the garage cos I had Moreno's cell phone number. There's a pay phone there, so I reckoned I'd better call him and find out what was going on."

"Did you get hold of him?" she asked impatiently.

"No, I tried, but it just rang then clicked into his message service. I wasn't sure what to do and I was hungry now, so I grabbed some breakfast. I was thinking of giving up, then decided I'd check one last time to see if Moreno's car was still there. Then, just as I was heading back across the road, I saw it turning left onto the highway. He had to drive right past me almost. I waved and yelled, but it just drove on."

"With Moreno driving?"

"No, it was the guy I'd seen by the pool. I never got a good look at him. All I could see were wide shoulders—he was hunched over the wheel and in profile to me."

"Then what?"

"So now I go back again to the building site. Figured maybe this guy was getting coffee or somethin' for Moreno. It was quite a walk, and I had a big bag to carry. All the guys were starting work. They were concreting over the bottom of the swimming pool for the lining."

"Did you see Moreno?"

"I asked if anyone knew where he was, but nobody had seen him. I finally gave up and went home."

"Did he contact you again?"

"No. I called his cell phone a few times, but it was dead." He shrugged. "That's it."

Sylvia was chilled to the bone, but she wasn't through, not after paying out five hundred dollars. She brought out the photograph of herself and David at the Christmas party. Her hand shook, partly from the cold and partly because she knew this might be the confirmation she had been looking for.

"Was this the man you saw at the building site?"

Clint looked at the photograph intently. There was a short pause and Sylvia held her breath.

"I think so. Can't be sure, though. Now I think of it, the guy I saw had reddish hair and this guy's blond, right?" He tapped Edward de Jersey's image.

She sat tensely. "Is this the man who was at the building site?"

Clint took a deep breath. "I'm pretty sure it is. But, like I said, it was dark, and when he drove past me I only got a profile. But it could be him."

"Could be isn't good enough," she said. "Please, really look at the photograph. It's very, very important."

Clint sighed. "It was a while back now, three months." He stared hard at the photograph. "Yes, it's him."

Sylvia replaced the photograph in her handbag and smiled. Her lips were almost blue it was so cold. No wonder de Jersey hadn't wanted to help her trace Philip Simmons. He'd threatened her, and now she was pretty sure that those threats had been designed to throw her off the scent, but she'd show him! Edward de Jersey, alias Philip Simmons, was going to pay her handsomely for what she had discovered.

CHAPTER

20

Over lunch a couple of days later, Christina told de Jersey that she was planning a dinner party.

"Who do you want to invite?" he asked, as he unfolded his napkin.

"I don't know. Maybe some of the jockeys and trainers, make it a fun evening." She ladled out the spinach soup. "What do you think?"

"Sounds good to me. We've not had a staff get-together for a long time." He broke up his bread and dipped it into the soup.

"Shall I organize it, then?"

"Sure."

He looked up in surprise as her roll hit his head. "What was that for?"

She glared at him. "Do you think I'm blind, stupid, or what? I want you to stop treating me like a child and start telling me the truth. The yard is like a morgue. The entire east wing is empty, and half of the staff are missing. We're in dire financial trouble, aren't we?"

"Ten points."

"Don't use that sarcastic tone with me."

"I wasn't aware that I was using any specific tone."

"God, I hate you when you're like this. It's like I'm sitting opposite a stranger. If things are bad, then we should discuss it like adults."

"And what could you do about it, my darling? Did your mother leave you a vast legacy?"

She stood up, walked round to him, removed his soup plate, went to the kitchen, and threw it into the sink. She returned with a large bowl of salad and banged it down on the table. "Help yourself."

"Thank you," he said. She returned to the kitchen and came back with a roasted chicken. She banged that down too, jabbed it with a carving knife, then returned to her seat.

"Throwing a tantrum, Christina, is not going to help. Pass me your plate and I'll serve."

It whizzed past his head and crashed against the wall. "I'm waiting for you to tell me what is going on," she said. "Or do you want me to go out and ask Donald Fleming?"

She poured herself a glass of wine as he carved the chicken breast. Eventually he said, "It's those investments I lost out on. The situation is worse than I initially thought. A lot worse."

"How long have you known?"

"Quite a while. I just didn't want to bother you with it. With your mother's illness, I felt you had enough to worry about without me adding to it."

"How bad is it, then?" she asked.

"Well, I've had to sell off a lot of the horses, and I'll probably have to sell more. Now is the time to do it. I shouldn't be away too long. Couple of days."

"Where are you going?" she snapped.

"To look at some auctions, maybe Dublin. I'm not sure."

"I'll come with you."

"If you want."

"What I want, Edward, is for you to be honest with me. If you're saying we're in financial trouble, why buy more horses?"

"I'm more than likely going to try to find buyers for the ones I have to let go. Does that answer your question?"

"Why are you being like this?"

He pushed away his plate and sighed. "Because it's breaking my heart."

"So you have to hurt me too?"

"Not intentionally. But I have a lot to think about and—"

"Maybe if you shared it, it wouldn't be so bad."

She was shocked when he met her eyes. His were brimming with tears.

"Oh, Edward," she said softly.

"Christina . . ." He turned away from her, and she got up to put her arms around him. "I'm sorry," he said.

"Darling, whatever happens, no matter how bad, if we see it through together we'll be okay. That's what's important, sharing it."

He drew her down to sit on his knee. "This is what happens when you marry someone old enough to be your father," he told her. "I should be taking care of you and the girls, and here I am getting tearful because it's all crumbling about my ears."

Christina hugged him tightly. "So, from the beginning. I know it started with David Lyons's suicide. I want you to tell me everything."

He sighed. "David got me into this mess. He stiffed me rigid. He delved into every account and proved to me how dumb I was to place such trust in him. He had carte blanche." He rocked her. "Let's continue this in more comfort. I need a brandy."

De Jersey walked with his wife into the drawing room. The fire was blazing, and she drew the curtains as he poured himself the brandy. He was working out in his mind how much to tell her. He lit a cigar and sat in the center of the sofa. He patted the cushion, and she curled up next to him, more like one of his daughters than his wife. She seemed so young and he felt so very old.

"I forgot to tell you. You must promise me that you'll be free on the second of May."

"What?"

"We have a school open day. They're doing *The Taming of the Shrew*, and Natasha's got the lead part. We have to be there at about six."

He took a deep breath. "I wouldn't miss it for the world."

"So, now that you have your brandy and your cigar and I'm sitting comfortably beside you, start with David Lyons's suicide."

He blew a smoke ring, then closed his eyes. "I can't believe you threw a roll at my head."

"Don't change the subject."

"Followed by a dinner plate." He laughed but stopped when he saw her expression. "I love you so much," he said quietly.

"Don't cut me out, Edward. Please. How bad is it?"

"Well, for me to lose one horse hurts like hell, so to lose an entire wing was a catastrophe. But I made enough from the sales to cover a substantial part of my losses. The estate is worth millions—the land alone is worth a fortune and I can sell some if I need an infusion of cash." He talked on, embroidering the lies for his wife, wishing they were true.

That following afternoon, de Jersey went into the yard with Fleming to look at the horses, particularly Royal Flush, who was being saddled for a training session. De Jersey stroked his neck. "How you doing, my son, eh?"

"He's a special one, isn't he?" Mickey Rowland, the jockey, had joined them. He was fixing the strap beneath his riding helmet. "He's been a bugger the last few days. If he gets downwind of the stud he's a right handful.

Couple of mares are in season, and you know what the young colts are like, randy sods."

De Jersey nodded. It was rare to have a racing stable and a stud in the same vicinity—a colt could smell a mare in season from a good distance away. This was why racing stallions did not go to stud until they had won enough races to make it worth the stud fees. Once they had mounted a mare, they became willful.

Mickey took the reins and could not resist kissing the horse's velvety nose. "I love him, he's a real character," he said.

De Jersey helped him into the saddle. "Yes, he's special, Mickey, and he's going to win the Derby."

"That's every racehorse owner's dream," Mickey said as he slipped his feet into the stirrups. "It's my dream too, Boss. I'd give a lot to ride him in the Derby."

"It's your ride, Mickey, but you've got to bring him in first at Lingfield, yeah?"

"Thank you, sir. I'll do my best."

De Jersey watched as his beloved Royal Flush walked out of the yard, Mickey talking to him as he tossed his head, eager to get to the gallops.

"Tony. *Tony!*"

Driscoll sat up in bed, his heart beating fast.

"What?" he yelled back.

Liz walked in with an invoice in her hand. "You've not paid the florist and they're saying that if we don't settle up they'll take legal action."

He flopped back onto the pillows. "Shit, is that all? I thought there was a bleeding fire."

"I'd like to throw you in one," she snapped. "The caterers are screaming too—and don't you hide under the duvet, cos I've not finished. I had Michelle on the phone this morning. She tells me an estate agent's been walking in and out of the villa showing buyers around. They're on their honeymoon, for God's sake!"

Driscoll closed his eyes. She sat on the edge of the bed and prodded him. "You'd better come clean with me, Tony. What the hell is going on?"

Driscoll burped, and she threw his antacid tablets at him. "I'm waiting. Have you not told me the full story about these bad investments?"

"I lost everything I invested."

"And how much was that?"

"A lot. We're in trouble now, but I'm gonna sort things out. In the meantime, though—"

"In the meantime you've got to pay these bills. It was your daughter's wedding, and you know how people round here talk."

"I don't give a fuck."

"Well, I do!" She paused. "Do you need the money from the villa to pay for the wedding?"

"Yeah. Soon as it's sold I'll sort out the florist."

"But it might not sell for ages—and what about all my stuff there?"

"I'm selling it furnished."

"But I worked my butt off doing that place up! I could have a real go at you, Tony. I really could."

"Oh, go and work it off with your muscleman. I can't take any more of your yelling."

"I'm not yelling. But I think we're gonna have to sit down and talk this out. I need to know just how badly off we are. We don't have to sell this place, do we?"

"Not yet."

"*Not yet!* I've got a garden party arranged for this summer. We *can't* sell. Please don't tell me we're in that deep."

He sat up and rubbed his head. "Can you just leave me alone? I've got a headache."

"You've had one for months," she said and stormed off.

Kevin was warming up when Liz came in. She was about to join him when she burst into tears.

"I've just about had my fill of him." She sniffled. "He's selling the villa without even asking me." Kevin handed her a tissue. "He's got into some terrible financial difficulty. It's just unbelievable that he's not said a word to me."

Kevin hovered. "Perhaps he didn't want to worry you."

"Worry me? He can't pay for his daughter's wedding. I'm worried all right."

Kevin took another tissue and handed it to her as she blew her nose. "I'm sorry. Do you want to leave the workout this morning?"

"No, no I don't. I want to work this out of my system. I want you to really push me this morning, Kevin. Take my mind off that husband of mine."

"I can think of a number of ways I can do that," he said, taking her in his arms. They went into a passionate embrace as he tried to peel off her red leotard.

"No, Kevin, we can't. He's in the house."

"So? He's been in and around before. It never bothered you then."

"Well, it does now. I'm just not in the mood. I'm sorry."

"That's okay, but you know sometimes? You should think about the way you treat me, like I'm just a hired stud."

"You know that's not true."

"Isn't it? You pay for me to train that body. How long's it gonna be before you start asking me how much I charge for a fuck?"

"Ah stop it. You know I care about you."

"So you say."

"I do. But I've got a lot on my mind."

"You said that about the wedding, so you didn't see me. Now it's something else, but I'm not taking it, Liz. This has been going on for almost a year now."

"Kevin, don't do this to me, please."

"It's my doing it to you that you said kept you sane. Your old man can't get it up, so is that all I am? Sex therapy? You said you two don't do it anymore. Well, what's going on, Liz? I care about you, you know that."

"Kevin, it's not the way it looks. I really care about you, I do. But he's my husband, impotent or not. He has been a real pain for the past six months. You know that. He's never home. I dunno what he's doing. He's hardly said two words to me."

Kevin flexed his muscles and stared at his reflection in the gym mirror. She came to his side and touched his arm, resting her head against his back, staring at their reflections. Kevin's body was honed to perfection. His hair was just starting to recede at the front, but he was handsome and he noticed her. If she had a new haircut, he noticed. When she had her nails done, he noticed. He'd even recommended the doctor who'd pumped her lips up and noticed when she'd had it done. Tony had asked if she'd got a cold sore because her lips looked puffy! Lately Tony seemed to be in a perpetual bad temper, burping and complaining about his stomach and snoring beside her every night, usually without so much as a good night kiss.

As she thought about her husband, Kevin gently eased her around to face him and began kissing her neck and stroking her breasts. He lifted her off her feet and laid her down on the bench press, stripping off her leotard and sucking at her nipples. If Tony tried to lift her in his arms, he'd put his back out! They became more passionate.

"Not here, Kevin. Take me into the sauna." She sighed and hugged him close.

The pair was having such a good time that neither heard Driscoll calling her name, or the sound of him at the sauna door. He opened it only a fraction, but he saw enough: his wife naked with her legs over Kevin's shoulders and her face flushed in pleasure. He shut the door, saying nothing. He left the house fifteen minutes later. His initial anger was gone; in its place there was a cold, seething calmness. He was going to be risking his neck in a few weeks' time, and in many ways he had been risking it for her; he had not wanted to let her down. Now he didn't care if he ever saw her again. Win or lose, he would do this last one for himself alone.

Driscoll drove to Chelsea and parked in the underground car park at Chelsea Harbor. He went into the apartments and up to number 204. The apartment was now on the market, but he'd not yet had time to tell Nikki, his patient longtime girlfriend.

Nikki opened the door and immediately wrapped her arms around his portly little body. "I've missed you. I've not heard from you in weeks."

"I know, darling, but I've had big troubles."

She brewed coffee the way he liked it with hot milk and then heated up some ginger biscuits. He also liked them hot. Driscoll, for all his fury against his wife and the trainer, never considered that his having a mistress was in any way a fault. In the good old days, when he had been flush with money, Liz had shopped till she dropped and he had screwed until he dropped.

"Nikki, I've got financial problems. I'm gonna have to sell this place. I'm sorry. There's no way round it. But if you go and live with your mum for a while, maybe . . . I can't say why or how, but I think I might be free and you and me can go off abroad to live together."

"Live with my mum?" Her pale face clouded and she started to cry.

Nikki was twenty-nine years old. He'd met her in the perfumery department at Harrods several years ago. For a while his wife received more gifts of perfume and cosmetics than most women would need in a lifetime. Three months later Nikki agreed to move into the apartment. They had been lovers ever since, on and off. He knew she probably dated other guys, but if so he never saw any sign of them and she never mentioned any other person being in her life. She simply focused on him when he arranged to see her. He paid money into a bank account for her every month, but now he had to tell her that he couldn't do that any longer either.

Driscoll managed to make love to Nikki. It was not a majestic performance by any standard, but as always, she made him feel as if he was the greatest stud in the world. They had some lunch and a bottle of champagne, and with a few more tears, she showed him out, promising that she would leave the apartment by the end of the month. She also promised she would show any potential buyers round when they called.

As the door closed behind him, she swore under her breath and went to the phone. She dialed her brother first, telling him to get a van round ASAP. She wasn't going to leave a single stick of furniture behind. Then she called her boyfriend and asked whether she could move in with him. Driscoll had been a "nice little earner" for Nikki, nothing more. She was just angry that she hadn't persuaded him to put the apartment in her name! She had a good mind to call his wife and give her an earful, but she didn't bother. Besides, she didn't want to tip the idiot off that she was doing a moonlight flit.

Driscoll met up with Wilcox at Kingston boat yard for some "shopping" for the heist. Wilcox was checking over a secondhand two-seater speed-boat for sale. It had seen better days and smelt of mildew as he hauled the tarpaulin off the trailer.

"It's been knocked around a bit. It's had a shoddy repaint job. How much are they asking?" Wilcox asked, looking at the For Sale card stuck on the windscreen. "I suppose we won't do better for this price," he said, but Driscoll was miles away, still deep in thought about Nikki.

"I mean, I couldn't say anything," Driscoll said. "But you know, if we pull this off, I'm gonna make sure Nikki does all right, take her abroad with me."

"What, leave the wife?" Wilcox asked, still more interested in the boat.

"Yeah, she nags all day. Caught her with her legs akimbo in the sauna today with her one-on-one trainer!" Driscoll said.

"How long have you had her?" Wilcox asked.

"Who, the wife?"

"No, the little girlfriend," Wilcox said as he bent down to check out all the rust. "This hasn't been under cover for a few years, never mind in the water," he said.

"She's been a fixture for four or five years," Driscoll said. "She's a lovely redhead. Tall, lovely long legs. You know, she's always there for me, makes me feel good, and she's great in the sack. Used to work in Harrods."

"You've been keeping her then?"

"Yeah, nice pad she arranged. Very tasteful. I used to love going to see her when I could. Needed her, know what I mean?"

"Yep, this is a real old boat. We do the business then torch it."

"Okay, what about you? You got any little dollies stashed away? You always used to."

"Nope. I had but they've been elbowed. Rika and I are on a good thing right now, and I don't want her to get her knickers in a twist just when I need to be chilled out."

"Right, yeah right. I don't want any aggro either. I'm just sorry I've got to sell the apartment. And me and Nikki'll get back together. She's gonna move in with her mother."

Wilcox nodded, not really interested. He fished in his pocket for some readies to deal with the boat owner. The bulbous-nosed elderly mechanic, wearing oil-streaked dungarees, had been hovering in the background, tinkering with another boat. Wilcox gestured for him to come over, and together they eased the boat off the trailer and down the few yards of slip road into the water. Wilcox started up the outboard, and he was surprised when it turned over quickly and appeared sound. He climbed out again as the old boy kept hold of the rope.

"Five hundred," Wilcox said, counting the fifty-pound notes.

"Nah, no way. Thousand quid, pal," the old boy insisted, winding the rope round a post, then wiping his filthy hands on an equally filthy rag.

"Six is my final offer," repeated Wilcox, still counting.

"Na, I'll go nine fifty and I'm doing myself an injury."

"Six hundred, take it or leave it," Wilcox said again. By this time he had the money stacked in a neat, tight wad.

"I can't do that. I'm giving you a good price. This is a fast boat. I worked on it myself. Nice seats too."

"You don't drive the seats though, do you? And with the amount of rust it's got, I'll be lucky if it stays afloat."

"Look, I'll come down to seven fifty, but that's it, that's my final price."

"Okay, thanks. Sorry not to be able to do business with you."

Wilcox opened his wallet, about to replace the money when the dirty hand made a grab for it.

"Six hundred, you bastards. Go on, take it!"

Wilcox climbed into the boat followed by Driscoll, who almost overbalanced and fell into the water. He then started the outboard and they set off up the river toward Richmond.

"We got moorings for this?" Driscoll yelled above the noise of the engine, his hair standing on end.

"Yeah, the Colonel's arranged it. Plus we've got another speedboat to check over. It's already at the boathouse."

It was blisteringly cold as they sped past Bucklands Wharf, then on toward Chiswick. Just past Teddington Lock the outboard coughed and spluttered, then cut out. Wilcox managed to get it going again, and they turned round, back up the river toward Putney.

"What a piece of fucking junk," Wilcox said, as they made it past the Putney rowing club and puttered on toward a boathouse a quarter of a mile away.

"We only need it for a few hours and, besides, it won't be us using it," Driscoll said, rubbing his hands.

"Right, but if it screws up they're fucked."

They passed beneath a willow tree. Wilcox maneuvered the boat into the boathouse, then switched off the engine. The boathouse was at the end of a garden. The house was up for lease, and the owners had let the boathouse and their speedboat for six months to a Mr. Philip Simmons. They had advertised it in the property pages on the agent's Internet site. The other boat was moored inside, covered with a tarpaulin. Driscoll stepped out onto some broken steps, then climbed up to the garden path. "I'll see you later," he said. "I'm going to get us some food—I'm starving."

In the boathouse there were gaps between the floorboards and holes in the roof. The water was murky and clogged with weeds and debris. Wilcox eased the doors shut and put on an overall to start work.

When Driscoll returned he was carrying two takeaway hamburgers, two cartons of soup, and coffee.

"You took your bloody time. This other one's rusted to hell and back too," Wilcox muttered, as he scraped then peered under the speedboat's steering column.

"I got you a cheeseburger," Driscoll said, handing him one, then sitting on an old orange box.

"This engine's been hammered into the ground, but I'm tuning it and it's sounding better." Wilcox opened his cheeseburger box, then looked at Driscoll slumped on the crate.

"You okay? Tony?"

Driscoll shook his head.

"What's happened? You get bad news?"

"No more than five hours; no, six. I only told her six fucking hours ago. It's unbelievable. She's even taken the fucking toilet-roll holder. The kitchen's like a war zone, all these fucking wires hanging out. I was selling it fucking furnished!"

"What are you talking about?" Wilcox asked as he stuffed the food into his mouth.

"Nikki. I went back by the apartment. I just wanted to make sure she was okay. She must have got a bloody furniture removal van there before I got the bleeding front door shut. She's cleaned the place out, the bitch!"

Wilcox couldn't help grinning, and Driscoll became irate. "What's so funny?"

"Well, you going on about this lovely redhead and now she's a bitch. Maybe she's gone with it all to her mother's."

"What? With a whole furniture van full of gear?"

Wilcox made his face straight and went over and patted Driscoll's shoulder. "Good riddance and better you find out now. If she had been around when you got the cut from this little job, she'd have screwed you over even worse, right? Best it happened now."

Driscoll sighed. He felt foolish and totally humiliated. It had been bad enough finding his wife with her trainer, now Nikki had betrayed him too.

"I tell you something, next woman I get is gonna be one hundred percent special."

"Hello?" Pamela's throaty, theatrical voice floated in to them, and she appeared at the door. In an oatmeal-colored coat, low-heeled fawn shoes, and a white silk shirt, she was looking much smarter than usual.

"What are you doing here?" Driscoll asked.

"Bringing you the mooring permits from our lord and master." She tossed over a large manila envelope.

"You look different," Wilcox said as he sipped his soup.

"I've been buying my wardrobe for the opening performance. I'm the perfect lady-in-waiting."

"Apart from the fag hanging out of your mouth," Wilcox joked, and she laughed, turning to leave.

"See you later, I suspect. Have a lovely day out on the river, boys!"

Driscoll checked his watch. "We should be going to the barn soon. How long you gonna be?"

"As long as it takes to fix the engine and see what gears it'll need. You go on ahead. I'll see you there."

When Driscoll entered the barn, he was still chilled from the river and blew into his hands. "Will somebody get those bloody heaters on?"

"You're in a pleasant mood," Pamela said, opening a bottle of water to fill the kettle.

"Yeah, well, I've had a bad day."

"Let's have a cup of tea and maybe you'll feel better." She opened the box of tea bags and looked around. "Have you heard from his lordship? He was supposed to be here before me." She lit a cigarette.

On cue the door opened and Westbrook entered. He smiled wanly, began to unbutton his coat, then keeled over onto the ground.

Driscoll stood above him. "Christ, is he pissed?"

"No, he's sick. Help him up. He gets these headaches that make him faint."

They assisted Westbrook to a chair. He sat down, shaking, and gripped his head. "I'm so sorry. Feel rather poorly today. Be okay in a while."

Driscoll turned away. It was fucking ridiculous. What a choice for the heist!

Pamela fussed over Westbrook, fetching him water, searching his pockets for his pills, and standing over him as he sipped. Then she helped him to the back of the barn, where he lay down on some sacking. "Will you marry me?" His voice was racked with pain.

Pamela stroked his head, which was glistening with perspiration. "I would have done like a shot, dear, once, but I'm too old for all that now. The best thing for me now would be retirement in the Bahamas. You could always be my houseguest."

"I'd like that," he said, hardly audible. Pamela watched over him until he drifted off to sleep. He didn't stir when Wilcox came in and banged the door. He was disheveled and freezing cold, and went straight to the heater to rub his hands.

Driscoll passed him his rubber gloves and nodded to Westbrook. "He fainted, flat on his face."

"Is he gonna be all right?"

"He's sleeping," Pamela said, as she put the kettle on the burner.

"Oh, that's brilliant," Wilcox said. "He's a fucking liability."

"Don't you swear at me, Jimmy, because I won't take it," Pamela said. "Tony is popping antacid tablets like mad, and you're not exactly a choirboy, so the pot's calling the kettle black, isn't it?"

Wilcox became irate. "I'm clean. What about *you*? Top yourself up with gin before you came, did you?"

"Stop it," Driscoll snapped at Wilcox. "Just shut the fuck up! Any problems we've got, we put before the Colonel and let him sort them out. Bickering's a waste of time and energy."

De Jersey stood outside the door, listening, choosing his moment. Eventually, he stepped forward and they saw him. "Problems?"

Wilcox pointed to where Lord Westbrook was sleeping. "Did a pratfall when he came in. Couldn't stand upright."

De Jersey went to the back of the barn, sat on his heels, and looked at the sleeping man. Westbrook's eyes opened. "I will not let you down," he said. "I'll make sure of it. I'll take the tablets before I go, not wait as I did today. It's just that I have to test how long I can go between these wretched attacks."

"What do they feel like?" de Jersey asked.

"Excruciating migraine, dizzy, sick. But my pills sort me out, really they do."

De Jersey patted his shoulder. "Okay, old chap, I believe you. Just rest here a while, and when you feel up to it, come and join us."

"Thank you."

De Jersey began to confer with Wilcox and Driscoll about the look-alike. "We take her straight to the Aldersgate warehouse. Try to keep her calm, maybe even let her think that that's where we'll be filming. Not until we have her secure inside do we give her the details. We need her standing by earlier to be sure, I'm thinking now maybe six o'clock, seven at the latest, so we can prime her. Meanwhile we need to get to her husband fast. There'll be no need for any rough stuff."

Pamela broke in. "If the Queen becomes troublesome, what should I do?"

"She won't if we're threatening her husband."

Driscoll snorted. "If it was me and you had my wife, I'd tell you to keep her!"

Later that evening, when everyone except Wilcox, Driscoll, and de Jersey had left, de Jersey asked them for their opinion. He believed he had come up with a solution to the panic alarms. He opened the diagrams he'd printed off from the CD. "The power source for the alarms is located here, in what would have been the old coal chute." He pointed to a spot on the diagram. "The on-street chute access has been cemented over, so the only way into it is from inside the house." De Jersey marked it as he spoke.

"How the hell do we get in there?" Driscoll asked.

De Jersey opened his cigar case and offered it to Driscoll and Wilcox, who shook their heads.

"Have another look at the information on the CD," he said. "The warehouse where we'll be is just a hundred yards from the safe house, but its cellar extends beyond the actual warehouse space. It's almost next to theirs. All these properties were supplied with coal using the same chute. If we enlarge the small chute door in our warehouse's cellar, we'll have access to the room at the bottom of the chute. At the other side there should be a similar door leading into the safe house's cellar. We open up our side and gain access to their cellar through this coal chute. We can't do it any other way. Marsh tells me they test the alarms every day at nine. After that we disconnect the lines. We will have only a short time because we're moving out the convoy at ten twenty-five, but at least we'll know that anyone pressing a panic button is not going to worry us. What do you think?"

"It might be the only way," said Wilcox.

Heartened, de Jersey outlined how long it would take and what equipment they would need, and both men agreed the idea was workable. They would use a high-powered laser gun to cut soundlessly through the cement, but as they would have to go brick by brick, their nights from now on would be busy. All he had left to work out was how to disconnect the alarms without them going off once they were inside. For this he would need Marsh again.

They turned to the getaway plan—they hadn't yet worked out the fine details of their own escape. They had to get rid of the Royal vehicles, then get themselves and the jewels away from the scene as quickly as possible.

By late evening, they believed they had a plan, but they wouldn't know until the day of the robbery whether it would work.

Christina was in the kitchen sorting through some of her mother's old letters and photographs when the phone rang.

"Could I speak to Edward de Jersey, please?" said an unfamiliar voice.

"He's not here. Can I take a message?"

"Where is he?"

"Who is speaking?"

"Sylvia Hewitt. Who's that?"

"Christina de Jersey. Do you want to leave a message?"

"When do you expect him back? I need to see him."

"In a few days. Does he have your number?"

"Thank you, and yes. Sorry to have bothered you, Mrs. de Jersey."

Christina hung up. She didn't know why, but the call unnerved her. She'd never met Sylvia, but she knew she was Helen Lyons's sister. She had been so abrupt, almost rude. She jotted down the message on a yellow Post-it and stuck it on the phone.

Liz Driscoll had just returned from a manicure when the phone rang. She picked it up. "Hello?"

"Could I speak to Mr. Driscoll, please?"

"He's not at home. Who's calling?"

"Sylvia Hewitt. Do you know when he'll be back?"

"He's out on business."

"When do you expect him?"

"Sometime this evening. Do you want to leave a message?"

"Just say I called. I think he has my number. Sorry to disturb you."

Liz hung up. This was the second time she'd taken a call from the woman, and if Tony was up to his old tricks again she'd really have it out with him.

Marsh was pleased with the new equipment. He had spent thousands in computer stores across London. The skimmer was well worth the five thousand he'd paid for it. He'd given his wife carte blanche to go shopping at Harrods with the fake credit cards he'd had a pal create using several numbers he'd got from the skimmer, and she had departed, leaving him to take care of their child.

De Jersey had traveled by public transport to Marsh's house. It was almost five thirty when they met. They discussed the phone conversations between Scotland Yard and the safe house. Marsh was still confident they would have no problem in gaining the IRA code word for the second of May. He played the tapes he had recorded of numerous IRA informants calling in to give the day's code word. It was usually an odd name, sometimes a place or object. The tapes reassured de Jersey that Marsh was as good as his word, and they played them again so that de Jersey could practice an Irish accent. Marsh also confirmed that there had been no changes in the Queen's official diary and the fitting date remained fixed. The Royal party was to depart from Buckingham Palace at ten that morning.

De Jersey looked around the room. "You're certainly spending the money I'm paying you. Perhaps you should slow down a bit. You don't want to make anyone suspicious about all this equipment you've got. You couldn't buy it on your wages."

"I'm watching my arse, don't you worry." Marsh swiveled round in his chair and looked at de Jersey. "Come on, what is it? There was no real need for you to come and see me today. What else do you want?"

De Jersey put his hand into his pocket and took out a thick envelope. "I need your help with something. Take a look at this. It's D'Ancona's visual display, the alarms, the panic buttons."

Marsh grinned. "You're something else, man, you really are." He took the CD and put it into his computer. "Fuck me! How did you get hold of this?" he exclaimed.

"Inadvertently via you. You set the cat among the pigeons when you tried to hack in, so they had to check all their files, and I have my contacts."

"This must have cost."

De Jersey smiled. "Not really." He tapped the screen. "My problem is this. I know how to get into this area here"—he pointed to the coal chute—"and I know that's where we can get access to the panic alarms. But I don't know how to deactivate them."

Marsh's mouth turned down as he peered at the screen. He scrolled down, then back up again. "Well, it's simple enough to unplug lines from boxes—it's just a matter of pulling them out."

"I can tell there's a *but* coming," de Jersey said.

"There is, and it's a big one. The second you pull any one of those plugs, all the others will activate and notify the call center. You'll have every copper in London down there in a jiffy."

"What do you suggest?"

Raymond tugged nervously at his cuffs. "I haven't a clue. You'll need to find a way to pull out all the plugs at the same moment. A fraction of a second out and it's bye-bye Crown Jewels!"

There was a moment's silence as the two men contemplated their predicament. Marsh clicked, and the interior of the safe house came up again on his screen. The silence was broken by his daughter, who started howling. He left the room, and de Jersey could hear him cooing and talking to her.

Then Marsh charged back in carrying the child. "I've got it! I think I know how we can do it—but she's filled her nappy so I gotta change her."

Rika had just put the twins to bed and was thumbing through the *TV Times* when the phone rang. She hoped it would be Jimmy. He'd been gone all day.

"Is Mr. Wilcox there?"

"No, he not back yet."

"My name is Sylvia Hewitt. Could you ask him to call me? He has my number. Tell him it's quite urgent, would you?"

"Who?"

"Sylvia Hewitt. Are you expecting him this evening?"

"Yes, I tell him you call. Sylvia who?"

"Hewitt. Please give him the message."

Rika got a pen and notepad. She started to write down the message then crumpled the paper and threw it into the bin. She was sure this Sylvia Hewitt was after her man. She had spoken so rudely, as if Rika was the maid.

De Jersey left Marsh's house grinning from ear to ear. A taxi passed him, slowing down. The inside was lit, and de Jersey saw that the blond-haired Mrs. Marsh was paying the driver. She had a vast array of boxes and bags, all with the Harrods logo. He watched until she had entered the house, and then, as the cab made a U-turn, he stepped out and flagged it down.

He asked to be driven to Wimbledon Station, and the driver beamed.

"That's lucky. I've just come from Knightsbridge. Didn't reckon I'd get another fare back." He switched on the clock.

"That was some shopping your last fare had," de Jersey said.

"Don't know where they get the dosh. Took two Harrods doormen to load me up. Said her husband had made a killing on the horses. Wish he'd give me a few tips."

De Jersey sat back against the seat as his driver gave a monologue about his lack of luck on the tracks. "You a racing man?" he asked eventually.

"No, I'm not," de Jersey replied.

"Best way to be. It's a fool's game," the driver said, then turned to glance at de Jersey. He was sitting in the shadow, his face virtually in darkness. "Not a gambling man, then, eh?"

"No."

"Don't take risks, eh?"

"No, I don't like risks." He closed his eyes.

CHAPTER

21

De Jersey was loath to do it, but he cut down on some more staff and sold six more horses. The yard was rife with rumors. All were concerned for the stable's future and their jobs, so no one felt it odd that just as the racing season was starting de Jersey was spending more and more time away. Fleming had told them only that he was in financial difficulty. However, de Jersey was monitoring Royal Flush as diligently as ever: he was now relying on the great horse to achieve big results. Luckily he had consistently improved during training, even if his temperament in the stable had not. If he felt like it, he could fly on the flat, but he was often a slow starter, not kicking in until halfway through the run, when Mickey said he could feel the animal's mood change. One moment he was sluggish, the next Mickey could hardly hold him. There was not a horse in the yard that could keep up with him.

De Jersey received a call from Pamela. Lord Westbrook's health had deteriorated and she suggested de Jersey visit him. De Jersey thanked her and hung up. He swore under his breath. Just as he thought everything was under control, something else had gone wrong. Christina had mentioned a phone call from Sylvia Hewitt, and both Wilcox and Driscoll said the woman had called them.

"I had to fish the fucking message out of the bin. Rika's convinced I'm fooling around with her," Wilcox told them.

"Leave it with me," de Jersey said. "I'll go and see what she wants."

"Maybe her money," Wilcox suggested.

* * *

It was just over two weeks to go, and Raymond Marsh had been busy. So had his wife. His purchases ranged from two dozen handmade silk shirts, suits, and shoes to computer accessories, TV sets, and furniture. Marsh was preparing to leave the country. After the robbery, he would decamp to South America. His credit-card frauds were reaching ludicrous proportions, but he needed hard cash to ensure that his departure was paid for and he had funds in hand. His house was on the market. He had not thought of how his behavior might affect de Jersey. Only one of the stolen credit-card numbers had to be recognized for him to be arrested for theft.

De Jersey still had not made contact with Sylvia, and Christina took another call from her.

"This is Sylvia Hewitt. Mrs. de Jersey, would you please ask your husband to return my call? When I said it was urgent I meant it."

Christina found her attitude most objectionable. "What is this about, Miss Hewitt?"

"Alex Moreno. Tell him I have some interesting information concerning a man called Philip Simmons."

As before, Sylvia hung up abruptly. Christina couldn't understand why the woman had been so rude.

In Monaco, Paul Dulay was ready. His boat was crewed up, and the engine had been tested. The weeks before the Crown Jewels fitting dragged, but his workrooms were prepared. Everything was ready for the green light.

He was sitting outside a harbor café in Monte Carlo, on his third coffee, when de Jersey approached.

"You're late," Dulay said. "I've been here over an hour."

"Sorry. I was looking over your boat."

"She's all set. Would you like to go for a spin in her?"

"I don't have time. Did you arrange the meet?"

"Yeah. He's only in Paris for two days."

"At the Ritz?"

"Yeah, and he didn't like me asking him to meet you. You know what these guys are like about honor. You have to do a lot of bowing around the guy. He's something else. And he's got this other guy that breathes down your neck the whole time."

"Odd Job."

"What?"

"Nothing. Is this guy his bodyguard?"

"Yeah. He's got a driver-cum-heavy as well. I said we'd meet him this afternoon at the Louvre. He's also into art. Do you know that if a Japanese person buys a painting and holds on to it for two years, it becomes his property even if it's stolen goods."

"No, I didn't. I want to meet him alone, Paul."

"What?"

"You heard me. The less we're seen together the better."

"I arranged the meet, for Chrissakes!"

"I know you did. But I still want to meet him alone." He reminded Dulay to anchor a good distance off the coast the day of the robbery. De Jersey also instructed him to test the watertight crate he had told him to acquire. They spoke for another few moments, then de Jersey left.

He caught a taxi back to the airport and hired a twin-engine plane to fly to Paris. He picked up another taxi and arrived at the Louvre just after two thirty. He had half an hour before his meeting with Mr. Kitamo.

Mr. Kitamo hardly ever looked directly at de Jersey. He maintained a slow walk, pausing at various paintings, sometimes stopping to read a plaque, then stepping back to gaze at the picture. He appeared to be interested only in the art on display and let out a soft sigh when they stood in front of the *Mona Lisa*. The bodyguard kept a discreet distance behind them.

Kitamo finally broke the silence. "To possess a painting of such beauty is very desirable, but there are many rumors that her enigmatic smile is whispering, 'Fake.' I will require one of my own people to check over the merchandise. Although I trust our mutual friend, I will accept the terms only if I am satisfied that the said item is authentic. We have agreed on the price, and I understand you wish to have a show of my intention." Kitamo turned his expressionless black eyes toward de Jersey. "One million U.S. dollars."

"Correct," de Jersey said.

"Agreed. Our friend will receive it as soon as I am informed that the item is in his possession. I will, perhaps, be prepared also to negotiate a price for certain smaller valuable pieces." Kitamo ended the conversation as quickly as he had started it. "I have enjoyed meeting you, Mr. Simmons." He gave a small bow, as if to conclude the meeting, and turned back to the *Mona Lisa*.

De Jersey, however, remained where he stood. Kitamo hesitated, then clicked his fingers to his bodyguard. Kitamo moved off, and his bodyguard stepped in front of de Jersey, withdrawing from his jacket pocket a white envelope and passing it discreetly to him. Then he joined Kitamo. De Jersey crossed to sit on one of the leather-covered benches and slipped the envelope inside the gallery's brochure as he opened it. It contained confirmation of a banking facility for over $250 million U.S. in Kitamo's name. It was issued by the Banque Eurofin. A contact number was provided.

De Jersey remained seated for a few moments. When he stood up and looked toward the end of the gallery, Kitamo, who had been watching him, gave a small bow. De Jersey inclined his head back and walked out. Mr. Kitamo, as Dulay had said, was a legitimate buyer and had the finance to purchase a good many of the jewels they were planning to steal. De Jersey was relieved to know this.

Back in England, the warehouse remained empty, but Wilcox and Driscoll timed the journey from there to the safe house several times. The date on which they would move all the convoy vehicles and the equipment was still undecided, although de Jersey planned to do it at night, one vehicle at a time, so as not to raise suspicion. After months of planning, the heist was only five days away.

Christina was at home watching television when she received a third call from Sylvia Hewitt. She again asked to speak to de Jersey and seemed angry when she was told that he was away.

"Where can I get in touch with him?" she asked.

"He usually stays at his club, the St. James's, but I know he's very busy at the moment, so if you would like to leave him a message—"

"I already have. I'll call the club. Sorry to bother you, but if he should return, can you pass on these numbers?" Sylvia dictated her cell, office, and home numbers.

"How is Helen?" Christina couldn't resist asking, just to hear Sylvia's response.

"Still grieving for David. So, will you pass these numbers to your husband?"

"Yes."

"Thank you," Sylvia said and hung up.

Christina had just settled down to continue watching television when Sylvia called back. "He's not there, and they said he was not expected this evening. Have you a mobile number I could call?"

"I'm afraid I don't know it. I'm so sorry."

There was a pause. Christina could almost feel the woman's impatience.

Sylvia sounded really angry when she asked again if Christina could get her husband to call her urgently. "Please make sure he knows that he really should contact me."

"I'll tell him."

Christina went into her husband's study to look for his cell phone number. She could never remember it. She had been worried to hear that he was not expected at the club that evening. She found the number and called it, but the phone was switched off. Frustrated, she called de Jersey's club. A moment later they were speaking.

"Christina? Is something wrong?"

"No, darling. It's just that David Lyons's sister-in-law called. She said it was very urgent. It's the third time. She's really quite persistent. I said you were staying at the club, and I think she called there."

"Oh, God, that wretched woman."

"The porter said you weren't there."

He laughed. "That's why I stay here. Good service!"

"Well, it's good that I caught you. She wanted your mobile number, but I didn't give it to her."

"Thank you. She's a real pain. Did she say why she wanted me so urgently?"

"Not really. Something about someone called Moreno, and I can't remember the other name she mentioned. She left an array of contact numbers. Do you want them?"

"No, I don't want to speak to her."

"Are you all right, darling?"

"Yes. Just had a heavy day. Back-to-back meetings. I'm not raising funds as fast as I'd hoped."

"Is there anything I can do?"

"Not really. I'm having dinner with an American banker this evening, so things may look better tomorrow. I'll call you later and give you an update. And perhaps after all I'll have the woman's numbers. I'll call and get her off my back."

De Jersey replaced the receiver, tense with anger. He thanked the porter and arranged a room for the night. The man passed him his room keys and told him about the call from a Miss Hewitt. "Thank you, John. If she calls again, tell her I'm in a meeting and can't be interrupted, would you?"

"Yes, sir. Good night, sir."

"Good night, John."

De Jersey showered and changed into a clean shirt, which he had brought in his briefcase. He lay down on the bed and closed his eyes. He was relieved that he had decided on a whim to come to his club. It had been pure coincidence that he had walked in just as Christina called. He wondered what the wretched Hewitt woman wanted. It was almost eight, though, so he decided to go to Westbrook's and deal with Sylvia Hewitt later.

De Jersey left the club unnoticed by the porter. He had already put a do-not-disturb message on his room's phone-message recorder. He hailed a taxi in Jermyn Street.

Westbrook was leaning against the rail looking down at de Jersey as he came up the stairs.

"Hi there. When you left the message that you wanted to talk to me, I didn't think you'd come in person. I was waiting for you to ring back," he said.

De Jersey put out his hand. "Well, we're pretty close to kickoff, so I thought it best to run over the finer details in person." They shook hands.

"Come in." Westbrook strolled ahead of him through the open door.

De Jersey didn't show how shocked he was by Westbrook's appearance. The man's face was haggard, with a yellowish, sickly pallor, and his clothes were unkempt.

"Can I offer you a drink?" Westbrook asked.

"No, thank you," de Jersey said, and his nostrils flared at the stench of alcohol and urine. "Stinks like a cat's litter tray in here," he said.

"I know, it's frightful, isn't it? There are two moggies. God knows where they are. I don't see them much. Live under the bed most of the time. But they're why I'm here. I agreed with my relative to feed them and empty their shitty bins." Westbrook slumped on the unmade bed. "I've not been out today," he said.

De Jersey sat on the edge of a once elegant, velvet-covered wing chair. On the mantelpiece stood rows of pillboxes and bottles. Stuffed between them were letters, postcards, invitations, and unopened bills.

"Have you not been out because you're sick or because you can't be bothered?"

"Bit of both. I'm sick as hell, so I've been staying in watching the soaps. They all have such dreadful lives, it sort of takes the heat off my own." He laughed, and de Jersey saw that even his teeth were worse than he remembered, as if the cancer was rotting his gums.

"You'd better get yourself together. You smell as bad as the cats' tray. What about clean clothes?"

Westbrook indicated an old walnut wardrobe, its door hanging off its hinges. Inside were racks of suits, plus sweaters and shirts on shelves. "Oh, I'm flush for clothes, thanks to you, old chap. It's just getting up the energy to get dressed. It's not been a priority."

"Make it one," de Jersey snapped.

Westbrook stared at him, then shrugged. "Yes, sir."

"What do you need to get yourself together? We have four days to go, and from the look of you, I'd say you're not going to make it."

Westbrook swung down his legs and glared at de Jersey. "I'll make it. I'll take some booster painkillers and some high-quality speed. I won't let you down. Believe me, this is all I'm staying alive for."

"All right, but if you fuck me over, it won't be your life I'll go after. Do you understand what I am saying?" He nodded at a picture of Westbrook's kids.

"I understand you perfectly."

De Jersey looked over the array of medicines. "Morphine," he said coldly.

"Yes," said Westbrook. "It's not prescription, but it dulls the pain. My old aunt Sarah used it for years for arthritis. Got to be careful not to take too much, though."

"I'll have it." De Jersey pocketed the bottle.

"Do you fancy a glass of wine? There's a reasonable wine bar on the corner up the road. Bite to eat on me?" Westbrook gave a wolfish smile.

De Jersey stood up. If he had been uneasy about Westbrook before, he was even more so now. "You use that money I'm paying you to eat, not to get pissed." He looked down at Westbrook's feet. He was wearing holey socks. "Use it to get some laundry done too, and a new pair of socks. And if you've got a toothbrush, use it. Your breath stinks as much as you do."

"I'm rotting away inside," Westbrook said, stepping away defensively, but de Jersey held on to his jacket lapel.

"I'm depending on you and I'm watching you. Four days is all I ask for you to hold on to being straight. Then you can stew in your own shit for all I care. Four days. Look at me. Can you do it?"

Westbrook somehow found the strength to push de Jersey's hand away from him. "Don't threaten me. I said I'd be up for it. I haven't let you down yet, and I have no intention of doing so now. Like I said, I have the drugs I need to keep me on my feet and my head clear. Take the morphine. I'll suffer for you. How's that?"

De Jersey felt compassion for him. "I'm sorry . . . but we're worried about you. I don't want you OD'ing on that stuff before the heist."

Westbrook made a big effort to straighten up. It was both sad and admirable. "I'm ready, and I hope to God you are, because I don't know how much longer I've got left."

* * *

Sylvia had decided not to go into work but to take another week off. By the following morning, with still no call back from de Jersey, she was furious. She put in yet another, this time to the estate. A blustering man answered. He said he was the manager and would pass on the message.

Christina was in the kitchen when Fleming tapped on the door. "Mrs. de Jersey, there was a call from a Miss Hewitt for the boss. It came through to my office. Rude woman."

"Oh, thank you, and yes, she is. She's called here numerous times. Did you say he was still at his club?"

"No. I just said I'd pass on the message, and I gave her his mobile number as she said it was urgent. I hope that's okay. I also need to have a word with him about scheduling some races. Can you ask him to give me a ring when it's convenient?"

"Sure. I'll call him now."

Fleming seemed very put out about something.

"Are you all right?" Christina asked.

He gave her a curt nod and started to leave, then paused, his back to her. "It's a tough time. A lot of the staff have been made redundant. It doesn't make for good staff relations. Some of the young lads are worried. I know it can't be helped, but like I said, it's not easy."

"I'm sorry, Donald, but Edward is trying to make himself financially more secure. It's why he has to spend so much time in London. In fact, he's meeting with bankers this week."

Fleming gave her a rueful look.

"He said he may have to think about remortgaging the estate," she told him. "If there's anything I can do, please don't hesitate to ask."

"Thank you, Mrs. de Jersey."

Christina left a message at the St. James's, then called her husband's cell phone.

He answered. "Hello, darling. It's a bit difficult for me to talk right now, I'm in the middle of a meeting. It's sounding as if I may have some good news. Is it urgent?"

"Not really. Sylvia Hewitt has called again, and Donald gave her your mobile number. He also wants to sort out some racing dates. Also, please don't forget the girls' school play. You promised you'd be there."

"Can we talk about this later?"

"Yes, sorry to interrupt, but I felt that Donald would really like to talk to you, and from what he said, Sylvia was angry that you hadn't returned her calls."

"I'll call them both."

She hung up, then went into her husband's study. On the desk was a large diary. She opened it and looked down the listed races and the horses earmarked to compete. Some had lines crossed through them. She turned a few pages. She noticed that May second was circled and that a memo about a race at Brighton had been written in. She saw her own note to remind him of the school play; she picked up a pen and printed THE TAMING OF THE SHREW. She replaced the pen in the holder and glanced over the neat desk. Then she hooked a finger through one of the drawer handles and pulled. It was locked, which niggled her, but she left the study and forgot about it.

Later, from the kitchen window, she watched the jockeys leading the horses out for their midday training. It was cold and the sun was bright. Royal Flush was playing up again, bucking and shaking his head. He kicked out, and then the long line of valuable horses was heading for the rolling acres beyond the track. It all looked so perfect, so affluent, and she sighed. She knew how much her husband loved this life. Christina threw on her fur-lined coat and dragged her riding boots out of the hall closet. By the time she reached the stable yard, most of the horses were out exercising, and she walked from stable to stable, then turned into the tack room. It was a hive of activity. The pungent aroma of saddle soap mingled with the fresh smell of hay and manure. For the first time she felt as if she didn't belong. She walked for an hour around all the stables, into the various yards and offices, and then to the garages. She stood by her husband's Rolls-Royce, which was being polished by one of the chauffeurs, ready to be sold. She asked where the driver she usually used was and discovered that he no longer worked for them. It was only now that she realized just how many of the staff had gone. It made her feel even more inadequate. No wonder Donald Fleming was concerned. So much had happened while she had been away. So much that she hadn't noticed on her return.

"How many horses have been sold?" she asked a girl she passed on her way back to the house.

"I think about twenty, Mrs. de Jersey," she replied sadly.

"Does that include the ones from the east wing?"

"No, Mrs. de Jersey, they went a while back. The latest ones went to the Tattersalls sales and over to Ireland," the girl continued. "But we've big hopes for Royal Flush," she added.

Christina gave her a wan smile and walked on. It dawned on her that perhaps her husband was not going to be able to get out of his present financial trouble. It was obvious that it was a lot worse than he had suggested. By the time she had returned to the house and removed her coat and boots, her depression had turned to anger.

Christina went back into her husband's study. Even there she felt like an outsider. The neatness and the locked drawers infuriated her. She went into the kitchen, found a screwdriver, then returned to the study. She wrenched open one drawer after another, took out the contents, and placed them on the desk. She was panting, half in fear, half in anger, as she set about sorting through them. To begin with she found nothing of importance: fees for trainers and purchases of horses, notes on horses he was considering buying, at least before the current financial crisis. However, there were also unpaid bills and outstanding accounts and a 155,000-pound VAT bill, with a warning that unless it was paid within a week legal action would be taken.

At the bottom of one of the drawers she found a paper with Edward's handwritten notes. She sat down in the desk chair and scrutinized the figures. He had been neat and meticulous. He had listed and dated everything that Lyons had invested as well as everything on which Moreno had frittered the money away: meals, houses, expensive office supplies. Seeing in black and white the losses, in not thousands but millions, she felt almost faint with shock. Her husband was virtually bankrupt.

Christina went into the kitchen and opened the fridge. Her throat was dry with nerves. She poured a tumbler of orange juice and went back to the study. She began to return the documents to the drawers, at first hoping she could replace them as she had found them, then not bothering. He would know by the marks of the screwdriver on the drawer handles and locks that she had broken in. She stuffed loose papers into the top right-hand drawer and slammed it shut, but it was too full so she snatched out a handful of papers and slammed it shut again. The glass of juice toppled over. "Shit." She ran from the room and returned with a wet cloth.

Back in the study she faced the front of the desk to scrub at the carpet on her knees. She half-rose and was leaning against the rim of the desk with the palm of her hand when it moved. She stood up. "Now what have I done?" she muttered. She tried to push the desk back into position, then saw a small hinge. She pressed it, and to her astonishment, the right-hand side of the front of the desk opened. She bent down to discover three more drawers. The lower ones were locked, and even when she attempted to open them with the screwdriver they wouldn't budge. She could see they had what looked like a steel rim.

"It's a safe," she said aloud. Then she tried the smaller top drawer, which opened. It contained envelopes full of documents about the estate mortgage. A brown manila envelope was tucked beneath them. Her heart missed a beat. Inside it, she discovered two passports. Both contained pictures of Edward but with different names. One was in the name Edward

Cummings, and there was a recent New York customs stamp inside. The other passport was Irish, in the name of Michael Shaughnessy. None of this made sense. Christina was certain her husband had been in the United Kingdom on the date marked in the Cummings passport. In another envelope, there were passports for herself and their daughters, all with different names. She sat back, unsure of anything anymore. She had believed de Jersey was in London after Christmas because he had told her so, but according to the passport he had been in New York. What else had he lied to her about?

De Jersey was in the warehouse inspecting Wilcox's work on removing the wall that separated it from the D'Ancona cellar. Wilcox had put the bricks back into position with a sugar and flour solution mixed with gray water paint for the right color to cover the missing cement. They would fall apart if a hand pushed hard against them. The work was good, and de Jersey was pleased. Then a call came through on his cell phone. It was Sylvia Hewitt.

"Mr. de Jersey, I had hoped you would call me."

"I'm sorry, Miss Hewitt, I've been very busy."

"So have I," she said softly. "I need to meet you urgently. I have just returned from New York. I believe you were there?"

"You must be mistaken."

"I don't think I am, and I'm not playing games with you anymore. This is a very serious matter, perhaps even for the police . . . or we could come to some financial arrangement. Either way, we should discuss my findings. I think you know what I'm referring to."

"No, I don't," he said coldly.

"Shall we say six this evening at my flat? You know the address, don't you, Mr. Simmons?"

She hung up. He stared at the phone in his hand, hardly able to believe what he had just heard. His heart was beating rapidly, and he felt dizzy. This was the worst thing that had happened so far, and he was going to have to sort it out fast. He slowly walked away from the coal cellar and into the grimy toilets. He splashed his face with cold water until he felt calm, then patted it dry with a grubby white towel. He stared at his reflection in the cracked mirror. He crossed to his overcoat, felt in the pocket, and took out Westbrook's bottle of morphine. He held it in the palm of his hand, as if weighing it. He would have to find out how many other people Sylvia Hewitt had told, then make a decision about the woman herself. He sighed. He would do it alone so that only he risked paying the ultimate price.

CHAPTER

22

Sylvia uncorked a fresh bottle of wine and set it out with two glasses and a bowl of peanuts and crisps. She'd already had a few glasses to celebrate what she felt would be a sweet victory. She had vacuumed, dusted, and plumped up the cushions. She felt excited and powerful, and a little light-headed from the wine as she looked over the "stage" she had set. She went to her desk and called Matheson. He listened as she told him she had received his final invoice and would be sending him a check. She also told him she had tracked down Philip Simmons in London.

"He's in the U.K., then?" Matheson asked.

"Yes, and I'm expecting him to come and see me now."

"Well, congratulations. Job well done. Does he know where Moreno is?"

"I presume so. All will be divulged soon enough. I'm sure I'll get my investment repaid, perhaps even more for all the trouble it's caused me." Sylvia was pleased with herself. "I might send you a little extra, Mr. Matheson."

The doorbell rang, and she stood up. "I have to go. He's arrived. Thank you so much again."

She was still pleased with herself as she ushered de Jersey into the drawing room, gesturing for him to sit as she took his coat. She had decided not to accuse him of Moreno's murder immediately. That was to be her trump card if everything else failed.

"Please help yourself to wine," she said, carrying his coat into the hall.

"I would prefer coffee," he said pleasantly.

"Oh, well, give me a moment, then."

De Jersey picked up the bottle of wine and poured some, then took out the morphine and emptied it into the glass. He had just started to pour some wine for himself when she returned with his coffee.

"It's instant. I hope you don't mind," she said.

"No. That's fine. The wine looked so inviting that I've poured some anyway."

She passed him the coffee, picked up her glass, and lifted it to her lips. "Cheers," she said and drank. Lowering the glass, she frowned and licked her lips.

"This is very strange," she said.

De Jersey picked up his glass and sipped. "Do you think so?"

She took another sip. "Yes, is it all right?"

He sipped again. "It's fine."

She reached for the bottle to look at the label. "I don't know, it's not cheap," she said and took another gulp.

He raised his glass. "Perhaps it should have been left to breathe awhile longer."

Sylvia reached for the peanuts, took a few, and munched them like a squirrel. "You must be eager to hear what I have to say. I'm surprised you could contain yourself."

He smiled. "Of course I'm eager to know, and I'm sure you're about to enlighten me. It's obvious that you've been very . . . active, shall we say? So, please." He sat back and gestured for her to talk.

She laughed. "Oh, you're a cool customer, Mr. de Jersey, but I don't think you've given me the credit I deserve. I knew how important my discovery was when I found out you'd been to East Hampton. You have control of Alex Moreno's properties, so you must be working with him, perhaps even helped him leave the country. His apartment and that estate he owned are worth millions, and I daresay you have no desire to share the proceeds with any of the other investors. But you're going to share them with me."

"Why would I do that?" he asked softly.

"Because I know who you are, and if you want that to remain our secret, I'll need a considerable amount more than the money I lost." She explained how she had discovered his identity through Moreno's lover, Clint. "Not that he knew your names. Either of them," she said and giggled. "I also showed your photograph to the site foreman at Moreno's property. He was not as forthcoming as Moreno's young friend, but gay men are so much more observant, don't you think?"

"How much do you want?" he asked.

"Well, I'd say it would be worth fifty-fifty, don't you? What you have been doing is highly illegal, and I would love to know exactly how you pulled it off."

"Well, it took a lot of work. Just getting a fake passport was hair-raising. You know, I've never done anything illegal in my life before this, but I was afraid of losing everything I had, and when you're desperate . . ." He got up and paced the room, continuing to talk about the stress he'd been under. Suddenly she felt hot, and her forehead became damp. She continued to eat the peanuts and drank the remainder of her wine.

Eventually she took a deep breath and interrupted him. "It's been hard for all of us. The reason I think you should agree to pay me, however, is the disappearance of Mr. Moreno. According to his gay friend, he was alive the evening before he had a meeting with . . ." She trailed off.

"Are you all right, Miss Hewitt?" he said.

"No, I am feeling very . . ." Her body heaved and she felt as if she was about to vomit, but instead she flopped forward. She gave a strange laugh as she tried to focus her eyes. "Too much wine," she said.

He stood up, collected his wineglass and coffee cup, and left the room. She tried to stand, but her legs gave way and she fell back into the chair. Now the room blurred and she felt dreadfully sick.

In the kitchen de Jersey washed his coffee cup and glass, dried them with a tea towel, removing all fingerprints, and replaced them on the shelf. He filled a glass with water, then took a small hypodermic needle from his wallet. He injected the water with ketamine, a horse tranquilizer, then re-placed the hypodermic in his wallet. He opened the fridge, put some ice in the glass, and carried it back to the living room.

"Here, drink this."

Sylvia seemed less drugged and held out her hand for the water. He made sure she had a firm hold of it before he returned to sit on the sofa. She drank thirstily, gasped, and looked at him in terror. "What have you put in this?"

He took the glass from her and checked how much she had drunk. "Just a little sedative, Miss Hewitt. My vet uses it all the time." He walked out of the room, taking her wineglass and the water glass with him, washed them, and put them away as the lethal cocktail of drugs flooded through her.

Putting on a pair of surgical gloves, de Jersey spent a considerable time gathering up Sylvia's correspondence with Matheson and any other documents relating to the investment case. Then he went back to the sink in the kitchen and set light to it all. He cleared up the charred remains and placed them in the waste-disposal unit, turned it on, and ground away every fragment. Then he cleaned around the sink, wiping away any possible remaining fingerprints.

When he carried Sylvia to the sofa, she was unconscious. He lifted her head onto a frilled cushion, then went into her bedroom, took a quilt from her bed, and tucked it around her.

Christina was in bed when de Jersey called her from his room at the club. He knew straightaway that something was wrong.

"We have a lot to talk about," she said rather coldly.

"Why? What's happened?"

"I'd rather not discuss it over the phone."

"Fine. I'll be home in a few days. I have to go to Ireland," he said affably.

"Why?" she asked.

"I'm sorry, sweetheart, I can't put it off. You know why."

"Where will you be staying?"

"I'll be moving around, but I'll be in Dublin first, then go to a few auctions. I've recently sold off a filly to a friend, so I need to settle her in." He gave no hint of the tension he felt.

"Well, don't forget we have the girls' school play on the second."

"I haven't forgotten, darling. I'll be home in plenty of time. Are you all right? You sound . . . What's happened? It's not Royal Flush, is it?"

"No, he's fine," she said. "We can discuss it when you get back."

"You know I love you," he said.

"And I love you." She hung up.

His hand rested a moment on the receiver. She had sounded odd. If something was troubling Christina, he would find out what it was, but it would have to wait. He cleaned his teeth, showered, and got ready for bed. He felt uneasy, however, so he called Donald Fleming. "Sorry to ring so late, but I'm up against it at the moment. I've just spoken to Christina. Nothing wrong up at the house, is there?"

"Not that I know of, but she was around the yard this afternoon. I think she's just worried like all of us."

"Yes, well, let's hope I come up with some extra financing. But keep your eye on her for me, would you? I don't want her unduly worried. We'll get through this, Donald."

"I will. I see you've earmarked a runner for Brighton on the second. You gonna make it?"

"Perhaps. Depends on a few meetings."

"But you'll be at Lingfield for Royal Flush's race, won't you?"

"Of course. I wouldn't miss it for the world. Oh, any news on the other matter?"

"She's going for a blood test in a few days," Fleming said. "We'll know if she's in foal then, but I think your boy may have done the business."

"Fine. I'll keep in touch." He hung up and sighed. He was tired to the bone, but before he settled for the night, he took out the bottle of morphine and the hypodermic needle with the ketamine. Sylvia Hewitt's glass of water had contained enough horse tranquilizer to knock out a carthorse permanently, so he reckoned one heavy slug of it along with the morphine was enough to ensure she would no longer be a problem. He refused to allow himself to contemplate what he had done and instead concentrated on getting rid of the evidence. He wrapped the bottle and the syringe in a hotel napkin and smashed them against the wall, Then he took one of the glasses in his room, dropped it on the floor, and added the broken pieces to the crushed bottle and syringe. He slipped out of his room, walked along the corridor and up another flight of stairs until he came to an unattended porter's trolley. He emptied the glass into the bin and tossed the towel and napkin in a laundry basket before he returned to his room. It was after eleven when he fell into a deep, dreamless sleep.

Over the next two nights they began to move the vehicles to the warehouse. They had disguised the Royal mascot on the Daimler so no one would be suspicious, but when it was driven to the warehouse in Aldersgate at four in the morning, there was hardly a soul around. The movement of the clothes and motorbikes was simpler but also done under cover of night. There was no looking back now, and de Jersey called Dulay. The *Hortensia Princess* was on its way to the South Coast of England with Dulay at the helm. All the months of preparation, the working out of timings and details had begun to gel.

On May 1, Royal Flush won his first race of the season at Lingfield by seven lengths. Mickey Rowland was sad that de Jersey had not been there to witness his victory; Fleming was surprised. They both received calls from de Jersey and gave him a second-by-second account of the race, how Royal Flush had not even been breathing hard afterward. He had traveled home calmly and eaten his feed, and both jockey and trainer were confident.

"You should have been there, Mr. de Jersey," said Fleming. "He did you proud. He did us all proud. You've got a champion there. You should have seen the Sheikh's trainer sniffing around him. We'll headline in the *Racing News*, I guarantee it."

There was an awkward pause, then Fleming went on. "With regard to the filly, Bandit Queen, she's in foal."

"Jesus God," de Jersey said, closing his eyes.

"You want me to ship her out to Ireland to this Shaughnessy character?"

"Yes, I'll call with the details. Well done, and thank you again."

Christina watched as the lads celebrated Royal Flush's win. Fleming had cracked open the champagne. He was drinking directly from a bottle. "Did you see him?" he asked Christina.

"Of course. It was on Channel Four. Did you speak to my husband? He told me that he had to go to Dublin."

"He was over the moon. If our boy wins the next one, he's got one hell of a chance at the Derby. Can I offer you a glass? The boss ordered a crate for the lads."

"No, thank you," she said, turning as one of the lads asked Fleming about arranging the horse box for Bandit Queen.

"Be over there later with the paperwork," Fleming called back.

"Are you selling her?" Christina asked, perplexed. Edward had bought the horse for her.

"Yep, she's being shipped out to Ireland."

"Oh, I see. Is that why he's going over there?"

"I guess so. She's been bought by a Michael Shaughnessy, old friend of Mr. de Jersey's."

"Well, congratulations to everyone," she said and went back toward the house. Then she changed her mind and went to her car. She drove over to where the brood mares were stabled and parked. She sat watching as the filly was led out of her stall while the lads drove up in the horse box. Christina got out and crossed to them as they were draping Bandit Queen in a blanket.

"Another gone," she said, half to herself, then moved closer to stroke the mare's head.

A young lad stood to one side holding the halter. "Sad to see her go," he said. "We had high hopes for her."

"Do you know this man Michael Shaughnessy who's apparently bought her?"

"No, Mrs. de Jersey, but she must have cost him a packet. Like I said, we had high hopes for her, and she won her maiden race almost as well as our Royal Flush."

"Thank you," Christina said and went back to her car. She drove to the house, and as she went into the kitchen, the phone rang.

"Christina? It's Helen Lyons."

Christina sighed. "Hello, Helen," she said. "How are you?"

"Oh, a little better now. I'm staying with a friend in Devon, and she's taking good care of me. Is this an inconvenient time to call?"

"Erm, no."

"It's about my insurance from the house. Sylvia was taking care of it. They still haven't settled, you know, since the fire."

"Good heavens! That is a long time."

"Well, that's what I thought, but with things the way they are between Sylvia and me, I don't feel I can call her."

"I understand, Helen, but it seems you're going to have to. Or perhaps you should write to her."

"I have, but she hasn't replied. I was wondering . . ." Her voice tapered off.

Christina said nothing.

"Well, as I said, I really don't want to speak to her, and I was wondering if you would be kind enough to call her for me as you knew David so well."

Christina sighed again. She could see no way out of it. "I'll call her for you, Helen."

"Oh, thank you. Please would you ask her to send me the details of the insurance policy. I'd be most grateful."

Christina took down Sylvia's number and Helen's in Devon and said she would call her back as soon as she had contacted Sylvia. She hung up feeling irritated. She had no interest in Helen or her sister, especially when she considered what David Lyons had done to her husband. She lit a cigarette before she rang Sylvia. There was no reply. She made another call to Dublin, to the Westcliffe Hotel, where her husband usually stayed. She was told that Mr. de Jersey had not booked in, and they were not expecting him. This time she slammed the receiver down. Another lie! She stubbed out her cigarette and lit another immediately.

The phone rang, and she snatched it up. "Yes?"

"Christina, it's Helen. Did you call her?"

"Yes, there was no reply."

"Did you try her office? I did give you her work number as well, didn't I?"

"No."

Helen gave Christina Sylvia's work number, thanked her profusely, and apologized again.

"Helen, I'll call you back as soon as I've spoken to Sylvia. So there's no need for you to ring me again. Good-bye now."

Christina hung up. She felt like weeping. She sat smoking one cigarette after another, then forced herself to leave the kitchen. She'd change
the beds and see to the laundry. After that she'd return to the study. She
would go through every document she could find. When her husband returned home she would be ready for him, and this time she wanted answers, not lies.

Once everything had been transported to the warehouse, they cleared the
barn. De Jersey and Driscoll spent hours cleaning up. They didn't leave a
scrap of evidence. The stove, the heaters, and the big lamps were all removed. They lit a bonfire to burn the waste, the paper cups, the rubber
gloves. With only twenty-four hours to go, it was the calm before the
storm.

De Jersey tapped the window of the Mercedes. In a chauffeur's uniform
behind the wheel, Driscoll lowered the window. "It's time," de Jersey said.
"Let's get the ball rolling."

The Mercedes was owned by Wilcox but had fake number plates and
would be driven to the crusher the minute they were done with it. Wilcox
gave the thumbs-up, and Driscoll drove out of the warehouse. It was four
fifteen in the morning on May 2. They left de Jersey alone to wait for the
rest of the team to arrive. As they drove away, he looked at his watch. In a
few hours the waiting would all be over.

"It's five o'clock," Eric Stanley said, a fraction before the alarm sounded.
His wife, Maureen, lay next to him, her hair in pin curls. She sat bolt upright.

"Breakfast?" Eric asked, standing next to the bed with a tray that held
a lightly boiled egg, two slices of buttered toast, and a cup of tea.

"You spoil me," Maureen said.

By six, Eric had his wife's little suitcase packed. She always took a few
changes of clothes to advertisement shoots, because if they supplied them
the skirts were always too long. For this one she had been asked to bring
her own anyway. She had chosen a blue tweed coat with a velvet collar. She
also had a hat in a box and a pleated skirt and blouse to go beneath the
coat. Although they usually supplied a makeup artist, she made up her
face carefully as she knew the exact shade of base and lipstick required. She
must never look overly made-up. That would be a dead giveaway.

Eric helped her into a raincoat. Though it was still dark, he could see
it was cloudy, and he handed her a small folding umbrella. "You all set,
darling?" he asked.

"I am. Is the car here?"

"I'll go and check." Eric opened the front door, walked down the path, and stood at the gate. A Mercedes was heading down the road.

Eric returned to the house and called, "They're here, dear, just coming to the drive." He turned as the Mercedes drew up behind his own car.

The driver stepped out, his hat pulled low, almost hiding his face. "Morning, I've come to collect—" At that moment she came out of the house, carrying the suitcase, hatbox, and handbag.

"I'm ready," said Maureen pleasantly and turned her cheek to her husband for a good-bye kiss. Another man stepped out and opened the rear door of the Mercedes, taking her case as he helped her inside. The driver asked Eric if he could use their bathroom. Eric gestured for him to follow him inside. In the car, the second man placed a rug around Maureen's knees, then closed the door and got into the front passenger seat.

"What on earth are they doing?" she asked after five minutes had passed and the driver had still not returned.

"He's had a bit of trouble with his prostate," the man replied.

At last the driver came out, red in the face, and closed the front door. As they drove out, Maureen looked back toward the house. "That's odd," she said. "My husband always waves me off to work. It's a little ritual we have. I'm a very lucky woman." She settled back. Sometimes his undivided attention got on her nerves a little. But, as Eric said so many times, his queen was worth taking care of.

Maureen Stanley had made her career as Queen Elizabeth's look-alike. She was almost the same age and, like the Queen, was cutting down on the amount of work she took on. Millennium year had been fantastic, and she had often had two engagements on the same night. She enjoyed the television work more, though, than the special appearances.

"Where are we filming?" she asked Driscoll.

"Close to the BBC radio studios."

After about ten minutes, Driscoll saw that she had fallen asleep, her head lolling forward. He looked at her and smiled at Wilcox. "Dead ringer, isn't she?" he said softly.

"Yeah. Did all go to plan back at the house?"

"Yep. He's comfortable, can't hurt himself. Tucked him up on the sofa." He glanced again at Eric's wife, who was unaware that her beloved husband had been drugged and tied up. Eric had been bending over the hall table looking at some leaflet that had been pushed through his letter box for window cleaning when Driscoll placed his left arm across the small man's chest and injected his right buttock through his trousers. Eric had tried to fend him off, but the sedative had acted quickly and his body had sagged.

"What . . . what have you done?" he'd gasped.

"Put you to sleep for a few hours, pal, nothing to worry about. You'll have a bit of a headache when you wake up, that's all."

At six thirty, the Mercedes arrived at the Aldersgate warehouse. As the doors closed behind it, Maureen woke up. "Are we here?" she asked, looking around the large warehouse in surprise. "This isn't the BBC, is it?"

Driscoll turned and smiled. "No, ma'am, it isn't. Would you like to get out of the car? There's coffee and doughnuts."

"Thank you, I've had my breakfast." She glanced around the vast warehouse.

"I'll take you to your dressing room, then." Driscoll opened the door for her. By the time she was settled, Wilcox was driving the Mercedes across London to be destroyed. Driscoll then set off again to pick up a rented furniture-removal van. It would play a major role in the getaway, and the team had prepared stickers to cover the name of the rental company and the number plate.

The dressing room was a small room off the main warehouse space, previously used for storing clothes and accessories. It contained a dressing table with a mirror, a comfortable chair, and a heater. Maureen was ushered inside and told to wait for someone to come and see to her hair and makeup. She nodded and put down her suitcase. She opened it to take out her clothes. A few items were already hanging on a rail. They were all expensive, with Aquascutum and Harrods labels, but she could see at a glance that they were too long. Why don't they get their facts right? she thought. The Queen is tiny.

Outside the dressing room, there was a lot of movement. The Daimlers were ready and being given a final polish. Pamela was next to arrive, and de Jersey gestured for her to join him at the back of the warehouse. He told her their Queen was in the dressing room still unaware of her role, and he wanted her kept in the dark for as long as possible.

Pamela seemed relaxed but was chain-smoking. She poured herself a coffee. "I'll go and get changed, keep her company." She surveyed the warehouse. "Westbrook here yet?"

De Jersey checked his watch. "He's due at eight. You all set?"

"Yes, of course. It's rather like opening night at the theater." She chortled.

De Jersey smiled. Pamela had been a great choice. "You're a special lady," he said softly.

"I know, darling. Pity I can't find a decent fella who thinks so too." She raised an eyebrow and sipped her coffee. "Maybe with all the loot I'll get from this I'll find me a nice boy-toy." Then she went to the dressing room, knocked, and entered.

Even though she had been prepared to see her coartist, Pamela was taken aback by Maureen's eerie likeness to the Queen.

"Morning, darling," she said. "I'm your lady-in-waiting. We've got to shack up in here for a while before they take us to the location." She plonked down her coffee and drew up the only hard-backed chair.

"Do you have the script?" Maureen asked, still fussing with her clothes.

"No, sweetheart, I don't. The director will let us know what we have to do."

Maureen nodded. She always liked to have the script well before they filmed so she knew what would be required.

"Did you want a coffee?" Pamela asked, taking out another cigarette.

"No, thank you."

As Pamela held the lighter to the end of the cigarette, she saw that her hands were shaking. For all her bravado, she was nervous. She knew she had to ignore the butterflies starting in the pit of her stomach. She had come too far to back out now.

"Do you play cards?" Maureen asked hopefully.

"I do, darling! Have you got a pack with you?"

Maureen produced one from her handbag. "Never without! These shoots are so boring. They always get you here far too early, don't you think?"

Wilcox and Driscoll returned in plenty of time. Wilcox couldn't help but admire the Daimlers, which were polished like mirrors. The bikes stood beside them. He turned sharply as the gate opened and the two bikers entered. Hall and Short gave him a cool nod, but Wilcox kept his distance from them. To all intents and purposes, they were hired villains and to Wilcox the most dangerous to security, but de Jersey and Driscoll had assured him they were reliable. They went to change into their police uniforms, leaving Wilcox to continue checking the Daimlers. He looked up as Driscoll appeared with coffee.

"You can't get them any cleaner," Driscoll said. He noticed the two bikers. "Nice to see they're on time." He moved closer to Wilcox. "The one on the right did twelve years for that Asprey and Garrard jewel heist. The one on the left was inside for fifteen. Same kind of gig but got out over the wall about a year ago."

Wilcox changed the subject. "The Colonel told me he was straight with that Hewitt woman." He tossed the duster aside.

"What do you think he meant by that?"

Wilcox gave a shrug. "Well, he paid her off, I guess."

"This has sure cost him a bundle."

Wilcox nodded. Then he smiled. "But what a payout we're in line for!"

They grinned and slapped hands, each man as tense as the other but refusing to admit it.

Westbrook arrived in a navy blue pin-striped suit, a blue shirt with a starched white collar and cuffs, his old Eton school tie with a pearl pin, and a rose in his lapel. He had washed his hair and combed it back from his high forehead. Even his teeth appeared whiter. His pallor, however, was sickly, and his luminous eyes were far too bright. He had taken his first hit of speed.

"Morning, Colonel," he chirped in the familiar upper-crust drawl. He executed a small pivot turn on the heels of his new Gucci loafers. "How do I look?"

"Good." De Jersey glanced down at his socks: no holes. "How are you feeling?"

"Fine, thank you. Is H.M. installed yet?" He fiddled with his kid gloves.

"She's in the dressing room with Pamela. She's not been told her script yet, so take care what you say to her and remind Pamela not to remove her gloves. That goes for you too. The place has been cleaned."

"Fine. Any coffee on?"

"Help yourself." De Jersey looked at his watch. It was coming up to eight o'clock. They would leave the warehouse at ten twenty-five exactly. He watched Westbrook stroll across to the coffeepot, and his heart went out to him. He was so well dressed it was hard to believe that he was the same messed-up creature de Jersey had been worried about. He just hoped to God that his lordship could keep up the pretense.

Westbrook tapped on the door and entered the dressing room, and de Jersey heard Pamela shriek at how gorgeous he looked. So far, so good. Everything and everyone was on time. De Jersey changed into a cheap polyester suit, black shoes and socks, a white shirt and black tie. He used a nasty silver tiepin and tucked a handkerchief into his breast pocket. He stared at himself. He looked every inch the private security guard, down to his large frame. He sat down, opened his briefcase, and removed an expensive wig of fine reddish hair. It was the one he had worn in the Hamptons, along with matching mustache and eyebrows. He spent some time carefully gluing the mustache into place and even longer adjusting the eyebrows and wig. Satisfied, he peeled off the surgical gloves, replacing them with soft black leather ones.

He spent another half hour spraying every surface that might reveal fingerprints or DNA. He had already sprayed and cleaned the coffee mugs and food area. The trash had been collected in a black bin liner, which he would incinerate. He wanted to be sure that there wasn't a single print or clue left to identify him or anyone else in the team. He put down his briefcase and clicked it open. It contained his cell phone—the vital link to Raymond Marsh. Now all Marsh had to do was get the right code word. If he didn't come up with the goods, they were screwed.

At ten to nine, he went into the dressing room. He gave Pamela and Westbrook a nod to leave him alone with Maureen. He apologized for breaking up the party and explained it was time to leave for the location.

"Well, I can't say it's not before time." Maureen started to gather her things. "What do you want me to wear? You're the director, aren't you? I've been here since just after six and I haven't even been shown a script yet!"

De Jersey stared at her. "I think the coat you're wearing would be perfect, if that's okay with you. Do you think you should wear a hat or a head scarf?"

"Well, that depends on the script. I mean, is it interior or exterior? She doesn't wear a hat all the time, but I've brought a selection."

"It's exterior moving to interior."

Maureen displayed her hats, but he chose a pale blue head scarf that matched her coat and gave the right casual feel for the occasion. He asked her not to wear it until they reached the set. Then he chose a large brooch for her to wear on the coat lapel before hurrying her to get into the car.

"It's just typical this, you know," Maureen complained. "I've been here since after six, and now it's all hurry-hurry. I've not even had my makeup checked. I need at least to freshen my lipstick. Will we rehearse?"

"Yes. I'd like you to come to the car."

She chattered on as he guided her to it. His lordship was seated in the front, and Pamela was waiting in the rear passenger seat with the door open. Maureen got in beside her, remarking on how unusual it was to be driven with the director.

"Oh, we're not moving yet. We just want to rehearse getting in and out of the Daimler."

"Well, I've certainly done that many times," Maureen said. She and Pamela got in and out as Westbrook oversaw the rehearsal.

De Jersey checked his watch and looked at Pamela. "I need to have a chat with the artist." Then to Maureen he said, "Would you please get back into the Daimler?" Maureen hesitated and looked at Pamela, then climbed in. De Jersey got in beside her, leaned back, and took a deep breath. He could smell the glue he had used to stick his wig and mustache in place. "Do you love your husband?" he asked quietly.

"Pardon?" Maureen said.

"I asked if you loved your husband," he repeated.

"Of course! We've been married forty-two years."

"Good. Now, I want you to remain as calm as possible and pay attention to what I'm going to tell you. Your husband is being held at gunpoint. He's perfectly safe and will not be harmed if you do exactly as I tell you. If you do not, he will be shot."

She stared, her mouth open. She blinked rapidly.

"Do you understand? It is up to you whether or not you see your husband again. If you cry out or give any indication that we are holding him captive, you will never see him alive again. If you obey to the letter what I am going to tell you to do, if you value your husband's life, you do exactly as I say, no harm will come to him or you. Do you understand?" de Jersey asked. "This is not a game. This is not a film. This is happening, right now. Give me your hand."

Maureen lifted it as if she were a robot, and he clasped it tightly. "We are all about to commit a dangerous robbery, and we need you to portray Her Majesty the Queen."

Driscoll glanced at the Daimler. They had been in it for ten minutes. He had heard no sound but the low murmur of de Jersey's voice. It was now almost nine o'clock. He reckoned they were taking one hell of a risk with the woman. What if she fell apart and couldn't keep up the act? He began to feel sick.

The car door opened, and de Jersey got out. He closed the door again, leaving the woman inside, and crossed to Pamela. "Go in and sit with her. Go through the routine." He nodded to Westbrook, who stood up. Wilcox looked at him nervously.

"She's going to be fine. Maybe a little drop of brandy will set her up, but she'll be just fine."

In the car, Pamela sat beside Maureen.

"Are you part of this?" Maureen asked, hardly audible.

"No, but I don't think they'll hurt us. We just have to do exactly as we're told and nothing will go wrong."

"They've got my husband."

"Yes, I know."

"Have they got yours too?" she asked.

Pamela turned and took her hand. "Yes, darling, so we're in this together. We just have to think it's a film. It's the only way we can get through it."

The door opened, and Westbrook passed in a small silver flask. "Have a nip of this, ladies, we've got about half an hour to go."

Pamela winked at him and unscrewed the flask. Maureen clutched at it with both hands and gulped down the brandy. It made her cough and splutter. Her hands were shaking and her knees were jerking. "I'm so frightened. This is terrible, terrible."

Pamela gripped her hand again. "Now stop this, stop it now. We have to do what they say. It's my husband as well, you know."

Maureen nodded and closed her eyes. "I need—need to redo my lip-lipstick," she stammered.

De Jersey's cell phone rang, and he snatched it up. "All on course, are we?" came Marsh's chirpy voice.

"Just waiting for you," de Jersey responded. He glanced at his watch. It was ten past nine.

"Well, I'd hit your coal bunker. I've just sensed activity on the alarm phone lines, which means they've done their tests. You'll need to do your IRA threat in about three-quarters of an hour."

"Fine, but what's the code word?"

"They've not phoned it through yet. Don't panic. I'm on to it."

"You'd better be."

"Over and out." Marsh clicked off.

De Jersey stood up. He knew that the wait would get to them all now; he also knew that, above all else, he had to show no sign of his own tension. He turned to Wilcox and nodded for him to get ready to climb through into the D'Ancona coal room. Wilcox was wearing an overall, thick gloves, and a helmet with a light attached. "How long have I got?" he asked.

"It's nine fifteen now. I'll make the threat call at ten, and Marsh will intercept to the safe house shortly after that. Then we've got twenty minutes before we move out."

Wilcox walked down into the cellar and made his way to the opening between the two buildings. He switched on his lamp and started to remove the loosened bricks.

"How we doing?" came a soft whisper. Wilcox whipped round. De Jersey looked like a ghost in a white paper suit to protect his clothes from the dust.

"Just breaking through now. How am I for time?"

"We're fine."

As de Jersey spoke, Wilcox pushed another brick loose, cringing as it dropped to the opposite side. He pulled bricks toward him onto an old duvet he'd laid on the floor to dull the noise.

"They're doing the final cleanup of the warehouse," de Jersey told him.

"Great," said Wilcox, working hard. Both men remained silent for a moment. "We're in," he said softly. "Shouldn't you be upstairs making a call, for Christ's sake?"

"I'm on my way. Just get in and see if it's going to be a problem."

"Bit late for that now, isn't it?" said Wilcox and crawled out of sight.

He had already seen inside the room when he opened up the wall, so he knew what he would find. Marsh had been correct. There was the box with all the lines plugged into it, each neatly labeled with the location of the related panic alarm, such as "under floor reception" or "vault walls." On the far side a steel door led into the safe house. D'Ancona had never suspected anyone would be able to gain access from the opposite side. That had been their mistake.

Wilcox was dripping with sweat. If one of the plugs was pulled a fraction earlier than the others, the police would be round in minutes and they'd be on the run without the reward. The technique Marsh had come up with for removing the plugs was brilliantly simple. At the end of each plug was a small loop where it met the cable. Wilcox took a piece of stiff wire from his belt and began to thread it through all the loops. He took his time. He didn't want to jolt any of the plugs. After five minutes the wire was in place. This was the moment of truth. He took hold of each end of the wire and pulled.

Driscoll was ready, pacing up and down beside the Daimler. The two bikers sat with their helmets in their hands. Wilcox seemed to be taking ages. Eventually he emerged, covered in dust, and gave a thumbs-up. The team heaved a collective sigh of relief, and Driscoll patted him on the back.

Westbrook checked the time. It was five to ten. He was starting to sweat and unsure if he should take his last hit of speed now.

"Is there a bog in this place?" Westbrook asked. Driscoll pointed to the rear of the warehouse. Westbrook walked off and let himself into the dirty bathroom. He was just a few minutes behind Wilcox and heard him snorting up a line of cocaine through the door. "I wouldn't mind a line if you have one to spare," he said quietly. Wilcox opened the door and beckoned him in. They huddled together as Wilcox chopped up two very long lines.

"For Christ's sake, don't let the Colonel know I'm doing this," Wilcox said.

"He knows I need it." Westbrook was already rolling a rather creased five-pound note in anticipation. Wilcox produced a short silver straw and Hoovered up his line. He was still wearing his overall, his face filthy from the dust.

De Jersey checked the time again and again. They had half an hour to go, and there was still no word from Marsh. It was insanity to have depended so heavily on him. He was starting to think about leaving the warehouse and killing the man with his bare hands when the cell phone rang. The IRA code word for that day was Boswell. With trembling fingers, de Jersey made the call. When someone answered, he said, in a mild Northern Irish accent, "Boswell, I repeat, Boswell." The officer taking the call did not question the authenticity and put the receiver down fast. De Jersey sighed with relief.

Marsh was listening in to a call from the commander at Scotland Yard to Buckingham Palace informing them of the IRA threat and putting a halt to the day's plans. His final task was to intercept the call from Scotland Yard to the safe house, which would inform them of the cancellation.

The team waited in silence. Wilcox had changed into his chauffeur's uniform in preparation for driving the second Daimler and stood chewing his lips. All were on edge for the last call to come in. When it did, everyone stared at de Jersey as he answered. Marsh had intercepted the call, and the safe house had no idea that the fitting had been canceled.

De Jersey checked his watch: it was exactly ten twenty. They prepared to move the short distance from the warehouse to the safe house. De Jersey climbed into the Daimler beside Wilcox. Driscoll took his position in the second Daimler containing Pamela, Westbrook, and the silent, terrified Maureen. The bikers lowered their helmets and sat astride their police bikes. The minutes ticked by slowly.

"Open the doors," de Jersey said. The biker nearest pressed the automatic button to slide back the warehouse doors, and they were on the move.

The convoy turned left. Maureen sat beside Pamela, clutching her handbag, her blue head scarf tied round her head, her lipstick badly reapplied.

She wanted to go to the toilet, but she was too scared to open her mouth. Her eyes were wide with fear. Pamela occasionally patted her knees, which were still shaking alarmingly.

"Well, we got the show on the road," de Jersey said, resting his arm along the back of the front seat, just touching Wilcox. "We got the show on the road," he repeated, when Wilcox didn't respond. He gave him a sharp look. "How much of the stuff did you take?" he asked.

"Enough to keep me steady. I needed it. My nerves were shot."

De Jersey stared at him and withdrew his arm. "Fuck up and I'll kill you."

Wilcox licked his lips.

"Bikers are still in position," de Jersey continued. He picked up his cell phone and dialed. "How's Her Majesty?"

"She's doing just fine," Westbrook told him.

They passed the traffic cones, which had been placed by the two bikers earlier that morning. This was the only road leading to the safe house. They passed the no-entry sign at the end of the street, again placed by the bikers to avoid any other traffic entering. The journey took less than three minutes.

De Jersey looked out the window, then spoke into the phone. "Stand by, we're there." He switched off the cell phone and pulled at his glove. Ahead he could see the security guard in his uniform and cap waiting at the entrance to the safe house.

"The show is on." De Jersey laughed softly, and Wilcox gave him a covert glance. He seemed relaxed, as if he was enjoying himself. De Jersey caught the look and patted his shoulder. "Three Musketeers, eh? Just like the old days."

Wilcox dropped down a gear to move to the side of the road just ahead of the entrance so that the Queen's Daimler could park with ease directly behind him.

"Good morning," de Jersey said to the waiting security guard as he climbed out of the car. The heavy, studded doors of the safe house were open, a red carpet placed on the steps to the entrance. Lined up inside the reception area were the D'Ancona employees. "The road should stay closed until we leave," de Jersey said to the guard in a quiet but authoritative tone. "One of my officers will stay out here to help you if there's any trouble."

"Yes, sir."

At this moment the head representative from D'Ancona appeared in the doorway, wearing a pin-striped suit and a rose in his buttonhole. He stood to one side, waiting. There was a fraction of a pause, just two or three seconds, which felt like minutes. Then Lord Westbrook stepped out of the front seat of the Queen's Daimler. He gave a cold, arrogant look to the guard. Then he opened the passenger door to allow Pamela to exit first. She stood to one side, holding Maureen's handbag, as Maureen stepped from the Daimler with a frozen smile.

The guard bowed, and as rehearsed, Pamela fell into position behind Maureen. Lord Westbrook stepped to her left, with de Jersey behind him, and Driscoll brought up the rear. They began to proceed into the safe house as one of the bikers, Hall, stepped forward to check the road and the buildings opposite for any signs of disturbance.

As the Royal party moved into the entrance hall, then down the stairs and out of sight, the D'Ancona security guard decided to go back to his workstation. Within four feet of the safe house main doors there was a cage, grilled on all three sides. Inside it were banks of monitors, all showing the Royal party heading slowly down the thickly carpeted stairs to the lower floor reception area. As the guard went to enter the cage, Hall, still with his helmet in place, moved in close behind him, so close that he unnerved the guard, who turned to find the muzzle of a handgun pressed into his neck. "Back into the cage and do exactly as I tell you or this blows your head off," Hall hissed.

The man put his hands up and obeyed but trod on a concealed panic button.

"Further in, pal. Move it!"

The Royal party was displayed on every monitor. They were now being led into the reception area. Other banks of monitors showed virtually every inch of corridor and office, plus the vault on the lower level, which was standing wide open. Hall's thuggish bulk came close to the guard. "Pull the fucking camera controls, pal. The alarms are dead. And so will you be if you make me wait another second. Do it!" The guard hesitated but got a rough push from the gun, pressed now in the small of his back.

One by one he unplugged the cameras, and the monitors went blank. Hall pushed him roughly into the chair, tied his hands and feet with tape, and gagged him. He then crammed the man's hat down on his head and turned the seat slightly so that anyone passing the cage would see him sitting "on guard."

Wilcox was still seated in the Daimler. Eventually Hall left the cage and signaled to him that the coast was clear. Wilcox turned on the engine and drove back to the warehouse. He opened the doors with the electronic buzzer and drove in. The Daimler had served its purpose; moving fast, he poured acid over the bonnet, removed the number plates, and stuffed them with the chauffeur's uniform into a black rubbish bag that already contained the paper suit de Jersey had worn. He carried it to the rear of the warehouse and placed it in a bin. He poured more acid into the bin, then replaced the lid and left it to smolder. Minutes later he walked out to take up his position in the driving seat of the second Daimler in front of the safe house. Spittle had formed at the sides of his mouth, and he kept licking his lips.

As the robbery was going on, Raymond Marsh walked out of the Scotland Yard telephone exchange and prepared to perform his last task. He traveled by underground to Edgware Road, then caught a bus to Kilburn. He let himself into de Jersey's flat and dismantled the satellite linkup. Once the connections to de Jersey's home computer were broken, he poured acid over the controls, the keyboard, and the printer. He took off his gloves as the acid was burning through the leather, then appraised the flat room by room. Nothing of a personal nature was left, just old newspapers and journals. He headed off to his own home.

His wife had already packed. Only his precious guitar collection and Elvis memorabilia were going with him and his family to Brazil. These items were crated up, ready to be shipped out. A friend had the house keys and contact number for the shippers. Simmons had his banking details. When payday came, his cut would be transferred to his account via the Internet.

Marsh had taken great care to look after number one, even down to arranging holiday time for himself and his family, but he knew he was still traceable. The police would discover that someone had had access to the phones to hack into the safe house and Scotland Yard lines. By then, however, he would be long gone. Like Ronnie Biggs, he had chosen Brazil as his first port of call. Unlike Ronnie, however, Marsh didn't run solo. He had first-class tickets for himself, his wife, and daughter, all under assumed names. He gave little thought to the men and women involved in the robbery as he prepared to make his getaway. He just hoped they would pull it off.

23

The line of expectant, well-groomed staff in the D'Ancona safe house reception area reminded Lord Westbrook of a school assembly. The two nervous secretaries were like his old headmaster's daughters, flushing and dressed in their best. Next to them stood a large-bosomed, round-faced woman, who held her plump arms flat to the sides of her ample body like a military officer. She resembled his old matron. She was, in fact, one of D'Ancona's chief gem experts and head of marketing. Three men reminded Westbrook of masters at Eton. They were all waiting to acknowledge Her Majesty as she passed by.

De Jersey was worried by the lineup: there were far more people than he had anticipated. He could feel the sweat breaking out as he wondered whether Hall had done his job. The only way de Jersey would know was by the stillness of the cameras. He glanced up at them. If Hall failed, they would all be caught on film. On his third glance he was relieved to see the cameras stop tracking them, their red lights disappearing.

The royal blue carpet swirled down the stairs and covered the reception floor. Vast displays of lilies were arranged prominently. The Royal party was greeted with polite bows from the two fitters, who wore immaculate pin-striped trousers and dark jackets with pristine white shirts and ties. They held white gloves, which they would put on when measuring and fitting.

"Good morning," Maureen said, passing down the lineup. She smiled, but her eyes were like a frightened rabbit's. Pamela remained close by, almost able to touch her. Lord Westbrook now took the floor, his charm and breeding shining like a beacon. His soft, aristocratic tone rang out as the party moved along the line, shaking hands and smiling.

The head representative, Mr. Saunders, a small and nervous man, took Westbrook aside. "The vaults are being opened. Her Majesty can view the jewels at her discretion." Saunders bowed to Maureen, who was frozen-faced. Her manner made the man even more nervous.

"If you would kindly follow me down to the lower level, Your Majesty, we have the vaults prepared for you."

Much to de Jersey's relief, as soon as "the Queen" began to move down the second set of stairs to the vaults, most of the staff dispersed. The matron figure ushered the girls toward the stairs, and de Jersey watched them with bated breath: if they passed back into the entrance hall, they might see the security guard bound and gagged. They didn't glance in his direction, however; instead they moved up a second flight of stairs to their offices.

The inner reception area was now empty, the outer hallway guarded by Hall. Short and Wilcox were ready to act as backup.

There were ten steps down to the vault with a polished brass rail on either side. They passed cameras poised at every corner and recess. None moved. Satisfied now that Hall had done his job, de Jersey hoped no one would notice that the cameras weren't functioning.

Maureen leaned heavily on the banister rail, Pamela close behind as she continued down. De Jersey and Westbrook kept her closely guarded. Saunders maintained a rather stuttering speech, detailing the security surrounding the vault. Fortunately he and the fitters kept their eyes directed deferentially on the Royal party. When they reached the basement, a man stood waiting beside a trolley laden with iced water, fruit, and coffee. Saunders suggested a pause for refreshments, but Westbrook smiled and tapped his watch.

The party now approached the vault, with steel doors and two protective inner cages. The first thick steel door stood wide open, and the shining steel bars inside it were also open. Above the steel door was the edge of the grille that would slam down if an alarm button were pressed, protecting the contents of the vault and trapping anyone inside.

Westbrook kept the tension to a minimum by maintaining a steady flow of conversation, which de Jersey hugely admired. He constantly referred to Her Majesty as he recalled anecdotes of when he had been a page at the coronation. Whether he had or not was immaterial.

The vault was enormous, with banks of steel boxes surrounding the large central cage. Inside it was a massive steel-framed display case, lined with black velvet, where the spectacular jewels had been laid out for viewing. The sight stunned all of them into a strange silence, which was broken only when Westbrook exhaled audibly, then whispered, "Dear Lord above!"

This quiet expression of awe somehow made it easier for de Jersey to continue in the same tone: "Ladies and gentlemen, do not call out, but remain silent and no one will be hurt."

Saunders half-turned, as if he had not heard correctly, and at that moment de Jersey revealed his automatic. "I need you all to lie facedown on the floor." He pointed at Saunders. "You first. Do not make a sound."

Saunders looked in confusion at his assistants, and his face drained of color. Driscoll opened his jacket and pulled out his shotgun. "Obey every word or I won't hesitate to shoot. Get down, facedown!"

Maureen dropped to the floor, twitching. Her bag fell open, and cosmetics rolled across the vault. Pamela drew out a fake gun from her own bag and directed it at Maureen's head. Driscoll ran back up the stairs, signaling to Hall to join them. He moved away from the door, and his position was taken up by Short.

Inside the vault, Saunders raised his hands and shouted, "You can't do this. For God's sake, *no!*"

"*Down!*" de Jersey commanded and took off his coat to reveal a large, lightweight rucksack. He tossed it to Westbrook. Driscoll and Hall held the staff at gunpoint as Westbrook lifted the platinum crown containing the Koh-i-noor Diamond and stashed it in the rucksack. De Jersey handed Westbrook the gun and began to drag more jewels from the display into a second rucksack, held open by Driscoll. When all the jewels were in the rucksacks, he gave the signal to move out.

The team backed toward the stairs as Driscoll shut the heavy steel doors, leaving Saunders, Maureen, and the two terrified fitters captive. Then the gang walked boldly up the stairs, through the reception area, into the small hallway, and past the bound security guard.

The bikers started their engines and moved off in different directions, although their destination was the same: the speedboats at the Tower Bridge Marina. Pamela and Westbrook left Newbury Street on foot. Neither could speak, and their legs were wobbly, but they walked toward the City Thameslink Station, looking over their shoulders as often as they dared, trying not to be too conspicuous.

Driscoll walked straight into Barbican Station and went down to the Hammersmith and City line. It seemed an interminable time before a train came, and he shook as he paced up and down. After three minutes he stepped into a carriage and cursed under his breath until the train's doors finally closed and it left the station. He was dripping with sweat.

*   *   *

Wilcox and de Jersey knew they needed to distance themselves from the crime scene as quickly as possible, but they couldn't leave the Daimler behind. It was too risky and time-consuming to take it back to the warehouse, and they didn't want to drive it through town. This was where the furniture van came into play. It was parked nearby on a meter.

De Jersey climbed into the Daimler with both rucksacks. Wilcox slammed his foot down, and they screeched round the corner, sending the no-parking signs and cones flying.

"Slowly!" de Jersey snapped. The last thing they needed was to be picked up for speeding. The tense Wilcox managed to slow down, and they drove through the back streets until they reached the van. De Jersey leaped out and opened the van's driving side, threw in the rucksacks, and got in. At the same time, Wilcox opened the rear doors, dropped the tailgate, returned to the Daimler, and drove it in. There was so little space to move that he took a while to squeeze out of the car. He drew up the back and shut the doors with himself inside, then banged on the front of the van for de Jersey to move off.

As de Jersey drove, he ripped off the wig, eyebrows, and mustache, keeping his speed to thirty miles an hour. It felt like a snail's pace. He headed toward the river, crossed it, and turned right to drive toward Battersea.

The getaway had taken only fifteen minutes so far, but he could already hear police sirens blasting in the distance. As they passed the heliport in Battersea, de Jersey saw his two decoy helicopters take off. He checked his watch: it was perfect timing. The confusion should provide cover for his own copter.

The officials locked in the vault had screamed and shouted to no avail. They could not get out, and the lack of air was becoming asphyxiating. Maureen was hysterical, screaming that they had got her husband. The others in the vault had realized at last that she wasn't talking about Prince Philip.

The staff from the upper floors carried on working, unaware of what was taking place downstairs. However, when the secretaries entered the reception area at the time the Royal party was due to leave, they were confronted by an overturned plinth of lilies and the bound and gagged security guard. With trepidation one of them opened the outer vault doors.

By eleven o'clock the City was wailing with sirens. No one could believe what had happened. It was one of the most audacious robberies in history.

The first thing the police did was send up their helicopters to monitor the area. They were on the lookout for two Daimlers and two motorbikes.

The entire area surrounding the safe house was cordoned off. De Jersey was still driving the furniture van and was now passing Kingston, moving on toward the A3. He still had a way to go before he would reach his helicopter to lift the jewels away from London.

At the same time, two speedboats raced from separate moorings near Tower Bridge. Hall had dumped his motorbike and placed his helmet and leathers into a holdall. He now wore a thick cable-knit sweater and a baseball cap. He had walked to the first boat, which had been brought from the old boathouse in Putney. Before leaving he had tied weights to his holdall and dropped it into the river. He steered the boat toward Putney, intending to stash it in the boathouse and catch the tube back to his east London home from Putney Bridge.

Ten minutes later Short followed almost identical orders. He left his bike in a car park near Blackfriars and changed in the toilets. He walked down toward Temple, pulling his cap low over his face. When he reached his mooring, he had trouble with the engine. After a few false starts, however, he got the boat going and sped off after Hall just as the sirens started. Short had to drop the boat at the boathouse, then use a can of petrol to set light to the building and its contents. They hoped the fire would provide another distraction.

Short set a bunch of doused rags alight and exited quickly. He was a good fifty yards away when he saw the flames take hold. He was to continue on foot along the New King's Road, catch a bus to Sloane Square, and from there take a tube to his flat.

Driscoll walked out of the tube station at Shepherd's Bush and picked up his car from a car park. He drove home, calm now although his shirt was soaking. He wondered if de Jersey had made it. He wanted more than anything to call Wilcox, to know that everyone was home and free, but he resisted the urge and kept on driving.

De Jersey had parked his helicopter at Brooklands airfield. It was used mostly at the weekend, so it was deserted now, with just a small office in operation across the car park. Wilcox jumped down from the back of the van, climbed into the driving seat, and drove out of the airfield, catching de Jersey's eye as he left. Both allowed themselves half-relieved smiles, but they were not in the clear yet.

An experienced pilot, de Jersey knew that there would be no problems with air traffic control. Contrary to popular belief, most low-level airspace in the United Kingdom is uncontrolled. He had used the Brooklands airfield a few times when he had horses racing at Epsom and Goodwood. Today he was expected at Brighton for a two-year-old's maiden race. He used the airfield's bathroom to wash off the wig glue, put on a camel overcoat and his brown trilby, stashed the rucksacks in two suitcases, and loaded them into the helicopter, which contained an incongruous-looking crate. It was watertight, lined with polystyrene squares held together with waterproof glue.

De Jersey saw only one person by the hangars, a man cleaning a glider who didn't pay him any attention. As he left the washroom, the caretaker, who was sitting in his office eating his lunch, asked if he had a tip for the races. De Jersey laughed and said perhaps an each-way bet on his colt, Fan Dancer, but he wasn't optimistic as it was his first time out.

As de Jersey started the engine and the propellers began to move, Wilcox was six miles away, heading toward the old barn. Once there he drove the furniture truck in through the large doors, drove the Daimler out, and removed the number plates. The registration number on the engine had already been removed. He used four cans of acid to destroy the seats, paintwork, and all the contents of the boot. He smashed every window with a hammer and attacked the dashboard. The exertion felt good. Then he stripped the stickers off the sides of the removal van to reveal its true identity. The "Double Your Time" rental company did not expect it back until later that afternoon. Their headquarters were in Leatherhead, so it was just a short drive back down the A3. Wilcox left the truck in a large car park and posted the keys into a box at the gates. Philip Simmons had hired it after seeing the company's advert on the Internet and had paid for it. Then Wilcox caught a train home from Leatherhead.

De Jersey's horse was running in the three o'clock at Brighton. It was the perfect opportunity to show his face and establish an alibi, but he had to do the drop first. As he headed for the coast, he looked down on the busy traffic heading in and out of the center of London. He wondered whether it was his imagination or there was a glint of flashing blue light in every direction. He didn't dwell on it, knowing that by now every airport would be targeted as a possible getaway route, likewise the ports. It would take a long time to organize a full search, however, and by then he hoped they would be home and free.

* * *

Pamela and the now sickly Westbrook had traveled from the City Thames-link Station to Brighton. There they switched to a second train for Plymouth. Pamela was concerned by Westbrook's depleted energy. He was sweating profusely and had twice staggered to the lavatory to vomit. His face was yellow, and sweat plastered his hair to his head. The journey would take at least five hours, and they would need a taxi to get them to the safety of her flat. De Jersey had instructed them to separate and Westbrook to return to London, but his Lordship was too unwell to be left alone.

When they reached the station, they flagged down a taxi. Pamela had constantly to feed Westbrook his painkillers so that he had enough energy to walk unaided to her flat. She had made the taxi stop two streets away, not wanting to give the driver her address. Westbrook hardly spoke, but when she opened her front door and helped him collapse onto the sofa, he gave a dry sob, his face twisted in pain. Her heart went out to him. "We made it," she said softly.

The helicopter too was reaching its destination. The yacht was anchored almost nine miles off Brighton Marina, and as he flew overhead de Jersey used his cell phone to call Dulay. He put the engine on remote control, slid open the side door, and tossed out the crate. He didn't wait to see it hit the water. Instead he did a wide arc, then headed for the helipad at Brighton racetrack.

Dulay watched the crate hit the water and bob to the surface. It was just a few yards off its marker. He gave the signal to start up the engines, and the big yacht moved majestically toward it. Dulay and two crew hauled the crate aboard, then they were on their way back to the Riviera. He spotted a small yacht a good distance away but realized he could do nothing about it and hoped to God that no one aboard had seen the drop.

Three boys were testing the little yacht for the nationals. They had taken it without their parents' permission and were smoking a large joint when the helicopter flew overhead. Through binoculars they watched in amazement as the crate fell out. At first they were unsure what they had seen, and they passed the binoculars around, wondering if they had witnessed a drugs drop. They did not, however, have a radio, and as the large yacht turned to head out to sea, they reckoned they were wrong. If it had been drugs, surely the boat would be heading inland. Suddenly they felt a flurry of wind and galvanized themselves to set sail back to the marina.

*   *   *

At the racecourse de Jersey went into the weighing room to see Mickey Rowland, surprising him. The jockey was heading toward the locker rooms carrying de Jersey's racing colors, ready to dress. He thought it was odd that his boss was here to see Fan Dancer when he hadn't made it to Royal Flush's race at Lingfield, but he didn't say anything. It wasn't his business where and when the boss showed up.

He shook de Jersey's hand and told him that Fleming was heading over to the saddling enclosure. He watched de Jersey stroll out, smiling and acknowledging a few of the jockeys he knew. He also saw him pause by the Sheikh's jockey and take him to one side. He wondered if his boss would go back on his word about his ride in the Derby.

De Jersey walked into the owners' and trainers' bar, acknowledging a few people he knew. He bought a gin and tonic but hardly touched it and, moments later, crossed to the saddling stalls. He stopped beside the Sheikh's trainer. They discussed a few race meetings, and the conversation came round to Royal Flush. Evidently the horse's progress was being monitored by everyone in the business. De Jersey felt a rush of pride and said casually to the trainer that it was his turn for the Derby. He paused as the trainer's quiet, almost lisping voice said, "Yours, Mr. de Jersey, or Royal Flush's?" It was an odd statement, and he would have replied to it but he saw Fleming waving to him.

He excused himself and joined his trainer. "Seen him fishing around. Any money he was asking you about Royal Flush. He's got his eyes on him, you know," Fleming said.

"So would I if I had his money and history of success." De Jersey was referring to the Sheikh's domination of the racetracks and his record of breeding champions. He had the finest stud in England, if not the world. The Arabs were well known for their love of the races. Their animals were kept in luxurious surroundings with the finest trainers and jockeys under million-pound contracts to race exclusively for them. One of their studs was not far from de Jersey's.

"What brings you here?" Fleming asked as they headed across the green toward their allocated stall.

"I missed my boy's last race, so I felt I should make an appearance. Don't want the gossipmongers spreading it around that I'm not taking an interest anymore."

Fleming saddled Fan Dancer, and together they went to the ring to watch him being led out to wait for the jockey. There were ten horses racing, so nine other owners and trainers stood waiting as well. Mickey walked out, fixing his helmet strap beneath his chin. He stood with de

Jersey and Fleming for a few moments, listening to last-minute instructions, which were to give Fan Dancer an easy race. He was helped into the saddle, and they went out of the parade ring to watch him canter up to the starting gates.

De Jersey and Fleming stood side by side in the owners' and trainers' stand. Fleming had to lend his boss his binoculars.

"I can't stay too long. Christina and I are due to watch the girls in *The Taming of the Shrew*," de Jersey said, monitoring Fan Dancer. "After the race I'm going to have to shift myself to make it." Then he focused the binoculars on the Sheikh's trainer, who stood nearby studying the racing form.

The horses were under starter's orders, and then they were off. Fan Dancer ran a good race but seemed to get boxed in early at the rails. De Jersey watched Mickey move him out, but the horse didn't like pushing his way between two others. Then Mickey moved him through a nice gap and, hardly touching Fan Dancer with the whip, rode him into fifth position. He dropped back to sixth, then moved up again to remain in fifth as they crossed the finishing line.

"He's no Royal Flush," de Jersey said, returning Fleming's binoculars to him.

"Few are" came the reply as they turned to walk back to the stables. De Jersey excused himself, asking Fleming to tell Mickey he'd ridden a good race.

De Jersey left the Brighton track at four o'clock and did not relax until he was alone. He gave his pocket an involuntary pat and felt the object cushioned against his leg. He knew the exact weight was 105.6 carats, but it had felt even heavier when he had prized it out of the crown. If they lost the bulk of the jewels he had dropped for Dulay, he would still retain the prize Koh-i-noor Diamond.

The City of London learned that the most daring robbery in history had been pulled off through numerous news flashes that interrupted TV programming for that day. The *Evening Standard* ran the story on the front page, and the police were stunned at the audacity of the raiders. They gave away little about the robbery, but Maureen was pictured on the front page dressed as Her Majesty with a fake crown and a frozen smile. She was currently under sedation and unable to speak coherently. Her husband, she had been told, was safe if badly shaken. Though she was hysterical, she had been able to tell the police how she had been kidnapped and her husband's life threatened. She had also given a description of the man she said headed the robbery. Although she had never heard his name, she described de Jersey as a "military kind of man." He was in his mid-fifties, she said, had red hair and a mustache, and was very tall.

The public marveled at the robbery, but most were confident that the culprits would be caught. The Metropolitan Police Special Branch and the Army announced that they would join forces to recover the jewels. Operation Crown began immediately.

Quickly the police processed the section of the security film that had been recorded just moments before Hall had forced the guard to pull the plugs. The team were caught on film entering the hallway and heading toward the reception. But when they got the film back from the labs they saw that there was a clear shot of Maureen but no single frame in which her lady-in-waiting could be seen because of the large hat the woman had worn. They could see only a partial profile of Driscoll and a shoulder and body shot of de Jersey, his face obscured by the only member of the team caught fully on camera. Lord Henry Westbrook was shown smiling and talking before the screen went blank. It was only a few hours before he was identified by a police officer who had been involved in his fraud case.

At a press conference, reporters were informed that progress had been made. There was a warrant out for the arrest of Lord Henry Westbrook. Meanwhile the staff at the safe house were all asked for detailed descriptions of the men and the woman involved in the heist. Their descriptions of Pamela varied, so the police were relying on Maureen for details. She was still sedated and in hospital, her husband at her side. He gave a description of the driver of the Mercedes that had picked up his wife. He could offer only vague details of the man's companion.

No one could provide a decent description of the two bikers as their attention had been focused on the "Queen." The sketches depicting the tall man hardly seen on the videotapes were confusing. All agreed that he had red hair and a mustache, but none could give a clear description of his face. Saunders maintained that this man was the leader. His voice was cultured, and he had a military manner. He had been the first to leave the vault.

A massive search for the cars was mounted, and witnesses were asked to come forward if they had seen the convoy driving toward the safe house, but no one called.

Christina was selecting what to wear for her daughters' school play when the phone rang. She pursed her lips, sure it would be her husband making some excuse.

But it was Helen Lyons. "Have you been able to contact Sylvia yet?" she asked.

"I've called her home and her office, who told me she's taking some time off in America. I told you this last time we spoke. I got no reply from her flat, so she must still be away."

"I'm sorry to bother you, but I'm really worried about my money situation. I'm not broke, but David always took care of all our finances."

"He certainly took care of ours," Christina snapped. "I've called your sister for you, and I don't want to get involved any further. I'm sorry, we have money problems too, thanks to your husband's misappropriation of our finances. The more I discover about how much David stole from us, the more I find these calls tedious. Now, I really have to go, please don't call me again!"

She replaced the receiver, then felt dreadful. She knew she was taking out her own anxiety on the poor woman—but what she had said to her was true.

Just after three she drove away from the estate to do some shopping.

De Jersey got home at five o'clock. He stashed the wig and mustache in a briefcase and hurried toward the house. He seemed calm and collected, but his adrenaline was still pumping. When Christina returned from her shopping, he had bathed and changed, and was in the kitchen.

"You're back," she said.

"I am, my darling. We have a date tonight, don't we?"

"The girls' play, yes. I thought, with all your problems, you might have forgotten it." She walked past him to unpack the groceries.

He turned, surprised at her tone. "You make it sound as if I'm in the doghouse," he said.

"You are, if you must know." She joined him at the table. "I might as well tell you, because you'll find out soon enough."

"Find out what?"

"I was in your study and broke . . ." She paused. She looked at him, frowning, then leaned forward and rubbed his sideburns. "You've got glue or something stuck to your face."

He backed away. "It's shaving lotion. Go on, what have you broken?"

"I haven't broken anything," she said petulantly, then faced him angrily. "Please stop treating me like a child. I broke into your desk drawers."

He hesitated a moment. "Really? And why did you do that?"

Christina chewed her lip, then took a deep breath. "I don't know—no, I do. I'm sick of your lies. I just wanted to know what was going on."

"When was this?"

"Does it really matter? Anyway, what I found upset me. I wanted to discuss it with you face-to-face. That's why I didn't mention it to you when you called. Why didn't you tell me, for God's sake? If you can't be honest with me after all these years . . . You're virtually bankrupt!" Christina said.

De Jersey relaxed a little. "Why don't we go and sit in the drawing room and you can tell me about it."

"You go ahead," she said. "I'll make some tea." He nodded and walked out.

She took a deep breath. Her nerves were in shreds, but she was determined not to let him off the hook this time.

De Jersey listened as Christina detailed her discoveries. "I don't understand why you would need fake passports."

"I've been using aliases off and on for years. It's been a sort of ploy to allow me to move in and out of the horse auctions without my real name attached."

"That can't be the reason," she said angrily. "You even had passports for me and the girls, all in false names. There are recent stamps in one passport to New York. You never told me you'd been to New York. What's going on?"

"I didn't know I'd be going there myself, and I got the passports for you and the girls just in case you accompanied me on one of these undercover buying trips. You know I hate being apart from you. That's the only reason."

"So what were you doing in New York?"

De Jersey decided to come partially clean. "I went to see the man who ruined me. I didn't want it to get out that I had."

"Why not?"

"He used me, Christina. As you know, he let his company go belly up and consequently did the same to my whole life."

"So you went to see him?"

"Yes, but I used a different name because I didn't want to alarm him or forewarn him. Turned out he still had some of my money invested in some properties out there. He was a cheap con man. I caught him just about to skip the country for South America. He got scared I'd get the cops on to him, so he coughed up. Not all of it, just a fraction, really, but enough to keep my head above water for a while."

"Does Sylvia know?"

"No. If I'd told her I would have had to pay her off, and then the other creditors would be hounding me for their cut too. This way, I got some of my losses back and Moreno took off, I hope never to be seen again." He shrugged.

"So how are things now, financially?" she asked.

"Well, not good, but they're a hell of a lot better with Moreno's cash. At least I'm not forced to sell this place, which I would have been if I hadn't got to the bastard."

"Did you have to do it illegally?"

"Of course. I had to carry the money back into England in a suitcase, which is another reason I thanked God I'd used a false name. It was all done to protect us. Legal or not, I did it, but who is Moreno going to cry to? Not the police. He's the criminal, not me. He committed a massive fraud that bankrupted a lot of people. I know I've told you a few lies, but darling, I had to do this on the spur of the moment. I didn't have any time to waste, and the fewer people who knew of my intentions the better."

"On the spur of the moment? Do you think I'm stupid? Some of the dates on the passports go back years. And who is this Michael Shaughnessy character?"

"Well, having a fake identity worked once, so I did it a few times. As I said, it was to protect myself. You buy horses in Ireland and it's all over the *Racing News*! The fewer people know what I'm doing the better."

"But I'm your wife!"

"And if I hadn't pulled it off, you'd have been run through the mill with me. I was only trying to protect you."

"Treat me like an idiot, more like," she snapped.

"If that's what you call protection, then yes. I didn't want to involve you in case it went wrong. I might have been arrested at Heathrow with the cash. Fortunately I wasn't, so there was no harm done. I also couldn't put the cash into a bank because I'd be hauled up for taxes. But we're not bankrupt yet, my darling, so as I said, no harm done."

"There is, though." He frowned at her. "You've made me feel inadequate and helpless. You were in trouble when we went to Monaco, but you never discussed it with me and instead bought me expensive gifts as if nothing was wrong, when all the time you were in dire trouble. How do you think that makes me feel?"

"Loved?" He laughed, but she turned away angrily.

"No, foolish. But it is still not making sense to me. For instance, you've sold Bandit Queen, and Fleming thinks she's been bought by this Michael Shaughnessy, which is the name on one of your passports. But that doesn't make sense because it's really you, isn't it? The passport had your photograph in it."

"Correct. It's simple. If I went bankrupt, Bandit Queen would have been part and parcel of the debts. This way I still own her."

"But she was mine! You bought her for me!"

"Well, that's true, but she still is in a way." He got up, put his arms around her, and kissed her neck. "You've had so much to deal with recently, with your mother's death. I just didn't want to worry you. And"—he looked at his watch—"if we don't get a move on, we'll both be in the doghouse because we'll be late for the girls' production."

She nodded and kissed him, then touched his face. "That is such a weird smell, like glue. Next you'll tell me you're really as bald as a coot and you're wearing a wig." He grinned, scooped her up in his arms, and carried her out of the room. The phone rang, and she shrieked, "Don't answer it! It'll be Helen Lyons."

He carried her up the stairs and set her down midway. His knee was throbbing. The phone rang and rang. He wanted to answer it in case it concerned him, but Christina caught his hand.

"She's called every other day. She's trying to get me to contact her sister for her."

"Why?" He looked over the banister rail to the hall table below, where the phone still rang.

"Because when she found out David and Sylvia were having an affair, she said she was never going to speak to her again. She asked me to call her on her behalf. Did you know about it?"

"What?"

"That Sylvia was seeing David, for years apparently."

"Good God! No, of course I didn't. What did she want? Is it to do with David or what?"

"It's the insurance money. Apparently Sylvia was handling all the claims, and now Helen is running short of cash."

The phone had stopped ringing.

"Did you speak to Sylvia?"

"No. I even called her office, but they said she was away. New York, I think. But when Helen called again, just before you got home, I couldn't contain myself any longer. I told her that, considering what David had done to us, she could damned well call Sylvia herself!"

Christina's mood changed. "I have felt very lonely while you've been away, Edward."

"I'm sorry, but I didn't have any choice." He stroked her face and kissed her gently.

"But is everything all right? I mean, truthfully. Please, no more lies. I hated prizing open the drawers like some demented, jealous woman, and then when it all became clear how badly off we are financially, I almost hated you for being so dishonest with me."

"The truth is that we're out of trouble now, and with the expectation I have for Royal Flush . . . If he wins the Derby, it'll put this place on the map. He'll be worth millions." He kissed her again. "We're almost in the clear, sweetheart."

"And you didn't have to remortgage the farm?"

"Nope. I got away without having to do that by the skin of my teeth. We're safe."

She leaned against him as they continued up the stairs. "Things have to change between us," she said quietly. "From now on, don't lie to me anymore."

"I won't. Hell, you might take a screwdriver to *me* next, never mind my desk!" He drew her close to him, and they walked up to their bedroom. He gave silent thanks that he had taken Philip Simmons's passport with him to Paris. If he hadn't, Christina would have found it with the others.

They left for their daughters' school an hour later and sat through a lengthy production of *The Taming of the Shrew*. Both girls were delighted that their father was there, but Christina did not tell them he had slept through most of the last act. They had wine and cheese with the other parents, then left. They listened to classical music on the car stereo rather than the news, and it was almost one in the morning by the time they reached home.

De Jersey was so exhausted he went straight to bed and fell into a deep sleep. Christina lay next to him, her eyes wide open, wondering how many other lies her husband had told her. She was so naïve, she realized, and this was the first time she had ever questioned their relationship or his past. She had never felt their age difference until now and wondered what he had done in the years before he met her. She looked at him now, sleeping like a baby, and felt intensely irritated. They hardly made love anymore, and he had not even kissed her good night. She flopped back on her pillow, the seeds of discontent continuing to grow.

Driscoll sat in the TV room with a large gin and tonic. He had been watching the news flashes, partly in amusement and partly in denial. They were not in the clear by any means. The biggest plus was that neither he nor Wilcox had been in trouble with the law before, so even if Maureen could describe them, she could look at mug shots until the cows came home: they were not in the books. The news flashes described the missing vehicles, and requests for information were repeated with numbers to call if anyone had information. A warrant had been issued for Westbrook's arrest. A parade of debs and his associates were interviewed on the news, telling tales of his womanizing and dealings in high society. His face was becoming as familiar as Lord Lucan's.

"What the hell were you doing all day?" Liz asked, setting down a bowl of raw carrots.

"Touting for business," he said, then looked at her as she started to crunch a carrot.

"Christ, do you have to do that?" he asked.

"I'm on a diet."

"Well, I'm hungry. I didn't have time for lunch."

She stood up. "What do you want?"

"Omelet. Nothing too rich. My gut's giving me hell."

"You should see another specialist. You want anything in the omelet or just plain?"

"Bit of cheese."

"That's fattening."

"I don't give a fuck!"

"Tony!"

"I'm sorry, but I'm trying to listen to the news." Suddenly he felt gleeful. "You seen it?"

"I only just got in. I've been having a mud bath at the new hydro clinic."

"Well, there's been a big robbery."

"Oh, I know about that. Sandra had the TV on. Do you want a side salad with your omelet?"

"Sure." He watched her walk out of the room. He wondered how Sandra would feel if she knew her last customer's husband had been in on the robbery of the Crown Jewels.

Shortly after Westbrook and Pamela arrived home, Pamela dyed her hair back to its usual auburn. Westbrook was on her sofa bed and continued to apologize for imposing on her, swearing that as soon as he recovered he'd make his own arrangements. He had a fake passport and cash to leave the country, but until he could stand up travel was out of the question. He watched the television all that day and night, but even the news flashes could not hold his attention and he dozed fitfully. Where on earth had they managed to get so many photographs of him, let alone of his so-called associates? He wondered where these close friends had been for the past year.

Wilcox arrived home in time for the twins' birthday party, which he'd forgotten. It was a bit of a pain; all he wanted to do was relax and watch the news. But he blew up balloons and sat out with the kids as they ate sausages, eggs, and chips. He left the chaos for a while to go to the local video store. He returned, arms loaded with Mars bars, Smarties, cartoons, sci-fi films, and all the evening newspapers he could lay hands on. The headlines all told of the robbery, and everyone was talking about it, even in the video store. The public seemed to view it as sacrilege. Later in the evening he sneaked away to his bedroom to watch the late-night television news. The hunt for Westbrook was on, but as yet there seemed to be no clues as to the identity of the rest of the team. Nevertheless, they gave out descriptions based on what little they had to go on. Wilcox sighed with relief. He wanted to call Driscoll. He ached to hear how he was coping and became paranoid that the police had to be withholding evidence. He chopped up the last of his stash of cocaine, and Rika found him snorting it in the bathroom. They had a blistering row, which somehow eased his tension.

After they had made love, Rika lay beside him, her body glistening with sweat, and he leaned on his elbow, smiling at her. "The kids had a great day. Thank you. They get on really well with you, Rika. Dunno what I'd do without you, but they're gonna go to boarding school soon. Their mother suggested they go and stay over with her for the next holidays and—"

She turned toward him. "Vhat you saying? You don't need me no more?"

"No, I am not saying that at all."

"Then vhy you say it?"

"No reason. Why do you question everything I bloody say?"

"I don't."

"Yes, you do."

"Vhy vere you so late coming home? I told you I needed things for the party."

"I hadda sell a car. In fact, I'm selling off most of them."

Rika pouted. "You still got no money."

"Yeah, but not for long."

"Ve get married then? You marry Rika?"

He closed his eyes. "Yeah, maybe . . . Just let me get some kip. I'm tired out."

Rika got off the bed and put on a robe. She tightened the belt and walked out. He sighed and picked up the remote control. He switched from one program to another and fell asleep with the remote still in his hand.

* * *

Not long after the robbery, the police discovered that the team had pulled the plugs on the panic alarms, and they backtracked through the coal chute to the warehouse base. It was two in the morning when they broke in with a search warrant. Now they had their next big lead. There, rotting in acid, was one of the Daimlers used in the heist. Fingerprint experts and twenty officers were shipped in to examine the warehouse inch by inch. They were also trying to find out who had rented the place, but it was a further five hours before they got the man's name: Philip Simmons.

The day after the robbery, Her Majesty made an unprecedented broadcast, asking for the public's assistance in apprehending the thieves who had taken the precious items of British heritage. The interview was followed by a documentary about the Crown Jewels, watched by 10 million viewers. That led to another breakthrough. An elderly man believed the Daimlers used in the robbery might have been the ones he'd sold in Leicester. He informed the police there had been two, and a chap had bought the lease on his garage more than six months previously. When questioned, he gave the best description of Wilcox his memory afforded him. The police matched the garage owner's description to that of the driver Maureen had given.

They had also discovered that Philip Simmons had rented the Aldersgate warehouse. After questioning the estate agents who had negotiated the transaction, they had yet another description of the man they now believed had led the gang. It was confusing, though. Most of the negotiations for the warehouse had been done by telephone, but the agent who had shown de Jersey the property was unable to verify that he had red hair as he had worn a hat. As far as he could recall, he had no mustache. Although the description was sketchy, he confirmed that the man was tall and well built, and spoke with an upper-class accent.

Operation Crown's initial hype was starting to fade. The description of Pamela had yielded no response. The police knew their biggest card would be the capture of Westbrook. The inquiry now fielded a force of over a thousand officers, all sifting through statements and calls from the public. Fifty telephone operators were working round the clock.

There had been hundreds of sightings of Westbrook on the day of the robbery and after the event. Some were at Heathrow Airport, some at the ferry in Dover, and others at various railway stations in the south. One caller said she was sure she had seen him on a train going to Plymouth with a blond woman. She also said he looked drunk or sick. As it had not been disclosed to the public that Westbrook had cancer, this was a valuable piece of information that might lead to the discovery of the lady-in-waiting too.

Two days after the robbery, the police gained their next vital clue. The three boys out sailing who had watched a crate being dropped into the sea off Brighton had subsequently told their father, who reported the incident to the coast guard. He thought that although it might not have been connected with the robbery of the Crown Jewels, it was an unusual event and should be reported anyway.

The coast guard felt the incident warranted reporting to the police. Anything that sniffed of drugs was treated seriously. The local police interviewed the boys, then contacted Scotland Yard. Operation Crown officers traveled to Brighton.

The boys had only the first part of the yacht's name, *Hortensia.* but told police that it had been flying the French flag. British customs were alerted, but there had been no further sightings of the vessel in any harbors along the coast. No customs officials had boarded her to ask why she was anchored off the Sussex coast.

The boys' report added fuel to theories about the robbers' possible getaway. The police had numerous helicopter sightings and were still checking with all the heliports on which helicopters had been used at the time of the robbery. When all the data were cross-referenced, they ascertained that four helicopters had been hired to coincide with the robbery. They had all had instructions to collect passengers from around the City of London, but the pickups had made no contact. What spurred the team up a notch was that the helicopters had been hired by Philip Simmons, who had now taken over from Westbrook as the most hunted man in Britain. His description and police identikit drawings were in every newspaper, and a computerized headshot of him frequently appeared on the daily television news coverage.

24

The police hunt was further aided by a much calmer Maureen Stanley. She was taken over and over through the details of the day of the robbery.

Meanwhile, the forensic experts working in the warehouse had not found a single fingerprint. The debris left by the robbers was so minuscule that it was of no use. The acid had burned the clothes and articles Wilcox had placed in the bin. The remnants, however, were taken to the lab. The acid cans were checked out. Yet again Philip Simmons emerged as the purchaser. The company from which he had bought the acid in bulk gave the police his credit-card number, which threw up an address in Kilburn. When the police arrived at the Kilburn flat, the landlord told them he had never met the occupant. All details had been given over the Internet.

As one team of officers drove across London with search warrants for Simmons's flat, a second team was trying to figure out how the robbers had been able to break into Buckingham Palace security and tap the phones of both Scotland Yard and the safe house. They knew whoever had done it had had access to the telephone exchange, so all employees were being questioned. One man with sufficient knowledge and authority had gone on holiday the day of the robbery. His name was Raymond Marsh. The second team headed for Marsh's house in Clapham. Those in charge of Operation Crown were confident that arrests would soon be made.

As the squad cars pulled up outside the house, they were greeted by a For Sale notice with a sold sticker across it. Lined up in the hall were crates to be shipped to Marsh in South America. All were tagged and carefully packed but with only a poste restante address.

The estate agent was unable to provide an address for Marsh and said the proceeds from the sale of the property were to be deposited in his bank account. She did not know anything about the crates. Marsh had said that a friend would collect them and any bits of furniture the new owners did not want.

"Do you have this friend's name?"

"No, I'm afraid not. As I said, we were just instructed to sell the property with the furniture. I presume whoever it is must have a key."

Robbie Richards did have the key, but he didn't have anywhere to store the boxes, so he had not got round to picking them up. He was supposed to have moved them on the night of the robbery and, in return for helping Marsh, take whatever furniture he wanted.

He was scared to death when he drove into Marsh's street to see the house cordoned off by squad cars and cops wandering around like bluebottles. He turned his borrowed van and moved off fast. He would not have been able to assist the police in the heist inquiry, but he would have been able to give a lot of details about Marsh's other illegal activities, such as the hacking and the credit-card skimming.

A team of officers broke into the Kilburn flat, but the occupant had long since departed. The damaged computer was taken away for tests, but it was deemed useless; the acid had burned through the plastic controls.

Maureen Stanley, after hours of questioning, ultimately proved unable to add to the array of sketches already drawn by the police artists. They had transferred the drawings to a computer-graphics program, layering in coloring and features to assist her, but this confused her even more. She constantly repeated that during the time before they left the warehouse she had been in a state of shock, frightened for herself and for her captive husband. She did say that Lord Westbrook was kind and considerate, and that the woman acting as her lady-in-waiting was called Pamela, or possibly Pauline.

Four days after the heist, led by their commander, the Operation Crown team assembled in their large office block. The press was now lampooning the inquiry as a failure. The culprits, who had once been vilified for stealing the Crown Jewels, were now lauded as antiestablishment heroes.

The police knew that the two Daimlers used in the robbery had initially been kept in the Leicester garage, but again a search by forensics teams had proved futile. The investigating officers were aware that the longer it took for them to sift through their findings, the more likely it was that the heist masterminds would evade them. Worse, however, was the possibility that the precious gems would be cut up and lost to the nation forever.

The most promising clue now seemed futile. Philip Simmons had organized his whole life over the Internet: setting up domestic bills, making numerous purchases, renting the warehouse and his flat. None of the apparently promising leads took them to the man.

The officers were instructed to spread their nets wider. The robbers had to have had a second, larger premises in which to prepare the vehicles and store them. Police press officers were instructed to continue to ask the public for assistance. They were looking for anyone in or around London who had leased a building large enough for the purpose. They still wished to question Philip Simmons, Lord Henry Westbrook, Raymond Marsh, and a blond woman possibly calling herself Pauline or Pamela. Sketches and computer images of Pamela and the other members of the gang were distributed widely and were continuously on the news.

Pamela was frightened. She watched the television updates like a hawk, and the computer image of her was closer than she had thought possible. Added to this, they now had her Christian name. She was also worried about Westbrook, who was dying but refused to allow her to call a doctor. His one fear was that, after all he had done, his son would not benefit. Pamela was adamant that, whatever the outcome, they could trust the Colonel. She knew his word was his bond. They had known it would take considerable time for the big payoff to come through. In the meantime the Colonel had given them all enough cash to live on well and safely. He had even arranged a flight for Westbrook. But this was of little use to his lordship now. Without medication, he was in agony.

Pamela bought some grass from a guy upstairs, and it seemed to ease Westbrook's pain. One evening she returned from shopping to find him stoned but dressed and trying to tie his shoelaces. He was shaking badly, and his hair was plastered to his head, making him appear skinnier than ever. He had hardly been able to eat, sipping only watered brandy.

"Papers are still full of it," she informed him.

"My face seems to be on every TV channel." He grinned boyishly, and she could see that his gums were bleeding.

"I'll put this through the mixer and see if you can keep it down." She held up a ready-made meal and popped it into the oven.

"No, don't. I'm leaving." He lit a cigarette and inhaled deeply. "I've been here too long, and I don't want to put you at further risk."

She was relieved but ashamed to show it. "Where the hell will you go? It's already six o'clock."

"Home." He tried to stand, but his long, thin legs shook violently.

"I'm sure you'll make it in that state." She couldn't help the sarcasm.

"Sure I will, sweetheart. I'll roll a joint, get a bit more energy up, and then you can call a taxi."

"I can't have you picked up from here, darling. That's too much of a risk."

"I know. Get it to pick me up at the station. I can make it that far."

"You can't even stand up."

He straightened and gestured with his free hand. "Course I can."

"But if you take a taxi to Pimlico, you'll be picked up within minutes."

"Not that home," he said softly and eased himself back down. "My real home. My ancestral pile."

"Are you joking? Isn't it miles away?"

"Yes, maybe the taxi isn't such a good idea. Just get me onto a train to Waterloo, and I'll sort something out from there. Please, Pamela."

She approached him and cupped his face in her hands. "Let me think. If that's what you want, we'll work it out somehow."

She left the flat and returned shortly with a wheelchair borrowed from one of the elderly tenants. "It's a long walk, but we'll make it. So roll up your joints and let's get moving."

Westbrook allowed her to shave him and give him a shirt left by a long-gone lover. He wore a polo-neck sweater over it, and she wrapped a blanket around him. She put a hat on his head and pulled it down low.

At eight she set off to walk the two miles to the railway station. Emaciated though he was, Westbrook was heavy to push, and she had to stop for a breather every now and then. His head bobbed up and down on his chest as she eased the chair across the pavements.

There was a train to Waterloo in fifteen minutes, so she bought a one-way ticket and wheeled him onto the platform. She didn't want to think about how he would get on and off the train. They sat together, saying little. To her astonishment, when the train headed into the platform he found enough strength to stand unaided.

"This is good-bye, fair Pamela. Take care of yourself. I adore you and cannot thank you enough for your care. Now, please go and don't look back. Just walk out before I blubber like a schoolboy. I never had much control over my emotions. Reminds me of saying good-bye to my mother when I went back to boarding school."

Pamela kissed his wet, yellow cheek and fussed with the chair to hide her own tears. She knew she would never see him again.

She returned to her room and began to clean up. When she had folded the soiled sheets and Hoovered around the sofa, she sat down and broke into sobs, partly out of relief that he had gone and partly because she would miss him. Then she heated the ready-made meal and poured a large brandy. She couldn't bring herself to switch on the television, fearing she might hear a report of his capture at Waterloo. When she found his unused plane tickets, with two thousand pounds that he had left for her, she broke down again.

Westbrook huddled in a corner of the train compartment and slept for the entire journey. No one paid him any attention. When the train arrived at Waterloo, he mustered the strength to walk the length of the platform toward the taxi rank. Pain forced him to sit down for fifteen minutes. Then, sweating profusely, he rose and hailed a taxi. He asked to be driven to Andover, a good two hours away. At first the driver refused to take him; then he saw Westbrook's cash and helped him into the car.

"You sick?" he asked.

"You could say that. I just had my appendix out." Westbrook rested against the seat, amazed he had managed to come this far. "When we get there, squire, wake me up and I'll direct you to the lodge." He closed his eyes. He knew that from the lodge he could get through the keeper's gate and possibly manage the quarter of a mile to the house. He was too exhausted to open his eyes but passed the time in counting how many steps it would take him to get from the lodge to the kitchens, into the main hall, and from there up the stairs to his bedroom.

His mind drifted back to the room he had known as a boy. He had always been terrified of the dark, shut up in the east wing. He had never received much attention from either of his parents. He could not recall his father showing him any form of warmth or understanding. His mother had tried, when she was sober, but when he had needed her most she was always at some society event. The one great love of his life had been the wondrous building to which he was on his way—the halls, the ballroom, the library, and the vaulted, hand-painted ceiling in his room, with round pink cherubs beckoning him to the clouds on which they rested. All his ventures had been disasters, but with the money from his last enterprise, he was going to make sure his son and heir, living far out of his reach, could return to his rightful home. It was a fantasy, but it kept Westbrook alive for the duration of the taxi ride.

He gave the driver a generous tip and watched him leave, then used the stone wall as an aid to make his way toward the lodge gates. The magnificent house loomed dark and silent as he walked to the kitchens, counting each step. He made it into the house and up to his bedroom, then lay down on the French quilt, his head resting on the rolled satin cushions with their gold tassels. The pink cherubs danced on the ceiling above him, their fingers outstretched. A white marble bust of his great-great-great-grandfather stood at the window. Lord Alexander Westbrook, his periwig curling to his shoulders, stared down at him with his sightless eyes. Westbrook gave a soft sigh of satisfaction. He was home, just in time to die.

Westbrook's body was discovered the next day by an elderly cleaning lady. By the time the doctor was called, two family retainers, now hired as cleaners by the commercial ice-cream company who rented the estate, had removed his soiled clothes and washed his body. They had called the police, who arrived with sirens screaming, as the doctor finished his examination.

The body was taken to the mortuary and an autopsy performed. The cancer that had been seeping through him had rendered his heart and lungs useless. When the body was released, one of the old retainers provided the funeral home with his lordship's uniform and sword. They felt it only fitting that he should be laid out in his uniform, even though he had been disowned by his regiment. He was Lord Westbrook, after all. His dress uniform had been on display in the hall for visitors. His family was summoned to England for the funeral. His soiled garments were taken by the police to be examined, and the retainers were questioned but released without charge.

Westbrook made headlines again, but he had left the police without clues. He had thrown away anything that might link him to the robbery or to Pamela. He died knowing that the Colonel would be impressed by his tenacity and care. But then he had always been a true gentleman.

De Jersey lowered *The Times* and allowed himself an appreciative smile. The article stated that Westbrook had died of natural causes, and his death was not being treated as suspicious. He had heard no word of Sylvia Hewitt, and nothing had appeared about her in any of the papers. He took this as a good sign. In fact, although the newspapers still carried front-page articles about the hunt, he sensed that they might be in the clear. He was not stupid enough to think everything the police uncovered would be handed to the journalists, but at the same time, five days after the robbery, they had not arrested anyone and did not appear close to doing so. Still, the daily requests for information regarding Philip Simmons, the artists' sketches and computer pictures posed some risk to him. He just hoped that all links between him and Simmons had been destroyed.

De Jersey continued his usual business on the estate, exercising the horses and discussing the future racing programs with Fleming. He was attentive to Christina, who seemed less anxious about their situation now that he was at home with her. As in the rest of the country, there were many discussions in the yard about the robbery, but eventually interest died down as the flat season got under way.

After going through a gamut of emotions, Helen Lyons had decided to telephone her sister. For all her faults, Sylvia was the only family she had, and Helen was lonely. Her friend in Devon had suggested that she try to sort out her finances and visit her sister, hinting that Helen had overstayed her welcome.

Sylvia, however, appeared to be away, or at least was not answering her phone. The office confirmed what Christina de Jersey had told her, that Sylvia was still possibly in New York. When she had not heard from her sister after a week, Helen caught a train from Devon, then took a taxi to St. John's Wood. She still had her own key to Sylvia's apartment. She unlocked the front door. "Sylvia," she called, ". . . it's Helen."

She entered the apartment and stepped over a stack of mail. As she walked into the drawing room, she noticed a pungent smell. Sylvia's body lay on the sofa. Helen ran to the caretaker's apartment. The caretaker didn't know what to do. Sylvia was obviously dead and had been so for some time, but they called the doctor anyway.

When the doctor turned up, he confirmed what they already knew and said that they would not know how she had died until a postmortem had been conducted. He called the police, and a young, uniformed officer took a statement from him and Helen. There was no sign of a break-in, and no items were missing or disturbed.

Helen had to wait for the body to be removed to the mortuary. She opened all the windows to get rid of the stench. There seemed no real reason for her to leave, and she discovered all the documents regarding the insurance on her home neatly stacked in a drawer of Sylvia's desk. She also found Sylvia's will and learned that she was the main beneficiary. The apartment was now hers, but until she took it over legally she would stay in the spare room where she had slept before.

There were some unanswered questions in the police investigation into Sylvia Hewitt's death, and the case remained open. The suspicion of suicide seemed to be confirmed when the postmortem revealed a heavy presence of morphine. What perturbed the pathologist, however, was the additional presence of ketamine. Helen was dumbfounded by this and collapsed in tears. The young sergeant sitting opposite her had to wait a considerable time before he could continue to question her.

Helen told him that it was incomprehensible that anyone could have wanted Sylvia dead, but it was possible she had taken her own life. "In the last couple of days, before I left her, I've learned that she lost a considerable amount of money on a bad investment deal," she said. "It was connected to my husband." Then the story of the affair tumbled out. Perhaps Sylvia had taken her own life after losing David, her savings, and her sister. She had also told her employers that she would not be coming into work.

Helen was asked if she knew of anyone who had seen her sister during the past two weeks, but she did not. The police, still dissatisfied, began to check phone calls Sylvia had made or received on the evening of her death. They also questioned friends and work colleagues. No one else they spoke to felt that Sylvia would have taken her life, and they told the officers of her trip to New York. This tallied with the last phone call Sylvia had made, to a private detective named Matheson in New York City. When Detective Sergeant Jon Fuller contacted him, Matheson was shocked. He explained that he had been hired by Miss Hewitt to trace a man called Alex Moreno, who they believed was involved in a fraud. He was also aware she had lost a considerable amount of money.

"Did she sound depressed?" Fuller asked.

"No, far from it," he told them. "She was very positive because she had traced the man she believed could help her regain some of her losses."

"Did Miss Hewitt give this man's name?"

"Philip Simmons."

"Did you know him?"

"I never met him, but I knew he had been in New York recently. In fact, we thought he was still here. He was Moreno's business adviser. Miss Hewitt also said everything was going well and she no longer needed my services."

"Do you have any idea where Simmons would be?"

"No. As I said, I never met him, but I think he was Canadian."

Fuller's report was passed to his superior and placed on file. He had concluded that, although it was probably suicide, Miss Hewitt's death still seemed suspicious. Why would a woman committing suicide with morphine and ketamine bother to clean her kitchen before she died, leaving no trace of how she had consumed the drugs? Why was there no suicide note? He also wanted to speak to the person who may have been the last to see her alive: Philip Simmons, the name entered and underlined three times in her desk diary for a 6:00 P.M. meeting on the day she died. As yet they had found no trace of him in her address books or office files.

Fuller was told to continue the inquiry, and Sylvia's body was released for burial. Even though the robbery squad had told the media that they were searching for a man called Philip Simmons, D.S. Fuller did not make the connection. The suicide of a woman in St. John's Wood was not the crime of the century. The name Philip Simmons was simply listed among many others they wished to interview in connection with Sylvia Hewitt's death.

The robbery squad took a big step forward when British customs, working with Interpol, traced a motorized yacht named the *Hortensia Princess,* owned by Paul Dulay and anchored in the south of France. They contacted their European counterparts, whose records showed that the *Hortensia Princess* had left Cannes four days before the sighting and returned four days later. They e-mailed a photograph of Dulay's boat.

The boys who had seen the yacht on the day of the robbery were questioned again by customs and asked if the boat they had seen bore any resemblance to the photograph of Dulay's vessel. They agreed without hesitation that it was the same one. Then the investigating team discovered that Dulay was a jeweler. Two detectives were sent to interview him and his crew.

The two crew members confirmed that they had picked up a box dropped by a helicopter off the English coast. When they hauled it aboard it had been full of junk, so they had tossed it back into the sea. They said a fault in the fuel gauge had occurred, which was why they were anchored off Brighton. They had been able to repair it themselves, then hauled up the anchor to return to France. When asked if the owner of the boat had been aboard, they said that he had and that he had instructed them to retrieve the package.

Paul Dulay was working in his shop when the officers questioned him about his trip. He kept his cool, saying that he had not been ashore in England. He gave the names of three companies he had called from the yacht to ask for assistance with the fuel gauge before they had managed to repair it. He didn't flinch when asked about the crate.

"Oh, yes. We saw a helicopter flying overhead and watched it drop something into the water. I instructed my crew to haul it aboard." He gave a knowing look. "It might have been drugs—anything, you know. When we opened it, it was full of empty bottles, a couple of jackets, and some other clothing. We tossed it back into the water. It's probably still floating around out there."

The police asked about the helicopter, but Dulay shrugged. He couldn't remember, possibly a twin engine as it was quite large, and there were two or three people aboard. The officers left, only to return an hour later with a helicopter manual showing different designs. Dulay took a long, hard look, then pointed to a Sikorsky S-76. "This one."

"Would you mind if we searched your boat?"

"No, of course not."

"We'd also like to look over your premises."

"I don't see why this is necessary, but by all means."

The two officers left Dulay in a cold sweat. He called the captain of his boat and told him to reiterate the make of the helicopter he'd identified and to say that three people were on board.

The officers reported that they had searched Dulay's boat, home, and workplace but had found nothing incriminating. They did note that Dulay himself cut stones and had a very well appointed workroom at the rear of his shop. He also had a successful business with influential clients. They said he had been helpful in every way and that they were not suspicious.

They were told to stay away from him until further notice but not to return to England. They were to keep surveillance on him and to make it obvious. He might not have given them reason to doubt him, but the coincidence of his profession and his having been near England at the time of the robbery and the business with the crate made him a suspect.

The same photograph of the helicopter was subsequently shown to the boys, who knew nothing about helicopters and were unable to confirm if it was the same make.

The team began to inquire into who in the United Kingdom owned a Sikorsky helicopter. They also contacted the companies Dulay said he had asked for help. All remembered the inquiry, so his story could not be disproved. Launches were sent out to find the crate.

Dulay was sure he was being watched, and his nerves were getting the better of him. He wanted to contact de Jersey but was afraid to. However, a few days after he'd been interviewed he received a call from the man himself. The newspapers were full of details of the helicopter, stating it was likely to have been the getaway vehicle, so de Jersey had known Dulay would be unnerved. He called from a pay phone at Kempton Park racecourse. He had just watched Royal Flush sail home first with ease, ensuring his place in the Derby. He had congratulated Mickey, avoided posing for photographs, and watched his horse get rugged up.

He was still on a high when he rang Dulay. "How are you?" he asked.

"They're on to me, I'm sure," hissed Dulay.

"Not if you followed orders."

"There's some witness who saw the drop."

"But you kept to the story?"

"Yes. They searched the boat from top to bottom. My house, the shop—"

"But it's well hidden, so you've got nothing to worry about." De Jersey maintained his calm.

"Yeah, but you're not the one being tailed. Man, I am shitting myself."

"Just carry on as if nothing's happening. Don't go near the loot, just stick to the plans. We don't collect until the heat's off. Go about your business and see how Mr. Kitamo is. We want that down payment."

"He's going to want to authenticate the Koh-i-noor, but I'm too hot right now to retrieve the jewels."

"Well, if he wants the diamond, he's just going to have to trust us. You tell him we want the million dollars before we'll let him see it. Unless he's completely out of touch, he knows by now there are some priceless gems to be had."

"I hear you. Anything happening at your end?"

"No. Still in the clear."

By the end of the call, de Jersey was edgy. He had not expected a problem so soon. Apart from the Koh-i-noor, the jewels were still in the crate, wrapped in tarpaulins and haversacks, hundreds of feet down in the ocean. A lobster pot marked the place where it had been dropped off the coast of Cannes, toward a small inlet and fishing harbor. When it was time to collect, Dulay would go in single-handed with a speedboat: no crew, no witnesses.

The coast guard retrieved a large, old wooden crate. It contained boiler suits, boots, two jackets, and a pair of shoes. It provided the robbery squad with no further clues and made Dulay's explanation seem more credible.

Dulay read on the Internet that the crate had been recovered, but the news did little to ease his mind. He had been lucky so far, but how long would his luck hold out?

Sylvia Hewitt's death looked suspicious to D.S. Fuller. He had removed her business diary and personal papers from her office, plus letters and files from her St. John's Wood flat. He discovered from her office diary that she had had numerous appointments for the weeks after her death and had made dates for dental and medical checkups the next day. This was not the pattern of a woman contemplating suicide.

He called Matheson again; the PI felt certain that when he had last spoken to her in New York Sylvia was not suicidal but determined to trace Moreno in the hope of recouping her losses. Matheson added that Moreno had disappeared.

Also in her office diary were the names and contact numbers of certain clients of David Lyons who had suffered similar losses. Among them were Anthony Driscoll, James Wilcox, and Edward de Jersey. These three were underlined, so Fuller decided to concentrate on them.

The first of the threesome to be interviewed was Tony Driscoll. He almost had heart failure when his wife came into his study to tell him a police officer wanted to talk to him.

"Sorry to bother you, sir. I'm Detective Sergeant Jon Fuller, and this is Police Constable Margaret Kilshaw. I am here concerning a woman named Sylvia Hewitt. I believe you were a business associate." Driscoll hesitated, but Fuller continued, "You should know that Miss Hewitt is dead."

"Oh, I'm sorry to hear that, but I didn't know her."

"Miss Hewitt recently suffered financial losses due to her involvement with an Internet company, and your name was listed in her diary."

"Ah, yes. Now I know who she is, but I never met her. I think she got my number from David Lyons, who advised me to invest in the same company."

"Could you tell me why she contacted you?"

"I suffered substantial losses in the same company, and Miss Hewitt asked if I would be willing to hire someone to help trace the man she believed was responsible. I was rather annoyed that she had got hold of my personal details, which I pointed out to her was illegal."

"And you never met her?"

"No, I did not. I'm sorry I can't be more helpful."

"Just one more thing. Do you know someone named Edward de Jersey?"

"No."

"Do you know someone called James Wilcox?"

"No."

"Philip Simmons?"

Driscoll's heart was fit to burst through his chest. "No. I'm sorry I can't help you. I only spoke to the woman once on the phone." He hesitated, then decided he had said enough.

Wilcox was tipped off fast by Driscoll.

"I warned everyone about that bloody woman," Wilcox said tightly.

"Yes, I know, but we've no problem. She's dead."

There was a pause as Wilcox took this in. "How come they came to you?"

"The bitch had my details in her fucking diary, so she must have yours and the Colonel's. I'll warn him too." Driscoll paused. "So far so good, huh?" he said.

"Yeah. Let's hope it stays that way," Wilcox replied.

When Detective Sergeant Fuller visited that afternoon, Wilcox denied knowing Sylvia Hewitt, Driscoll, or de Jersey. "Did you know that David Lyons committed suicide?" Wilcox asked the sergeant innocently.

"Yes, we are aware of that. Just one more thing, do you know a Philip Simmons?"

"No. I didn't mix with Lyons socially, so I didn't know any of his other clients. All I do know is we all lost a considerable amount in this Internet company we invested in. Maybe he was one of the losers."

"Via a Mr. Alex Moreno?"

"I believe so. But I think he did a runner. I know we have little hope of recovering any money."

As he had said he would, Driscoll made a short warning call to de Jersey, who was abrupt and noncommittal. When he replaced the phone, Driscoll was aware of a dull sensation in the pit of his stomach. He was sure that de Jersey had played some part in Miss Hewitt's demise, but as with Moreno, he hadn't asked and he didn't want to know. He was just relieved that she was no longer a problem.

However, both Driscoll and Wilcox needed cash injections. Driscoll decided to put his house on the market, unaware that Wilcox was contemplating the same thing.

Jon Fuller and his P.C. now made the journey to de Jersey's estate. If Fuller had been impressed by the properties owned by Driscoll and Wilcox, de Jersey's took his breath away. The patrol car drew up beside the west wing stables. Fuller asked a boy if he could tell them where they would find de Jersey and was pointed to a vast, semicovered arena with a horseshoe-shaped swimming pool for exercising the horses.

De Jersey was watching Royal Flush swimming around the perimeter of the pool. He had seen the patrol car enter the yard and paid it no attention. As the officers approached, he continued to call out instructions. "Keep him going. Give him another two half circles."

"Good morning, sir." Fuller showed his card and introduced his companion.

"This is my pride and joy, Royal Flush," de Jersey said, gesturing to the swimming stallion. "Put your money on him for the Derby," he advised and gave the officers a charming smile.

He walked with them back to the house, where he told them he had met Sylvia Hewitt twice, once at her brother-in-law's house and a second time when he had visited her at her apartment in St. John's Wood.

"Miss Hewitt was found dead in her apartment," Fuller said.

"My God! When did this happen?" De Jersey stopped in his tracks.

"Two weeks ago. We believe it was suicide, sir."

"Well, that's dreadful, but I fail to see how I can be of any help. I didn't really know her." He added that he was surprised Sylvia would contemplate suicide. Then he paused. "I don't know if I should go into this, but her brother-in-law, as you must know, also committed suicide quite recently. The reason I am hesitant to say anything derogatory about Sylvia is that I had a great affection for David and his poor wife." He paused again. "I believe Sylvia and David had been lovers for some time." He sighed. "I am deeply sorry this has happened. In some ways I wish I had known her better. The loss of certain investments was deeply disturbing for me, but in comparison . . ."

"Did you ever think of taking legal action?" asked the detective.

"Well, my father always used to say, 'Never invest in anything you don't understand,' and I wish to God I had taken his advice. This chap Moreno ran off with whatever he salvaged out of the mess."

"Did you ever approach Moreno?"

"Good heavens, no. Sylvia was trying to find him. She wanted me to help, but private detectives can't be trusted, and I just felt it was best to forgive and forget. David was dead, and that was the end of it as far as I was concerned."

"And you do not know an Anthony Driscoll or a James Wilcox?"

"I'm afraid not."

"Have you ever met a man called Philip Simmons?"

At this moment Christina appeared in the doorway with a tray of coffee.

"Darling, do come in." De Jersey rose and made the introductions. She put down the tray and shook their hands. De Jersey handed round the coffee as he explained the reason for the officers' visit.

Christina sat down, shocked. "Good heavens. How terrible. I must call Helen," she said.

De Jersey put his arm round her. "Yes, of course, we should."

She gazed at him a moment, then smiled at the officers. "Excuse me," she said and left the room.

* * *

Outside the study door Christina waited to hear her husband tell the police whether he knew Philip Simmons. "I don't think I do. Was he one of David's clients?" she heard him say.

"We're not sure," replied Fuller. "It's just that there are various notes in Miss Hewitt's diary with regard to this man and, according to the detective in New York, she felt that he was connected to Alex Moreno."

"I can't recall meeting someone of that name, but then I do meet a lot of people at the racetracks."

"Have you been to New York yourself recently?"

"No, I have not."

Christina remained listening until they began to discuss racing. Then she went slowly up to her bedroom. She could understand why he had lied. He had done something illegal in New York, he had told her that. But how on earth could it be connected to Sylvia Hewitt? She went to the window to see de Jersey ushering the officers out and watched as they walked to their parked patrol car.

A few moments later de Jersey came into the bedroom. "I wasn't expecting you home for a while," he said.

Christina watched him. He frightened her.

"How much did you overhear?" he asked.

"Well, I heard them ask you about being in New York."

"And I was not likely to admit I was there, and you know why," he said, sitting beside her on the bed.

"But they'll find out, surely." She avoided his eyes.

"Why should they? I'll destroy those passports if you like."

"I would if I were you, but I don't understand why all this subterfuge is necessary."

"I explained it to you."

"I know you did, but why did Sylvia Hewitt have notes in her diary about this man you went to see?"

"Because, sweetheart, she was trying to trace him to get her own money back. I've told you this. In fact, it was David who suggested I use a pseudonym when traveling to buy racehorses. He even got the passports for me. As soon as sellers know my name, they put up the price. I would say the reason she kept on calling here was that she might have found out and wanted to squeeze money out of me. She really was a very unpleasant woman."

"She's dead, for God's sake."

"I know, and by her own hand. She was not a nice woman at all, carrying on with David behind Helen's back. Her own sister!"

"Suddenly you're coming over all moralistic," she said in disbelief.

"Not really, but she was only concerned about getting her money back. She had probably discovered that she didn't have a hope in hell of seeing any of it again, and it must have been too much for her."

"How did she do it?"

"I have no idea. We didn't get into those kind of details."

"Did you go and see her, then?"

"What?"

"I said, Did you go and see her after she kept calling?"

"No, I put it off. I had enough to think about—and considering that that son of a bitch David has virtually bankrupted me, I would think you could understand my reasons for not wanting anything to do with her."

"Did you?"

"Did I what?"

"Have anything to do with her?"

"Why on earth are you asking me that? I just told you I didn't go to see her. I don't want to discuss this any further. It's finished." He walked out, slamming the door.

De Jersey was treading on dangerous ground, and now the person he cared most deeply for might also be the most dangerous to him. He was angry with himself for having left the passports to be found, angry that the one area he had felt was secure was now vulnerable. He had to find a way to sort it out quickly and efficiently.

Raymond Marsh, unaware that he was under investigation, had arrived in Rio de Janeiro without a hitch. Almost immediately he had a reaction to something in the climate that gave him blinding headaches and a rash all over his body. His wife and daughter booked into a hotel with him, but he decided he wanted to move on. South America was not to his liking. He called his friend Robbie with instructions on where to send his packing cases. When he was told that cops were swarming around his old house and his face was plastered all over the newspapers and on television, he slammed the phone down. It was imperative to get out of Brazil. The police might have discovered from Robbie where he was. He paced up and down the hotel room, itching and sweating, trying to think where they should go, when his wife walked in with their screaming child.

"She's got a rash too. It's the heat."

Marsh looked at her and grinned. "Let's get out of here then. Tell you what, why don't we visit your place?"

"What are you talking about?" she asked, sticking a pacifier into the baby's mouth.

"New Zealand," he said.

Anything can be bought in Rio, and within one afternoon Raymond Marsh had new passports. At ten in the evening, he, his wife, and his daughter flew out on tickets booked through their illegal credit cards. During the flight he began to feel worse, and by the time they landed he had a high temperature. They moved into the best hotel in Auckland, and a doctor was called. Marsh's allergy subsided, but the fever and aches persisted. He was diagnosed with a virulent form of shingles. He remained in a darkened room under sedation for two days. He felt so ill that he didn't even watch TV.

His quick exodus from Rio meant there was no clue as to his present whereabouts. When the detectives traced the poste restante address on his boxes to Rio, they set off with a warrant for his arrest but returned empty-handed.

In London, the headlines now blasted on about the police's failure to capture Marsh or to trace Philip Simmons. The articles made their way to the hotel where Marsh was staying. By the time he saw the papers, the story was a week old.

Marsh read the coverage with relief. It was believed that he was still at large in Rio. He was amazed at the photographs they had used of him, which had been taken from his packing boxes. Some were in Elvis mode, others showed him in school uniform. He knew he must not use any of the credit-card numbers from the United Kingdom.

Marsh studied himself in the mirror. Since he had been ill he'd not had time to fix his hair, and it was stuck together in unattractive clumps. He went into the bathroom, put his head under the shower, and shampooed it three times to get the grease and old mousse out. It had taken years of practice to style his hair into a teddy boy quiff, but now it was receding badly and hung limply to his chin. He picked up a pair of nail scissors and chopped it short. He was near tears. It wasn't just his hair he had lost but all his memorabilia. The crates containing his hero's guitars and his autographed pictures were now in the hands of the Metropolitan Police.

His wife barged in with a dirty nappy and had to sit on the edge of the bath, she was laughing so hard. When she stopped giggling, she wiped her eyes with a tissue. "Christ, Raymond, you don't half look different!"

"I'll get a transplant," he snapped.

Marsh calculated they would have real financial problems soon, but he knew that to contact Philip Simmons was tantamount to suicide. He would have to monitor the papers and lie low. He moved his family into a small apartment in Wellington and applied for a job with a local computer company. It was a far cry from the life he had hoped for, but at least he was free.

Sylvia Hewitt's funeral took place within days of Lord Westbrook's. The latter was a more public occasion, with press and photographers lining the streets outside the family estate. His ex-wife, his son and heir, and his two daughters had returned to England for the occasion. The ice-cream company now running the house and grounds allowed them to use the chapel and crypt, and the mourners were old family friends and various distant relatives. Displays of lilies sat on either side of his photograph. The police officers seated at the rear of the tiny chapel looked on with disgust: this man had been a petty criminal and then part of a robbery that still stunned the nation.

Lord Westbrook had dreamed of his son returning to the ancestral seat. The boy stood beside his mother in a gray suit. Neither he nor his mother knew of Westbrook's dream. More distant relations told the press they were appalled by his actions.

De Jersey was relieved to see the funeral on the news. It meant one major risk was gone, but he would honor his promise. When payday came, Westbrook's son would receive his father's cut. Whatever else de Jersey was, he was an honorable man. He had still not seen anything in the papers about Sylvia Hewitt's "suicide" and hoped to God they had closed the inquiry.

Pamela saw the televised snippet of Westbrook's funeral and sobbed. She wished she could have been there. She had sent flowers with a card that simply said, "From your lady-in-waiting, with love and fond memories." She paid for the bouquet in cash.

The police filmed the entire funeral, hoping that people linked to the robbery might show their faces, but no one did. They also examined the flowers. Pamela's message was obscure, perhaps from a mistress or a lover, though "lady-in-waiting" seemed to refer to the robbery. The florist was contacted and remembered that a bedraggled, red-haired lady with a refined voice and sophisticated manner had placed the order. Unfortunately she had not left an address or contact number. When shown the computer pictures of Pamela from Maureen Stanley's description, the florist gasped. "Oh, my God, this is the woman wanted for the Crown Jewels robbery. I don't believe it." She took another look at the photo fit and shook her head. "No, it wasn't her. The woman I met was much older."

* * *

The police were at yet another dead end, and the robbery was dropping out of the headlines. They felt their next best move was to have it profiled on a television crime program. *The Crime Show* had given over an entire fifty-minute episode to the case, and a private benefactor had offered 25,000 pounds for information leading to a conviction. As the program closed, the phones were ringing. The following morning, the calls were still being followed up.

Chief Superintendent Dom Rodgers, the officer overseeing Operation Crown, was feeling ill. He had been coughing for a couple of days and feared he had caught a virus. Now he felt red-hot, and he took himself to his G.P.'s surgery in Maida Vale. The waiting room was chilly and uninviting, and the two patients ahead of him both had streaming colds. He sat feeling wretched, wishing he had remembered to bring his morning paper. His cell phone rang, and he fished it out of his pocket. "Rodgers," he answered, then listened. "What?" he said in amazement. "Look, I'm not far from their station. I'll get right over there."

He snapped off his phone, left the surgery, and drove straight to the St. John's Wood police station. His chest hurt and he was sweating beneath his overcoat, but his excitement put his ill health to the back of his mind. He asked to speak to the officers involved in the Sylvia Hewitt inquiry.

Detective Sergeant Jon Fuller's hand shook as he spooned sugar into a beaker of tea. "I'm so sorry, sir, but we had a list of David Lyons's clients Miss Hewitt had named as losing in the crash of the Internet company and—"

"Just get to the fucking point, Sergeant. Philip Simmons. You called the robbery squad and"—he banged down a small tape recorder, then gestured with his hand—"go on, you've lost me enough times already, son. Philip Simmons."

Armed with the details of the Hewitt case, Rodgers returned to Scotland Yard, where his team was waiting, having received the call from St. John's Wood station earlier that morning. He tossed over his tape recorder.

"Listen to this prick, then come into my office. We've had a development we could have had fucking days ago."

25

Other developments now materialized in the wake of the television program. A taxi driver was sure he had picked up Lord Westbrook from Waterloo Station just before he died. He said he had driven him to his family estate but at the time did not recognize him. He was unable to say what train Westbrook had alighted from, but they had the date and time, so they could begin checking which trains had arrived around then. A hotel barman was sure he had seen Westbrook in the company of a man similar to the one described in the program, but he was more dark blond than redheaded. He could not recall the exact day but knew it had been sometime in January. A railway porter recalled seeing someone fitting Westbrook's description on Plymouth station and said that he had arrived in a wheelchair pushed by an elderly, red-haired woman. A train had left Plymouth to arrive at Waterloo just before Westbrook was picked up by the taxi driver. The description of the woman wheeling the chair matched that of the woman who had purchased the flowers for Westbrook's funeral.

The inquiry was buzzing again. An estate agent said that a man named Philip Simmons had rented a boathouse close to Putney Bridge. The transaction had been done over the Internet, and he had never met Mr. Simmons. The boathouse had burned down on the day of the robbery.

Officers were sent with frogmen and equipment to drag the river in and around the boathouse. They hauled up the wreck of a small speedboat. An identical boat was photographed and appeared on the front page of the *Evening Standard* with a request for anyone with information about a boat of this description to contact the police directly. This produced the mechanic who had sold the boat to Wilcox. He gave a description of Wilcox, whom the police identified as one of the men who had picked up

Maureen Stanley, and who had purchased the two Daimlers. The mechanic, however, had never met anyone by the name of Philip Simmons.

All of this information made it look as if the robbers had escaped via the river, and appeals were made for anyone who had seen these two boats on the Thames to come forward. More officers questioned the owners of the vast number of boats along the Thames. This investigation yielded the location of the mooring facility rented for the two speedboats, and the name materialized yet again: Philip Simmons.

The Operation Crown officers were certain that Philip Simmons was the cyber-identity of their number-one man. But the most vital clue to his real identity came as a result of the death of Sylvia Hewitt, which now became part of the inquiry. They had the names of the men who had suffered extensive losses in the fall of the Internet company: James Wilcox, Anthony Driscoll, and Edward de Jersey. Could these three be connected in some way to Philip Simmons?

Pamela became frightened by the headlines—POLICE ABOUT TO SWOOP—and holed up in her grimy apartment. She felt cut off and alone. She wore a head scarf and dark glasses when she left to buy a dark brown hair dye. Then she went to the nearest off-license and bought a large bottle of vodka. When she returned she locked and bolted the front door, put the rinse on her hair, and left it for half an hour. She began to drink the vodka and chain-smoked, watching television from her bed. Her recent adventure seemed a far-off fantasy, except that the six o'clock news had implied it was just a matter of time before the robbers were arrested.

Driscoll and Wilcox were in the same boat as Pamela, albeit a more comfortable one. They both watched the news bulletins and read the papers from cover to cover. They had each watched *The Crime Show* with equal trepidation, their confidence dented. Their women put their bad moods down to financial pressures. Unlike de Jersey, Wilcox and Driscoll rarely left their homes. They felt more terrified with every phone call and knock on the door. The waiting was becoming unbearable, and eventually each decided independently that he had to flee the country.

Driscoll went to Spain, telling Liz that he needed to secure the sale of their villa, and after a quick phone call, Wilcox agreed to join him. They were breaking the Colonel's rules, but they were unable to deal with the pressure alone. Still, they resisted the urge to contact de Jersey.

The latest developments had given Chief Superintendent Rodgers fresh energy, but by late afternoon on the day after he had interviewed Detective

Sergeant Fuller, his temperature had risen again and he was forced to go home. The doctor insisted he spend at least two days in bed. The police press office assigned to the robbery now put out a statement saying that they had acquired vital new evidence and were confident arrests would soon be made. Rodgers warned, however, that not one of the three men's names was to be divulged until they had more evidence. Above all, they didn't want them tipped off. They knew that they were still in England from the statements taken by the young officer, but Rodgers made the mistake of delaying the requestioning of Wilcox, Driscoll, and de Jersey when he took to his sickbed.

Although Liz Driscoll knew her husband was going to Spain, Rika had no idea that Wilcox was leaving. He put the twins in his car, saying he was taking them to stay with their mother for a few days, and never returned.

De Jersey occupied himself with his horses. The friction between him and Christina had not eased and was a constant source of worry to him. It came to a head on the night of the television documentary. Christina was watching it in the bedroom, while he saw it in his study with brandy and a cigar. Halfway through he clenched the cigar in his teeth, switched off the television set, and got to his feet.

Christina heard her husband leaving the house and watched him drive away in the Range Rover from the bedroom window. She waited for a full ten minutes, but he did not return, and by the time she went back to the program it was over. The constant references to Philip Simmons had terrified her because, although the man was described as having red hair and a mustache, it had also been suggested that this might be a disguise. The man they wished to question had either worn a wig or dyed his hair. Although the computerized pictures of Britain's "Most Wanted Man" did not look like her husband, the description of his size, demeanor, and military bearing made her suspicious.

Christina went into de Jersey's office and closed the door. The room still smelled of his cigar, and the brandy glass was half full, as if he intended returning shortly. She went to his desk and tried the drawers. All had been fitted with new locks and handles. Christina was of two minds whether to force the locks again. Then she saw the keys on the desk. She opened the first drawer on the left side. It contained a few papers but nothing of importance. The next drawer contained veterinary and feed bills, and a stack of brochures for horse auctions in Ireland. The next had details of sales at Tattersalls, all of which she had already seen. She then turned to the right-hand side of the desk, opened the secret compartment, and removed everything, placing it on top of the desk. The envelope with the passports was no longer there. In its place was the last will and testament of Edward de Jersey. He had left his estate to Christina and their daughters. Also included were many donations to charities and detailed lists of personal mementos and monies to be paid to his staff. The will must have been drawn up a long time ago, not just because of the date but because she knew there was now no money for donations. She found nothing incriminating, except that he had removed the passports. Had he found a new hiding place for them?

She relocked the drawers and replaced the keys on the desk. She was calmer now but still disturbed. She kept telling herself that she was being paranoid. As if she was on automatic pilot, though, she began to search her husband's dressing room. She went first to the underwear drawers, then to his socks and the shelves containing his cashmere sweaters. She felt underneath them. She searched his jackets, his shoes and boots. It was a waste of time. She stood up in a rage and swiped at the hangers. Jackets fell noiselessly to the floor, and the ineffectiveness of the search made her scream with frustration.

She returned to the bedroom, opening bedside cabinets and drawers, then threw herself on the floor to look under the bed. By now she did not care about covering her tracks and frantically searched everywhere, even the girls' bedrooms. All she wanted was something, anything to stop the nagging fear that her husband was somehow involved in the robbery of the Crown Jewels.

It was after twelve when Christina, exhausted, went downstairs to get a whiskey. She had looked just about everywhere, but as she passed the cloakroom, she paused. De Jersey's riding caps and jackets were stacked near the rows of Wellingtons and boots. She picked up one after another, turning them upside down. Something was lodged in the toe of a muddy riding boot, hidden beneath a thick, rolled-up sock. As she took out the sock, her heart pounded. Resting against the wall, she withdrew an object wrapped in an old cloth, then sank slowly to the ground as she looked at the glittering stone: the Koh-i-noor Diamond. There was no denying it. She had found what she had been looking for.

De Jersey returned at about one fifteen. He was carrying a black briefcase and entered silently. He went into his study and put the case beneath his desk. He looked down at the drawers, picked up the keys, and weighed them in his hand for a moment. Then he hurried to the cloakroom. He didn't have to turn on the light to realize that the coats had been searched. He turned and made his way up the stairs. All the bedroom lights were on, and he prowled from room to room before entering his own bedroom.

There was only a small bedside lamp on, and from the doorway he could see the disturbance.

Christina was waiting in bed for him, a pillow behind her head. He leaned against the doorframe and smiled. "Did you find what you were looking for?" He came to stand at the end of the bed, his eyes boring into hers as he eased off one shoe, then the other, and kicked them aside.

"You didn't answer my question," he said. Christina turned away from him. He took off his jacket and unbuttoned his shirt, then walked into the bathroom and closed the door. She could hear the shower being turned on, and off a little later, the clink of his toothbrush in the glass, and then his electric shaver buzzing. It was over fifteen minutes before he walked out wearing a white towel robe. In his bare feet, he crossed to his dressing room, glanced inside and saw the fallen clothes and coat hangers, then went to the dressing table.

"You have been busy," he said mockingly as he combed his wet hair, looking at her reflection in the mirror. Then he turned.

She wanted to hide from his eyes, and at first she couldn't work out why she felt that way. Then it came to her. It was because she found him so sexually attractive, more than she had for a long time. His presence filled the darkened bedroom, and she was not afraid of him anymore.

"We need to talk." Her voice was surprisingly calm.

"Not yet." De Jersey pulled the duvet off her. Now her eyes met his and, contrary to her misgivings, she opened her arms as he knelt on the bed and moved toward her. He touched her, gently at first, kissing every part of her body before tearing off his robe and pulling her tightly into his arms. This time his kiss was harder and deeper, and she responded, moaning softly, as he began to make love to her, hard and fast, pinning her arms behind her head until they climaxed simultaneously. He rolled onto his side, his breath coming in harsh gasps.

"Well, that's made me feel better," he said and reached to the bedside table to pour a glass of water. He gulped almost half, then offered the glass to her.

She shook her head and drew the duvet around her naked body.

"First, let me tell you that I love you, I always have," he said, replacing the glass.

"I don't know you!" She had tears in her eyes.

"No, I don't think you do—well, not all of me." He said it so matter-of-factly that she curled away from him. "But it's too late now."

"What have you done?" she said, afraid.

"So much, my darling, but like I said, it's too late. It would take too long to explain." He lifted his right arm. "Come here."

"No."

"Come here," he said firmly and drew her into the curve of his body as if she were a child. "It's safer if you know as little as possible. You already know too much, and I don't know how you will be able to deal with knowing more."

"I found what you had hidden in the toe of your boot," she said and leaned up on her elbow. "What is it?" He looked into her frightened face and smiled, but he did not answer her. She turned away. "I watched the program tonight, about the robbery."

"I know."

"Please tell me it isn't what I think it is."

He said nothing, and she rummaged beneath her pillow, then withdrew the stone. "I could feel it, hard against my head, when you were fucking me," she said, holding it tightly.

He reached across, and she clenched her fist over it. "Give it to me," he said.

"No, I won't. Not until you tell me what it is. Not until you tell me why you have it."

He leaned over and almost crushed her hand as he took the stone, then held it up to catch the light. It sparkled.

"Mountain of Light," he said softly, and his face was like a boy's as he looked at the stone. "It is the most priceless diamond in the world."

"Why have you got it?" she said in awe.

"Because I needed it."

"You have to return it."

"Do I?"

"You can't keep it."

"I can't?"

"No, you must be insane even to think that you can."

"Why is that?"

She sat up angrily and looked at him. "It's stolen."

He gave her a glance that chilled her. She moved away from him, and the fear she had felt earlier returned. At first it was fear for herself, but he had softened again and he reached out to her.

"No, please don't touch me. I don't want you near me. I can't deal with this." She got up, reached for a robe, and wrapped it around her. "What did you have to do with Sylvia Hewitt's death?"

"Nothing," he replied.

"But the police want to question this Philip Simmons, and I know it's you. He was the last person to see her alive, that's what they said on the program. Why would they say that if you were not involved?"

"How do you know it's me?" he asked, almost mockingly.

"You fit the description."

"Along with how many thousands of other men?" he asked. "Besides, you know where I was on the day of the robbery. First at Brighton race-track and then at the girls' play. I couldn't be in two places at once, sweetheart, could I?" He placed the diamond where he could see it. "I had nothing to do with Sylvia Hewitt's death. At the time they are claiming she died, I was at my club, I even spoke to you from there. If you don't believe me, ask the porter."

"So if you had nothing to do with her death, why do they want to speak to you?"

"I have no idea. Maybe it's connected to David Lyons. He topped himself, and it looks as if she did the same. He lost her savings as well as mine, and as I told you before, I didn't get in touch with her because I had a good idea she was trying to hit me for money. On and on she went about hiring a private investigator, and as for this"—he nodded to the stone and turned back to her—"it's a crystal replica I bought when we went to the Tower of London with your parents. I intended to give it to one of the girls. I carried it around in my pocket and forgot about it until I was going out riding, so I slipped it into one of my old boots." He chuckled. "For God's sake, darling, don't tell me you thought I was involved in the Crown Jewels robbery. You *can't* have thought that." He chuckled again as she stood at the end of the bed and flushed. "Oh, my poor darling. What have you been doing all evening? Trying to find the rest of them?"

"Not to begin with. I was looking for the passports you had. Where did you go tonight?"

"For a drive. Then I parked the car and walked for a while. How long is this interrogation going to go on, Miss Marple?"

He laughed, tossed the stone in the air, and caught it. The light from the diamond cut shafts across the room.

"Give it to me," she said and snatched it. She crossed to the dressing table mirror and slashed at it with the stone. When it cut into the glass, she began to tremble.

"I wish you hadn't done that," he said softly, and he was no longer smiling.

"Oh, God. Oh, my God," she said, and he took a deep breath.

"It's going to be all right, sweetheart, but now that you do know I'm involved, I will have to take great care of you. I won't let any harm come to you. I'll have to work out just how I can keep you and the girls out of it."

"Will you go away?" she asked.

"No. No need as yet, but now you know why I had the passports in your name and the girls'. We might have to do a moonlight flit. We'll have to have a serious talk about what we should do, but right now I don't think we have too much to worry about."

"How can you say that? If I recognized you, how long do you think it will be before someone else does?"

"You are my wife, dearest."

She swallowed. His calm made her even more afraid.

"Did you . . . I mean, did you do it?"

"Do what?"

"For God's sake, the robbery."

"Yes," he said simply.

Then, as if nothing had happened, he walked casually to the door, tying his robe. "I'm going to put on some tea. Would you like some?"

"No." Her throat felt as if it was burning.

"I'm starving. I think I'll make a toasted cheese sandwich too. Maybe I can tempt you," he called as he left the room.

She remained huddled on the bed, listening to him moving around downstairs, and her head started to throb.

De Jersey busied himself in the kitchen. He took some of Christina's sleeping tablets from the pocket of his dressing gown, crushed them into powder, and layered some under the melting cheese, then put the rest into her tea.

She was sitting up in bed when he returned with the tray, plus the brandy bottle, and he poured some into both their mugs as he sat cross-legged on the bed.

"Can I tempt you?" he asked teasingly, and she shook her head, but her mouth felt so dry she picked up a mug and drank.

She pulled a face at the tea, not liking the brandy he'd put in it, but he encouraged her to drink it. Then he started to eat a sandwich, and she took one too.

"This might be our last meal together," he joked.

She turned away from him.

"I'm teasing, you know that."

Christina turned back to him, and tears filled her eyes until she shook her head. "I am so frightened," she whispered.

He put aside the tray and took her in his arms. "Listen to me, everything is going to be all right, and now I can tell you the truth. You must have pieced it together anyway by now. I have plans. We'll have to leave England. Are you listening?"

She nodded as tears streamed down her cheeks.

"I love you," he said softly, and he made love to her again. He held her until he heard her breathing deeply. He lay beside her, gently stroking her hair until he was sure she wouldn't wake. He tucked the duvet around her and checked that she had drunk most of the tea and eaten half of the sandwich. He reckoned that would be enough. He packed quickly, and put the diamond in his pocket. He went downstairs to collect the briefcase. He left no note and didn't look back as he let himself out of the kitchen door. He walked across the silent stable yard. It was three thirty in the morning, and no one was awake. He entered Royal Flush's stable and cradled the horse's head in his arms. The bond he felt with the great stallion crushed him, and he was almost in tears. "Good-bye, my son. Wherever I am, I'll be watching you."

The sound of the helicopter woke a few of the lads, and one sat up swearing, but silence soon returned.

Christina slept on throughout the next morning as trailers drew up at the estate and took away the horses. They had been bought by the billionaire Sheikh, and the jewel in his crown was Royal Flush.

26

The estate was in turmoil when it became clear that de Jersey had sold up, lock, stock, and barrel, but the staff were informed that they could continue to work for the Sheikh. The stable lads watched the great horse being led into the trailer. As always, he was kicking and biting. Even his blanket had been changed, to one that bore the colors of his new owner, who stood, smoking and inspecting his purchases, then walked around the estate with the shattered Donald Fleming.

Christina slept until midday, unaware that the mansion too had been sold. When she awoke she felt as if a lead weight had been tied round her neck, and her fear returned. Looking out the window, she saw all the movement in the stable yard and presumed her husband must be exercising the horses. She showered, dressed, and went to the kitchen to make herself some breakfast. There she found out what had been happening. The new owner had left a courteous letter asking her to vacate the premises with her possessions and furnishings within a week. She also discovered the almost empty bottle of her sleeping tablets where de Jersey had left it along with the loaf of bread he had used to make their toasted cheese sandwiches.

By the time she discovered from the staff what had happened, she was too upset to talk to anyone. She returned to the house and ran to the sink to throw up.

Christina could not admit that, along with everyone else, she had not been privy to her husband's intentions. At first she had expected him to return and explain everything to her. By mid-afternoon, still shocked, she called her daughters' school, only to be told by the headmistress that the girls' fees were outstanding. If there was a problem, perhaps Mrs. de Jersey would arrange a meeting to discuss her daughters' future. Christina, at a loss, asked if she could speak to her elder daughter. She kept control of her emotions as she told Natasha that she would like her and Leonie to catch the next train home and she would collect them at the station. She told her she could not discuss the reasons over the phone.

When Christina called the bank to discuss paying her daughters' school fees, she learned that the joint bank account was virtually empty, and payments on certain loans had not been made. She also discovered outstanding bills from the grocery and wine merchants, as well as those for horse feed and veterinary visits. The phone rang constantly until she took it off the hook, unable to listen to any more queries about unpaid accounts. The papers she'd found in her husband's desk revealed only a fraction of the truth about their debts.

Drawing on what little energy she had left, she went to see Donald Fleming. He was as shocked as she was. Now she discovered that wages were owed to most of the staff. She felt so ashamed that she couldn't continue talking to Fleming, who broke down in front of her. "How could he have done this? Not to even discuss it with me," he said.

"I'm so sorry," she replied. "I'm so very sorry."

He looked at her, shaking his head. "I can't believe he'd do this, not take me into his confidence. It's just . . . I worked for almost twenty years alongside him," he said.

"I was married to him for that long and . . ." She felt her chin tremble. "I'll come back later. We'll talk. I'm sorry, I can't think straight right now."

She ran from the office. Entering the house, she couldn't even find the strength to take off her coat. The more she began to understand the severity of her situation the more it forced the realization of what her husband had done. She was forced to face the probability that he had planned his departure for a considerable time and it was doubtful that he intended to return. She couldn't bring herself to think about the previous night and how he had made love to her. She sat at the kitchen table sobbing. Every time she dried her eyes, the tears flowed again.

Christina forced herself to go upstairs and get ready to face her daughters. But when she entered the bedroom, her loss swamped her again, and she lay facedown on the bed, where she could still smell her husband's scent. The sobs tore upward from her belly.

When Christina finally stopped weeping, she changed and drove to collect her daughters. She was calm. She didn't tell the girls what had happened until they were back at the house. Then she said that it was possible their father had not just left home but left them too. She found herself in an awkward position. If he did intend to come back and take them away, as he had promised, the less the girls knew the better. She went over and over in her mind their conversation of the previous night: his promises, his protestation of love. But she also knew that he had drugged her.

Christina was unable to tell her daughters everything she knew, but she tried to soften the blow by saying that their father had been in dire financial trouble and had been unable to deal with it. Their confused, sad faces broke Christina's tight hold on herself, and she was again unable to stop the tears.

Twenty-four hours later, de Jersey had still made no contact. Christina began to earmark anything of value to sell, but her husband's betrayal hung over her like a dark cloud. It was while she was in this vulnerable state that two patrol cars entered the drive. It had been decided that the uniformed officers would start questioning the staff around the stables while Chief Superintendent Rodgers, with Detective Constable Trudy Grainger, interviewed Edward de Jersey. At the same time, Rodgers had allocated officers to interview Driscoll and Wilcox at their homes.

As they pulled up, Rodgers saw the furniture-removal vans outside the house. "I don't like the look of this," he murmured, getting out of the car and stretching his legs. He walked flat-footed, his feet pointing outward, his head jutting forward like a turtle's, but he had one redeeming feature: incredibly bright blue eyes. Eyes that didn't seem to miss anything, eyes that could feel like they were boring into your head, eyes that crinkled up when he smiled and made him appear to be a jovial, kindly man. In many ways he was, but underneath it he was as tough as they came.

Rodgers knocked at the open door. When he received no reply, he walked into the hallway, bypassing cardboard packing cases, some open and some waiting to be made up.

"Hello," he called. He went into the drawing room. The radio was tuned to Classic FM, and Christina was wrapping crystal glasses in newspaper.

Rodgers knocked loudly on the door.

"If you've come for the silver, I'm not ready," she said.

Then he showed her his ID. "I am Chief Superintendent Rodgers," he said, "and this is D.C. Grainger."

"Have you come about my husband?" she stuttered.

"I'd like to speak to him," Rodgers replied.

"So would I, but I'm afraid he's not here and I've no idea where he is." She wiped her newsprint-stained hands on her apron.

"Could I talk to you?"

"Yes, but I have no idea where he is. He sold the farm and the house, so as you can see, I'm moving out. I have no other option. The new owner has given me only a week."

Rodgers smiled, trying to calm her. "Mrs. de Jersey, do you mind if I turn down the radio?"

"Not at all." She took off her apron and burst into tears. Two teenage girls appeared, carrying silver candlesticks, and Christina almost shouted at them, "Just leave those where they are."

Rodgers nodded and moved toward Natasha. Before he could ask either girl anything, Christina put a protective arm around each of them. "These are my daughters, Natasha and Leonie. You won't need to speak to them, will you?"

"Not immediately," Rodgers said and watched as Christina ushered the girls out of the room.

"They have just got home from school," she said. "They don't know anything about"—she took a deep breath, catching herself—"the sale."

Rodgers led her into the kitchen, where he asked if his officer could brew some coffee.

"Go ahead," she replied, distracted.

He sat at the kitchen table. Even in this room there were packing boxes and crates of china stacked and ready to be taken out.

"I've decided to put what I have left into storage and go and stay with my father," she said. "My daughters are very distressed. As I said, they have only just returned home and don't know anything." She took out a tissue and blew her nose. Rodgers bided his time, talking gently to her about the effects of moving. But from the few things she had said, he knew she was privy to something he needed to hear about her husband.

At last, after some coffee and a cigarette, she seemed more in control. "I need to ask you some questions." he said.

"Is it about debts? He owes money everywhere. In fact, I had to take the phone off the hook. As soon as it became known that the estate was sold, it's not stopped ringing."

"I am not here about debts," Rodgers said and waited while she dried her eyes again. She couldn't meet his steady gaze.

"Do you know Sylvia Hewitt?" he asked.

Christina nodded and said that she also knew she was dead. "She was the sister-in-law of my husband's financial adviser."

"We had been treating her death as a suicide, but certain matters have arisen," he said and opened a notebook. He asked if Christina knew

Anthony Driscoll or James Wilcox, but she shook her head. Then she paused and said that, if she remembered correctly, they had also been clients of David Lyons.

"How well did your husband know Miss Hewitt?" he asked.

Christina shrugged. "I think he did know her but not well," she said flatly.

"Do you know if he ever visited her at her St. John's Wood flat?" Rodgers asked.

"No," she said, averting her eyes.

"So he might have been to see her, if only to discuss the loss of his investments?"

Christina didn't reply.

"Miss Hewitt also lost a considerable amount, I understand," Rodgers continued.

"I believe so, but not as much as my husband. In fact, he was always very dismissive of her. I don't think he liked her."

"Do you know where your husband was on the night Sylvia died?"

"Yes, I do," she said. Rodgers was taken aback by the abruptness of her reply. "He was staying at his club, the St. James's. He said he was there all night."

"You seem very sure about that."

She kept her eyes on her hands in her lap. "We just happened to discuss it."

"Why was that?"

"No real reason." She reached for her coffee cup. He saw that her hand was shaking.

Rodgers tapped his teeth with his pencil. "Did you ask him about her death?"

"I don't understand. What do you mean?"

"Why do you remember where your husband was on that specific night?"

Christina was silent.

"Mrs. de Jersey, could you answer the question, please?"

"Well, I had tried to contact him, and he hadn't returned my calls, so I called the club. I just remember it was that night."

"Do you know where your husband was on the second of May?"

She frowned and twisted a sodden piece of tissue. "Why that date?" When she looked up, her eyes reminded Rodgers of those of a frightened animal caught in a trap.

"Well, Mrs. de Jersey, if you need a reminder, it was the day the Crown Jewels were stolen," he said pleasantly and waited.

"If you'll just hold on, I'll fetch our diary." She rose and went into the hall. She stood with her hands pressed to her eyes, her whole body shaking. She had to take deep breaths before she returned with the book. "I know he was in Brighton racing in the afternoon, but he was back here by early evening. Our daughters were performing in a school play, and we both went from here at around five o'clock."

"Do you know anyone named Philip Simmons?" Rodgers caught the quick intake of breath and watched Christina closely. "Philip Simmons," he repeated.

"I know the name," she said and looked up, her eyes now bright and clear. "I watched the TV program about the jewel robbery, and I know the police want to question him."

"And that is how you know the name?" Rodgers asked.

Christina reached for his pack of Silk Cut and took one out. He leaned forward to light it for her.

"They mentioned it on the program," she said.

"So where do you think your husband is?" Rodgers asked.

Christina shrugged and turned away. "I have no idea." She inhaled deeply, then turned back to him. He noticed yet another swift change of mood. The trapped animal was fighting back. "My husband left me. I have to leave the house. He's sold everything. He took off in his helicopter. He left no note. I have not stopped working since then. Anything to keep my mind off the way he . . . I discovered he had sold our home from a note left to me by the new owner. My husband has also left me in tremendous debt, so if you do find him, be sure to let me know." She stubbed out her cigarette in the ashtray and sat back in her chair, clasping her hands tightly. "Why are you here? If it isn't about Sylvia Hewitt, what is it about? Why do you want to see him?"

Rodgers turned over the cigarette packet. "It is about Miss Hewitt. I'm speaking to whoever knew her." Although he was being polite, he was watching her like a hawk.

"No other reason?" she asked.

"Possibly. I am also trying to trace Philip Simmons."

"So you believe this man is involved in Sylvia Hewitt's death?"

"Possibly."

"I thought she committed suicide. Helen, her sister, told me it was suicide," Christina said.

"Possibly." He gave nothing away. "I would like the details of your husband's helicopter," he said, tapping his notebook. "And if you have any thoughts about where he might have gone, I would be grateful to hear them."

Christina remained silent.

"So you don't expect him to return?" Rodgers said.

Christina's eyes filled with tears. She sprang to her feet and fetched another tissue.

Rodgers gave her his card. "Call me anytime if you think of anything that would help me."

"I will."

He left her looking drained and defeated. He felt sorry for her, but he was sure she was holding something back. He was not finished with her yet.

Christina watched the officers from the kitchen window, saw them moving across the yard, stopping the stable girls, conferring with the jockeys, then entering the manager's office. Apart from the faint hope that de Jersey would get in touch, she hadn't said anything because she was afraid that what she knew might endanger not only him but herself and her daughters. She decided to leave as soon as possible for Sweden. They would be safer there than in England.

Rodgers sat in Fleming's office looking at the lists of forthcoming race meetings, the array of cups and awards the yard had won, and the largest photograph hanging on the wall. It was of de Jersey standing by his beloved Royal Flush. He then glanced over the other photographs of de Jersey with various champions and of de Jersey close to the Queen at Royal Ascot.

"He's a big chap," Rodgers stated quietly.

"Yes, over sixteen hands," said Fleming.

"No, I meant Mr. de Jersey," Rodgers said, pointing to the photograph.

"Yes, about six four." Fleming sighed and joined Rodgers, who stood looking closely at one photograph after another.

"Did Her Majesty ever come to the stables?" he asked, peering closer at one photo.

"Good heavens, no! That was taken last year at Royal Ascot."

"Did anyone from the Royal household ever come here?" he asked.

"Not that I am aware of. Like someone from the Queen's racing stables?"

"Anyone, really, who was connected to Her Majesty's household."

"I doubt it, and I've worked here for almost twenty years. Why do you ask?"

"No reason. It's quite a place," he said, changing the subject. As Fleming returned to his desk, Rodgers removed one of the photographs and slipped it beneath his coat. He was taken aback by the emotion in the man's voice.

"I'll never understand how he could just walk away from this stallion in particular." Fleming pointed at a picture of Royal Flush. "He was his pride and joy, and we reckon he'll win the Derby. He's an extraordinary horse." Fleming swallowed.

"Why do you think he's done a runner?" Rodgers asked conversationally.

"Money. He lost a fortune on some Internet company. He never picked himself up from it, and running a place this size costs thousands a week. He just couldn't get out of the hole he'd dug for himself. But it still doesn't make sense to me. I thought he'd at least have told me, if not the rest of the yard."

"Apparently he never even told his wife," Rodgers said.

"Yeah, so I hear, and he doted on her. But the love of his life was Royal Flush. He was obsessed with him. That's what doesn't make sense. I can understand flogging the rest, but selling that horse off must have broken his heart."

"Did you like him?"

"Who? The boss?" Fleming asked, more in control.

"Yes. What kind of a man was he?"

"Well, I'd have given him my life savings. He's a man you thought you could trust one hundred percent. A man of his word, until now that is. But at least most of us will still be employed. Maybe that was part of his deal."

"Deal?" asked Rodgers.

"He's sold up lock, stock, and barrel to a sheikh, but we'll all apparently have work if we want it. He saw to that."

"How much do you think he would have got for the place?"

"The stables?" Fleming asked warily and moved papers around his desk. "Well, I dunno how much he owed on it. I think he'd mortgaged it to the hilt. Who knows? Either way, I'd say the farm and his horses were worth about forty million. Royal Flush alone cost over a million, but he'd been selling off some of his best for months, along with his cars. He'd already let a lot of staff go."

"Do you know a Philip Simmons?"

Fleming shook his head. "No."

"Do you know a James Wilcox?"

"No."

Rodgers shifted his weight. The photograph was still hidden beneath his coat. "Have you ever met a man named Anthony Driscoll?"

"No, I've never heard of any of them. You know, there's a lot I should be doing. Is there something you need from me? I would like to get on with things."

"On May second of this year, do you know where Mr. de Jersey was?"

"Well, not all of the time, but for part of the day he was at the races with me. We had a runner in the three o'clock at Brighton. He had to leave straight after the race as his daughters were in some play."

"How did Mr. de Jersey travel to Brighton?"

"By helicopter. He flies it himself now. He used to have a pilot, but he went months ago."

"What make of helicopter is it?"

"Erm . . . I don't really know. A small one, I think," Fleming said, looking pointedly at his watch.

"Where do you think he is?" Rodgers asked, his hand on the door.

"I have no idea, I'm sorry."

Rodgers smiled and thanked him for his time. Just as he stepped out, Fleming said, "I'll give you a tip, though. I know where he *will* be."

Rodgers turned back.

"The Derby. No way will he miss seeing Royal Flush win that race. Back the horse now and you'll get a good price." Four more uniformed officers remained to question the entire staff from the stables.

Rodgers returned to his car, patiently awaiting D.C. Grainger. They drove out in silence, with Rodgers flicking through his notebook, which was resting on the photograph of de Jersey.

"He's either done a bunk with the cash he got from the sale or he's holed up somewhere with a bottle of pills," he said flatly.

"Or he's run off with the Crown Jewels," said the driver, but Rodgers gave him an icy stare.

After another lengthy silence, Rodgers flicked through his notebook again. "Mrs. de Jersey was covering something." He tapped the book and suggested they check out de Jersey's alibi for the night Sylvia Hewitt had died. Then he rested back on the seat and shut his eyes. "Something stinks in this, and it's not horse manure. We'll put out an interest report on PNC on him, see if we can pull him in, if only for his wife's sake. She's quite a looker. It must have been difficult to walk out on her." He opened his eyes. "Unless he hasn't and she was covering for him." He glared through the window and ground his teeth. "What if the man we want is de Jersey? I reckon he could be. The descriptions we've got of Philip Simmons resemble de Jersey." He balanced the photograph on his knee. "Would a man with his face in the papers at every race meeting—a man who mixed with the Queen, for Christ's sake—risk pulling off the biggest heist in history?"

Rodgers stared at the photograph and fished in his pocket for a tin of peppermints. His cell phone rang. "Well, we'll soon know if Maureen Stanley recognizes him."

"Rodgers," he snapped and listened, chewing a peppermint. When he was told that both Driscoll and Wilcox had left the country the previous day, he swore. He should have hauled them in the moment he'd had the tip-off. This was going to look bad.

De Jersey knew that time was running out. He had flown to Paris using Shaughnessy's passport and booked into a small pension. From a call box he contacted Dulay to say that they needed to meet. He wanted the buyer's down payment.

Paul Dulay, still under surveillance, drove to Paris. Leaving the car, he went on foot and public transport until he felt certain he had lost his tail. He was an hour late for his meeting with de Jersey in a small bar across from Hôtel de la Tremouille. He had brought half of the million dollars with him in a small leather holdall, retaining the other half for himself.

"If you knew the runaround I've had to go through to get this cash— and I got it with those arseholes on my butt."

"What did Kitamo have to say?"

"Well, he never says a lot, but he knows what must have gone down and he's asking when he's gonna see his goods."

De Jersey instructed Dulay not to attempt to haul up the loot. It was to remain attached to the marked lobster pot. It could stay there for months, if necessary.

"How long do we expect Kitamo to wait?" Dulay asked.

"However long it takes. Don't give him the Koh-i-noor until the heat has died down. As for the other stones, tell him he'll get them in dribs and drabs. You don't go near that crate."

"How will I give him the diamond if I can't go near the crate?"

De Jersey answered by taking it out of his pocket and covertly handing it over.

Dulay was speechless. "Holy Christ, is it. Where in Christ's name am I gonna put it?"

"Stay calm and lower your voice. Hold on to it until I give the word, and let him know that he'll be transferring the next payment via the Internet. The day it clears we pass over the stone. Not until then."

"I like your use of the word *we*," snapped Dulay. "It's me who's gonna be carrying the fucking thing around." Dulay was scared and he was drinking heavily, but de Jersey remained calm. "Where the hell do I stash it? They've been over my shop and my home like a goddamned rash!"

De Jersey laughed and leaned in close. "I'll tell you exactly where you're going to stash it."

De Jersey returned to his hotel and stacked in a large wooden crate the money from Dulay alongside the cash he had received after the mortgage for the estate had been redeemed. The rest he had instructed to be placed in two banking facilities he'd arranged over the Internet in New York. On top of the false bottom of the crate were three large paintings from a small gallery close to the Hôtel de la Tremouille. They were individually wrapped in oilskins and thick rolls of bubble wrap. It was then nailed down and was to be sent by sea to New York with the gallery's name and a valuation of the contents clearly posted on the side. The paintings were to be dispatched to the Hamptons, to be stored by his solicitors until his arrival. It was too risky to return to his helicopter, and he'd arranged storage for it at Orly airport. He knew his chances of escape depended on a solitary run. He could not afford to speak to or contact anyone. He was hoping that Christina had not divulged the names on his fake passports, because he intended to use them both.

After the crate had been collected by the shipping company, labelled for Shaughnessy, he changed his identity and switched passports to become Edward Cummings, the English art dealer. He dyed his hair dark brown and put on a small goatee, tinted to match his hair. Last he added a pair of horn-rimmed glasses. As the plane left Paris for New York, he stared out the window. Somewhere below, bobbing on the sparkling sea, was a small lobster pot attached to a crate containing the Crown Jewels.

Christina returned to the home she had loved, which was now stripped bare. She had admitted to her husband that she did not know him, and she remembered word for word what he had said. It was devastating to stand in rooms they had furnished together and realize the extent of his betrayal. She walked around the almost empty house until she reached their bedroom. She could hear him, his voice, his laugh. She remembered how he had said he loved her. It was torture, but she needed to feel the pain, the force of his lies, to do what she had in mind. If he had provided for her, shown some care that the love she had given him for twenty years meant something, it would have eased the hurt. But he had given her nothing and walked away with millions of pounds in cash.

Christina headed slowly down the stairs and into his study. All the furniture was gone, but his cigar smoke had left a tangy smell clinging to the walls and it made her feel as if he was there to witness what she was about to do. She bent down to the phone. It was still connected, and she took out the card given to her by Chief Superintendent Rodgers. She was calm and cold with anger. She dialed his direct number and waited.

"Rodgers."

"It's Christina de Jersey. I would like to speak to you with regard to my husband."

CHAPTER

27

Maureen Stanley was not shown the picture removed from de Jersey's office, but the police lab had blown up the section of the photograph that showed his face and shoulders. It was placed among seven other black-and-white photographs of men with similar build and hair coloring. They didn't yet have photos of either Wilcox or Driscoll.

Chief Superintendent Rodgers waited as she stared at one photograph after another. She frowned and pursed her lips. She laid all eight in front of her as if she was playing patience. "I've got a good memory for faces." She had now recovered from the kidnap ordeal, and bathing in the continued media interest, she was enjoying herself.

Rodgers interrupted her impatiently. "Mrs. Stanley, do you recognize the face of the man who held you captive? The man you claim to be the leader."

"Oh, yes, without any doubt!"

"Could you please indicate to everyone here which of these eight photographs you believe to be this man?"

Maureen nodded, her hand poised over the photographs. "Without any doubt, that's him!" she said triumphantly and held up the picture of George Ericson, one of the officers attached to the inquiry.

Rodgers closed his eyes.

Tony Driscoll signed the papers for the sale of his villa in Marbella. The estate agent was a glamorous blonde with an all-over tan and plunging neckline. The villa was going to a dapper Italian, who had agreed to pay cash. That, minus the agent's cut, plus all the contents, left him with 130,000 pounds. Driscoll knew it was worth more, but for the sake of being paid in cash, he accepted the loss.

He was preparing to return to England when he received a call from his wife. She was hysterical. The cops had been round. "They were asking all this stuff, Tony, about this woman Sylvia Hewitt. Then—oh, my God, Tony—they were asking about the Crown Jewels robbery. Where you were on the day, where you are now. They got a search warrant, they're all over the house."

"Get off the phone, Liz."

"What do you mean, get off the phone? What the hell is going on, Tony? *Tony?*"

But Driscoll had slammed down the receiver. He went to find Wilcox on the patio. He sat down on the sun lounger beside him. "We've got trouble," he said quietly. "The cops have been round to my place asking questions, and they've got a search warrant." Wilcox's eyes remained closed. "Did you hear what I said?"

"Yeah." Wilcox removed his shades.

"What do you think?" Driscoll asked.

Wilcox got up, reached for his towel, and slung it round his neck. "I'll go down to the harbor and call Rika, see if they've been nosing around my place too."

"Then what?"

"Well, we'll have to think what we do next."

"I know what I'm doing, pal. I'm getting the fuck out of here. Stupid cow told them I was here, so how long do you think it's gonna take for them to come and pick me up? One call to the Spanish police and we're nabbed."

"What did they want?"

"They were asking about Hewitt, then slipped in the date of the fucking robbery. Not hard to put two and two together. They're fucking on to us."

"We don't know that for sure."

"Well, I tell you one thing, I ain't going back to find out."

"What are you gonna do?"

"Move on, lie low, and wait, I guess."

Wilcox kept his cool. "You mind waiting until I speak to Rika?"

"Sure, but get a move on. We should separate, fast." Driscoll went back into the villa.

Wilcox drove Driscoll's Jeep to Puerto Banus harbor. Once there, he went into a bar and called Rika. He said little but listened as she told him that not only had the police been round asking questions but they had also returned later with a search warrant.

"Vhat are they looking for, James? Vhy you leave me? Vhere are you? Tell me vhat you do."

He hung up and dialed his ex-wife, Françoise. He could hear his kids shouting in the background as he said he would not be able to return to England for a while and the boys should stay with her. Françoise hit the roof. He hung up on her and walked out of the bar. He drove back to the villa, his nerves in shreds.

As he parked the Jeep in the drive, trying to think what his next move should be, Driscoll came out, his bags packed. "I'm out of here," he said flatly.

"Where you going?"

"I dunno, but I'm not staying around to be picked up, and if you've got any sense you'll get out too."

"On what?" snapped Wilcox, slamming the car door.

Driscoll sighed. "Look, I'm not ditching you in the shit. I've left five hundred quid on the kitchen table."

"Big deal. How far am I gonna get on that?"

"It's not my problem, Jimmy. We can't risk staying together."

"Well, it's all right for you. You just made a packet on this villa, but five hundred's not gonna last me long, is it?"

"Take the Jeep—all the documents are in a drawer in the hall—then go visit one of the chicks you've been hanging out with. Leave the keys on the table in the hall. The agent's got another set, but you can't stay on here for much longer. The new tenants are moving in at the end of the month." He walked away without a backward glance.

Driscoll walked down the green gravel drive, past the kidney-shaped swimming pool, and into the half-completed lane beyond. The authorities had been "finishing" the roadway to the plot of villas since he had purchased his fifteen years previously. At the end of the potholed road he turned right and headed toward a small row of shops where he called a local taxi to take him to the airport. He still had no plan, but he called his wife and told her to sell the house. He told her not to ask any questions but to wait for him to contact her. Driscoll said little to comfort her, just that he was unable to return to England. He didn't know how long he would be away and told her that she was to buy herself a house and leave a contact number with the estate agent he had used to sell the villa. He felt wretched to leave her sobbing and scared, but he reckoned that if they were on to him they'd have tapped his phone. And they knew he was in Spain now.

Using a false name, he hired a private plane to take him to Palma, Majorca. It was the only place he could think to go without having to show his passport. Once there he rented a run-down apartment overlooking a pottery factory. Not until he was installed in it did he relax. At least without Wilcox he felt less vulnerable. He did some grocery shopping and hurried back to the apartment. Having spent many summers with his family in Spain, he had a good grasp of the language, but he still sounded like an Englishman, and worse, he knew he would stick out like a sore thumb if he didn't change his appearance. He decided to grow a beard, get a good suntan, and hide out. He knew he had to use his cash sparingly; there had been no big payday yet, and there might never be one. After reading all the English newspapers from cover to cover, he felt sick. Most were a day old, but they made no mention of the robbery, which scared him more than big headlines. It was always that way before the police swooped in.

Wilcox took from the villa anything he could sell: bed linen, cutlery, and Driscoll's clothing. He loaded up the Jeep, knowing it would have to be the first thing he sold as it was licensed in Driscoll's name. His main problem was where he was going to hide out, and he had to resolve it fast. Taking Driscoll's advice, he wondered about shacking up with one of the girls he'd met on his first night there. Sharon was a waitress in a cocktail bar down on the harbor. If not her, there was Daniella, a masseuse who worked at the Marbella Country Club. She'd come on to him in a big way, and he'd arranged a date for that night.

Wilcox drove toward Sharon's villa in the hills, but at the last minute he decided against it as she shared with two other girls. He turned round and headed for Daniella's. By that evening he had sold the Jeep to a rental company, signing it away as Anthony Driscoll, and bought an old Suzuki for cash. He drove to Daniella's small apartment on the outskirts of Nueva Andalucia. Even though Daniella was unsure how she felt about her new houseguest, he was charming and persuasive, and she finally relented. She warned him, however, that if he messed around with her he would have her brothers to deal with. As it was, they wouldn't like her cohabiting with him.

He gave her money toward the rent immediately to show that his intentions were honorable, and that night he was introduced to Daniella's family. He did not mention that he had six children and an irate mistress in England but gave an elaborate story about falling in love and wanting to make a new life with Daniella, outlining his intentions to look for work the following day. One of Daniella's brothers offered him a job in his holiday apartment block as a general handyman, painting, decorating, and cleaning up after the clients had gone home. It was a far cry from what he was used to, but at least he felt safe, for now.

Neither Wilcox nor Driscoll had attempted to contact de Jersey. Wilcox decided that he should not even contact Françoise or Rika for some considerable time. At least the boys were with their mother, and he felt sure that Rika would not stay solo for long.

Christina was nervous but so hurt and betrayed that she felt her salvation lay in what she was about to do. Once confronted by Chief Superintendent Rodgers and three senior officers, however, she became flustered and tearful. She was offered tea or coffee but asked for water. She remained silent, head bowed, as Rodgers gently began trying to encourage her to talk. She agreed to the interview being tape-recorded.

"Why have you come to see us today?" he asked.

"I feel compelled to voice my suspicions of someone's involvement in the robbery of the Crown Jewels and the death of Sylvia Hewitt," she replied in a flat, unemotional voice.

Rodgers glanced at his officers. "Who are you referring to, Mrs. de Jersey? We have asked for the public's assistance in many areas."

"Philip Simmons." She did not look up.

"Do you know who he is?"

"Yes, I think so." They waited as she coughed and sipped the water, her head still bowed. "I think he's my husband." She looked up then and began to talk quickly, explaining how she thought she had recognized him from the television program but she had not wanted to believe it.

"I'm sorry to interrupt, Mrs. de Jersey, but until you saw that program did you have any reason to believe your husband was Philip Simmons?"

"No, not really. He had been worried about money and—"

"Once you'd recognized him from the depictions on the TV program, what did you do?"

"I'm sorry?"

"Well, was he at home? Did you confront him?"

"Yes."

"So you confronted your husband and accused him of being this man we are trying to contact, is that correct?"

"Yes."

"You asked him if he was Philip Simmons?"

"Yes."

"And what did he say?"

"He said he wasn't."

"He denied it, then?"

"Yes, to begin with, until . . ."

The tension in the room was almost palpable, and Christina hesitated. "Until . . . I found the diamond."

Rodgers sat back in his chair with disbelief. "Mrs. de Jersey, are you saying you found the stolen jewels?"

Christina's hands were clenched. "One of them. It was in the toe of one of his boots." She described how she had found the stone and said she was now sure that it was the Koh-i-noor. She told of how she had confronted her husband, how he had said it was a fake, and how she had then used the stone to cut the dressing table mirror, proving that it was real.

"What did he do then?"

"I asked him point-blank if he was involved in the robbery."

Rodgers and the other officers leaned forward. "And what did he say?"

Christina paused. "He said he was."

The silence in the room was deafening. This was the confirmation they had all been waiting for. She continued, "When he told me . . . I didn't know what to say. It was like I was in shock. He made me some tea and . . ." Tearfully she explained how he had laced it with sleeping tablets and how she'd awoken to discover he had left during the night in the helicopter. Then she broke down, and Rodgers called for a break.

Once they resumed, she was questioned again about Sylvia Hewitt and was able to recall the night of the woman's death.

"Are you aware that Sylvia Hewitt died from a mix of morphine and ketamine?" Rodgers asked quietly.

"I didn't know how she died. I believed it was suicide. I told you this when you came to the house."

"Ketamine is a strong horse tranquilizer, and vets also use it for putting smaller animals to sleep."

"I didn't know that," she said, with a dull-eyed stare.

"Would your husband have had access to this drug?"

"I suppose so . . . he did run a racing stable. You should ask Mr. Fleming. I don't know."

"You say he fed you sleeping tablets the night before he left?"

She looked up, shocked at what he was suggesting.

"Did you suspect that he may have been trying to silence you? You have told us he left the same night."

"Yes, that is correct, but there were pills left in the bottle, and if he had wanted to kill me he would have used them all." Her voice rose.

"So, you do not think your husband meant to harm you?"

"No!"

Rodgers remained silent, then leaned close to her. "When we came to the house, you said nothing of this to me, Mrs. de Jersey. Not a word about finding the diamond, not a word about confronting your husband, not a word about his admission of guilt. And that makes me suspicious."

For the next hour, Christina was forced to repeat many times the moment she confronted her husband. When she was accused of aiding his escape, she stood up. "I didn't know! I didn't know! *I didn't know!*" she yelled and broke down sobbing. "I didn't think he would leave me," she cried, and it was Trudy Grainger who took Rodgers aside and said that Christina should be allowed to rest.

Rodgers was fully aware that the woman was in shock, but he felt only excitement at the advances they'd made. The old adage that hell hath no fury like a woman scorned was giving them their biggest break to date.

They stopped for lunch, and the team assessed the information. They were worried that they might have lost the big fish as they had received no word from Interpol. As for the other stolen gems, Christina had no clue where they could be. Unknown to her, a search warrant had been issued. To the consternation of the new owner, an army of police officers had arrived to search the house and stables. The same scrutiny was also directed at Tony Driscoll's property and James Wilcox's house.

That evening the police gave a statement to the press saying they were now able to name Britain's most wanted man as Edward de Jersey, also known as Philip Simmons. Additional warrants had been issued for the arrest of James Wilcox and Anthony Driscoll. The police said that both men were possibly residing in Spain.

On the following day, accompanied now by her solicitor, Christina began another lengthy session with the police. They asked detailed questions about her husband's trips abroad. When they learned of the trip to Monaco, they looked again at the inquiry into the *Hortensia Princess* owned by Paul Dulay, who had been under surveillance for weeks. Until now they had had only his confirmation that he owned the *Hortensia Princess* and his explanation of the "drop" witnessed by the boys.

Dulay was arrested by the French police. At first he was adamant that he had had an innocent reason for being anchored off Brighton. However, they were now armed with the fact that de Jersey had been at the Brighton racecourse on the afternoon of the heist and that he had arrived there shortly after the eyewitnesses said they had seen the drop. Under pressure Dulay refused to answer questions without a solicitor.

Dulay's shop and home were searched again, and under further questioning he began to break. His lawyers agreed to a deal if he gave information and admitted his part in the robbery. He took the police to the small cove and pointed out the bobbing lobster pot. The cove was jammed with sightseers and reporters as the launches set out to make the collection.

The crate was returned to the shore and taken to the local police station, where it was opened. In it they discovered all the stolen jewels, except for the fabulous Koh-i-noor Diamond.

Dulay was questioned round the clock and at last gave details about the sale of the diamond, and the Japanese buyer was traced. At first he refused to be interviewed, but then, on condition that there would be no repercussions, he admitted to having given a large down payment to Dulay for the diamond but said he had not yet received the stone. Dulay was questioned again, with the British police present, and admitted to paying Edward de Jersey half a million dollars in Paris; the rest he had kept for himself.

Now the police feared that the stone had already been broken up. They persisted in their interrogation until Dulay cracked. They could hardly believe it. The stone was hidden among pebbles by a waterfall in his garden.

When British officers reached the waterfall, they found a mermaid spouting a trickle of water from her outstretched hand. Beneath her tail fin, gleaming among the rockery stones, was the Koh-i-noor. As the water bounced off it, refracted rainbows danced in the sunlight.

In England the excitement of the jewels' return was dying down, but reporters had given heroic stature to the men they believed were behind the theft. Edward de Jersey's name was on most people's lips. The police were sent on one wild-goose chase after another. Two weeks later there were no arrests except for that of Paul Dulay. He had spilled his guts, but it became clear that he had known only so much. He had never met Driscoll or Wilcox or any of the others involved in the heist, he maintained, but when he was shown the photograph of Edward de Jersey, he identified him as Philip Simmons. He remained in a French prison until he could be brought to England to stand trial.

After naming de Jersey as the main operator, Dulay was returned to his cell. He had not disclosed that he had met Anthony Driscoll many years before. The police still had no notion that Dulay, along with de Jersey and his team, had been behind the bullion robbery. Dulay asked for notepaper and a pen. Then he tore up his shirt and hanged himself in his cell. The note he left for Vibekka and the children asked them to forgive him. His death was a severe blow to the police. It was four weeks from the day of the robbery.

Chief Superintendent Rodgers insisted that he would not give up searching for the robbery suspects. He stated that he would arrest the culprits within the next few months. However, de Jersey's trail had gone cold. A man on the run with nothing was easy to pick up. But de Jersey had more than enough money to buy a new identity, a new face if he so desired. Even with the efforts of the FBI and Interpol, they had no leads. He, like Wilcox and Driscoll, had disappeared.

The team of detectives decided to focus their search in Spain and try to pick up Wilcox and Driscoll. Armed with photographs of their suspects, plus a substantial reward for information, they headed off.

After days of interrogation Christina collapsed. She spent two days in a private clinic, and her father came to England to care for his granddaughters. At last she was given permission to return to Sweden with the girls. The Swedish authorities agreed to put surveillance on them all in case de Jersey made contact.

Christina had been in Sweden almost a week before she went to the bank. She had her own account there, with money left to her by her mother and some small items of jewelry in a deposit box. She wished to sell the jewelry as she had decided to remain in Sweden. She spoke briefly to the manager, who took her to the vault. She unlocked the box in private. In it she found a letter addressed to her. She knew from the writing on the envelope that it was from her husband. With shaking fingers she ripped it open and read the single sheet.

My Beloved,
By the time you read this, either I will be a man you despise intensely or you may have found it in your heart to forgive me. I had no option but to sell fast and make no indication to you of my intentions. I did not ever want to implicate or harm you and our children in any way. I love you as much now as I did when we were first married, and I love my daughters wholeheartedly too. I also respect you and know you will bring them up to be as beautiful and admirable as yourself.

I know you would never betray me, but to safeguard your life and ensure your future happiness, the best possible scenario is for me to disappear. I have made provision for you all. The keys enclosed belong to a lovely house I chose with you all in mind, as I knew you would return to Sweden. I will love you until the day I die, and I thank you for the most beautiful and perfect twenty years. God bless you.

She held the letter loosely, reading and rereading it as the tears welled in her eyes and dropped onto the page. The keys were attached to a small card with an address on it, and beneath that was a thick envelope with bank cards and accounts in the name of Christina Olefson, her maiden name. They contained one and a half million pounds. The house was valued at three quarters of a million.

Later that day Christina sat on the stripped-pine floors of her new home, staring out at the gardens. He had thought of everything, as always through their marriage. He had loved her, and she had not trusted him. He must have known she would not, and guilt now replaced the pain she had carried for weeks. But there were no more tears: she had wept too many. She got up and pressed her face against the cold windowpane. She drew a heart in the condensation on the glass, wrote her name and his, then slashed an arrow through it. She walked out of the room as the heart dripped tears. She knew now that their life together was truly over. She had loved him so much, perhaps too much, and it had made her blind. Christina would not have cared if they had been penniless, but he would have, and that was why he had jeopardized the happiness of his family.

Christina intended to keep secret the money she had received. She did not ask the bank manager when or how her husband had accessed the deposit box. She preferred not to know. She asked her father to move in with her and the girls; then it might be thought that her father had bought the house or at least part of it. The police, she knew, were still monitoring her, perhaps hoping de Jersey would make contact. But now she was certain he would not.

She enrolled her daughters in the American school in Stockholm and began furnishing and decorating her new house.

It had been one of the coldest Mays on record, but Royal Flush was in peak condition, ready for the Derby on June eighth. The massive stallion had lost his frantic, often dangerous edge. He had been groomed until his coat looked like black patent leather. He left the other top-class horses a good furlong behind in training, and as the buildup to the flat-racing season started, Mickey Rowland became confident that, although the owner had changed, he would still have the ride of his life. It had been written into the deal de Jersey had struck, and for that Mickey could forgive his boss's sudden departure and the salary he was still owed.

Royal Flush's new owner kept his prowess under wraps. No spectators were allowed to watch his training sessions. Having won his two trial races with ease, he was the hot favorite for the Derby, even more so because he had been Edward de Jersey's horse. The most wanted man in Britain was about to see taken from him the prize he had coveted.

*   *   *

To Chief Superintendent Rodgers, the lack of sightings and of public information regarding Driscoll and Wilcox, even with a large reward, was unfathomable. Clues to the whereabouts of Pamela Kenworthy-Wright had also borne no fruit until they received a call from Plymouth police. A woman had been badly burned in a fire at her flat in a run-down area known as the Fort. She had apparently fallen asleep while smoking and drinking. The neighbors had seen smoke coming from beneath her door and tried to break in. Unable to do so, they had called the fire brigade. Pamela was found in a sorry state on her bed, badly burned and suffering from smoke inhalation. When the paramedics had tried to take her to hospital she became hysterical, but by then she was sinking into a coma. Beneath her bed the police discovered a large tin box containing three thousand pounds in cash and a variety of articles that warranted suspicion. There was a shirt with Lord Westbrook's monogram and a gold signet ring with his family crest on it.

Chief Superintendent Rodgers and two officers caught the train to Plymouth, and a squad car picked them up at the station. Within fifteen minutes of their arrival at the hospital, Pamela died. It was a bitter blow that they had been unable to interview her, though her part in the robbery was later confirmed by Maureen Stanley, who identified her as the lady-in-waiting.

They spent a considerable time sifting through Pamela's belongings but came up with no further clues. She had been as diligent as de Jersey had instructed her to be, except for Westbrook's ring, which he had left her along with the cash.

Alone, and with little contact from anyone, Pamela had taken to drinking heavily as she read the exploits of the police in their hunt for the raiders. But even that began to mean little to her as she drank more and ate less. Poor Pamela. She had died a horrible death, but she made front-page headlines, and the papers showed a photograph of her taken years ago in a touring production of *The School for Scandal*. In the photographs from her old scrapbook she looked beautiful, so at least she was saved the disgrace of anyone seeing her raddled, drink-blotched face and carrot red hair. She died as Lady Teazle, and even long-lost friends who had known her as an actress came forward to give eulogies about her talent and her wonderful nature and humor. She would at least have liked that part.

In Spain, Wilcox was tanned and had grown his hair and beard. He was still working for Daniella's brothers. One positive outcome of his new modest lifestyle: he was getting his cocaine addiction under control. One lunch break, Daniella's brother held up a Spanish newspaper. "There's a horse here that was owned by the guy they say did the Crown Jewels robbery," he said, stabbing at the paper. "It's called Royal Flush."

When the young man had gone, Wilcox read the story about Royal Flush. He turned the page to see a picture of Edward de Jersey, still at large, and yet another lengthy article about the jewel heist. He stared at de Jersey's impassive face. It would be just like him, Wilcox thought, to turn up at the Derby, bold as brass, and watch his horse run. He wondered whether the police had thought the same thing. He could not resist touching the image of de Jersey's face and sending up a silent prayer that he did not.

Driscoll was flicking through the U.K. satellite channels. Eventually he settled on one where they were discussing the forthcoming Derby. At first he paid little attention as he had never been a gambling man. When he had worked in Ronnie Jersey's betting shops, the old boy had warned him to keep his money in his pocket and let the punters lose theirs. Driscoll had religiously followed his advice. Then the program focused on a horse called Royal Flush, once owned by Edward de Jersey, and he gave the TV his full attention. Driscoll had not allowed himself to think about de Jersey, but hearing his name brought it all back. He rarely left his apartment for fear of being recognized and had grown a full beard. He had lost a considerable amount of weight, partly as a result of living on his nerves and partly thanks to the fresh salads and vegetables he bought at the market. The stomach pains and indigestion he'd lived with for years had abated, and he was much fitter thanks to the nightly jogs he took to pick up newspapers left on the beaches by the tourists. Over the past couple of days he had been in a panic: his own face was plastered over the papers along with Wilcox's. He sent up a silent prayer that for his sake, for Jimmy's, for the old Three Musketeers, de Jersey would stay hidden.

By late May, Christina knew that the hype for the Derby would soon pick up, and this Derby would have special implications for her. She would not place a bet—she never had—but for de Jersey's sake, she hoped Royal Flush would win. Like Wilcox, she wondered if he would risk watching his horse race. This was the race her husband had wanted so badly to win, with its connection to his long-dead father, though exactly what the connection was she did not know. All she hoped was that he would not surface.

CHAPTER

28

The police were still maintaining a large team on the hunt for de Jersey and were armed with recent photographs of Wilcox and Driscoll. Liz Driscoll had no idea where her husband had been on the day of the robbery, and Rika said she was certain Wilcox had been at home because it had been his sons' birthday party. Up to this point no physical evidence had connected either of the pair to the heist, but they had set themselves up for suspicion with their absence. The hunt for them was stepped up.

After nearly a month of wild-goose chases around Spain, the police came up with nothing. Chief Superintendent Rodgers was now looking into leadingleisurewear and Alex Moreno. But Moreno had disappeared off the face of the earth. Rodgers was feeling depressed when he called a meeting to update his top officers. He knew he had to remind the public that de Jersey was still at large—he needed their help—but even the press were no longer eager for bulletins. At his last weekly session with the big chiefs, they had hinted about bringing in a fresh team to review the situation.

He stood up, pushed back his chair, and went to the meeting room where the twenty male and two female officers on the inquiry sat waiting for him. He entered with a scowl on his face and stood in front of the rows of photographs assembled on one wall. "Well, I'm going to have the rug pulled out from under my feet if we don't make some bloody arrests," he snapped. "They're still at large, and anyone with any bright ideas, now's the time to spill them out."

Sara Redmond, a small, pretty, blond detective, raised her hand. "It strikes me, gov, that the one lead we do have is this name, Philip Simmons.

Why did he use that name? Maybe there's some historical reason, some link to his past. Or perhaps he's used it in other crimes. It's worth a—"

The phone rang. Rodgers picked it up and listened, his face changing from drawn gray to deep red. As he hung up, he hit the table with the flat of his hand. "We've got a guy held in Newcastle, brought in after a burglary went belly-up. He's asking for a deal." They looked on in anticipation. "He's admitted to being in the heist."

The room erupted with a cheer, and they scrambled to their feet. Sara Redmond's comment was forgotten.

In exchange for a reduced sentence, Kenneth Short had given a statement in which he admitted to being one of the bikers on the raid. At first he had denied knowing his partner, but eventually he gave the second name and the police picked up Brian Hall from the farm in Dorset where he had been hiding out. Short had been paid in cash by a man he knew only as Philip Simmons, twenty thousand up-front with a second twenty thousand to come after the stones had been sold. After reading in the press that the jewels had been recovered, he knew he would never see the second payment, but he had already got himself into debt on the strength of it. He had arranged to burgle a factory office, but he had been caught by a security guard with a dog.

Hall and Short described how they had used the boats as getaway vehicles, then set fire to the boathouse. Both motorbikes were recovered from where the men had left them. They also took the police to the barn, which still housed the second Daimler. In addition to providing the team with fresh evidence, the two men's arrest put the robbery back on the front pages, and the police hoped for further developments.

Neither of the men arrested could give details of the setup for the robbery, but they told the police that they had been brought in by Tony Driscoll. Hall had worked for Driscoll years back but had met him again when he was hired to work at his daughter's wedding. Both men identified Wilcox as the driver. Now the hunt for Driscoll and Wilcox intensified.

Wilcox and Driscoll were forced to sweat it out. Spain was crowded with British holidaymakers, and photographs of the two were placed in every Spanish police station, in bus shelters and airports, with REWARD in red letters printed above their faces.

The next lucky break came from a prisoner who also wanted to make a deal. He said he had heard a rumor that a guy in Franklyn had had something to do with it, a Gregory Jones.

Jones was unforthcoming. He was in for life and knew he would not get a more lenient sentence, even if he cooperated. He agreed to talk only when they promised to put in a good word for his transfer to an open prison. From Jones the team learned how he had told Edward de Jersey, posing as a solicitor named Philip Simmons, about the Royal household's security procedures. Jones did not indicate that he had been paid.

Reviewing the outcome of the work, Rodgers was back on form, his energy renewed. And his officers were more confident now. They felt they knew both Wilcox and Driscoll, having spent hours interviewing Liz Driscoll and Wilcox's live-in girlfriend and his ex-wife. Trudy Grainger and Sara Redmond, the two women attached to the team, had both been very visible when they and Christina de Jersey had been interviewed.

"We may be getting to know Driscoll and Wilcox, but Edward de Jersey remains an enigma," Trudy said as she checked over the recent statements.

"What do you mean?" Sara asked.

"Well, he doesn't fit into the same pattern as either Wilcox or Driscoll. He's a different kind of man, and you can almost understand why the press make such a meal of him, of all three of them. I mean, they didn't use any violence during the robbery. Nobody got hurt."

"You want to bet?" Sara said.

Trudy continued, "They didn't use violence. It's a fact. All right, they put the fear of God into the security guard at D'Ancona, ditto the staff, but in the long run it's benefited that Queen look-alike. She's getting a lot of mileage out of the kidnapping. She's in the *News of the World* every week, and her husband is acting as her manager! Last Sunday they gave her a full-page spread in the magazine section on how to wear twinsets or some such crap. Like I said, nobody got hurt and they got the jewels back, so that's why the public doesn't give a toss."

"I don't agree about nobody getting hurt. Ask the wives—in particular Christina de Jersey—how they feel. They were lying bastards all of them, especially Edward de Jersey. He didn't give a damn for his wife or his two kids. How do you think they're coping?"

"Probably loving it," snapped Trudy, irritated because she knew Sara was right.

"Loving it?" Sara asked. "No way. He walked out on them, and got away with millions. He's not a hero to me. He's a lying, two-faced son of a bitch, and I hope we catch the bastard."

"Okay, you made your point. But for all his faults we can't seem to get a single person to say anything bad about him."

Sara leaned against Trudy's desk. "No, that's not quite right. It's not that no one will say anything bad about him, it's that they don't want to say anything at all. Maybe because they're afraid. But someone's got to know him, got to be able to lead us to him."

Trudy smiled. "Well, maybe you'll find them now. I've got to take these in to the gov, so excuse me."

Sara returned to her desk and sat doodling on a notepad. All the men arrested had spoken freely about Driscoll and Wilcox but seemed reluctant or unable to divulge much about Edward de Jersey. They said he spoke little, was always polite yet acted like an army officer. They had never seen him angry: he had always been pleasant, well dressed, and courteous. Brian Hall had said Wilcox and Driscoll hung out together, rarely talking to anyone but de Jersey; both men always referred to him as the Colonel. Sara drew a pin man with a big head and a curling mustache and printed under it THE COLONEL. Then she tore it into fragments and concentrated on looking over all the statements from Brian Hall.

Sara was not the only person who had picked up on Hall's reference to Edward de Jersey's nickname. When he was receiving all of the other information, Rodgers had not paid it much attention. But now it intrigued him, and he stepped out of his cubicle. "Sara, can you print up Brian Hall's statements for me?"

"Sure, just going over them myself, gov."

Rodgers sat down again in his swivel chair, his desk empty but for a telephone and a notepad. He detested clutter as much as he loathed computers. He was hemmed in by boxes and filing cabinets. It was as if the hunt for the jewel thieves had been going on for years instead of weeks.

Sara placed the statements on his desk and watched as he thumbed through them. "You looking for something specific?" she asked.

"Yep. It was something Hall said. It's lodged in my brain. Did he say that Driscoll and Wilcox called de Jersey by a nickname, something like the Colonel?"

"Yes, gov. It's on page four, about five lines in."

Rodgers looked up, surprised. "Thanks. That's all for now."

She walked out, and he frowned, rereading the sentence in Hall's interview as a bell rang in his mind. He closed his eyes and thought back to his days as a rookie officer, days when stories abounded about a mythical, untouchable robber known only as the Colonel. Could de Jersey have been that mastermind? He was the right age. Suddenly Sara Redmond's suggestion that de Jersey had used the name Philip Simmons for a historical reason came flooding back to him. Could it be that if he looked again at the robberies attributed to the Colonel—the Gold Bullion Raid and the Great Train Robbery—the name Philip Simmons would crop up there too?

Rodgers walked into the main incident room. "I need a car. I want to go to Edward de Jersey's place. Is Trudy around?"

"No, sir. She's just left to check out Gregory Jones's bank statements. She's going to interview his mother and—"

"Never mind. You come with me. Right now."

Rodgers headed out to the estate again. This time he wanted to talk at greater length with those who worked there, those who had been in day-to-day contact with de Jersey. Up until now Rodgers had concentrated on the physical evidence and myriad leads, but now he knew he would have to understand the man. One thing everyone mentioned fascinated Rodgers: de Jersey was obsessed with Royal Flush. He had treated the stallion like a son, they said, had given him more attention than his own daughters.

At the estate, Rodgers was surprised to see so few people. But there were heavy cement trucks and building equipment: the new owner had begun renovations. In the stables Rodgers went from one empty stall to another, and Sara trailed after him. It was obvious that the staff, or most of them, had left. Rodgers came across Fleming talking to the vet.

"Afternoon," Rodgers said. "Could I just ask you a few questions?"

They returned to Fleming's old office, stripped now although the photograph of de Jersey with the Queen remained on the desk. The vet told Rodgers that de Jersey had been beside himself when Royal Flush was injured and ill. He said that de Jersey himself had tended the horse's injured leg. Fleming told Rodgers that de Jersey seemed able to communicate with the horse better than anyone else. He recalled de Jersey's outright refusal when it had been suggested they geld Royal Flush due to the vicious temperament that might destroy the horse's concentration on the racetrack. Fleming decided not to mention the "arrangement" he had had with de Jersey or his payment of ten thousand pounds. He was too ashamed of it and knew it would not help the inquiry. As much as de Jersey loved the horse, he had risked his performance in the Derby. But Fleming now understood why de Jersey had used the stallion illegally to cover his champion dam. He had known that he might lose him and wanted the chance to own another racehorse as great as Royal Flush.

The vet left, and Rodgers with Sara, who had not said a word, remained in the office. Fleming was uneasy.

"Nobody wants this, then," Rodgers said, picking up the silver-framed photograph of de Jersey with the Queen.

"I do," Fleming said softly. He gave a glum smile. "The Derby was the race he always wanted to win. He had entered many of his horses over the years. It was something to do with his father."

"What about his father?" Rodgers asked. "Did Edward de Jersey inherit this from him?"

Fleming looked surprised. "No. His father was an East End bookie."

Rodgers was stunned. "A *bookie*?"

"Yes. I think his first name was Ronald, not that he ever said much to me about him. The boss wasn't the kind of man you had lengthy personal conversations with. He went to Sandhurst, but I only knew him as a racehorse owner. He hired me over twenty years ago."

"Did you like him?" Rodgers asked. He waited as Fleming hesitated, then repeated the question.

"Did I like him?"

"As a man," Rodgers persisted.

"I don't know how to answer that. It's hard to, after what's happened. They were a special couple, though. Ask my wife."

"I'm asking you." Rodgers stared hard at Fleming.

"Well, I just answered your question, didn't I? You don't work for a man for twenty years and feel nothing for him. I respected him and . . ."

"And?" persisted Rodgers.

"If he did what he's accused of, then I must never have really known him, because he was always on the level with me, until right at the end. But I put that down to him having money troubles. Listen, I've got nothing more to add, and I'd like to get on with things, if you don't mind. Still got some loose ends to tie up for the new owner."

"Well, thank you. I appreciate you talking to me. I need to get to know the man I'm trying to track down."

"I gathered that, but I don't wish you all that much luck. I hope he stays free."

Rodgers stood up, looking angry, and nodded to Sara, who had still not said a word. "Well, *I* hope he doesn't. When it boils down to it, he's a thief. A cheap con man. And he's not going to get away with it." He walked out. Sara gave a nod to Fleming and followed.

Alone now, Fleming picked up the silver-framed photograph his old boss had been so proud of. He did have more to say about de Jersey, but he couldn't because it would implicate himself. Right now he and his wife were looking for a new place to live. He had discussed working for the

Sheikh and had been offered a job in their offices. It was a comedown, but it would pay the rent and also provided accommodation. His retirement would be a considerable time off, and now he had no bonus or pension. When de Jersey had hit his financial troubles, he had stopped paying the pension scheme for his staff. Suddenly anger welled up inside him. Fleming wondered where de Jersey was hiding out and felt a rush of fury that he had put so much trust in his old boss. He smashed the photograph against the desk.

After his last meeting with Dulay, de Jersey headed back to Ireland using the passport in the name of Michael Shaughnessy. He owned a smallholding in that name, which was managed by a local Irish horse breeder. De Jersey had visited whenever he was in Ireland, but always in disguise. It had been his little secret. Bandit Queen, now in foal, was there.

The mare had cost 125,000 pounds and had been purchased from Tattersalls in 1999. She had raced only three times in the de Jersey colors. While the hysterical manhunt for Edward de Jersey continued, he was calmly arranging to send Bandit Queen to America. First he chartered a flight and paid shipping agency and export testing fees. He arranged the Weatherbys papers, listing Royal Flush's brother, a stallion called Royal Livery, as the sire. He did everything he could to conceal that Royal Flush had been put to stud illegally. Bandit Queen, in foal by Royal Flush, was transported in a horse box to the airport. She would be held in quarantine in America, for which he had also paid, then taken to East Hampton. De Jersey hired a boy to travel with the horse and paid him well to make sure he took the greatest care of his precious cargo. De Jersey, as Shaughnessy, then flew from Ireland to Virginia. From there he took a flight to New York.

After arriving at JFK, de Jersey traveled on, still as Shaughnessy, to East Hampton on the jitney bus. He had only one suitcase and stayed at the Huntting Inn. He checked that Bandit Queen had traveled well and was undergoing tests at Cornell. He was certain they would find no discrepancies with her papers or blood tests. As with everything, he had covered his tracks well. He rented a cottage near Gardiners Bay in Springs, East Hampton. He rarely left the property but ordered anything he needed over the Internet as he planned how to regain ownership of Moreno's property. He was careful, knowing that by now the U.K. police might have traced his connection to it, but he was not prepared to walk away from millions of dollars.

The hands at the Cornell quarantine stables led Bandit Queen down from the trailer, impressed by her size and obvious quality. She had a smallish head, almost Arab, with a powerful neck and a strong, muscular body. The foal she was carrying was not showing to a great extent. She was checked by a vet, who found that the long journey had not upset her, and she ate her first feed hungrily. Her coat gleamed in the late-afternoon sun.

By the end of May, de Jersey, now comfortable with his new name, contacted the law firm to which he had sent the crate of paintings, saying he would collect it personally. He drove there in a rented Jeep, walked into their offices, handed over his documents, and paid for the delivery. Then he drove to a warehouse they used for storage of their clients' possessions. This was not an unusual transaction; the nomadic nature of many home-owners in the Hamptons meant that lawyers acted as "house carers," pay-ing bills and monitoring properties during the winter months, when they were vacant. De Jersey put the crate into the Jeep and returned to his house. He took out twenty thousand dollars, then hid the rest in water-proof plastic bags beneath the floorboards.

Over the last month he had aged considerably and lost a substantial amount of weight. Like Driscoll and Wilcox, he now had a full beard. He hardly went out unless to buy groceries. He bought from the local farmers' markets and ate good, fresh food, trying to build up his strength, and every day he called to check on his unborn foal. At the quarantine stables they became used to the soft-toned voice of the man they had never met. "Hello, this is Michael Shaughnessy. How's my lady?" he'd ask. He said he was hoping to leave Ireland shortly and gave no indication that he was al-ready living in East Hampton.

De Jersey looked around for a property where he could eventually sta-ble the mare and foal. Beneath the floorboards he had more than enough to keep him for many years, and when he eventually discovered a way to get his hands on the Moreno property, he would retire in luxury. His long-term plan was to open a racing stable in Virginia. Until then he was con-tent to bide his time. The locals were aware that there was a new resident along the bay, but they made no approach. That was part of the joy of the Hamptons, the privacy: you could be social if you liked, or remain incog-nito. It was an artists' colony, too, and the gaunt man with the long coat and beard fitted in. The beaches were always empty, and he took early-morning walks to watch the sun rise. He clambered over the rocks and sat contemplating his life, his future, and thinking of Christina, of his daugh-ters, wishing that it had turned out differently. This, however, was the only way he could stay free, if lonely.

De Jersey had plenty of time to think about Driscoll and Wilcox, but there was no remorse. In fact, he had none for anything he had done, ex-cept perhaps Sylvia Hewitt, but that had been necessary. Believing that helped him come to terms with her death. He had no intention of returning to England, or watching the Derby, whatever anyone hunting for him might think. He had no need to go home. Bandit Queen was expecting his champion's foal. He was certain that he had got away with it and that one day he would win the Derby with Royal Flush's foal.

His conversation with Fleming and the vet was further confirmation to Chief Superintendent Rodgers that he was dealing with a complex man in Edward de Jersey. His father had been a bookie, yet de Jersey was able to mix with Royalty at one moment and steal the Crown Jewels at the next. As the squad car drove away from the estate, he looked at Sara. "What do you think?"

She gave a rueful smile. "I don't think anyone really knew him."

"Well, I'm damn well going to, because I'm gonna catch the bugger. Then I'm gonna retire."

Rodgers decided he had to go back into the past to find out what made de Jersey tick. De Jersey had no previous criminal record, but Rodgers found old news coverage and articles on his father's betting shops and the feuds between rival East End gangs. There was little information about either father or son, but there had been a memorial service for the well-liked bookie. He had asked for his ashes to be spread over the Epsom racecourse on Derby Day, but permission had been denied.

Rodgers, again with Sara's assistance, now checked out births, marriages, and deaths, and discovered de Jersey's birth certificate. He was older than Rodgers had believed, which fueled him to unearth even more about the man. He checked medical and school records. He checked Fleming's comment that de Jersey had been at Sandhurst and found out that he had been discharged due to a complex knee injury that had required delicate surgery. It was Sara who discovered that James Wilcox had been at Sandhurst at the same time as de Jersey and, like him, had been forced to leave, although for different reasons.

At night, in the privacy of his home, Rodgers pieced together the paper trail; it fascinated him. Sara helped to uncover further details of de Jersey's past on the computer, and Rodgers studied his career in the estate business. Sara acquired tax records, which showed his growing affluence, but nothing told them how he had acquired wealth enough to buy the luxurious estate. Now Rodgers concentrated on finding a past link between de Jersey and Driscoll. After hours of checking and cross-referencing, he was certain he was on to something: both Driscoll's and Wilcox's affluence coincided with de Jersey's, all shortly after the Gold Bullion Robbery. Before he discussed his findings with his team, Rodgers instructed Sara to try to find when de Jersey had acquired the "de" in his name. She produced details of his first wife, Gail, whom he had married when he was still called Eddie Jersey. Remarried twice, she was now divorced and living in a mews house in Chelsea. Sara gave Rodgers her phone number.

The ex–Mrs. Jersey did not at first agree to be interviewed but eventually acquiesced. Rodgers hung up and looked at Sara. He would take her with him. After all, it was she who had put the idea of tracing de Jersey's history of crime into his head. "You busy?" he asked.

"I was just about to type up the interview statement from the farmer who leased de Jersey the barn," Sara said. "The forensic team is still at work, though it's looking like their efforts aren't producing much."

"Trudy, can you take that over? Sara, I want you with me."

Trudy pulled a face. "I can," she told Rodgers, "but I've got information that Philip Simmons, a.k.a. Edward de Jersey, paid money into Gregory Jones's mother's account. Fifty grand!"

"Good work, and if that lying bastard thinks he's going to a cushy open prison, he's got another think coming." He turned to Sara. "I need you for maybe a couple of hours, okay?" he said, and she closed down her computer. "Order a car for us, will you?"

Sara hurried out after Rodgers, who was pressing the lift button. "I need you to come and interview de Jersey's first wife with me. She's agreed to see us."

"Why? You think she knows where he is?"

"I just want a clearer picture of the man."

The small but expensive house was in Glebe Place, and Gail Raynor herself opened the front door. She was rather brittle and unforthcoming as she led them into a pleasant sitting room. She did not wait to be asked but went into a terse speech, saying that she realized they had come about her ex-husband but that she had not seen or had any contact with him for over twenty-five years. She had read the news coverage regarding his connection to the robbery, so she had thought they might want to speak to her, but she was not harboring him, she assured them. "And if he did make contact, I would waste no time in calling the police. It was a despicable crime, and I'm glad it failed. The stolen gems are now back, I hope, in safer hands than they were before."

It was obvious that at one time she had been beautiful, but she had not aged well. She had tinted blond hair, arched eyebrows, and vivid blue eyes. She seemed to prefer to talk about herself rather than her connection with de Jersey. She had married young and soon realized that he wanted her more for her contacts than for love. Her father had owned estate agencies around Chelsea and Fulham, and de Jersey had taken over the running of them. Following the death of her father, he had control of the business. She was still disgruntled, despite the generous divorce settlement she had received.

"Did he buy the estate then?" Rodgers asked.

Gail shrugged.

"It was worth forty million," he said softly, and her jaw dropped.

"The lying son of a bitch. Forty million! Jesus Christ." She ran her fingers through her hair.

"Can you tell me anything about his background, his family?" asked Rodgers.

"His father was a bookie. He apparently made a killing on Derby Day, which enabled him to open his first betting shop, but apart from that I know nothing. In fact, oddly enough, Eddy didn't have many friends. Forty million! I know the estate must have increased in value since he bought it, but it's just unbelievable. He told me he only earned fifty thousand a year from Daddy's business."

Rodgers's theory that de Jersey had acquired the estate using illegally procured funds seemed to hold water, and a knot of excitement formed in his belly. "So where do you think he got the finance to purchase it?" he asked, tentatively.

"I have no idea. He sold all Daddy's agencies, so probably from them. I really don't know. He always had money, though, very good at investments. He remarried some model young enough to be his daughter."

"Did you ever hear anyone refer to him as the Colonel?" he asked.

"The Colonel?" Gail repeated. "He went to Sandhurst for a while but got kicked out. Injured his knee or something. He was always complaining about it, but that was his only Army experience. He was never a colonel. Though, knowing him, I wouldn't put it past him to say he was. He may have played one once, I don't really know."

"Played one?" Rodgers asked.

"His mother was in some amateur dramatic society, and he used to be in their productions when he was a kid. I don't know much about it, but he had some photographs of himself in costumes and wigs. He didn't do it when he was married to me. Too keen to get on Daddy's good side." She stood up and looked toward a small antique desk. "I've got a photograph, I think. I'm sure I have."

She opened a drawer and began searching for a photograph album. "I'm sure I had it somewhere." She looked around the room, then crossed to a bookcase.

"Did you ever meet James Wilcox?"

"James?" Gail asked. "Yes, I knew him from the days we used to hang out in the clubs. He introduced me to Eddy."

"Tony Driscoll?"

"I read about him in the papers, but I never met him." She continued searching along the shelves, then pointed to a row of books. "There it is."

Sara, who was taller than Gail, reached up and took down a leather-bound album. She handed it to Gail, who began to turn the pages.

"Maybe I'm wrong. After he left I made a point of throwing out any-thing connected to him. Ah! I've no idea why I kept this, but here it is." She lifted the plastic covering off three black-and-white photographs. "It's a production he was in when he was a kid. See for yourself. He's standing at the end of the row."

Rodgers looked at the picture.

"They did *A Christmas Carol.* He's the one next to the little boy on crutches."

Rodgers could see no resemblance to the man he was hunting in the tall, thin boy standing shyly to one side. He turned the picture over, and scrawled on the back were the names of the actors in the show. He passed it to Sara. The one listed as playing Tiny Tim was H. Smedley, and de Jersey had written "Me" for himself. She gave the photograph back to Gail. "Thank you."

Rodgers knew instinctively that Gail didn't have any more useful in-formation so he stood to leave and thanked her for her time. But she hadn't finished her tirade. "He walked out on me, you know. He never had the guts to say to my face that he was leaving. I woke up and found he'd packed and gone. The worst part was that he'd been preparing to leave me for ages. My lawyers said he must have spent at least six months arranging it all. That's what kind of person he is, a devious liar."

Rodgers murmured his thanks again, then said, "Well, I hope we catch him this time."

To which Gail replied, "No point, really, is there? I mean, he's almost a national hero, according to the press, and they got the jewels back. It's not as if he killed anyone." She gave them a watery, blue-eyed stare as she closed the door.

"Do you believe that?" Rodgers asked Sara as they returned to their car.

She hesitated. "No, I don't. I think he killed Sylvia Hewitt. I also think he might have killed Alex Moreno."

"Why do you say that?"

"Well, I know everyone thinks Edward de Jersey is some kind of hero, but to me he's just a thief. Maybe he's been one for many years, and the more I hear about him, the more I uncover, the more I get this nasty feeling about him. I wouldn't trust him an inch, but if I met him I think I might just as easily fall in love with him. That's why he's so dangerous. I'm certain that if Alex Moreno did steal from him, he wouldn't let him get away with it."

Rodgers gave her a sideways glance. "Lemme tell you something, Sara. Maybe I think the same, but if we start an investigation in the United States, they'll get in on the act. We've come a long way to catch this bastard, and I want to be the one who does. I'm retiring after this, and no one else is gonna get the credit. I'll get this son of a bitch. I'm close to it. I know it."

"Unless he's in the U.S."

He gave her a dull-eyed stare. "If he tries to get his hands on the Moreno property, we'll know about it. I've got the contractor over there keeping an eye open for us. Right now, all I'm interested in is catching the bastard myself. I honestly think I know Edward de Jersey now, really know him. He's a cold fish. He dumped his first wife and did the same with his second."

"He does sound ruthless. To do that to his two daughters is just unbelievable," Sara remarked.

Rodgers unlocked the car doors. "Yes, he's ruthless, but he has one vulnerable area. I realize that now."

"His daughters?" she asked, getting into the car and slamming the door.

He got in beside her. "No. Somewhere, somehow he was able to cut out normal, everyday emotions like that. Sure he must care about them, but the man is calculating. He spends months working out every little detail. The planning of that robbery was a work of art."

"So what's vulnerable about him?"

"His racehorse Royal Flush, and if my gut feelings are correct, the bastard won't be able to stay away from the race of his life."

She gave him a sidelong glance. "I've got a little straw number," she said.

He frowned, not understanding.

"I'll need a hat for the races."

He gave an odd, snorting laugh. "Get a good one on expenses. If he's there, he might be in the boxes. I'm thinking of getting kitted out with a top hat and tails."

She laughed, and he turned to her with a scowl. "I'm not joking. If he's there, the bastard won't be crawling like a rat in and out of the punters' legs, he'll be moving with the high flyers—and, knowing the fickle aristos of this world, they'll probably welcome him, just like they covered for Lord Lucan. They'll think it's all a good laugh."

She nodded. "I hope to God the laugh's not going to be on . . ." She was about to say "you" but instead she said "us."

"It won't be, I'm sure of it. He's going to be there, and it's not gonna be funny. He's going to get thirty years just like the Great Train Robbers, and I'll be right there watching him as he's taken down. That'd wipe the smile off anyone's face."

"I wouldn't know." She smiled sweetly. "I wasn't born when that happened, gov."

"I was," he said softly. "I remember it all. I was also around for the Gold Bullion Robbery." He took a sharp breath. He had been about to say they had never caught the man nicknamed the Colonel, but he stopped himself, knowing he still could not prove his suspicions. But what a retirement bonus he would get if he could!

Two weeks before the race Rodgers asked Christina to be at the Derby. She tried to refuse, but he was insistent. Who would be better able to identify de Jersey than her? She did not want them to look too closely at her financial situation, so she agreed but did not tell her daughters. She looked over the invitations that had been sent to her and was touched by how many people had asked her to join them in their boxes. Until she had been contacted by the police, she had planned to refuse them all. Now she accepted one, saying how much she appreciated the hosts' kindness in asking her and that she looked forward to seeing them.

The police operation was planned and outlined. They would have the racecourse covered with officers in plain clothes, mixing on the lower levels, wandering around the tick-tack men, hanging out in the oyster and champagne bars. They would be by the main Tote betting shop. They would even be up in the Royal balconies. They would be in the restaurants and private rooms. They would be, as Rodgers said, everywhere de Jersey might appear. They had installed several cameras at the finishing line, covering the winner's enclosure, the owners' and trainers' sections in the stands, the bars, and the small helicopter landing pad. It was a massive operation to catch one man.

29

It was after one of de Jersey's morning walks that the unexpected happened. The beautiful weather at the beginning of June had changed to a thick, muggy heat, and the constant rain made the house cold and damp. The sound of the sea crashing against the rocks below, which usually filled him with a sense of freedom, now got on his nerves. Checking the calendar, he saw that there were only days to go before the Derby. For the first time since he had been on the run, he felt the loss of his family, the life he used to lead, and was enveloped in a deep depression. For months he had been moving and under pressure, but now he felt listless and empty.

He found it difficult to raise his head. The tears that had never come before now trickled down his cheeks, but he made no move to wipe them away. He could hear Christina's voice when she told him she had found the Koh-i-noor Diamond in his boot. He had already planned his departure by then, as he knew they were closing in, but he had not anticipated what losing her or his daughters would feel like. Slowly he got to his feet and walked to the window. The mist hung there like a dark gray blanket.

He had no notion of what had shaped him into the man he was, and he did not know why he had done what he had done. The only thing in his life that had held him was winning. The emotion he felt when he saw his horses pass the post first was exhilarating in a way that nothing else was. He began to pace up and down the room. He'd got away with it, he was free, he had won, he would win again. But this was not about money, not about what he had stashed beneath the floorboards, not about what he would get from selling Moreno's house.

As he paced, the darkness lifted. He'd give anything just to glimpse his beloved Royal Flush again. The adrenaline pumped into his body like a bolt of electricity. Gone was the restriction that felt like a tight band around his brain, gone the depression, and his body tingled. He snorted out a strange, guttural laugh, because it truly felt as if he had the last laugh. De Jersey knew they would all be waiting for him at the Derby. He also knew that if he showed up he would be arrested within moments, but it amused him to think of the furor it would create. And Bandit Queen would be not his future but his last laugh—even more so if Royal Flush won the Derby. Her colt or filly would be unstoppable.

He longed to attend the Derby, to hear the massive crowd. As at no other race meeting, they were as integral a part of the day as the race itself: the gypsies and punters, the tick-tack men, the boxes, the women in their extravagant hats, the men in their toppers and tails, the smell of chips, cockles and mussels, the pop of champagne corks. He had been taken there as a kid by his dad, thronging on Gypsy Hill with their East End friends and their beer and their picnic hampers. He had never thought then that one day he would be on the other side, greeted by the Queen. He could hear his father weeping with joy, cap in hand, as the horse he'd bet his life savings on romped home. His father had sworn that he would never lay another bet, that with his winnings on the rank outsider he would open his first betting shop. He had been true to his word. But the one race Ronnie Jersey would not miss for the world was the Derby. Now, to own the odds-on favorite, to have trained him, and to know in his heart that nothing was going to stop that horse passing the post first hit de Jersey harder than he would have believed possible.

"How's my lady?" came the familiar voice to the stable girl.

"Is this Mr. Shaughnessy?"

"It is, just calling to check on my girl," he said, and she could almost feel his smile through the phone.

"Well, sir, I have to tell you she's incredible. She eats like a Trojan, and she's getting to be a fair size. We had the vet check her out, and she should be out of quarantine soon. He thinks the foal's gonna be a whopper, but she's a big mare, and he thinks there'll be no complications, even though she's got another four months to go."

"But she's not too big?" he asked, with concern.

"He says there's no worries, and we had her scanned as you wanted."

"I'll come by this afternoon," he said abruptly.

The staff at the quarantine stables were somewhat surprised by the tall, gaunt man in his old overcoat. He drove up in an equally decrepit Jeep, covered in mud. He wore thick boots and looked as if he'd not had a good meal for a while, but his manner didn't match his appearance. He was authoritative when he asked to be left alone to view his mare.

The word went round that Shaughnessy was at the stables, and they watched as he entered the manager's office. There was a lengthy conversation, after which Shaughnessy returned to his Jeep, and drove off. The manager walked out, shaking his head. "He wants the mare and the foal shipped back to England when it's born."

"Where's he living? Is he local?"

"Says he's leased a house on Gardiners Bay up in the Springs, but he's going back to London." He checked his watch. "He's cutting it fine. He'll only just make it. Says he's going back for the Derby."

The Derby always drew a massive crowd. The Royal Family's own security was tight. Their Daimlers and Rolls-Royces drew up, and the occupants were ushered out and into the Royal Enclosure. Their boxes were hemmed in by security guards and police. The same amount of security would be present in all the car parks surrounding Epsom, and extra officials had been hired to check and double-check all the passes. All major parties hiring buses and other means of transport were to be checked out, as were the gates, though monitoring the thousands entering the track would be difficult.

The Queen had a horse running. It was the second favorite. The favorite, with days to go, was still Royal Flush. It was hardly ever mentioned that the horse was now owned by the Sheikh. It was always referred to as the Royal Thief's Horse.

The bookies would have a field day if Royal Flush didn't win. The punters were betting on him frantically, and the bookies had been asked by the police if they would tip off any single bet that might have been laid by de Jersey. They retorted that it was against the privacy laws to disclose a private gambler's bets, and any card-carrying member of Ladbrokes or any member of any of the established betting brokers would adhere to the code. The police did, however, gain possible confirmation from the United States that any substantial-size bet placed on Royal Flush from that side of the ocean would be reported.

Christina came from Sweden to stay at the Dorchester, giving herself time to purchase a new outfit. She had traveled alone and was met by officers at the airport in case she was pestered by journalists, but none were there. She moved into her suite. Alone in London, she felt a terrible sense of loss. If she saw de Jersey, she had no notion of how she would react. And if he did show, she was expected to give him up. Now she did not know if she could do it.

The officers were ready. It was still only an outside bet that de Jersey would turn up, but it was one on which Rodgers was risking his career. The cost of the investigation and the massive surveillance operation to take place at the racecourse were under review, as were his actions. He had rented his morning suit with his gray silk top hat. At least he would go down looking like a gent, or up looking like one, depending on the outcome of the day.

At last it was Saturday, June 8—Derby Day. The Derby was the fourth race. The first race had been over for twenty minutes, and the horses for the second were cantering to the start. There had been no sighting of de Jersey, but there was a bigger crowd this year than ever before, swelled by the press's anticipation of a win by Royal Flush and the fact that everyone felt sure the most wanted man in Britain would be there. Some hoped to see a dramatic arrest. Others hoped he would be seen but get away.

De Jersey walked up to a rather drunken reveler and offered him two hundred pounds to exchange suits with him. When the man hesitated, he upped it to three hundred. They went into the men's cloakroom, and while they switched clothes the flushed boy asked why he hadn't got a suit already.

"Because I'm Edward de Jersey," he said and walked out. He disappeared into the crowds.

The boy became hysterical. He forgot to do up his flies because he was so eager to find someone to tell and grabbed a uniformed officer, who tried to fight him off. "He's here, that man they want, the guy from the jewel robbery!"

"What?"

"What about the reward? Will I get the reward? I've just seen him!"

"Oh, yeah, right, you and two hundred others, mate," said the copper.

"I'm telling you the truth. He's wearing my bloody suit."

The rumors started, and the police were galvanized into searching the men's cloakroom and surrounding areas, but by this time de Jersey had made his way over to the saddling area. He approached his former trainer. "Hello, Donald, it's me."

Fleming turned and almost dropped the saddle. "You're crazy. The place is crawling with cops."

"I know, but I wanted to give you this. It's ownership of a certain horse. She's in the States, Donald, in quarantine, and the foal's doing well. The foal is yours and Mickey's. It's gonna make you both rich."

Fleming didn't know how to react or what to say. Suddenly he was close to tears. "I'll tell Mickey. His wife's pregnant and—"

De Jersey moved off without another word. Fleming had not even had time to shake his hand.

They had de Jersey on camera, heading out of the saddling area, but when they got there he had disappeared. The next sighting was at a booth selling cockles and mussels. He bought some and paid with a fifty-pound note, telling the vendor to keep the change. Rodgers, accompanied by Sara Redmond, was apoplectic.

The Derby runners were now being paraded in the ring as the jockeys came out to meet the owners and trainers. There was uproar as Royal Flush's jockey walked out. No matter what he thought about his former boss being a jewel thief, de Jersey had secured him the ride as part of the contract, and Mickey wanted to show his respect. He rode out carrying de Jersey's colors, holding the silk shirt high above his head. He waved it around madly before it was wrenched away from him by the Sheikh's bodyguard, but it had been caught on camera, seen by the crowd and by TV viewers around the country.

The police continued searching for de Jersey, but it was like hunting for the Scarlet Pimpernel. He was sighted virtually all over the track as the riders assembled at the start.

Christina, in a box belonging to a major racing family, watched the television broadcast. It was obvious that de Jersey was there, but where? Very distressed, she sat down by the TV screen as an officer entered the box and asked if she had seen her husband.

"No, I haven't. Please, leave me alone."

He left, but two officers were positioned outside. If Christina walked out, they would be right on her tail, but she remained seated, holding an untouched glass of champagne, her eyes on the screen. When she had seen Mickey Rowland wave her husband's colors, she had almost dropped the glass. The owners of the box had given up attempting to make her feel part of their celebrations. To some extent her presence made everyone anxious, and the thought that her husband might appear heightened their excitement to fever pitch. In the end Christina excused herself and said she was going to the cloakroom.

She knew she was being followed, and when she got to the ladies' room she turned to the officers and gave them a charming smile. "I won't be a moment, but I don't think it would be in order for you to join me in here."

She went into one of the cubicles, closed the door, and leaned against it. The tension was unbearable. She talked herself calm and walked out to look in the mirror. The face that gazed back at her was pale, and her eyes seemed overlarge. Her hands shook as she reapplied her makeup and adjusted her wide-brimmed hat. She took a deep breath and walked out. The two officers stood aside as she joined them. "I think I'd like to go and watch the race in the owners' and trainers' stand."

"Okay, Mrs. de Jersey, but we will have to accompany you."

"I understand."

They moved off, and the crowds knew something was up. Even if they didn't recognize the beautiful woman with two uniformed officers at either side of her, they moved aside to allow the three to pass. A steward tried to bar their entry, but the officers showed their ID. One used a walkie-talkie to report that Mrs. de Jersey had requested to watch the race close to the fence.

The horses were under starter's orders, and the police now had twenty-five sightings of de Jersey. What they didn't know was that he wasn't in the boxes or on the balconies. Instead, he had made his way toward Gypsy Hill, where the buses, the funfair, and all the East End families were gathered. He stuck out like a sore thumb. No one else there was in top hat and tails, and folks started to call his name as they ushered him closer and closer to the rails to watch the race. Among his own people he felt at home, and they gathered around him in an almost protective circle.

One man pushed, shoved, and elbowed his way toward the tall figure. He had broken out in a sweat in his eagerness to get to de Jersey, to touch him, to let him know he was there.

"Eddy, Eddy," he shouted, standing on tiptoe. He bent down and tried to squeeze between the pressing bodies. "Eddy. *Eddy!*" He could just see his quarry through the crowd.

"Eddy, it's me! *I know him, let me through!*"

De Jersey, hemmed in by men and women, some asking for his autograph, did a half turn and saw the round, sweating face of Harry Smedley. "Let my friend through," he said and raised an arm as Smedley reached his side.

"It's me, Harry Smedley," he gasped. "We was at school together. Remember me?"

De Jersey looked down and smiled. He still had no recollection of the little man. "Of course. Come on, Harry, the race is about to start."

* * *

This was to be the greatest day of Harry Smedley's life, standing right next to the most wanted man in Britain. His wife was not going to believe it, or his sons and grandsons. "I got two hundred quid on the nose," he yelled as he was jostled and pushed.

The crowds grew even more boisterous as de Jersey opened his wallet and threw fifty-pound notes to those around him. "Royal Flush is going to win," he shouted, and they scrabbled for the money as they cheered.

On the other side of the track, the police telescopic cameras finally picked him out, but with the race about to start, it was impossible to get cars and officers across the track. All the officers positioned in and around Gypsy Hill were instructed to move in and arrest him. The newscasters and racing correspondents were having the day of their lives.

"Added to the excitement felt around this wonderful race is the news that the most wanted man in Britain is here, mixing with the crowds. His horse, Royal Flush, is now at the start, and until the race is over it seems that there is nothing anyone can do. And they are under starter's orders, and they are *off*."

Royal Flush came out of his stall badly, pushed to one side by the horse to his right. He took a while before he gathered his stride. Rounding the bend, he was in sixth position but holding the ground well. De Jersey stood, surrounded by men and women like those his father had known, his infamy forgotten as they concentrated on the race. Smedley cheered and shouted until what little voice he had left became a croak. Most of them had bet on Royal Flush, and the cheers and yells for the stallion to come forward were deafening. The horses rounded the bend, then faced the hill climb, but it was starting to look as if Royal Flush would be left far behind if he didn't make his move.

Smedley was almost in tears. He looked up at de Jersey, who stood as if frozen. He was willing his boy to move up, willing him with his hands clenched at his sides. "Come on. Move him up, Mickey. Come on, my boy, come on, my son," he whispered.

Then the big stallion eased forward, whipped on by the jockey; he was now lying third. As he took second position, the crowd roared their approval.

De Jersey stood immobile. Not until his beloved Royal Flush moved up into first position did he begin to yell with everyone else. Royal Flush was neck and neck, and then, there he was, out alone, winning easily and with such force that the roar of the crowd was deafening. It had been worth it. Seeing him cross the finish line would surpass anything that was to come.

Smedley was weeping, leaning over the rails. "He did it. He did it," he said, but when he turned to de Jersey, it was as if he had disappeared into thin air.

De Jersey couldn't have pushed his way back through the crowds behind them. They were twenty deep and, being so tall, he would easily have been seen. Smedley turned back in confusion, and then his heart stopped. "Oh, my God, he's gone over the fence!"

"And the winner of the 2002 Derby is . . . Royal Flush."

As the Sheikh entered the winner's enclosure to be honored with the most coveted award horse racing could offer, a solitary figure was seen climbing over the barrier at Gypsy Hill, walking with his hat raised high. He swaggered along the track and was cheered almost as loudly as the winner.

"We got him," said Rodgers, red-faced and sweating as he spoke orders into the radio microphone to pick de Jersey up.

"No, we didn't," Sara said, holding on to her flowered hat. "He gave himself up." She sounded strangely close to tears. She turned to look at Christina de Jersey, still between the two officers. She was standing close to the rails by the winning post.

Rodgers had made sure his wife was visible, certain de Jersey would try to see her. He now watched her as de Jersey walked closer and closer. He crossed to ask her the unnecessary question. "Is that man Edward de Jersey?" he asked.

She turned to face him, but he couldn't meet her eyes. They were full of pain. "Yes, that is my husband," she said.

They all turned back to the track to see the officers streaming from all sides toward de Jersey, who was still audaciously acknowledging the cheers.

De Jersey was arrested on the track, surrounded by plainclothes and uniformed officers. Once he had been cautioned, he was handcuffed and removed from the ground in a police van to be taken to Scotland Yard for questioning.

"Do you want to see him?" Rodgers asked Christina, but she shook her head.

"No. I want to go home." She was led away, and he ordered the officers to shield her from the photographers. He felt such compassion for her, and admiration at the way she had behaved.

Her Majesty had also witnessed the arrest. She gave no indication of what she felt but seemed annoyed that her own horse had been placed fifth.

Edward de Jersey spent months in prison waiting for trial as bail was refused. He never named any of his associates and never spoke on his own behalf. He was not charged with Sylvia Hewitt's murder as there was insufficient evidence. He was sentenced to twenty-five years.

EPILOGUE

ANTHONY DRISCOLL is still at large. He lives with a Spanish woman named Rosa. She works in a local restaurant, and he is employed as a night watchman for a local pottery factory.

JAMES WILCOX is also still at large. He is now married to Daniella and has a baby daughter. He continues to work for Daniella's brothers, refurbishing holiday apartments.

CHRISTINA DE JERSEY divorced her husband after he was sentenced. He refused to see her or his daughters, encouraging them to start a new life. Christina subsequently discovered that he had placed $3 million in an account in the North Fork Bank in East Hampton, to be given to his daughters when they reached the age of twenty-one.

RAYMOND MARSH is still at large, now working for an IT consultancy company in New Zealand.

HARRY SMEDLEY was paid 10,000 pounds for his exclusive story in the *News of the World* based on his childhood memories of Eddy Jersey. His book was entitled *My Friend Edward de Jersey.*

ROYAL FLUSH went on to a stunning career, winning at Royal Ascot and Goodwood. He was then shipped out to Dubai, where he won the great Dubai championship. Returning to England, he suffered abdominal pain, sweating, and fine muscle tremors, and acute grass disease was diagnosed.

He died never having been put to stud. Bandit Queen's colt was Royal Flush's only progeny.

BANDIT QUEEN'S colt was born safely in the United States. He was a healthy, magnificent foal and was later shipped to England to his new owners, Donald Fleming and Mickey Rowland. He was turned out to graze until he was ready to be trained. His photographs dominated the cell walls of the man who had bred him illegally, the man who, unlike most men, had seen his dream come true. That, in the end, had been the fulfillment he had always coveted.

CHIEF SUPERINTENDENT RODGERS retired from the Metropolitan Police after watching Edward de Jersey sentenced. He had spent many hours interrogating de Jersey and was pleased to see him go down, yet he remained dissatisfied that two of the robbery team members remained at large. As they were about to lead away the handcuffed de Jersey, Rodgers asked if he could have two minutes alone with him. He knew that even if de Jersey admitted it, there was little he could do with the information, but he asked him anyway. Was he the Mr. Big behind the Great Train Robbery and the Gold Bullion Raid? De Jersey looked Rodgers straight in the eye. After a long pause he smiled and held up his handcuffed hands. "You'll have to wait for my autobiography."

ACKNOWLEDGMENTS

I would like to thank the many people who helped research and authenticate much of the action in *Royal Heist*. Very special thanks go to John Gosden, Annette and Andy Dive, Emmanuel Coste, Peter Middleton, Clive Driver, Jessica Cobham, Ann Duggan, Dr. Ian Hill, Stephen Ross and Andrew Bennet-Smith, Matthew Tucker, and Steve Nicholls.

I would like to thank my steadfast team at La Plante Productions: my personal assistant, George Ryan, whose brains and beauty hold me together, and the boss of bosses, Liz Thorburn, who keeps us all in control with deft charm and wisdom. I also thank Lucy Hillard, who runs the research department at LPP and had the key job of coordinating the research contacts for me to meet. Thanks as well to the script editor Richard Dobbs.

As always, a thank-you to my wonderful literary agent, Gill Coleridge, and all at Rogers, Coleridge and White, and to my U.S. literary agent, Esther Newberg. And my thanks to Random House for their terrific support and constant encouragement, especially from Susanna Porter, her assistant, Evelyn O'Hara, and Benjamin Dreyer.

A special thanks to Alison Summers for anchoring my book as it crossed the Atlantic, and also to my film and television agent and good friend Peter Benedek at the United Talent Agency.